Rough

Riders

BarbarianSpy

FOR LITERARY HEAT

This book is copyright © habu 2013
Published by BarbarianSpy in 2013
Cover design © S Bush 2013
Cover image: Copyright © Rangizzz
http://depositphotos.com/portfolio-1026550.html
ISBN: 978-1-922187-41-3
All rights reserved

BarbarianSpy
Jindalee St
Toronto, NSW 2283
AUSTRALIA

Rough Riders

habu

Table of Contents

Preface

It isn't just the act of sex alone that can be rough for a gay male, although this BarbarianSpy anthology includes quite a bit of rough taking. The relationships involved and the whole circumstance in which one male comes together with another (or more than one) male to satisfy basic hungers can be explosive in both physical and emotional terms. In this compendium of fifty short stories, habu hones in on giving readers some scintillating examples of tales and circumstances—and sexual acts—that are on the rougher side in more than one dimension. This collection isn't for the faint of heart—but it's a must read for those who like their GM stories rough and raw, both physically and emotionally.

This book from BarbarianSpy is an expansion of the anthology originally published by eXcessica Publishing LLC as *Rough Rides*.

9:30 Bus from Abilene

Sometimes I think I was born with a "fuck me" sign painted on my butt. But then, I seem to have been born with that young and vulnerable look that turns some men on, and I'll have to admit that I love being touched—especially in one particular sensitive spot below and to the left of my navel, where I have a blue rosebud tattooed. Ever since I started having sex, if a man touched me there, I hardened right up and softened to anything he might suggest. I'd just lay down and open my legs to him and let him do whatever he wanted. It didn't help that, no matter how much I fought it, I loved being cocked. And so I had the spot marked with a tattoo for reference. If I really, really liked the guy I'd move his hand there myself to short-circuit any early indecision on his part.

I was trying to fight my impulses just to lay down for whatever man who wanted me that morning I caught the 9:30 bus from Abilene headed up to Denver. Dave didn't want me to go. He agreed to drive me down to the bus station, but up to the very last minute I'm sure he didn't think I really was going. However, I'd pole danced in Dave's men's clubs for a couple of months now, which was as long as I'd stuck around anywhere since I'd gotten old enough to hit the road. And as nice as Dave's cocking was and as good as the tips for the extra service to the men in the club were, I had gotten myself in an old familiar rut, and I had started to tell myself that there must be something else out there for me to do other what whoring in sleazy little bars.

And something got into my head that if only I could get to Denver, I could start a whole new life and that this weakness in me—these urges, this vulnerability to the wants of other men—would just go away.

Just before I got on the bus in Abilene, Dave tried his last ploy. He pulled me around to the side of the station and pulled me in close to his chest. A hand sneaked up under the hem of my athletic T, and he pressed a thumb into that blue rosebud tattoo. His lips clamped down on mine, and I involuntarily danced on his pole for a few moments. First one leg went up around his hip and then another, and then he was dry humping me up against the wall—and I was loving it.

I was saved by the loudspeaker calling the "all aboard" for the 9:30 bus from Abilene, though, and I managed to break away and head for the bus without a look back. Instead, I looked up along the windows in the bus and saw that two cowboys were eyeing me real close. I wondered what they could have seen in the shadows at the side of the station house.

I climbed up into the bus and found a seat near the back on the side away from the platform. I didn't want to see Dave out there. I was fighting with myself, telling myself that life with Dave and in his sleazy little clubs wasn't what I wanted. That I wanted something more from life. But I was afraid if I saw Dave out there, looking oh so forlorn, as Dave was so good at when he wanted something from me, I'd lose my resolve to leave Abilene.

The bus started out, and I felt a sudden sense of freedom. It was going to work. I knew it was.

As the bus moved out into the dusty countryside outside of Abilene and headed north, I looked around to see what there was in the way of travel companions. An Hispanic family, a man and his wife and three children, the oldest a sullen-looking teenage boy of fifteen or sixteen, was sitting near the front. From the way they were dressed, I thought maybe they were field workers moving north to start the harvest up there and to work their way back to Abilene again over the season. A couple of elderly ladies, all dressed out in their Sunday best—off on an adventure. A young woman who always seemed to be huddled close to the window and asleep. And the two cowboys I'd seen in the bus window from the station platform. They must have been together, because they were sitting side by side on a row about two thirds of the way back until the bus got started and then one moved to the window seat in the same row on the opposite side of the bus. One was older than the other, wiry with ropy muscles. Clean shaven, graying at the temples, with startling pale blue eyes in a deeply tanned and weather-lined face. Piercing eyes when he stared at you—eyes that told you you'd better do what he asked if he told you to do something. The other, younger one, was dark-complexioned, probably half Hispanic, equally tanned, but chunkier than the older one. Not fat by any means, but heavily muscled. Both were in checked shirts and jeans, with fancy leather cowboy boots and big fancy silver belt buckles. Both had tattoos running up their arms and the hint at the neckline of more on their chests. And both were looking back at where I was sitting occasionally and then whispering to each other.

Buses weren't popular anymore as a means to move long distances, but what with the cost of gas and the overall economic conditions in the States at the moment, I thought they'd probably come into their own again. I had chosen the bus because I'd never owned a car, couldn't afford the plane fare, and there were no rail connections between Abilene and Denver that didn't go hundreds of miles out of the way and that didn't, in the long run, take longer—and cost more—than the bus.

I don't know why I picked Denver. I just had seen posters of it sitting right there next to the snow-capped Rocky Mountains and it looked so prosperous and clean and open that it had become somewhat of a Holy Grail to me, the symbol of a new, cleaner, less-complicated life.

We stopped at a gas station–convenience store just off the highway in the middle of nowhere for a lunch break. There was a small dining room off the lunch counter with only three tables. The young woman didn't leave the bus, but the elderly ladies took one table and the Hispanic family another, and I sat down at the third after I'd gotten my burger and fries.

13

The two cowboys sat down at my table.

"Hi, I'm Tex," the older one said as he sat down. "This here's Dusty." They were both wearing the traditional ten-gallon cowboy's hat and Dusty just tipped his hat at me without saying anything. But he had a big grin on his face.

"Hi, I'm Glade," I answered.

"Glade. That's an unusual name," Tex said.

"Yeah. I sorta picked it out myself," I said. "Didn't much care for what I'd been called before that." I didn't tell them that it was my stage name. All of us pole dancers picked out names that the customers would find intriguing and easy to remember. Most picked out suggestive or downright explicit names. I had wanted to be a bit more subtle with mine.

"Goin' far?" Tex asked.

"All the way to Denver," I answered.

"Dusty and me are gettin' off in Durango. We work a cattle ranch west of there. Been down in Abilene to see the sights. Were you in Abilene long or just passing through from somewheres else?"

"I was there a couple of months," I answered. I was feeling a little disconcerted. Dusty wasn't saying anything, but his leg was touching mine, and I felt those old yearnings building up inside me. Dusty was a real hunk. The strong silent type. And he was touching me. Any man who touched me set me going.

"Found something to do in Abilene, did you?" Tex asked. He was eyeing me with those piercing blues of his. It made it scared to lie.

"Oh, this and that," I answered.

"You look kinda familiar, like we've seen you before. Dusty was remarking on that when we saw you climb into the bus. Spent any time around the tenderloin district? That's mostly where Dusty and me sat drinkin' our beers. Place called Rapier mostly. Any chance we'd have seen you there?"

"I've heard of it," I answered in a rather tight voice. More than heard of it, it was one of three clubs Dave owned. I'd pole danced there. I wondered if Tex was establishing something with me—not just about me, but about him and Dusty too. You didn't go into the Rapier looking for women.

Tex started to say something else, but the bus driver was tooting his horn, and it was time for all of us to make that last rest stop and to return to the bus.

When we climbed back into the bus, Dusty returned to his seat, but Tex followed me back to where I'd been sitting and sat down in the aisle seat right next to me.

The driver started up the bus and got back onto the road. I tried to settle my nerves. Tex's leg was right up against mine, as was his upper arm. I could feel the hardness of his lean body through his checkered shirt. I was wearing an athletic T, so my biceps were bare. Just a thin layer of shirting between me and Tex's hard, warm skin.

"Born and raised in Texas?" Tex asked.

"No," I responded. "Lived here and there before that—mostly in the Midwest."

"Family in Texas or in Denver? Going to Denver to visit family?" Tex asked.

"No. No family," I answered. "No family anywhere."

"None at all?" Tex asked. His face was turned to me and his pale blue eyes were full of sympathy.

"No. I was an orphan. Floated around a lot. A couple of foster families, but not anything I'd want to talk much about." I certainly didn't want to talk about those foster families. If I'd gone down a bent path, it could all be traced back to that part of my life. I'd had a pretty rough life up to now; it looked like the only way I could go from here was up. I turned my head toward the window. My eyes had suddenly gotten a little watery, and I didn't want Tex to see that.

"No one at all waitin' for you in Denver, either?" Tex asked. His voice was soft, full of concern.

"No. No one at all," I answered. "Just startin' out again. I do that a lot. I start out again a lot."

I was still looking out the window, but I could see the reflection of Tex's face in the window, as I thought he could see mine.

He had a hand on my thigh, just above the knee now, and I'm sure he could feel me trembling.

"Just relax, Glade," he was whispering to me. "You're so tense. I can help you with that."

15

His voice had gotten low and guttural and his hand had moved up my thigh and was gripping me hard.

"Nice name, Glade," he was murmuring. "An unusual name. I think I saw that on a poster at the Rapier. Not a name you'd forget too fast. Not a body, either. Some even had distinctive markings. Dusty and me like tattoos. We've got 'em all over our bodies. Would like to show them to you. Would you like that?"

My trembling increased. He had fingers at my waistband now, very near my belly, with the grip of that other hand still on my upper thigh.

"Tex . . ." I said in a choked voice.

"Shush, it'll be fine. No one can see us back here." Tex stripped off his shirt to reveal full-body tattooing in a riot of colors and patterns against a rock-hard muscled chest. "Do you like my tattoos, Glade? If I remember rightly, you have a very nice one yourself. Somewhere near here, wasn't it? That's what I remember of you on that pole, dancin' away. That nice little tattoo. A rosebud, isn't it?"

He was pulling the T out of my shorts and a finger was moving across my belly and his thumb was on the rosebud tattoo. He was rubbing it and his other hand was on my basket, and I was falling apart.

"Happy day. You're just aching for it, ain't you?" Tex muttered through his heavy breathing. "Hot damn, you harden up fast." His hand snaked under the waistband of my gym shorts and he was pulling them down below my balls. My dick was standing straight up, betraying my arousal from his thumbing on my rosebud tattoo.

"Tex . . ."

"So tense. We must do somethin' about that," Tex was whispering. His ten-gallon hat came off and he dropped it onto my lap and fisted my cock under it and started to slow pump me. I turned my face to him and he could tell from the look in my eyes that I was lost to him. He leaned over and gave me a kiss and then he just pulled away and we sat there, staring into each other's eyes from six inches away, our cheeks resting on the nubby material of the seat backs, and he slowly beat me off,

16

enjoying the look in my eyes as I was transported by his hand job.

"You can touch my tattoos, Glade. Go ahead."

I tentatively, involuntarily reached out with my fingers and ran than over the markings on his hard chest. His nipples were taut—ready for me. He could feel the trembling of my fingers as I got lost in the sensuousness of his tattooing.

When I had jacked off up into his hat, he gave a little laugh and leaned over and kissed me again. Then he stood up in the aisle and rummaged around in the overhead compartment. He opened a duffle bag he had up there and took something out and then reached up and pulled down a blanket.

"Time for a little nap, don't ya think?" he said, and then he winked at me.

What he'd gotten out of his bag was a condom packet and a small tube of lubricant. When he sat back down, he leaned over and pulled down on the waistband of my gym shorts and, out of instinct, I raised my hips for him so that he could strip them off.

I knew what was happening, but still I made some effort to resist. I was trying my best to get beyond Abilene. "Tex . . . No, I don't think . . ."

"Shush," he whispered. "I wanted to do this back in the Rapier. But you'd gone off with some other customer before I could get to you. Come on. You know you want it. Look at what I got for you." He unbuttoned his jeans and fished out a nice plump cock, already hard. Tattooing wound down around that too, and I moaned.

But still I fought the cravings. "Here? Now?" I asked incredulously. "There isn't much room . . ."

"Hush. We'll manage. Just don't do much yelling. They always yelp for me. Just try to keep it quiet like. Too bad it's dark in here and we have to use the blanket. They always like to see the designs on my pecker disappearing into their holes. You know you can see them through the rubbers. I buy ones that you can do that with."

"Tex . . ."

But he just kept going. I watched as he opened the condom packet and rolled the transparent condom on his cock.

Then he slathered himself with lube. He covered us with the blanket and turned me toward the window onto my hip and I felt the cold lubricant at my hole and searching and stretching fingers. The palm of his other hand was on my belly and his thumb was on my tattoo and he was rubbing it. All of the resistance drained out of me. It was almost as though he knew that that was the key to my ass channel.

I shuddered as he worked his hips under mine, both of us turned toward the window. And then we was entering me, slowly, but relentlessly—showing me that indeed we could do it in bus seats. He slowly pumped up into me. His thumb was stroking my rosebud tattoo, and I was moaning and sighing softly for him. My head was against the cool window, and I watched the desert landscape drift by, as in another dimension I could also see the reflection of Tex's face and see how deeply he was enjoying the fuck.

I pretty much cleared my mind, enjoying the fuck myself, but being frustrated that I was doing so. Why was it so hard to leave Abilene and all that was Abilene so far behind, I wondered.

Tex left me under the blanket with no more than a kiss on the neck and a pat on my naked butt cheek. He pulled his shirt back on and buttoned up and went back up and sat down with Dusty, and the two of them whispered in low tones and laughed.

Near dusk we stopped for dinner and a change in drivers at a stop almost identical to the lunch stop, and I got my burger and fries from the fast food counter and took it out and ate it standing up by the gas pumps. As I ate, the young woman stumbled out of the bus, looking dazed and her eyes all puffed up. She came back moments later with a sack of food and climbed back up in the bus. I wondered what her story was and whether it was any rougher than mine. It made me feel a little better, if a little guilty, that there may be folks in the world worse off than I was.

In my case, I enjoyed the cocking. Couldn't get enough of it really. What I was having trouble with was the guilt of enjoying it and wanting more of it. That and the somewhat downtrodden feeling that I was being taken advantage of all of the time. What I really needed and wanted was just one guy. An

18

older man, maybe. One with a good income who would stick by me and give me a somewhat normal life. I'd want him to be virile and have a nice cock, though. I knew myself enough to know I didn't want to stop the cocking. Maybe in Denver. Surely in Denver that's what I'd find.

When we got back on the bus, I waited until Tex and Dusty had gotten on and settled themselves before I climbed into the bus. I wasn't in the mood for Tex to visit me again—at least not this soon. He cocked real well, though, and those tattoos of his were a real turn on, so I wouldn't mind having him again at some point.

Dusk turned into night, and I managed to go to sleep, huddled under the blanket that Tex had covered us with earlier in the day.

It was quite dark when I felt a nudge on my shoulder and swam up from a groggy, unsatisfying sleep into the grinning face of Dusty.

"Come on," he whispered. "Want to show you something in the back of the bus." He'd already stripped off his shirt and he was almost as tattooed as Tex was. He was covered in swirled, some of which curved under the bulge of his pecs and made them stand out and emphasize how well-defined he was there.

I struggled up, knowing full well what he wanted to show me, but he was already reaching down and palming my belly under my T, and the touch was enough for me to want what he was going to give me.

He followed behind me to the backseat of the bus, a bench seat that stretched the width of the bus carriage, with the palm of his hand on my belly and his forefinger rubbing that rosebud tattoo. My knees were going to jelly, and I was whimpering, my dick hardening and forming precum, the rim of my hole already puckering.

When we reached the back of the bus, Dusty scooted into the seat all the way into the corner, pulled me down onto the center of the seat, a good two and a half feet from him, unbuttoned the fly of his jeans, and pulled a thick, stubby cock out. He reached for one of my wrists and pressed my palm to his chest so I could feel how hard his nipples were for me and he moved my other hand to the root of his cock. Then he wrapped a hand around my neck and brought my face down to his cock and I gave him head. I was good at it.

He didn't say anything. He just sat there and moaned and sighed softly, with his hand on the back of my head guiding me, and his hips slowly rolling up as I deepthroated him and his stubby cock slowly became not in the least bit stubby.

After I'd gotten him all hot and bothered, he turned me, full length on my belly on the backseat, one of my legs hanging down, the ball of my foot leveraging on the floor of the bus to keep me steady in the tossing and turning motion of the bus, which was pronounced at the back. Then he pulled my gym shorts off my legs, crowned his cock with a condom, and straddled my hips and fucked down in me to his ejaculation. He had both of my arms pinned behind my back, holding my wrists together with one strong hand, holding me quite immobile and giving me the feeling of being taken almost against my will in a dark, enclosed corner of the world, which gave me a little thrill.

We were both breathing hard when he was done, but I knew he wasn't finished. I knew these young, virile cowboys with their hard and hard-worked bodies. I'd had them by the hundreds, it seemed, in Abilene on their one night a month off and coming into town to get their rocks off. He'd shot off, I could tell, but he was still hard. I'd known of guys like him who could recharge and fountain off three times before they went soft. Just one night of relief a month that wasn't self-initiated for a young cowboy can build up a whole lot of cum.

And, sure enough, He was pulling me up. Not dislodging his cock, which had lengthened out to gigantic proportions. He struggled up into a sitting position, with me lapped, his lips and teeth working my shoulder blades and the hollow of my neck, his hands wrapped around my belly, a finger pressing into that rosebud tattoo. Almost in a frenzy myself again, not least at watching the muscle roll on those tattooed arms encase me, I started fucking myself on his impaling cock in long strokes. One of his hands snaked around and fisted my cock, and we came almost simultaneously, all the time softly moaning and groaning, careful not to project the sounds of sex toward the front of the bus.

I looked up as we climaxed—and into Tex's eyes and then down to his naked, tattooed chest. He'd come back to watch the second fucking and was leaning over the seat, knees in the seat bottom, and face almost touching mine. His pale blue eyes were alight with lust and he leaned in and took my lips with his as I spouted off onto the back of the bus seat in front of us.

Dusty pulled out from underneath me and, after a little whispering session with Tex, moved back up the aisle. When he got to my seat, he picked up the blanket and brought it back and draped it over the aisle between two seats a couple of rows up from the back. Now, in the darkness anyone from the front of the bus couldn't see what was happening in the aisle beyond that blanket, and the interior of the bus was so dark they couldn't even have told the aisle was blocked unless they were coming back to use the bathroom in the rear corner.

Tex pulled me over and planted my butt in the center of the backseat, lifted my ankles to the tops of the separated aisle seats in front of the backseat, crouched between my thighs, and fucked me long and deep. Dusty sat there, turned around in an aisle seat in front of the backseat, and watched the action. And when Tex was done, Dusty replaced him again, turning me and pressing my head and chest into the center seat of the backseat, my rump pointed up the aisle, and doggy fucked me.

They left me wondering if maybe they hadn't had any success in getting their rocks off while they were in Abilene. And leave me they did, to stumble back to my seat on my own, exhausted and stretched and sore—but well-fucked and happy. This wasn't anything I hadn't endured on any given night in Dave's clubs.

The next morning, after breakfast at a small way station where there was another change in drivers and the two elderly ladies got off—in the middle of nowhere, as far as I could tell—Tex followed me back to my seat and sat with me and jacked me off again while murmuring in my ear about how nice I was—and how really sweet I'd been the night before.

"We'll be in Durango this afternoon," he said when we were finished and I was laying back in the seat, mellow and satisfied.

"Will we?" I murmured.

"It's pretty expensive in Denver, you know," he said from out of the blue.

"Is it?" I asked.

"Sure you got enough to get started there?"

"There's never enough, I've found."

"Could you make good use of, say, two hundred more?" he asked.

"Who couldn't?" I responded. I was just making small talk. Tex gave great hand jobs.

But Tex wasn't just making small talk. "You know you can stop off in Durango and get on the bus later on the same ticket?"

"Can you?" I said.

"Yes you can. You know, I've been thinkin'. Dusty and me had promised to bring something back to the boys at the ranch from Abilene and we plumb forgot to do that."

"Did you?"

"Yep. We got a pole in the middle of our bunk house. You could stop over for a day or two and give them guys a pole dance. I'm sure I could collect at least $200 for that. What do ya say to that?"

What I was thinking was that no matter how far down the road this bus had taken me, I was still in Abilene. But what I said was, "Sure, why not?" As I said, Tex gave the best of hand jobs and there he was, hand on my belly, stroking my rosebud tattoo with his thumb while he was making his proposition.

The ranch was a good hundred miles out of Durango in the direction of nowhere, but the bunk house did, indeed, have a wooden pole holding up the center of it. There were six interested cowboys out there in nowhere in addition to Tex and Dusty. I danced for them to a scratchy record on an old-fashioned record player, wearing one of the sparkly gold G-strings I'd brought with me from the Rapier. I wowed them and then they fucked me—all eight of them in succession over a three-hour period. A few had seconds.

I heard Tex telling them how turned on I got when my rosebud tattoo was rubbed, and they all made sure to give it attention, and thus they all got enthusiastic fucks.

They may have gone another exhausting round, but the foreman broke up the party and extracted me and helped me hobble out of the bunkhouse and into his cabin—where he bent me over a chair and satisfied his own need.

I made $350 off that afternoon of work, and Tex suggested that I stay on for a while—that the cowboys worked harder with a daily fuck and that there was plenty of money from where the $350 had come from.

But I really, really wanted to get out of Abilene.

Tex was good for his promise; he drove me back to the bus station in time to catch the next bus rambling through from Abilene to Denver. We left early, though, because he stopped behind a rock formation before dropping down into Durango and fucked me again in the backseat of the ranch's station wagon. He gave me another fifty for that, though.

The bus between Durango and Denver was more crowded than it had been on its initial leg into Durango. We were getting closer to big towns. And there was much more of a variety of people getting on and off as we rumbled along.

In Colorado Springs, a middle-aged guy in a business suit got on. He caught my attention, because he looked like someone who should be driving a Mercedes rather than riding in a Greyhound bus. He was smartly dressed; was in good, and obviously pampered condition; and was flashing a big diamond ring. It struck me that this looked like just the sort of guy I was looking for in Denver.

He looked around the bus as he got on. It was half full, although most of the passengers were in the front half. His eyes caught mine, and thinking what I had been thinking about how he was the type that filled my Denver bill, I probably gave him a more welcome smile than was absolutely necessary. I thought I saw his eyes sparkle up and he returned my smile, and then he was moving toward me. I was surprised when he came all of the way back to where I was sitting and sat down in the aisle seat next to me. There were lots of vacant seats back here, but he was sitting next to me. He'd taken his suit coat off and slung it into the overhead bin before he sat down. His warm arm was rubbing up against mine, and his thigh was touching mine, and I felt like I was going to hyperventilate. I looked down and was somewhat distressed that if he looked in my lap too, he'd see that I was tenting up.

But he wasn't looking at my lap, or so I thought. He came on with a briefcase and had taken some papers out of it and was sifting through those, looking for something.

The bus was out on the highway now.

"Wouldn't you know it?" he was muttered.

"What?" I asked more out of politeness than curiosity.

"They gave me a receipt back there at the garage, and now I can't find it. It had their telephone number on it. I'll need that to find out when the car will be fixed."

"The car?" I asked. He was on a bus.

"Yeah. My Merc broke down back there in Colorado Springs. God, I haven't had to ride a bus in years. But I needed to get back to Denver by this evening and the bus station was right there by the garage. It would have been more complicated to get a rental car. You come from far away?"

"From Abilene," I answered.

"Working there, were you?"

"Yeah, a place called the Rapier." I have no idea why I told him that. Being disconcerted by him touching me put me off center, I guess. That and assuming he'd have no idea what the Rapier was.

"Ah, I see," he said.

And, for a moment, it seemed like he did, indeed, see. He had turned to me and was looking at me real hard.

To try to cover, I asked him about where he lived and what he did for a living.

"I'm a few miles out of Denver. Out toward the mountains. Run a specialty service of sorts."

I didn't pursue the question further.

But then he settled back in his seat and started talking to me about his family.

"Adolescent girls," he snorted as his monologue moved along. "Daughters are such a challenge. You have any girlfriends with tattoos?"

"No girlfriends," I answered. I was trying to keep my answers short. I was sure that he was able to hear my arousal in my voice if I said too much.

24

"Well then, boyfriends perhaps?" He'd let it come out straight, as if there was nothing behind it. But I saw him eyeing my tented lap now, and I was beginning to figure out he was building up to something. I said nothing, but I know he could feel the intake of my breath and how tense I'd gotten.

"Tattoos aren't so bad," I said after a pause.

"Oh, you got any?" he asked.

"One," I answered.

"Somewhere I can see it?"

"Just here, near my navel," I said, and I raised the hem of my T-shirt to show him my blue rosebud tattoo. And he touched it with his finger, and I fell apart and my gym shorts tented up even further—and noticeably. And he was looking now. No doubt.

He looked into my eyes for a moment and then said, "Go back to the restroom at the back of the bus, and enter, but don't latch it. If I'm wrong just stay here and I'll move to another seat."

Dumbly, knowing already what would happen, I stood up and walked by his legs as he swung them into the aisle and unsteadily—not only from the rolling gait of the moving bus—walked back to the compact bathroom at the back corner of the bus and entered it.

Shortly afterward, the door opened, and he was inside with me. He'd rolled a condom on before coming back and he merely unzipped himself again, reached down and pulled my gym shorts and briefs off my legs and pulled my T-shirt over my head. I was naked. He wasn't but he unbuttoned his shirt so that our chests would be my bare skin against his hairy chest, and then I climbed his hips with my legs and he was holding me there against the back paneling of the bus restroom, his legs straddling the toilet basin, and he fucked me hard and deep by pulling me up and down on his cock with a broad hands palming and spreading my butt cheeks, giving him deeper, wider access in my channel. He had obviously done this before, and he was good at it.

I turned my face toward the mirror over the basin and watched his other thumb strumming my rosebud tattoo, and I ejaculated up his belly.

I returned to my seat first, leaving him to try to clean up the damage to his shirt. I looked around the bus as I moved up the aisle, but no one was showing any interest. No one had noticed.

Soon thereafter, he plopped back down into the seat next to me and reached into my gym shorts and pulled out my cock and slowly stroked me.

"That was nice," he said. "You know what you're doing. You mentioned the Rapier in Abilene. A professional, are you?"

"A dancer. A professional dancer, yes," I answered between sighs brought about by what he was doing with my cock.

"And other things too?"

"Yes . . . OK . . . yes. I've done other things too."

"A professional rent-boy too?"

I didn't answer.

"You're good. You're really good. I like that little thing you have going of turning on quickly when your tattoo is touched. Genuine is that, or an act?"

"It's what happens," I said.

As if he was rechecking, he reached over and pressed a finger from the hand not working my cock into the tattoo, and I shuddered and collapsed into myself and moaned for him.

"Sweet. How well can you give head? I'll give you a twenty for a blow job." He was unzipping himself and pulling my head down to his cock, and I showed him that I was an expert in that.

"Very nice," he said when I was done and had pulled out a twenty that I pocketed without comment.

"That special service I said I operated in the hills above Denver. It's a men's club. A special men's club. Would you be interested in working for me up there. At, let's say, $1,000 a week plus any tips you get, for starters?"

As far away from Abilene as I traveled, I still never could leave Abilene, it seemed.

But now I had a goal, even if it was, in some ways, a lot shorter goal than I had thought I would have.

26

All That Glitters

I was bent over on my belly on the conference table and the hunky blond attorney was riding me hard from behind. I still had on my tie; my shirt, unbuttoned; and my shoes and socks clipped to supporters wound just below my knees. But otherwise I was naked. He started a maddening rotation of his cock inside me, and I was giving little urping sounds. To let the others see the pain and ecstasy this master cocking brought to my facial expression, he pulled my head up by pulling on my tie, which he had spun around to my back to give him reins for his hot ride of my ass. All the time he was telling me what a hot performer I'd be in his nightclub act.

My own boss and the two Japanese businessmen were sitting there, mesmerized by the exhibition the blond and I were putting on, their hands in their laps, working their own meat. The blond released the tie, and his hands went to holding my hips still as he stroked hard in and out of me. I could feel his gold cock ring kissing the sides of my inner canal as he pumped me.

The golden blond was telling me what a good fuck I was—that he wanted to have more of me. He was asking me how I was enjoying the ride, and I was panting and groaning my approval of his eight inches working hard inside me.

My boss rose from the table, engorged cock in hand, and came over and tweaked one of my nipples while he kissed the blond deeply. Then he told the blond that it was time for the Japanese businessmen to take over with me and that he wanted the blond's cock in his own ass now.

The blond withdrew from me, the Japanese businessmen already eagerly standing in line behind him, and a large cock was exchanged for a medium-sized one, which, however, was more active and inventive in its exploration of my ass; the other Japanese businessman knelt between me and the table and started playing my cock and balls like a flute with his sensitive mouth.

The blond had planted my boss on his back across the narrow conference table from me, and my boss and I engaged in deep kissing and exploration of each other's torsos with our hands, as the blond spread my boss's legs and plowed into his ass. I lifted my head up from my boss's as the blond brutally entered him, and I held my boss's head between my hands, both of us connecting on what was happening in our asses with a variety of expressions on our faces.

When the Japanese and their blond attorney were finished sealing our multimillion dollar deal, they left my boss and me there on the table, consoling and rejoicing in each other and at our success at and on the conference table.

In parting, the golden blond came back to me and gave me a kiss. He flipped a business card out and said that I should visit his nightclub for the experience of my life—that the card would give me a free pass and free drinks and that he would throw in another wild, free fuck as well if I was interested.

Try as I might I couldn't get the blond out of my mind. He had ridden me hard and rough, but he hadn't finished me off. I developed an obsession that he finish me off, that I feel the explosion and bathing of that eight-inch ring-headed cock of his deep inside me.

* * * *

Three nights later, the blond's business card in hand, I was standing at the dimly lit walk-down wooden door under the iron porch of a brownstone on a dark street. Only the blinking sign announcing "Club Pan" beside the door assured me I was in the right place. At my ringing of the bell, the door opened just a crack, but enough for me to show the business card, with the scrawl of the blond across it. Then the door opened enough for me to slip through, but then it shut again with a solid sound of finality. The vestibule was dark, black drapery on black walls, ceiling, and floor. The half man who admitted me was also dark.

I say half man, because he was togged out as a wood nymph, or a satyr, or whatever they call those horned men with the legs and feet of a goat. This one was slender as a reed, with black curly hair, a small goatee, little pointed horns above his temples, black eyebrows curled up at the ends, and an interesting array of black tattooing on his naked torso. The most prominent of these, as I could see when he turned to guide me beyond a beaded curtain into a large step-down, smoke-filled room, was a chain of interlocked heart shapes descending from the hair line at the back of his head down to where the goat's pelt started just above his crack at the bottom of the small of his back. His legs, as I already indicated, were pelted like a brown goat's, and his feet coverings were made out like cloven hooves. Most distinctly, though, was that his cock and balls hung free and there was a fairly wide circular opening in the pelt at his rear where his asshole lurked.

The nymph swished his tail saucily as he guided me through the dim, smoky room to one of four long bars by the back walls on either side of what looked like a small dinner theater, with three tiers of descending levels going down to a circular stage in the center. Everything was black. The bars were black, the carpets and walls and ceiling were black, and the couches set around on the descending tiers, more like the lounges in those Roman banquet movies, were also covered in black material. Even the stage was black; it was square but had a round, revolving platform set into it. And standing up from this platform was an eight- or nine-foot high, widely spread X-shaped apparatus, with the cross-over set so that the upper portion of the apparatus was larger than the bottom. This was made out of some sort of transparent Lucite-type material. Near the four corners of the stage, rising to the ceiling, were poles made out of the same transparent material. The poles were some sort of hollow tube filled with a liquid in which glittery gold confetti floated.

The theater was dark, although I could hear the sound of moaning and activity that told me that something was happening down on those lounges on the descending tiers—and as my eyes adjusted to the dimness, I could see that there were pairings and small groups of men dotted here and there, becoming very well acquainted with each other. It must have been early, however, as the theater was only about a fourth full of these fully occupied patrons.

The nymph whispered something to the bartender, yet another satyr, but a larger version than the young man who had admitted me to the club—indeed all of those serving the patrons were decked out in the same motif. The younger man pointed to the business card that I carried and then told me I could order anything I wanted—that the bartender was at my beck and call. That was very nice to hear, I thought, as I checked out the very presentable, broadly smiling bartender, not leaving out a peek over the bar at what he was packing between his legs. There was nothing there for him to be ashamed of.

As I sat back and drank my first drink and observed the atmosphere, I saw that activity had started down on the stage. The four poles now were occupied by male dancers—all young, lithe nymphs just like the doorkeeper.

Strobing yellow-white lights started to work the room, and I now was getting a sparkly feeling of glitter everywhere. That's when I noticed the decor of the room. Cylinders of glittery gold hung on wires above the stage area in thick profusion, and as the lights strobed, they bounced off the glittery gold sparkles and brought the arena to life. I noticed then that the lights were picking up glitterings on the tiers down to the stage as well—just here and there, but enough to make my eyes dart around the room, increasingly picking out very intimate embraces and activity going on at the lounges.

A few of the glittering cylinders were on the floor of the stage, and I assumed that they had fallen from the wires. But I felt a chill and a tinkling sensation going down my spine as I realized otherwise. From the third tier in front of me, my eye caught a naked figure rise from one of the lounges, and I caught the bounce of strobe light off gold glitter as he glided down to the stage and came up with one of the gold glittery cylinders and threw it down on the stage floor. Condoms. These were glittery gold condoms. Used condoms, merging the activity in the audience with the entertainment on the stage. The club's decoration was both evocative and functional. I watched in awe as the figure pulled another cylinder off a wire hanging down toward the stage and glided back up to the third tier, no doubt for another round of pleasure.

Four beefy satyrs had arrived on the stage now and were cuffing the pole dancers who had preceded them to the poles and, one muscled satyr to one lithe pole-dancing nymph, were beginning to perform a duet of love dance for the patrons. Each of the muscled satyrs was outfitted with a glittery gold condom.

The club was beginning to fill up now, and all of the patrons I saw coming in were handsome and well built. The club had developed a winning clientele. The performers on stage were turning me on. Already one of the beefy satyrs had filled his glittering condom and had thrown it to the floor and was pulling another one down from an overhead hanger and sliding it on his hard, curved up tool. He quickly was ready to resume his dance with—and inside—the younger nymph, who was contorting his body around the pole, seeking a new and interesting position to be taken by his partner. All of this for the enjoyment of those in the audience, most of whom were so absorbed in filling out their own glittery tubes to give full attention to the floor show.

I felt my tool pushing against the fabric of my trousers, and I reached down to stroke myself, only to find that I'd been so absorbed in the atmosphere around me that I hadn't notice there already was a hand there. I turned to see a nice, square-jawed face with bedroom eyes. But I only caught a glimpse of the man who had taken interest in me when the bartender said something gruff to him and he was gone. I was a little annoyed, because I hadn't asked the bartender to run interference for me.

Two satyrs appeared almost immediately, one on either side of me. They were even taller and hunkier and more hung than the bartender—more like the brutes down on stage were. They embraced me from either side, and I was so taken with them that I didn't struggle. Neither did I struggle as one took me into a close kiss, rubbing his erect cock against my thighs and belly as the other one slowly stripped me of my clothes and used his hands intimately to make me hot and moan.

I was thinking that the one who stripped me was about to put me in a position wherein the one could mount me—something that I strangely wasn't resisting—when the lights went brighter on the stage and the heart-stopping golden blond who had invited me here appeared. He was decked out in leather, but it was all of a glittery gold color, from the chain criss-crossing his chest, to the boots, and arm bands, and a riding crop with a billy club-like handle—but no other body attire except for the glittery gold condom trying its best to cover his abundant inches of horse-hung meat.

He walked the four corners of the stage briefly, flicking bottoms here and there with his riding crop and inserting hands into this and that undulating position, and then he came in front of the revolving transparent X apparatus and spread his arms wide, muscles rippling in the strobe lights, and all action on the stage stopped in mid fuck.

"Do we have a volunteer this evening, gentlemen?" he asked the now-filled house in a booming voice.

The strobe lights revolved wildly around the theater and then all merged—on me.

Before I had time to react in any way, I was being bustled down to the stage by my babysitting bartender and the two hunky satyrs and was finding that the transparent X apparatus had cuffs on it that, when I was trussed up, stretched my arms and legs out wide and securely in place.

I had become a focal point for the floor show. For the next half hour or more, as the satyrs returned to pole fucking the nymphs and the well-used glittery condoms from the audience and the corners of the stage continued to build up on the floor of the stage, the blond god teased and tormented me. He prodded and pinched and kissed and tongued me endlessly and to distraction, as I revolved on the turntable at the center of the arena, cuffed to that transparent X. He flicked me with his riding crop and applied love slaps to my butt and hips and thighs and chest. He twisted and pulled at my nipples and balls until I screamed my awareness of the sensual cruelty in him.

And then he fucked me with the greased butt end of his riding crop, stretching and preparing me for his even longer and thicker gold-glittered tool. All the time I was revolving, giving the club patrons a look at the glorious torment from all angles, writhing and bucking with and against the butt end of the riding crop, testing the rock-solid holding strength of the X apparatus.

The tiers running up from where I was being displayed were a teaming mass of undulating bodies and young, naked men descending to the stage and tossing their offerings of spent glittery gold condoms at my feet and then grabbing a replacement off the handing wires and remerging with the slithering pile of man flesh stretched around the room.

The golden god was behind me now, his hands on my shoulders, and his glitter gold cock slapping on my butt cheeks and working its way up and down across the puckered, moist rim of my asshole as he stroked up and down inside my butt crack. The bulging head of his dick came ever lower as he stroked up and down inside my crack, with each stroke now more centered at my hole, until with one long stroke he entered me deeply, strongly, and painfully. I lifted my head and howled to the ceiling and a cheer went up around the theater.

There was more of a hush now, much of the attention on the blond god and me rather than on each other, as two of the satyrs—the two who had handled me at the bar—left tormenting their nymphs and uncuffed my legs and held them higher and stretched out more as the blond relentlessly pumped my hole with long, deep thrusts, giving all in the audience a good view of my plowing as the stage revolved slowly around and around.

I was not shy in voicing being well fucked, and another cheer went up as my ejaculate shot out across the dozens of glittery-gold used condoms littering the stage below me.

The golden god also yelled his delight and joy when he had come deep inside me, and he swiftly parted from me, jerked off his spent condom, and tossed it out into a roaring audience. Then he strutted around the stage, flicking the poled nymphs playfully with his riding crop as, one after the other, the six muscled satyrs plowed me and added their glittery gold condoms to the offerings at my feet.

When they had done with me, my wrists were uncuffed. But then I was pushed to my knees, with my heaving chest forced into the V of the X apparatus, and my wrists were cuffed again at a lower position. The blond then presented his cock to me, me knelt on one side of the X and him standing at the other side, and I sucked him to life again as the stage continued its endless revolutions to show the entire audience the full effect.

When he was once more in engorged full-eight-inch fucking form, I was uncuffed and simply sank to the floor, exhausted. But once more the golden god's tool was adorned with glittering gold and he took me one last time on the floor at the base of the X apparatus. He lifted my hips to his pelvis and fucked down into me deeply and strongly as I lay whimpering and moaning on my belly on a pile of used glittery gold condoms on the revolving stage—loving every golden stroke he took.

I was carried to the blond's dressing room and laid on a studio couch. When he appeared, he had the decency to look at least a bit concerned.

"I hope that wasn't too much. I did tell you that if you came to the club, you would be fucked—and I had already seen you put on a string in your office, so I didn't restrain my men, but—"

"Yes," I interjected. "It was more than I expected . . . but glorious more."

"So, you weren't taken too much?" he asked.

My answer was to flip a golden condom to him that I had taken off a wire when I was being carried from the stage and to open my thighs, roll up my pelvis to give him a good angle, and, placing my palms on my butt cheeks, to pull them apart to spread my channel.

Batavian Duel

I lay, panting, on the sandbar amidst a sea of similarly wet and miserable, yet grateful still to be breathing, passengers and crew members and watched the pride of the Dutch nation, the greatest ship ever afloat up to the first quarter of the seventieth century, list over and go onto its side on the sand bar. At high tide it surely would slip under the waves. Only about two-thirds of the souls who had set out to test the fortieth parallel—known as the Roaring Forties—crossing from Africa to the East Indies on the great ship *Batavia* had made it ashore on what I later would be told were outlaying islets of the Abrolhos Islands, off the dimly seen in the distance coast of some vast expanse of land that none of the explorers had yet ventured to—or, at least, had boasted of reaching.

I was more fortunate than most of the other survivors of the shipwreck in that I had received a first-class education and had been kept informed of the track of the *Batavia* from the docks of Antwerp around the Horn of Africa and out onto the great sea en route to Batavia in the East Indies and a new life—a chance to make my own mark. As the bastard second son of the Graf von Hoensbrouck, I had no prospects in the old world. But as a favorite of the graf, I had been raised in the palace and given a classical education. And when I had come of age, the graf had given me the best of opportunities available—he'd apprenticed me to his friend, the merchant, Galo Needham, who was embarking for the new world in the East Indies.

Even a ship as large and fine as the newly masted *Batavia* was hard pressed to contain 360 passengers and crew members, and Needham's stature had won us no more than a small room of a cabin with only one narrow bedstead. I was considered quite comely and well formed and Galo Needham was in his prime and robust—and the journey long—and somewhere along the coast of West Africa, Galo had been moved by my groans of trying to find sleep on the hard and pitching patch of decking beside his bed in the small, stifling-hot cabin and had invited me into his bed. And he had opened up a whole new world to me when his touching, first with wandering hands and in time with lips and tongue into increasingly more intimate recesses of my body, had encourage me to open my thighs to the strong and wondrously large and hard member at his center and to feel him moving deep inside me.

Of this, Galo urged me to say nothing—even though after my first deflowering I wanted to shout my glorious release to world. Such knowledge between men, he admonished me, was a capital offense, even on the high seas, where life is precarious and opportunities for release limited—and, it must be said, where sexual congress between seamen was quite common, if furtive. If such a relationship became public knowledge, Galo told me, the offenders were subject to be marooned on any remote island being passed at the time of discovery.

Thus, we had to keep our lovemaking secret. And this was very difficult for me. Although Galo was a gentle and sensitive lover, his cock was overpowering and the experience new and exhilarating for me, and he often had to stopper my mouth with his lips and tongue as I lay on my back with my legs raised and locked behind the small of his back, his hips moved against my pelvis, and his cock explored my channel at great depth, because his throbbing movement inside me made me want to moan and groan loudly enough to be heard in the cabins adjacent to ours.

As it was, halfway across the track of the Roaring Forties, I was afraid that we had become undone, because the occupant of the cabin adjacent to the head of Galo's bed, a butcher seeking a fortune in the new world where the skills of knowing how to dress and preserve the flesh of animals was highly prized, as, indeed, it was in the old world as well, began to sniff around me with knowing looks and furtive touchings that I spun away from as quickly as I could.

On that night, having moved from embarrassed, "can't help it" furtive couplings in the night, I had become wanton and pushed Galo onto his back on the bed and straddled his hips with my thighs and impaled and fucked myself on his erect cock. And he had been too late in rising up and seeking to lock my lips to his to prevent the long, low, loud, guttural moan that had risen involuntarily from my lips as my channel sank on Galo's pulsing member. Galo had brought his knees and chest up to me, sandwiching my body between them, and moved his hand between his belly and mine and stroked my cock while I rose and fell on his. But he had not been quick enough to take my lips with his to prevent me from announcing the unmistakable sounds of aroused sex from the surrounding cabins.

I did not connect the suggestive attentions of the butcher, Saam Bleecker, with the dangers of that night coupling until a week later when I returned to our cabin earlier than usual to retrieve paper and pen for Galo, who was engaged in some computations of supplies for *Batavia*'s captain, Francisco Pelsaert, and heard sounds coming from Bleecker's cabin that were very like what I wanted to make whenever Galo imprisoned my mouth to prevent me from making. The sounds were in a much deeper voice than mine, but they unmistakably spoke of sex. The door was ajar and I could not help but look into the cabin. A young seaman, of no greater age than I was who I knew to be named Also, as we had had some pleasant conversations, was seated on Bleecker's bed, his shoulder blades digging into the rough timbers of the curved ship's siding, his doublet ripped open to expose his heaving chest, and his lower extremities naked. His legs were thrown out wide and his hips turned up. Bleecker, his back to me and his breeches discarded on the decking, was crouched between Also's flung legs and was fucking into Also with long, rapid strokes. The butcher had his hands around Also's neck in a chokehold that was leaving Also nearly breathless.

The expression on Also's face was of mixed signaling, his cheeks had a bluish tinge and his tongue was hanging out, but there was such a smile of satisfaction on his lips and a flash to brilliance in his eyes that I knew that, as cruelly as Bleecker was fucking him, Also was being transported into another, more glorious world than the stinking bowls of the *Batavia*.

I felt my cock rising in arousal, but I also felt my body shudder and go all atremble. I couldn't take my eyes off the brutal but exotic and totally sexual taking for some moments, but with a moan of fear I pulled myself away and retrieved Galo's writing implements and went back up on deck by a different route.

That was not the last time I saw Bleecker fucking Also, though, and Also always came back for more cruelty, which left me in a quandary of just what was the nature of what a man could do brutally to another man and still have the power to bring his prey back to him. I could not get out of my mind another scene in which I saw Also bent over the bed, with Bleecker fucking him hard from behind and pulling on a leather belt he'd looped around Also's neck and slapping Also hard on the bare buttocks—almost as if Bleecker was riding Also hard in a full-out gallop across the flat plains of northern Germany.

But from that moment forward, when Bleecker touched me and looked into my eyes in a special, questioning way, although I moved away from him as quickly and unobtrusively as I could, I was atremble not only with the fear of what he might say of what he'd heard between Galo and me in our cabin but also with the fear of my going with him to be able to feel the ecstasy of the rough fuck that Also seemed to seek—and the even greater fear that I would enjoy it and seek it henceforth as Also did.

Just as the Dutch mariners had speculated, the Roaring Forties filled the many sails of the *Batavia* and sped the mighty ship across the Indian Ocean at record speed. But this was a case of fatal overachievement, because the *Batavia* reached the area of the Abrolhos Islands a full week before anticipated and Captain Pelsaert did not have lookouts posted in the top sails. In the middle of the night, the progress of the ship was abruptly brought to a halt in a jolt that sent me spinning off Galo's cock and out into the corridor. When I recovered from the shock, I lifted my head to see water pouring in from the end of passage. The *Batavia* had been holed on a sandbar off the Abrolhos.

The next several moments, which seemed like hours, were a nightmare as more than three hundred frightened and barely awake passengers, already weakened from months of stormy passage around the horn of Africa, stumbled and clawed at each other to get out onto the decks as water poured down the gangways at them.

I somehow lost contact with Galo and slipped and fell below the rushing water as I was reaching for the ladder to freedom. But strong arms gathered me up. I was being borne up the ladder and out onto the deck with the aid of strong and steady arms. I was being held close by a hard body, which, despite my shock in the midst of an unexpected ordeal, included the realization of a hard cock pressing in at the small of my back. Once on deck, when I tried to struggle away from my savior and, by mistaken instinct, to scramble in the wrong direction, the man holding me in his embrace clopped me across the chin. I was stunned into semiconscious, and the next I knew I was in one of the *Batavia*'s few lifeboats along with more of the other passengers and crew than the boat really should hold and heading toward a small barrier island with a broad sandy beach.

I turned my eyes to identify my liberator who was still holding me close to him and rubbing his cock up and down on the small of my back—to discover that I had been saved by the butcher, Saam Bleecker. I willed myself to shrink from him, but images of what he did to Also and the expression on Also's face when he was doing it made me shudder and feel every touch of his cock at the base of my spine. I went hard, and I knew that Bleecker had seen that he had had that effect on me.

When we were stretched out on the beach, side by side, as the dawn was creeping in from over the thin strand of a distant land to the east and shone on the foundering wreck of the mighty dying *Batavia*, and after I had managed to fill my lungs with air, I turned and thanked Saam for saving me.

"Aye, I would not let a nice piece like you go down with the ship, lad," he answered with a growl. "You must not forget that I have saved you. I will take your thanks, but I will take it in my own way."

I shuddered at the thought of what that meant. I struggled up, thinking to put some distance between us amongst the teeming mass of sputtering, sodden survivors struggling up on the beach, but he reached out and grabbed my leg and pulled me back down in the sand beside him. He was lacing the fingers of his hand at the waist of my soaked breeches, and I had the sudden fear that he meant to pull them off me and fuck me right there on the beach in the middle of the heaps of sputtering humans and detritus from the wreck of the ship washing up on the shore, but just then I heard the cry, "Dane. Dane! Oh thank the Lord, I have found you. You washed away from me in the hold of the ship and I was so afraid . . ."

My master, Galo Needham was struggling down the beach toward us.

"Lay off now," Saam Bleecker spoke out as he stood and squared off with Needham. "I have saved the lad, where you would have let him drown. He is mine now. Get thee off."

"You are daft, man," Needham retorted. "Do you not know this is a bastard son of the Graf von Hoensbrouck consigned to my protection? If Captain Pelsaert lives, he would have you in irons for what you claim on this young man."

"I have seen the nature of your protection," Bleecker answered darkly. "One word from me and you both would be marooned."

Needham laughed at that. "Lest you have not bothered to look around, brother Bleecker, you might do so now. We are all already marooned. And as for informing on me, there are those enough who know you are fucking the seaman Also to his death. Your threats are nothing to me." Then Galo turned to me, and gently said, "Come, come with me, Dane. I have heard that Captain Pelsaert has survived and been seen off in that direction. Much of what was on board the *Batavia* has washed up with us and mayhap more will be recovered before the ship sinks under the waves. Our services will be needed."

Bleecker was glowering at us, but all he said as we struggled off along the beach was, "Remember, Dane, lad, that you owe me your life and I will have my reward rights."

He perhaps would have said more, but as we were leaving, he espied the young seaman, Also, coming up the beach. It was with much joy that I saw that Also had survived. I was drawn to him and would have been much distressed to know that he was not among the survivors. Some way down the beach, I turned and saw Bleecker dragging Also toward the small island's treeline. I could only imagine what Bleecker, in his frustration at having me there and then taken out of his reach, would be doing to Also beyond the fringe of those trees.

A good number of the passengers and crew had survived the sinking of the *Batavia*, and many of the supplies on board were recovered before the ship turned over. Captain Pelsaert, angry and embarrassed at coming this close to East India and having lost the world's most costly ship on its maiden voyage, almost immediately decided to press on with the heartiest of the crew members in the least-damaged longboat. He left his first mate, Jeronimus Cornelisz, in charge to organize the survivors and maintain them until Pelsaert could return from the city of Batavia in the East Indies with a replacement vessel—in the unlikely event that he and his men could reach Batavia in a longboat. Many a man of the remaining survivors cursed Pelsaert before he had even shoved off in the longboat, as Cornelisz was well known to be a fanatic and unstable.

Cornelisz lived up to this reputation immediately by deciding that the supplies and what could be found on the island combined were only enough to sustain fewer than half of the survivors present, and he took the direct and easy route to solving this problem. He organized a small group of willing and armed crew members and proceeded to systematically cull out the weak and those with skills that may be at a premium in East India but not on this remote island. This small band also was careful to save the fairest of the young maidens, whom they used mercilessly for their own sport.

Some of the passengers, realizing they would not survive the culling, quickly organized and seized three of the remaining longboats and stole off to a smaller, nearby barrier island, thus setting up two opposing societies that raided each other for the next five months where and when they saw an opportunity to acquire useful provisions or to take advantage of weakened defense.

Luckily for Galo, his skills in organizing and helping to ration out the remaining supplies were high on the list of immediate needs—which protected me as well, as his trained assistant. I may have been saved in any event, as Cornelisz, who had been second in command to Pelsaert, most certainly knew my parentage and the quality of my protection.

As a butcher and preserver of meat, Saam Bleecker also had an important place in the new order. Game in near sufficiency, if not abundance, had been found in the heavily forested interior of the island and in the surrounding waters. And to Bleecker's credit, he protected the sailor Also, as well, although, as time went by, Also seemed to be becoming weaker and weaker, no thanks to the beatings and sexual demands Bleecker made on him.

This craziness of society at its raw edge and most primitive lasted for five long months before, miraculously, Captain Pelsaert, having reached Batavia in the longboat, sailed back to rescue the now significantly diminished collection of colonists who had been counted on to make the East Indies blossom with Dutch civilization and culture.

During this time, Needham and Bleecker set up a running warfare of words and posturing over me. Bleecker became obsessed with taking his reward for having saved my life, and Needham met this with determination to fulfill his concept of protecting me as charged by the Graf von Hoensbrouck. Although my heart was with the gentle and loving Needham, the man who had introduced me to the joys of man-to-man sexual congress, my mind recognized the right of Bleecker's claim and also recognized the cynicism of Needham protecting me under the instruction of Graf von Hoensbrouck by having taken my virginity and regularly relieving his lust inside my channel.

Thus, when Bleecker finally had me, I did not tell Needham, and when Captain Pelsaert returned, Bleecker had been fucking me for two months without Needham's knowledge. I knew the relationship between the two had become murderous, and I shunned any part of bringing it to a burn. Some things were best unknown by Needham as long as I was there to lay under him and open my legs to him and take his cock in the nighttime. And it was not only Bleecker and Needham who were fucking me in those last weeks. Before the end, I was enjoying the young, heavy-flowing cock of Also as well.

Needham, in fact, brushed off the first several attempts by Bleecker to have me.

For instance, one day, while Galo was busy inventorying the provisions, Bleecker came up and said to me, "I have been directed to lead a party into the forest to gather wood. Come along with me, Dane von Hoensbrouck. I require your assistance."

Needham rose from his stool and stood tall, his hand on the handle of the dagger at his waist. "I require Dane's aid here with the inventory. Take the sailor Also with you. I know what you are really about in this gathering of wood. Also is accustomed to gathering your wood. Take him."

Bleecker's hand went to his dagger as well, but just than Jeronimus Cornelisz walked by and cast his dangerous eye on Bleecker and said, "I told you to be off getting wood, Bleecker. Do it now."

Bleecker glowered at Needham, but his hand came off the dagger and he turned and strode away, motioning the sailor Also to follow him. When they came back hours later, Also was struggling under the weight of most of the wood they had found and he had been beaten about the face and was walking with bowed legs as if he had taken a tree trunk up his arse.

Weeks later, though, I wasn't as lucky. I had journeyed into the forest myself to help search for small game when I came across Bleecker fucking Also belly down on a mounded rock by a pool of water. They were both wearing their billowy shirts, but their breeches had been pulled off. And Bleecker had removed his red cravat and was choking Also with that within an inch of his life while he was strongly stroking his cock in and out of Also's hole.

This choking that Bleecker seemed to love to do had fascinated me from the first time I'd seen him fucking Also in his *Batavia* cabin. Driven by curiosity, I had asked Also about it, and he had said that it was fearsome and awesome experience. That each time he had thought he was going to die, that all of the breath would be drawn around him—but that when he was on the edge of unconsciousness, all of his senses were magnified. Bleecker's plunging cock became three times the blinding fuck that Also had enjoyed from any other man and in any other circumstance.

We discussed the danger of it—and that the cruelty of Bleecker might lead him to take Also over the edge someday, and Also admitted that he feared that it was so.

"So why do you let him do it?" I asked. "And the beatings. Why do you let him abuse you so in the fucking?"

"Ah, I cannot explain it," Also had answered. And I could see in his face that, in fact, it was a concept that was well beyond his control and understanding. "But you would know why I do it if it happened to you, I think. There is no better fucking than what Saam Bleecker gives me. I may hurt after, and I may black out from his choking during, but when he fucks me, I . . . am . . . fucked. I cannot explain it otherwise."

This was not an answer that comforted me or kept me from being unsettled—and both fearing and wanting the experience at the same time. I could readily understand how it confused a simple sailor such as Also.

It was thus with curiosity and a sense of arousal that I watched Also's face turning blue and his eyes rolling back in his head at the same time that he was crying out in ecstasy at the fucking and choking Bleecker was giving him. And it was with complete disregard for myself, and thus what happened then was really my fault.

Bleecker saw me watching, and he had let Also go and had pounced on me before I had the chance to turn and run. He carried me, struggling and crying out in fright, back to the rock and slammed me down hard on my belly on the rock where Also had been lying. Also had fallen off to the side and was panting, trying to regain his breath, the red cravat still wound around his neck.

Bleecker was stripping all of my clothes off. Having regained my breath from being slammed down on the rock on my belly, I turned and tried to struggle away from Bleecker, but he hauled a great fist back and gave me a controlled punch in my face that stunned me and rattled my teeth but didn't do any real structural damage.

"Fight me further and you get what for," he growled. "I can make that pretty face of yours ugly with one punch." I believed he could, but still I struggled.

"You owe me," he said stubbornly. "I saved your life. Your sweet arse is mine by rights. And I have been patient. I could take your lover Needham any time I wanted. I think you know I can. Let me have my rights, or I will cut up your precious Needham and still have fucked you. I will have you now regardless."

Already riddled with guilt at recognizing that he, in fact, had a claim over me, and with the added threat to Galo, all of the struggle went out of me and I collapsed over the rock. "Have me then, and God curse you," I muttered. "I would that you hadn't saved me to hold this over my head. But you did. So, take your reward. I'll not fight you. But know that I'll never be yours. I am linked to Galo. He is my love."

Bleecker uttered a curse and slapped me on the buttocks hard and pulled my buttocks back so that I was standing away from the rock, but my sternum was pressed into the cool, hard stone. Then, as punishment, he thrust his cock strongly into my arse without further preparation other than the lubrication he had from fucking Also.

I gasped and cried out in pain and indignation, which only served to make him laugh.

"Here, Also. Make yourself useful," he growled. "Get under him there and suck him off as I do my work."

Also moved between me and the rock and moved his lips over my cock and gave me suck as Bleecker pounded away at my hole.

I tried to object in terror as I felt Bleecker's hands close around my throat, but nothing came out but a strangled croak. I was writhing in agony and increasing ecstasy on his hard, impaling pole as the pressure increased and I began to fight for breath and my eyes began to bulge in their sockets. I was growing faint, and there was a buzzing in my ears, and Bleecker's filthy-language commentary of how hard and long he was going to fuck me and how sweet my arse was began to sound like it was coming from far, far away. I could feel my windpipe being cut off and Also sucking at my cock, but the overwhelming sensation that was taking over and expanding over my whole being was of Bleecker's cock turning into a tree trunk, a veritable stately oak, and my channel stretching and stretching and of the throbbing and searching cock exploring farther and farther up my channel—seeming to move up into my intestines and soon to burst out of my mouth. At the edge of consciousness, I ejaculated down Also's throat, and Bleecker spouted deep inside me in fountains of cum that burbled up between cock and channel walls and dribbled out of my hole—and Bleecker released his choke hold on my throat, and oxygen and the pain of returning from the brink flooded into me. My knees gave way, but I remained impaled by Bleecker's cock, which was still hard and big enough to hold me up.

"Now you fuck him," I heard Bleecker saying in a voice that still sounded like it was on the far side of a vast, echoing chamber.

Also was weakly objecting, but I heard the crack of the slap across his face and then Bleecker was pulling out of me and Also was entering me. And he was doing so more slowly and not as fillingly as Bleecker. And I had the sensation of something more like the cock of Needham than Bleecker—a loving cock— a bulb that lingered on my prostate and made love to it that made my cock seep although it had been fully milked just moments before. One that was exploring my channel and caressing me at every nock and cranny. Slowly pumping me; not overpowering me and slamming into me, but encouraging me to join it in the rhythm of the fuck, which I did. A young, strong chest was caressing my shoulder blades, and I felt the sweet kiss of lips at the hollow of my neck.

This only lasted briefly, though, because Bleecker had positioned himself behind Also, and he was fucking Also now as Also was fucking me. And then he was choking Also with the red cravat still wound around his neck, and Also lost control of his cock, which now was plunging wildly inside me as Also

46

scrabbled at the red cravat with his claws and fought for breath. His flow was strong and came in three jerks.

And thus was my initiation into both Bleecker's and Also's worlds as lovers. Each was entirely different from the love that Galo made to me at night. And Galo made his love in the misconception that he was my only lover and that all of my energy was saved for him.

However, Bleecker was demanding as well. And I had grown to understand what Also meant about the thrill of Bleecker's choking fuckings. I was still in love with Galo, but the cock that I loved was the giant oak tree trunk cock that Bleecker's edge-of-unconsciousness fucking gave me. And having taken Also's young cock and body, I sought solace with him on occasion as well. We would steal off to one of the pools in the forest with the excuse of the need for cleanliness, and while bathing, I would swim over to him in the shallowness of the pool, where he would have crouched down, forming a lap, with an upright hard cock for me to impale myself on, either facing or facing away from him as the mood struck, and enjoy a cocking from one as young as me who could produce semen that could flow up throughout my body and make my eyes swim in lust—and who could harden again immediately and take me to paradise again before I had left it the first time.

I had reached an accommodation with this new society and with my role not only in the function of society but also in the adjusting of three men to circumstance, two of whom were vital to the maintenance of a balance of life on this small island. And then one bright morning the sails of Captain Pelsaert's replacement vessel were sighted off the outlying island of the Abrolhos. Miracle of miracles. Not only had Pelsaert managed to reach the East Indian capital of Batavia in a longboat, but he'd also managed to find his way back to the shipwreck island that was in previously uncharted waters.

But if Pelsaert had truly been brilliant, he probably would not have lost his original vessel to begin with, and his return certainly started off without much promise. His assessment of the situation on the two islands the survivors had populated wasn't any better than his judgment in having left the fanatic Jeronimus Cornelisz in charge to begin with. Pelsaert was, at first, duped into believe Cornelisz' version of what had happened, and he prepared to attack the other island of survivors who had only distanced themselves to avoid slaughter by Cornelisz and his men.

However, Galo Needham and Saam Bleecker, in rare act of cooperation, took Pelsaert aside and gave him the real story of what had happened after Pelsaert had rowed off in his longboat. Getting it right at last, Pelsaert had Cornelisz and six of his most bloody henchmen hanged before nightfall. However, in revenge, Cornelisz, in his final declaration, publicly denounced both Needham and Bleecker as sodomists—and me and Also by association as well.

Reluctantly, but wanting now to keep the cleanup operation neat, Pelsaert placed the four of us in a rowboat and pointed us toward the hint of a land horizon to the east and pushed us off of the small sand island that had been our home for five months. He and his men stood at the water's edge with muskets and declared that we would be shot dead if we tried to return to the island and to the amenities we had contributed so heavily to establishing there.

Needham was resolved to our fate, and, handing an oar to me, he and I went to the stern of the little rowboat and pointed it toward the east and started to row. Also was too weak to do much of anything. Bleecker had broken his arm in unusually rough sex two weeks earlier, and Also was black and blue from stem to stern from Bleecker's beatings and as close to death as to life. Bleecker was livid and fired off curses to all and sundry as we rowed away from the island.

He built up to such a state of agitation that, while Needham and I rowed, he turned Also on his back, his head banging against the bow of the boat, and spread the young sailor's legs wide, and fucked him in hard thrusts that felt like they were propelling the boat to the distant shore with as much force as Needham and I were managing with our oars.

It took us two days to reach the pristine shores of a landmass that was far broader than any of the islands we had seen in the Abrolhos island chain. Sometime in the night, however, while we were all dozing, Also had gone over the side of the boat and disappeared forever. I will always wonder

48

whether he finally succumbed to the cruelty of the life that Bleecker had thrust upon him and slipped over the side on his own, or whether Bleecker, realizing that he had almost completely used Also up, had ended it all for the young sailor.

However, Also's disappearance from the equation brought life—and death—to a head for the rest of us. Now there were two takers and only one giver.

We didn't last a day.

We landed in a sandy cove in the morning. In one of their rare agreements Needham and Bleecker agreed that the tree fringe in this cove was as good as any to attempt a settlement until we could decide what we were going to do to try to survive in this virgin land. However, Bleecker started erecting a shelter on the south side of the cove, so Galo and I moved to the north side to build ours.

Right off the beach, Bleecker made his move on me, commanding me to come with him to the south side. Such was his domination of me in sex by this time that I started to move off as commanded. But Needham laid his hand on my arm and said, "Do not listen to him, Dane. Beware of him. Haven't you seen how he drove one man to his death with his demands? And a hardened sailor at that. Come with me. Your place is with me."

Bleecker said nothing, and I did not want to see a confrontation occur any sooner than it had to happen. But I knew what Needham didn't know. He may possess my heart, but Bleecker now possessed my arse. And Needham also didn't know that I already was further down that path to slow death by rough cocking than he could ever imagine. I knew now why Also submitted to it. And although I genuinely sighed and moaned for Needham when he was fucking me, I was lost to a much higher level of passion and satisfaction when Bleecker was fully possessing me.

I felt my only chance at survival would be if the domination of Bleecker was no longer a choice.

So, I went to the north end of the beach with Needham and helped him build the initial shelter good enough for two—at least good enough until the next day and the next when we had all of the time in the world to improve it.

At dusk, Bleecker appeared at the opening to our shelter.

49

"I have come for the lad, Needham. He is mine by rights and by possession."

"What do you mean by possession?" Needham declared. "You cannot live on the claim that you saved him from the *Batavia* sinking forever. There is no one to say that he would not have survived anyway."

"I mean that I have known him. I have fucked him, and he cannot live without my fucking. I can see it in his eyes, and I wonder that you have not seen it too. Whereas he can forget such as you can give him all the time my cock is working inside him."

Needham recoiled in shock and turned to me. "Be this true, Dane, lad? Has this man cocked you? And if so, do you wish to go with him? Is his cock tastier than mine?"

I hung my head and said nothing.

"Answer me. Answer me now. This man would have you dead inside a month. You have seen what he had done to Also. Tell me."

"I cannot tell either one of you," I muttered. "You both have something I need and want. Do not ask me to choose." And then almost as an afterthought, "Cannot we live together in peace? I shall not deny either one of you."

The two looked at each other in looks of belligerence that intensified, each one placing his hand on the hilt of the dagger at his waist.

"I love him. I cannot sit by and watch you fuck him to death," Needham declared.

"I must have him all, and I cannot be given limits on how I take my pleasure," Bleecker muttered. "There is nothing left for anyone else when I have taken my fill. I will not share."

They stood, glaring at each other, the atmosphere palpable. I gave a sob and tears came to my eyes. If there was anything I could do to make peace between these two men, I would do so. The skills of all three of us were needed if we were to survive, let alone thrive, in this untested environment.

"On the beach. Now," Bleecker declared.

"So be it," Needham responded.

Both left me alone as the sun sank over the ocean.

Some minutes later, I heard rustling at the edge of the forest line and looked up, through tear-stained eyes. And there he stood. Bloodied, but cock hard and proud, ready to claim me for his own. Resolute, I lay back on the small of my back and opened my legs to him.

Being Fussy

I was going back home from throwing some hoops with the guys one afternoon when I decided to drop in on Charlie and see how he was doing. He was a little high strung and had been having trouble with his latest live-in of late. Denny, the live in, was a real cocky asshole, so sure of himself and going directly for what he wanted—and usually getting it—and taking advantage of everyone along the way. And he was messy. Charlie was so fussy about neatness that I knew this arrangement with Denny wasn't going to work out from the beginning.

The most irritating thing about Denny was that he had every reason to be cocky. He was a professional model and had the perfect body—with an unbelievable long and thick cock to match. He made my knees tremble with desire as much as the next guy and I disliked him doubly for this reason.

Denny answered the door, decked out only in a bath towel.

"Charlie's not here," he said, "But he should be back soon. Come on in and wait. He'll be a pissy little bitch if he misses you."

"No, that's okay, I'll—"

"I said come on in," and he pulled me across the threshold and closed the door.

I perched on a sofa near the door, as Denny padded back toward the hallway to the bedrooms.

"I was just taking a shower. You can entertain yourself . . . ," and he turned in the doorway to the hall and let his towel drop, revealing his horse-hung cock and, with a big grin, said, ". . . or you can shower with me and entertain me."

"Naw, thanks," I croaked. "I'll just wait for Charlie. You know how upset he'd be if he found one of his friends messing around with you."

"Ah, well, your loss, stud," Denny said with a laugh and turned and padded down the hallway to the bath at the end, twirling his towel in an outstretched hand and showing a luscious bulbous butt.

Less than ten minutes later, I heard Denny calling me from down the hall.

"Could ya come here, please? I want to show you something."

I sighed and stood up and walked half way down the hall way. The bathroom door was open. Unexpectedly, Denny entered the hallway from the door to a bedroom close at hand. He was wet and still naked.

"What?" I started to say.

"This is what I wanted to show you," he said with a grin. He was wanking his dong, which had hardened out to a good nine inches. He had a tube of lubricant in his hands and was already greasing up his shaft. "You wouldn't take a shower with me, and all I could think of was bonking you while I was in the shower. And see what you did to me? So, what are you going to do about it?"

"Hey look, Charlie is—"

"Charlie isn't here," Denny interjected. "And I don't want Charlie right now. I want you." With that he pushed me up against the hallway wall with a strong forearm, my cheek against the cold plaster, and he worked long fingers under the hem of my gym shorts and up between my butt cheeks to my asshole. All I was wearing under my shorts was a jock strap. Although I was dressed, he had easy access to me. He was lathering up my asshole with the lube and obviously was just looking for a quick fuck. And, naturally, he was thinking of his need and pleasure only.

"Here, pull your butt back to me and spread those legs a bit," he commanded. "We're going to do this."

I did as he asked, numb to any thought of questioning his authority—or his right to use me—and he started working his huge tool into my ass. To take him in I had to widen my stance even further and pulled on my butt cheeks myself to open to him. Tears came to my eyes, and I wanted to scream in frustration as much as in pain at his initial slide into me. But most of the frustration stemmed in how much I wanted Denny to do this to me and how I had wanted it for so long but had held back because I knew Charlie would be devastated. And Charlie was expected to return at any moment.

When he'd worked his way into the root and he'd started a slow pumping action, Denny arms came around me and his hands explored my torso up under my T-shirt and my engorging cock bursting against the jock strap and gym shorts.

"Nice," he murmured. And, ashamed, I glowed at the compliment.

He left me fully dressed, not even giving me the thrill of my flesh on his perfect body, and laughed when he was able to make me come quickly. He continued pumping me from behind for a good long time before he came, and then he just held there until we heard a noise on the porch and the scraping of a key in the lock.

Denny quickly extricated himself from me and glided into his bedroom. I barely was able to make it back to the sofa, my innards awash in Denny's semen, before Charlie, arms full of grocery bags, crossed the threshold into the room.

"What the fuck?" Charlie said as he entered the room.

I rose from the sofa, totally embarrassed, assuming that Charlie had discerned what Denny and I had been doing.

"Denny," Charlie yelled. "You were supposed to clean up this cesspool while I was gone. I can't take this any . . . Oh, hi, Kevin, I didn't see you there. Sorry for the mess."

I collapsed back on the sofa from relief that Charlie clearly didn't suspect what I'd been doing with his live-in lover.

"Denny, come out here," Charlie yelled.

A still-naked Denny padded back out to the door of the living room and leaned up against the doorframe, his arms crossed and a silly grin on his face. "Hi, Charlie," he said, not paying a bit of attention to how angry Charlie was.

"Denny, I can't live in a pigsty like this anymore, and you are three months behind in your share of the rent. Get dressed and get out—Now!" Charlie, trembling and looking quite angry, marched into the kitchen with his bags of groceries.

Returning, he took a belligerent stance, hands on hips, and repeated "Now," in an emphatic voice.

Denny sauntered over to Charlie and came up real close to him, face to face. He gathered Charlie to him with one arm around his back and used his other hand to unbutton Charlie's shirt and explore his chest. The two backed up to the dining room table.

"Denny, don't," Charlie was saying, as he arched his back and Denny's mouth went to his nipples. "I mean it this time. You're a pig, and I want you out."

Denny's mouth came up and covered Charlie's mouth, and his hands went to Charlie's butt cheeks and pulled his groin into Denny's pelvis. I could see that Denny's rod was beginning to rise again.

"Denny, no," Charlie said weakly, as Denny came up for air from the kiss. But his actions belied his statement, as he took Denny's head in both of his hands and brought him back for a deeper kiss. Denny's hands came around to the front of Charlie's pants and unbuckled his belt, pulled down his zipper, and pulled his pants and briefs down off his legs. He held Charlie's dick with his with one hand, while his other hand went behind Charlie and brushed the dishes on top of the dining table unto the floor, only adding to the clutter that Charlie had been objecting to. He then spun Charlie around and pushed his torso down on the top of the dining table. Going down on his knees behind Charlie, Denny attacked his lover's asshole with his mouth. He was squeezing one butt cheek with one hand, and milking Charlie's cock with his other hand. Charlie turned his head toward me, and I could see the wild sexual desire in his eyes.

In short order, Denny had Charlie's ass wettened up to his desire and he rose and positioned his cock at Charlie's asshole and dove in. Charlie lurched and screamed in pain, but his eyes were still on mine and were still filled with desire. They contained a look of almost satisfaction and victory that I could not fathom.

Denny pumped away at Charlie, as Charlie grunted and yelped. Denny buried his fist in Charlie's hair and arched his back, bringing Charlie's lips to his and brutally possessing him in a kiss.

When he had pushed Charlie's head back onto the table, he said, "Now about me leaving. You still want me to leave? Cause' I can pull out right now and go pack."

"No," Charlie whimpered. "I don't want you to leave."

"Then what do you want me to do?"

"I want you to keep fucking me. Deeper. Oh, yes. Deeper still. Ohhhh. Yes!"

"And you don't care how messy I am?" Denny pulled his dick out of Charlie's ass.

"Oh, no, don't leave me. I don't care how messy you get."

Denny rammed his cock into Charlie again, pushed in to the hilt, and just held there. "And the rent. Do I owe you anything for the rent?"

"No, nothing. Don't leave me like this. Fuck me. Finish me."

"Well, you'll forgive me if I'm tired. I've got to take a break, but I'll finish you all right. In the meantime, Kevin, strip down and get your ass over here."

"Who, me?" I asked dumbly.

"Yes, you, stud. Who else? Get up on this table and let Charlie get you hard again." Denny turned Charlie onto his back on the table top while keeping him skewered with Denny's long, thick cock.

I stripped and climbed up on the table, dangling my cock over Charlie's mouth, as directed.

"No, I don't think I want to . . ." Charlie started. But as Denny sighed an "Oh, well," and started to slowly pull his cock out of Charlie, Charlie capitulated with an "OK, OK," and took my cock into his mouth.

Within minutes Charlie had me hard and Denny pulled out of Charlie and directed me to plow Charlie for a while. Charlie started to object, but Denny said he'd only finish Charlie off if he let me take an interim go at him.

All of my senses numb except for my urgent sex drive, I moved down and topped Charlie. Our eyes locked, and I watched Charlie's desire sharpen as I pumped him. He was enjoying me as much as I was enjoying him. I had never thought of fucking Charlie before, but now he became the focus of my attention, and I sought to both give and receive the maximum enjoyment from this encounter.

"Rub your chest on his; kiss him," Denny directed me. And I complied. Charlie's mouth willingly opened to mine, and our tongues entwined in a deep kiss.

It was then that I felt Denny enter me for the second time that day. I was still floating in his semen from earlier, so there was little pain as his long, hot dong worked its way up my ass. He was driving me wild, and my mouth and cock were working overtime on Charlie while Denny was plowing my field in a counterpunch action.

Charlie was sighing and moaning for me while I was sighing and moaning for Denny. I came in a flood of semen that had my scream of ecstasy melding with Charlie's. Immediately thereafter, Denny pulled out of me, pulled me up and out of Charlie, and pushed me over against the wall at the side of the table. I just lay there in a heap, completely spent.

Denny, however, slid back into Charlie and pumped him deep. Charlie's grunts and groans for joy heightened, and I could tell the instant in which Denny flooded Charlie's ass canal with his man juice. The two of them lay on the table, panting at their exertion for several minutes.

Then Denny rose off the table, simply said, "Let's not hear anymore about messy or rent for a while," and sauntered back to the hallway to the bedrooms, not really paying any attention to Charlie's weak, "No, of course not" response.

We heard the shower start up and Denny singing to himself in a self-satisfied way.

"Why do you stay with him?" I asked in a tired voice. "He's just taking advantage of you. It's all you giving and him taking. You're right. He's a pig."

"Him all taking? He's got that magnificent cock, and I'm not getting anything?" Charlie responded with a hoarse laugh. "Dude, I don't care about the mess he makes or whether or not he pays rent. He's got the longest, thickest, most satisfying dong I've ever had in me, and the only way I can get him to give it to me hard and deep is to threaten to throw him out. I didn't hear you objecting when he had it up your ass."

And then he started laughing—weakly at first and then more jovially. I couldn't help myself; I joined in the laughter.

"Of course, your dong is nice too," Charlie said at length. "I wouldn't mind having that up me again."

"We'll have to set a date for that," I answered, tears rolling down my cheeks from the laughter.

"How about now?" Charlie asked. "You've had time to reload haven't you?"

"We'll see," I answered, as I rose and climbed up on the table and side-split Charlie in a long, tender fuck that included much kissing and fluttering of hands and tongues on willing flesh.

Black Box

One might ask what I, a young American, was doing in a seedy bar and male bordello on a dusty street in Peshawar, Pakistan, walking down the stairs from the rooms overhead after having serviced a Pakistani military officer. And, indeed, that's exactly what the fine-looking fellow in a well-pressed safari suit who was lounging against the bar asked me when I reached the bar and positioned myself at the perfect nonthreatening, but possibly available, distance from him.

He was quite presentable indeed, and an American himself, as revealed by his accent, and he was giving me a friendly smile, so I picked one of my less acerbic responses. "I'm here having a drink, if anyone is paying."

That, of course, was the very shortest version of how I came to be here. The longer version was rather painful and wholly unflattering, so I didn't talk about it much. The truthful version is that I had been working in male porn films in Jersey City, of all places, and the director of one of my movies said he was taken with me and my commanding stage presence, and did I know that the best pay for male porn stars was to be had in Karachi—of all places?

I didn't know that, and I didn't take into account that the director was a South Asian himself and one with a particularly shifty-eyed appearance. He offered to pay my way to Karachi, saying he happened to be going there himself, and I bit. Barely there, he promptly sold me to a chieftain in the unmannered tribal areas in the north, along the Afghanistan border, and I spent a good three months in his harem being defiled by all and sundry. What the director also hadn't told me was that South Asians could immobilize a guy in a position resembling a pretzel and fuck him hard for days. When the tribal chieftain had grown tired of me, I was dumped on the streets of Peshawar one early morning to look out for myself. I was saving for airfare back to the States, and this bar and bordello was where I was doing the saving, such as it was. It certainly was a step up from being tumbled on a dirty rug in a mud hut by sometimes two burly men at once—although not much more than a baby step up.

You thus could say that I was in pretty desperate straits and open to almost any half-way reasonable suggestion for changing my lot even slightly for the better. And that's why Steve's proposition, when he got around to pitching it, didn't sound half bad.

"I'm standing drinks over here, if you're interested, yes," the handsome, well-muscled man of about thirty said. "My name is Steve, by the way. And you're . . .?"

"Ken. You can call me Ken," I said, as I moved over beside him, close enough for him to make a move if he wanted to. "And I'd do almost anything for a gin tonic," I added, remembering one of my most frequently used pickup lines.

"Almost anything?" Steve asked right on cue, and the palm of his hand went to the small of my back.

"Well, 2,000 rupees plus that gin and tonic would get you anything," I said. I turned and smiled at him, and he grinned back at me as his hand moved down to cup my buttocks.

He fucked me on the same narrow bed in the small room upstairs where I had sucked off the military officer not more than thirty minutes earlier.

Steve was a fast mover at the bar after our signaling was over; I hardly had time to down my gin tonic before he had me twisted to where he was letting my butt know he had a raging hard on—and quite a good-sized one too—and he had one hand

62

on my basket and the other running up under my shirt and searching for my nipples.

There were only a couple of other men in the bar. A few were enjoying the view, but none were showing any surprise, having seen me more or less in this position a couple of times a day. I'd seen the dicks of everyone I could see from the bar myself on days when they could scrape up the necessary rupees—and had most of them inside me too.

When we got to the room, he told me to strip—all of the way—but quickly, if you please. He wanted to see me in the altogether, he said, but time was short. While I undressed, he did so as well, neatly folding his clothes. He had an athlete's body, tanned and perfect except for a few scars on an arm and his side that could be either gunshot or stab wounds.

Perhaps I should have put a halt to everything then. But I didn't. He already had money out and on the nightstand—somewhat more than the requested 2,000 rupees.

"Do lube and condoms come with the quoted price?" he asked.

I opened the top drawer of the nightstand, and he leaned over me and reached in and took out a professional-size tube of lubricant and two condoms. He held the condoms up for me to see.

"Twice. I put 6,000 rupees down," he said. "We square so far?"

I nodded and leaned back against the side wall, my shoulder blades touching the cool, moist mud brick; rolled my hips up at the edge of the bed; and spread my legs.

He fucked me hard and fast and deep and expertly. And I gasped at the thickness and depth and rapid pistoning and came a long time before he did.

"Stretch out on your stomach," he said in a low voice after he'd spent his first condom. I did so and he sat on the bed beside my hips and started massaging my back and thighs and butt.

It felt nice, something I didn't usually get from a client except for the few who fancied they were in love with me and thought they could, eventually, convince me I was in love with them too if they treated me right. This mostly meant they

63

wanted their fucks for free. I could have been in love with an exotic prince if he'd swept in and taken me away to his mountain palace. But none had ever ventured into the bordello in this section of the city to my knowledge.

Steve ran his hand between my thighs. I sighed and opened my legs to him. No problem here; he'd paid for two. I knew a second one was coming. He encircled my cock in a fist and started rubbing my piss slit with a lubricated thumb.

And while he was slowly masturbating me, he offered to be my saving prince.

"You married to this place?" he asked.

"Not particularly."

"I'm taking a walk in the mountains and could use a companion. Fancy some fresh air for a couple of days?"

"Last time I checked I wasn't due a vacation," I answered.

"It would only be for a couple of days."

"I don't have hiking . . . ahhhh, yes, yes, like that . . . I don't have hiking boots."

"I'd outfit you," he said. "And it wouldn't be a vacation, really. I'd pay you 20,000 rupees."

"And fuck me how many times for that?"

"Oh, maybe five times—unless you wanted more, of course. That would be double pay."

"I don't know . . . yeah, maybe." Business had been slow; it was the wet season, and the men were out watching their women work the fields during the day and coming home exhausted in the evening from seeing how hard the woman worked.

"In that case, here's another 2,000 rupees," he said as he reached over and took more money out of his wallet and laid it on top of the 6,000 already on the nightstand. "Sit up and blow me. I want to know how well you suck before I'm sure about taking you along."

Steve stood up beside the bed, and I sat up on the edge and palmed the hollows below his hips and beside his hard-muscled buttocks and opened my lips to his erect cock. I sucked on just his glans and flicked his piss slit with my tongue until he groaned and palmed the back of my head and forced my lips

64

farther up his shaft. I didn't think I'd be able to take him all in, but he proved me wrong to a bit of objecting and gagging on my part.

He was breathing heavily and I could feel him shuddering—always a sign that I was delivering satisfaction—when he pulled away from me, made me roll the second condom on his cock, and told me to lay belly down on the bed again. I opened my legs as I felt him pull my cock up between my thighs. And then he gave my cock some attention with his mouth as he crouched between my legs. His lips and tongue went to my hole, and despite all advisories from me that I was close to coming again, he tongue-fucked my channel and slowly pumped my cock with his fist until I did, indeed, come.

He took up a pillow that had fallen to the floor and inserted it under my belly, raising my pelvis to him.

"Uh, I said."

"That was you coming, not me," he replied. "I still have a rubber that hasn't seen the inside of you."

I just grunted and opened my legs. He stretched out on top of me, closely fitting his body to mine, and I widened my stance as his cock slid into me. He quickly encased my thighs in his, though, causing me to gasp and groan at the tight filling of my channel by his thick cock, and plastered his lips to the hollow of my neck as he slow fucked me for an eternity.

After that there was no question whether I was going with him.

I didn't count on how cold a walk in the mountains along the Pakistan-Afghanistan border north of the Khyber Pass would be.

He was as quick and insistent on getting off on that hike as he'd been about getting me into bed. He didn't even give me a chance to ask him why he was taking that walk.

I really should have thought about asking him that before we set off.

We took a Land Rover as far up into the foothills as we could and then hiked for a while and stopped at a rest station built for mountain climbers at the base of a mountain that looked pretty much like the Rockies to me. But maybe a bit higher. OK, looks can be deceiving. Probably a great deal higher.

After dinner, taken in silence because I was already exhausted just by the short walk from the Land Rover, Steve disappeared outside. I stepped out into the cold to see what he was up to and found him holding some sort of beeping metallic box and turning it in different directions, listening to the change in the beeping. It had a needle on it too that seemed to insist that it wanted to point up the mountain. I saw Steve smile and then he turned and saw me, and I saw him give a little frown.

I started to ask him questions about the beeping box, but he bustled me inside, threw me down on one of the cots and fucked all of the questioning out of me, leaving me a heap of satisfied sighs—at least for the moment.

It was still dark when he woke me up again with his cock plowing my depths. And when he'd spent another condom, his own this time, we bundled up and started our slow hike up the mountain.

We made remarkably good distance, entirely, I'll report, because of Steve relentlessly driving us on. Twice on the trail he stopped and told me to go take a piss or something over to the side, and I saw him open his little beeping box and take bearings again.

Before nightfall, we had reached another rest stop cabin on the side of the trail. I heard Steve mutter, "Ah, good, they're still here," which was my first clue that we no longer were alone on the trail.

Three men were in the cabin when we entered it. All of them were hulky and bulky and Slavic looking. They were speaking Russian, which, I'm happy to say, I heard a lot of in Jersey City, so I know how it sounds when I hear it. Can't understand a word of it, of course. Which was too bad, because the three were looking us over real good and muttering to each other.

Surprise, surprise, Steve spoke Russian too, and then I found out that the man who seemed to be their leader, a muscle-bound dude who stood a head taller than the other two and whose name was given as Sergei, also spoke passable English.

I don't know what Steve told them in Russian, but they settled right down and became quite friendly.

They had brought vodka. And, more important, they were happy to share. Steve said no thanks, he didn't drink vodka, but when he produced chocolates from his backpack, the Russians seemed to forget any tendency to take umbrage at his failure to drink with them. I did drink with them, though. I didn't get drunk, but I got tipsy—too tipsy, in fact, to be much use to myself for what came later.

While we all shared dinner rations, Steve took me over to the side and gave me a serious look.

"Listen, you are a loyal American, aren't you?" he whispered.

"Well, yes, of course," I said. "I'm not really in Peshawar because I have anything against America. Just circumstances, you know."

"What I'm going to tell you now can't go any farther than you. You must never tell anyone. If I thought you would, I'd have to kill you."

"No, really?" I said, amused. But then I wasn't all that amused anymore. He was smiling—grimly, though. But it was his eyes. They weren't smiling at all.

"These guys are Russian spies," he whispered. "They're after something I've been sent by U.S. intelligence to retrieve, and I . . . we have to make sure I get there before they do. Can you understand that?"

"Spies? Get where?" I muttered back. "Does this have anything to do with that beeping box in your backpack."

"Yes, of course," Steve responded, his voice laced with exasperation. "But we can't talk long; they'll get suspicious. I'll just tell you straight out and you nod your head if you're with me. If you're a loyal American. This is very, very important."

I nodded my head—not really for practice, but he was so intense and had such a strong grip on my arm that I wanted him to know I'd die for America, if I had to. I'd even sing the "Star Spangled Banner," it that would help—although even in these circumstances I couldn't guarantee I'd hit that high note in the song.

"A plane went down on the mountain. A reconnaissance drone. Something so new and different that almost no one knows about it. It was locating Al-Qaeda leaders. And it went down. And somehow the Russians know about it too, although only I have the homing device to be able to walk directly to it. I've got to get to the plane first. There's a black box and some other gear that I must retrieve. Understand?"

I nodded my head. One of the Russians came over and refilled my vodka cup. Both Steve and I smiled sweetly to him, and then he went back to where the other two Russians were huddled. Sergei had his hand high on the thigh of the sitting Russian, and the other one leaned down and planted a kiss on Sergei's lips as he squatted and folded himself into the bundle.

Steve gave a low whistle. "OK, that's it. I was told that was it, but now I know. Here's what we are going to do. Ken, Ken. Focus, look at me. Read my lips. I have to say this fast and very low."

I turned to him and focused on his lips. There seemed to be two sets of them, though. I obviously was drinking too much vodka too fast.

"I have to go on ahead tonight to the wreckage and retrieve what I can," Steve whispered. "You have to stay here and occupy the Russians. Understand? Try to keep them from noticing I haven't come back from taking a leak. I'll be back as soon as I can to pick you up and we can go back down the mountain while the Russians go on up looking for what's no longer there. Understand?"

I started to nod my head and then realized it didn't make complete sense to me.

But before I could say anything, Steve had reached over and pulled my sweater over my head. He then put his arms around me from behind and palmed my nipples and called out to the Russians, "Say, Sergei. You like my friend here?"

Sergei looked up—in fact all three looked up—and I could tell that they did like me, that they liked me a lot.

"Ken here is a male whore," Steve continued in a friendly, casual tone. "I bought his time down in a bar in Peshawar. Brought him along so I could fuck him in the evenings."

I started to object. But then I had to clamp my mouth shut. Everything Steve had said was true. And now I knew why he'd picked me. And I also knew what I was supposed to do to keep these dudes occupied while Steve did his thing retrieving that black box.

Three sets of Russian eyes widened up to saucers. I could tell that they all understood English well enough.

"You want to fuck him tonight? Only 20,000 rupees and you can all have him. I'll go outside. I'll sleep in the shed outside. You can all fuck him all night long. Only 20,000 rupees. What do you say? Look at this chest. Young American piece. You should see his nice hole. Good fucking, I can assure you. You can double him if you like. He loves cock."

I never saw 20,000 rupees appear so fast. And with only mild vodka-impaired objection and struggle from me, which the Russians enjoyed immensely, they did, indeed, fuck me in relays most of the night, with one Russian cock barely vacating my channel and my mouth before another plunged in and started pumping away. They were so engrossed with me and with each other that none of them ever showed any curiosity about where Steve was.

It wasn't so much that the Russians had big cocks as it was that they had a lot of stamina and had their timing down perfectly so that my channel didn't lack company for more than a few seconds at a time all night. And they'd taken Steve's offer literally. They didn't let me get cold—they very thoughtfully sandwiched me between two of them from time to time and let both of their cocks vie for position inside my channel at the same time.

Toward dawn, they were all exhausted and in a stupor from having imbibed more vodka than I had and doing more vigorous fucking than they should have done in the thin atmosphere, and at last, saying I had to take a piss, I painfully rose and pulled on whatever of my warm gear I could find in the dark—the Russians never having bothered to make me take off my hiking boots while they fucked me—and hobbled out the door.

My timing was perfect. I was still creating yellow snow not far from the door to the cabin, when a bright light on the side of the mountain, a good bit farther up than where I stood, blossomed up and caught my attention. Seconds later I heard a low, rumbling boom. Not loud enough to wake the Russians, I am happy to say, but loud enough in combination with the slowly waning bright light up there outlining a hump on the mountain to know that Steve wasn't just retrieving a black box and some portable secret gear from that crashed plane up there.

I also wasn't dumb enough to believe that Steve was coming back this way to pick me up.

I felt in the pocket of my parka and found that Steve had stowed the Russians' 20,000 rupee in there. At least he'd done that much. This, with the 20,000 he'd given me back in Peshawar, might be enough to get me as far as Karachi—a good two centuries forward toward civilization. That is if the Russians didn't get suspicious when they woke up and found that Steve wasn't here anymore.

"Ah, well, that's life. My life, certainly," I muttered and, with a sigh, turned my nose downhill and started off at a slow, painful gait, hoping that Steve had left the keys in the Land Rover—knowing, though, that he either had not, or that he had every intention of getting there before anyone else did.

Body Snatcher

"I agree that it sounds peculiar and there may have been some foul play involved, but I can't understand exactly why you have come to me, Mr. Reardon. Whatever it was, it's over and done with and no ransom was ever demanded—or at least you say none was demanded and paid that you know of. As you say the police told you when you went there, it would be very difficult to establish that a crime has been committed—especially as your son, Robert, won't cooperate."

"I want something done about it. My son hasn't been the same since he came home. He was missing for three days. There were rope burns on his wrists—and who knows what else? And he just drags around the house with a faraway look on his face."

"So, again, what can I do to help?"

"You're a private eye, aren't you, Mr. Gant? And I've been told you are good at it. I want to know what happened—who did something to my boy. He hasn't even shown any interest in returning to college. And he's stopped with his bodybuilding routine. He had been happy in college—and was very active. And bodybuilding was his passion. I want to know what happened. And if someone did this to him—did something to change him in those three days he was missing—I want to know who it was and how I can locate them."

"Yes, I can understand—but to what purpose? If your son won't—?"

"You need not be any part of what happens after that. I will take care of that part."

"I could look into it for you. It would be difficult to have any idea where to start, though, if your son won't help with the enquiry."

"I can give you a couple of places to start. First, you can talk with a family named Connaut. I can give you their address and telephone number. I've already talked to Harry Connaut, and although their son doesn't want to pursue this either and they don't have the money to, I do have the money to, and Harry is willing to help."

"Their son?"

"Yes. Their son and my Robert know each other—they work out at the same gym. And this is one reason I want to track down what's happening. The same thing happened to their son the week before my son went missing. He was at the regional bodybuilding competitions over in Boynton that week—and disappeared after leaving that. Again for three days, and his father says he has completely changed personality as well."

"And what does this young man have to say for himself?"

"Nothing more than my Robert does. He was missing for three days and then he reappeared and wouldn't say anything to account for his missing time. And Harry says his wrists have rope burns on them too. Mr. Gant, we think our sons have been held prisoner somewhere and have been molested."

"Molested?"

"Yes. In quizzing them, we pursued every angle of possibility. And they both closed right down and looked both embarrassed and guilty when we broached the questions of physical molestation. They both panicked when we suggested that they have a medical examination."

"Yes, that gives me some place to start. You say they worked out at the same gym? Can you give me the information on that?"

"Yes. And there is another point of similarity. Robert was attending another regional bodybuilding competition—over in Rawley—when he went missing. And I have another name for you. Chet Tarbell, over at police headquarters. He wanted to help, but, as you said, he couldn't put the name of a crime to whatever happened to justify an investigation. But he's the one who gave me your name. And he said that you could contact him."

Chet Tarbell, I thought. I wondered when our paths were going to cross again. He'd been after me for months before I broke off any possibility of getting it on—although I was sorely tempted. He was a real hunk—and I was into handcuffs just like he proposed to me. But I'd been seeing someone else at the time.

I'd have to telephone him and see what he could add to this to get me started on unraveling what was both strange and intriguing at the same time. And I wasn't seeing someone else now, so . . . who knows?

* * * *

"Hello, Chet? It's me, Dale Gant. I understand—"

"Decided to take me on, have you? Got just the set of cuffs for you."

I ignored this. This wasn't about deciding to "take Chet" on, as he said. But I certainly wasn't ready to say "no" to that idea either. I hadn't made up my mind, and I didn't want to be rushed into a decision on that.

"This is about the Reardon kid, Robert Reardon. His father said you put him on to me about this possible kidnapping, and he said you'd tell me what the police have on the case."

"Did he tell you that the kid won't cooperate and that we can't officially do anything about it until a claim or some physical evidence of a crime is lodged?"

"Yep. He told me that. But he also told me that you'd be anxious to help."

"Well, I am, but it's not a police matter, so I can't do it on department time. You'll have to meet me after work."

"OK, guess I can do that. You got a favorite tavern I can—?"

"How about my place? At 9:00 tonight? You game for that? Maybe you can provide some beer."

I hesitated. Suggesting his place rather than a public spot likely meant that he wanted to help himself as well as help me. But I had to start somewhere on this case. And Chet and I had been waltzing around each other for a couple of months now. I had to start somewhere with Chet too—or just walk away from what he was making clear he wanted. He had me on the handcuff deal, though. That was one of my fetishes. I could go hard if he was just sitting there and twirling a pair of handcuffs.

Chet lived in a trailer out Canyon Road. There were other trailers around his, but what once had been a bustling park was less than half occupied now, and the trailers were set around almost haphazardly. His trailer wasn't too close to anyone else's, and I would have missed finding it except for the weak-wattage yellow light he had on beside his front door. His Mustang and motorcycle were sitting next to his single wide, and he was standing in the door when I drove up—just in gym shorts and flip-flops. And from the backlighting from the trailer's interior, he was looking really good—all muscled up in chest and arms and a slim waist and tight abs.

I was wearing just jeans and a tight T-shirt and loafers myself, and he whistled at me when I walked between his Mustang and the cycle and into the light from his doorway.

I held up the six pack of Bud I was carrying, and said, with a chuckle, "I assume you're showing approval of the beer."

"That too," he said. Then he withdrew into the trailer and motioned for me to sit across from him in a dining alcove that had a small table surrounded on three sides with benches.

When we sat down, he raised his feet, without the flip-flops, on either side of my thighs, which might have given me a trapped feeling, but instead sent a shiver of sensuality up my spine. His toes were long and fat, which set off my imagination about how other appendages were built.

"About the Reardon case," I opened with, as I handed him a beer and flipped the top off one for myself too. "Do you believe something happened to these young guys?"

"I do. Did Reardon tell you about the Connaut kid too?"

"Yep. Think their experiences are related?"

"I do. These aren't the only similar cases that have been reported. The department is interested, but neither of these young guys will interview, so our own department has nothing going to take on the pursuit."

"But something similar happened before—in another jurisdiction?"

"Yep. Up in Springfield. A young guy was snatched during a regional bodybuilding competition there—he was a spectator, not a participant, although he was into bodybuilding."

"Like the two cases here?"

"Yep."

"And he talked?"

"Bingo. He has held for two nights and a day. Bound."

"And?"

"Fucked repeatedly by a masked man in total darkness. He didn't like it much. After the second night, he woke up unbound and in a room of a shut-down motel not more than a couple of miles from the competition venue. And he just hobbled out of the motel and headed straight for the police."

"So, what are you thinking about these two guys? That they were snatched from other regional competition events and molested too?"

"Yep. And either enjoyed it or were made too scared to talk—or don't want anyone to know their cherries were popped."

I was breathing a little heavy now. It was partly because of the image of the case that was forming up—and it was partly because Chet now had his feet between my thighs, and I had unconsciously opened to him. One foot was rubbing on my crotch, and my cock was appreciating that—and Chet could feel that it was. He pushed the toes of his other foot under the hem of my T and had the sole of his bare foot on my belly.

"Uh, those are some talented feet you have there, Chet," I said, with it coming out as sort of a croak. I took the top of the foot at my crotch in a hand and massaged his toes and the sole of one foot as his heel continued rubbing on my cock through the material of the worn jeans.

"You haven't seen nothin' yet, unless you stop me. You're not going to stop me, Dale, are you? I haven't read you wrong, have I? You agreed to meet me here tonight."

"About the Reardon case. So, there's nothing official you can do yet, but if I do some stakeout—like at the regional competitions being held where they've gone from here and come up with something you can use, you'd be happy to hear about it?"

"I'm always happy to hear from you, Dale."

And what he heard right then was a moan, because when I'd removed my hand from his foot, he was managing to pop the button of my jeans open. He was massaging my belly with his other foot.

"Reardon said, though, that you seemed to be particularly interested in this case." I'd said it as a statement, trying my best not to whimper at what he was doing with his feet, but it was really a question. And Chet took it as such.

"Whoever this guy is, he's crimping my style."

"Crimping your style?"

"Yes. What the guy who would talk had to say was that the guy who fucked him repeatedly was muscle bound, had one monster of a cock, and great stamina. And he was rough."

This wasn't helping me ignore what Chet was doing to me with his feet. "And this crimps your style because—?" I asked.

"It crimps my style. 'Cause, as you can see, I'm muscle bound, and as we'll be getting into, I have one big motha of a cock, great stamina, and I fuck rough."

I swallowed hard and tried not to look impressed.

Chet continued. "The only thing he doesn't do is use these."

He clumped down a pair of padded handcuffs on the table between us, and I almost lost it. I'm sure he could feel the effect on my cock. I tried to ignore them.

"And this has anything to do with you because . . . ?"

"Because I go to the same body shops these guys getting kidnapped do—and these sweet young things are what I like bringing home and fucking. He's taking my . . . gawd, Dale, you ain't wearin' nothin' underneath."

76

"No," I whispered. "I'm not."

He knew that because after popping the button open, he'd managed to get the zipper pull between his toes and pulled it down. My cock responded by springing out of the open fly and leaving no doubt that I wanted him.

He also knew something else, although he fished for confirmation.

"We're not just bullshitting here, are we? You came ready to play, didn't you?"

"If the mood strikes," I answered.

"I'm good at creating the mood," he said with a mischievous smile. He was leaning forward like he just now realized that he was going to get what he wanted.

He got the base of my cock between his toes then, and I pushed my jeans down and off my legs. One of my own feet went to his crotch after I was free of my jeans. He pulled off his gym shorts as well, and I handled his nice-sized, engorged cock with my foot as best as I could. I wasn't anywhere as skilled as he was as he was now pulling on my cock at the base—but I didn't have any trouble getting him to engorge.

He leaned over the small table and I leaned in toward him as well. He lifted my T over my head and his hand went under my arms and held me at my side with his thumbs stretched around to thrum on my nipples. Our mouths met across the table.

He moved his face up into my right pit and snuffled and licked me there. When he was working on my left pit, I shot a load onto the top of his foot.

Chet laughed. "Come on into the bedroom with me, and we'll see if I can make you come again. Not with the dexterity of my feet but with the strength of my cock. I've wanted you for some time. I've been told you take cock and that you liked 'em my size. That's not wrong, is it?"

"No, that's not wrong," I said.

As we both stood up and I came around the table, I reached for the pair of handcuffs on the table.

"Won't need those," he said. "I'm not into that bondage shit. I just heard that you were, and I wanted to impress you. A guy's gotta want it when I fuck him—and there's none of this 'he made me' shit when I fuck a guy. You do want it, don't cha? Even without the cuffs?"

"Yes," I said, still in a small voice—a voice that I hoped didn't reveal the disappointment I felt. I like the bondage. I like being taken hard and made to feel it was being forcibly taken from me. I'll happily wrestle a guy and continue to writhe after he'd cuffed me—and then change on a dime and not get enough of him as soon as he got his cock bottomed in me. The guys I fucked usually seemed to like that as well. That's why I hung around cops. That's what I thought I'd get from Chet.

I laid back on the bed, my rump at the edge and spread my legs for Chet. He came in between my thighs and began feeding his cock into my hole as he took my ankles in his fists and opened me even wider to him. He had great technique and worked me well, with me coming a second time before he did his first—and then we managed to come nearly together yet another time after finishing off the six pack. And I knew I'd let him fuck me again if he wanted to—but the full satisfaction just wasn't there, and I knew I wouldn't be pursuing him.

"Good for you too, huh?" He asked when I got to the door.

"Would have been better with the cuffs," I answered. I saw no reason not to be truthful. I didn't think we'd be doing this again.

He wasn't looking too happy or as confident as he had been when I left.

As I drove through the dark for home, I thought about those young men and whether they indeed were being kidnapped, bound, and fucked. And I couldn't help think that, if the guy doing it gave good fuck, that I'd probably not be complaining much in their position either. The one guy had cooperated with the authorities because he quite definitely wasn't into any of the shit. But these other two . . . maybe there were some reservations about complaining about it. I certainly know I would have had them. I guess I was just fucked up that way. But maybe these young men were fucked up in the same way and their families should just be letting it ride. The young men would either recover or become resigned to this being what they wanted. I'd be the last to criticize them if they did the latter.

I didn't have to drive more than seventy miles to catch up with the next venue of the regionals for the national bodybuilding championships. They were being held in a pretty seedy part of the town in a boxing gym that must have been in continuous use since the 1930s and not cleaned very often or well since then. It had the heady smell of male musk—and I'll have to admit that it was a smell that aroused me. It had been the smell I was exuding when Chet couldn't get enough of me. He'd said my scent was driving him crazy.

The light was dim, except for a couple of portable spotlights that were hung from the ceiling and trained on a wooden stage, also apparently portable, that ran the length of one narrow side of the room. The boxing ring had been removed, but its footprint was clearly discernible, the square of dark-varnished floorboards under where the ring had stood standing out in stark contrast to the different kind of shine of the gym floor around it, which was stripped of color and polished by decades of male sweat and shuffling bare feet.

The stage was backdropped in black velvet, with large, false gilt frames lining the wall in which the bodybuilders posed for the judges and cameras, and the platform floor was covered in a red runner carpet. Rusty folding chairs must have initially been spaced in rows on the floor of the gym, facing the platform, but by the time I got there, they had been haphazardly pushed to the back and sides.

I quickly could see why. The guys—and a few gals— there to watch the parade of oiled, nearly naked, highly toned muscle preferred to move around the floor, eyeing the meat on display from every angle and forming tight little groups and commenting on whatever it was they liked to comment on with these homoerotic pretenses that the arrangement of muscles "just so" was what this was all about.

They had gotten beyond the bantam weights and were into the light-heavy weights by the time I arrived. Nearly in total those milling around on the gym floor—most of whom were in some stage of body development to dream of being on stage themselves—were giving their full attention to the guys mugging for the judges. This regional was male only, and I could tell from the stares the guys and gals around me were giving the contestants, the most important muscle to a good many of these gawkers was the one the contestant had between his thighs, which was the only covered part of his body.

I didn't give more than a glance to these watchers. What I was watching for was someone in the audience watching the other audience members rather than the stage.

I quickly saw two such guys. One was a young guy with a pretty good body, but with a couple of hard years of effort in front of him to make the competition stage. He was scrutinizing all those around him—and when he saw that I was doing the same, he gave me a hard look and turned his eyes a couple of times toward the shadows at the opposite end of the hall from the stage, where two other young guys were standing and making some effort not to show their faces. Because they obviously didn't want to be seen, I did what I could to see their faces and burn their images into my memory banks.

After running my eyes over the cruising young guy a couple of times, though, I started looking elsewhere. He was too young and trim to fit the bill for what I was looking for.

But then I saw him. Mr. Universe of body. I could tell, even though he was wearing street clothes, that he probably could have been a competitor—in the heavy weights—on the stage if he'd wanted. The only downside was that he was as ugly in the face as an ogre. It looked like someone had taken a hatchet to his face and tried to rearrange the important parts—and for all I knew that might have been what had happened to him.

I first noticed him, because he was looking at the young, trim guy who was looking at the audience members more than at those on stage himself.

And I thought maybe he was about to make a move toward the younger guy. But then he saw me. We played a game of furtive "I see you, but you don't think I do" with each other, but then I saw him break off and slowly move through the crowd—in an indirect path that I could tell was a direct move to the back of the gym. When he got to the back wall, I was startled by the sudden blast of light—coming evidently from a door he'd opened to the street. He turned and gave me a bold look, and I made it known I would follow. If this was my guy, he was getting increasingly bold—which means he was becoming increasingly dangerous.

I followed. When I reached the door, now closed again, I looked around for evidence of someone showing interest in my movements. But I saw nothing out of the ordinary. So, I slowly cracked open the door and slipped out of the gym—and into a back alley. It was a narrow, dirty space lined with trash barrels. I could see normal activity at the head of the alley on a street that would be outside the main entrance to the gym. The other end looked like a dead end in dark shadows, I turned and walked toward the street.

I'd gone no more than ten feet when I both sensed and heard a movement behind me, and had time only to turn half way toward the sound, when strong arms were wrapped around my neck, putting me in a choke hold that had me dead to the world within seconds—and without an opportunity to make a sound.

* * * *

When I came to again, it wasn't to a cheery good morning, or sunlight streaming through the windows as the butler put my morning coffee tray down and pulled the velvet draperies away from the French widows. It was with the pain of a monster cock forcing its way into my channel. And believe me, I knew the difference between the two sensations.

I was in pitch darkness and somehow had been bent belly over a padded saw horse type of contraption, with my wrists bound to my ankles as well as to the legs of the contraption, which had me spread-eagled. The heavy weight of a man was folded over me from behind. I felt hard, full-muscled chest muscles, expanding and contracting with heavy breathing on my shoulder blades, and heavy fingers with jagged nails were digging into my butt cheeks and pulling them apart, as, with much effort—surprising to me as often as I'd been fucked—my assailant was forcing a telephone pole of a cock inside me.

I felt the strain of my balls being distended toward the floor with heavy weights—at least that's what I guessed they were—not having ever had that done to me before. But it was so arousing and drove me to such distraction, that I was game for the experience.

I also was game for the rapid, deep, and full-stretched fucking this guy—whoever he was—was giving me. He no doubt would not have been as interested in the fuck if I let him know that I was having a ball—that this was the way I liked it and that he was giving it to me beyond my wildest dreams.

Over I don't know how long a period in total darkness, accentuated only by his groans and heavy breathing, and my moans and whimpers, he fucked me in that position three times, each time for what seemed to be forever, and with very little time for his recovery between fucks. I came more often than he did—until I feared that my aching balls would just pop off my body and fall to the floor.

Fat hands went around my neck and I could tell his fingers were searching for just the right position . . . and then I blacked out again.

When I came to, it was still pitch-black dark, but I was on my back on some sort of hard mattress. My arms were extended outward and above my torso and were bound to something at the wrists. My legs were extended up and spread-eagled and bound as well. The Fucking Monster—which is what I had come to name him—was straddling my torso with his knees, facing me. He had the fingers of both hands buried in the hair at the back of my head, and he was pulling my head up, relentlessly, and my mouth onto his cock.

I gagged at the width and length of him, but I gave him what he wanted as I deep throated him, and I sucked him to ejaculation.

Then at least three more times, with little relief between, he was standing between my legs and brutally ramming my ass with his cock in hard, deep fucks that took my breath away.

He released my arms and legs after the third fuck and picked me up bodily. I took what opportunity I had to feel his musculature, and I was sure then that he had been the divinely constructed heavyweight I'd seen eyeing the audience at the gym—and that, from the talkative victim's description, he was the mass molester we were after.

At that moment, the case was solved as far as I could tell of what had happened to the Reardon and Connaut young men and also why the Fucking Monster was doing this. They said nothing, because they couldn't admit that they had reveled in the fucking they got. And the Fucking Monster did it this way because he was so butt ugly in the face, he thought he had to do it in the dark and didn't think any man would take him willingly.

This was nonsense, of course. With the cock he had on him, serious bottoms would stand in line to be fucked—and if darkness was required, they wouldn't see that as a problem. But rationality obviously didn't trump delusion in this case.

Where he carried me next was into a smaller, still-dark room, where he locked me in. It had a bed and a shower and a toilet. I have no idea how long he let me rest. But in time I heard the turn of a key in the lock and the squeal of a door on its hinges, and he was reaching down for me.

That's when I gave him the surprise of his life. As he leaned over me, I raised one arm and wrapped it around his neck and brought his lips down to mine and gave him a deep kiss. My other hand went to his monster cock, which was already erect, and I moved that between my thighs and to my hole. With a thrust of my hips, I impaled my channel on his cock and wrapped my legs around his waist.

I started the rhythm of the fuck myself, and I felt him trembling on top of me and his chest heaving as if he was about to cry.

I disengaged our lip lock and whispered to him. "If you want to do it in the dark, that's fine. If you want to bind me, that's fine too. If you want to get rough, I'd like that. But I want you to know that I love your fucking and can't get enough of you."

We fucked for hours then, in various bound positions, and a couple of times with my hands free so that I could explore the deep curves of his body with my hands as his cock continued its work inside my ass or mouth, and he gasped and moaned as I'd done for him the day—for surely a day had passed—before.

I spent several hours alone, as before, in the smaller room. And then we fucked again. His fucks were slower now and not so frequent, and we spent more time massaging each other with our hands. I could tell, however, that as new as the experience of a more-than-willing partner this was, his libido—his need to body snatch to fuck—was lessening.

After I was placed in the small room a third time, he didn't come to me again. I tried the door and it opened. The room beyond was empty too, I found out as I found a light switch and brought light into the room—into an empty room. Whatever devices he'd used to restrain and position me in before were gone.

I went over to a window and pulled the heavy drapes aside, not only letting in more sunshine, but also seeing that I was in the building that was immediately adjacent to the gym building I'd gone to for the regional bodybuilding competition. The alley from which I had been snatched was right below me.

I found my clothes neatly folded and stacked by the outer door, and I just put them on and hobbled down to my car—finding three parking violation tickets on the windshield.

I drove home and called no one. But I did look up where and when the next regionals were to be held.

* * * *

At the next event in the regionals, I found more than I expected to find. Fucking Monster was there—but so was the young guy who had been scanning the crowd the day I was snatched. I stayed well into the shadows, where neither of them could see me.

On a hunch, in the ensuing days since I'd been let free, I asked to see photos of the Reardon and Connaut sons, and that had panned out. They were the young men I'd seen the guy with the roving eye looking at where they stood in the shadows. I went even farther in my preparation then and asked Chet Tarbell to get me a photo of the guy, Greg Ivey, who had been molested and hadn't appreciated it. This guy at today's event was older and slightly different looking—but not so different that it didn't

84

make me think he was an older brother or cousin of the Ivey guy.

As most of those in attendance watched the bodybuilders on the lit stage, I watched the guys whose eyes were roving the crowd. I caught the moment that Fucking Monster's attention became focused on Greg Ivey's near look-alike—and, at the same moment I saw the look-alike studiously look away from the Fucking Monster. I also caught the movement of the Reardon and Connaut sons to and out of the main door of the venue.

The look-alike slowly headed for a back entrance—slowly enough to be sure he was drawing Fucking Monster in. The look-alike went through the door, evidently to a back alley, and the Fucking Monster went through the same door about a quarter minute later. I was cracking the door and looking out into the alley thirty seconds after that—in time to see Fucking Monster bundling an apparently unconscious look-alike in the back of an old Jeep Cherokee.

As I watched, though, the Reardon and Connaut sons showed up at the scene and sprayed something—probably Mace—in Fucking Monster's face and, when he'd knelt down and gone to his eyes with his fists, handcuffed his hands and, in turn, bundled both FM and look-alike into yet another vehicle—a Chrysler Sebring convertible.

I barely made it to the head of the alley fast enough to catch the license plate number of the Sebring and to jot down the license number of the Jeep—and to jump into my own Mustang—and keep the Sebring in sight as it moved off.

Trying my best to keep sight of the Sebring in the traffic ahead of me, I snapped open my cell phone and punched in Chet Tarbell's number.

"I'd hoped you'd call," he said when he answered. "Ready to go another round?" The tone of his voice told me that he'd thought I'd done just fine when we last met.

"Whenever you call," I answered. "But not right at this minute. I've hit pay dirt, I think, on the Reardon case."

"Oh, yeah? Speak."

"Let's take this progressively," I answered. I wasn't sure why I didn't want to turn this all back to the police at this point.

But I didn't. "You check the names and addresses for a couple of licenses for me, and if I still think I have a handle on what's what, I'll tell you more."

"OK, shoot, and I'll call you back as soon as I have something. You on your cell?"

"Yep. You've got the number?"

"Yep. After the other night I put you at the top of my punch list." He laughed at his unintended double entendre.

I clicked out without further comment and concentrated on keeping well back but keeping the Sebring in my sights. It left the town limits and was climbing up onto the mountain overlooking the town, where I could see that people had vacation cabins.

My cell phone buzzed.

"Got your names. The Sebring belongs to Greg Ivey's older brother, Joe. The owner of the jeep is a guy named Sid Bailey. He's got a record that makes me ask if maybe you've fingered him as our body snatcher and molester."

"Yeah, maybe," I answered.

"And if you're pairing him up with Greg Ivey's brother, my guess is that there are going to be some fireworks that require police help."

"Yeah, maybe. Gotta go now, though, or I'll lose them. Just stay by the phone for me, Chet, and maybe I'll have something for you soon—and if you hang in with me on this, I'll have something for you tonight too, if you want."

"Dale. I think it's time—"

"Gotta go, Chet. Just stay by the phone for me—and maybe set up some police response in Springdale for me—maybe toward the mountain overlooking it."

"Dale—"

I clicked off and concentrated on following the Sebring, which, a short time later pulled into an almost-hidden dirt drive. I drove several yards above the turnout and turned the Mustang and parked it on the other side of the road, ready for a quick getaway, if that was required. Then I started walking as silently as I was able up the narrow, forest-edged drive.

I got to a clearing, where there was a small log cabin, in time to see Joe Ivey being lifted from the back of the Sebring by three guys and, awake now, but obviously still groggy, being helped up the porch stairs and toward an open door. The Reardon and Connaut sons had now been augmented by Greg Ivey, who must have stayed at the cabin, waiting for them.

The Fucking Monster—I suppose I should now refer to him by his name, Sid Bailey—was nowhere to be seen.

I waited for them to get settled in the cabin and then I worked my way around to the back, where the window ledges came down almost to the ground, as the cabin was set into the slope of the mountainside.

Looking in the window, I could see that the four guys had Bailey stripped naked and spread-eagled on his back on a bed, with his wrists and ankles tied to the four bedposts.

He was being tormented by the four—sexually—and Greg Ivey already had a fat zucchini half stuffed up Bailey's ass. He wasn't enjoying the attention all that much.

I went around to the front and walked boldly inside.

"You guys don't want to do this," I said, hoping I had surprised them enough that they wouldn't just decide to tie me up as well.

"I know who you guys are and why you're doing this. I was hired by your father, Robert, to get to the bottom of this problem. I know who this guy is, and I've already notified the police, who will be coming to get him."

"If you'll press charges, identifying this guy as your assailant, Greg," I said, turning toward Greg Ivey, making sure he knew I knew who he was, "that will get this done. The police are anxious to get it stopped. But there's no need for you four to go down too on the same charges. Clear out now, and there'll be no connection on him being apprehended and the four of you. Believe me, he'll get his in prison where he'll be branded in the most uncomfortable ways for the nature of his crime."

I had spoken fast and with authority before they could get their thoughts organized, but none of them headed for the door.

"You've got about ten minutes to be down the mountain before the police arrive," I then said. "You did good to track him down. Don't make it worse on your parents to have you up on charges too."

"Come on, guys," Joe Ivey, the oldest of the four and probably the brains for what they'd done, said. "He's right."

"How do we know he isn't just a friend of this guy's?" Greg Ivey piped up.

"My dad did hire someone named Gant," the Reardon son interjected.

"He snatched you too, didn't he?" Joe Ivey said, turning back to me. "I saw him do it."

"Yes, he did," I answered, "So, I have as much reason to want him taken down as you four do. His name's Sid Bailey. Here, I'll write his address down, and you can visit him if the law doesn't put him away. There's no reason not to stay out of it, though, if they do put him in prison. And now you have about five minutes to be gone. What's it going to be?"

I stood at the door to the cabin and watched until the Sebring and the other car, a Camaro, that Greg Ivey must have driven to the cabin were out of sight. Then I turned and looked at Bailey, who was looking back at me.

"You acted like you wanted the fuck," he said in a tone that tried to assert authority but had an edge of hysteria to it. "You let me go and I'll fuck you good."

"Oh, I think you'll fuck me good, anyway," I said, as I started stripping off my clothes. That done, I mounted his hips and impaled myself on his cock. I reached back and started twisting the zucchini still stuck in his channel, and he screamed out in frustration and pain as I screwed it further up into him. But he also stayed hard as I rode him to two ejaculations.

It was twilight before I called Chet to tell him where the police could pick Bailey up—and that they should contact Greg Ivey for a start on a formal pressing of charges.

"Oh, and Chet, if your guys ignore the state in which you find Bailey, I'll be extra special nice to you tonight. I'm sure your guys won't mind a bit of revenge having been taken before he was handed over to you. If you think otherwise, I won't tell you where he is."

Chet said he didn't have a problem with that. He also said we could use handcuffs that evening if I wanted. I told him that I wanted.

I dressed and left Bailey there, the zucchini well up into his channel. As I walked back to the Mustang, I was almost sad that I had to turn him in rather than keep him as a toy.

Bring on the Ruggers

It is all working just as Rod and I planned. I was visiting him in Napier after he had taken up the position of physical therapist for your Maori exhibition rugby team that had been formed for the Sydney Olympics and had proved to be so fearsome that it is now permanently organized and homed in Napier, New Zealand, and taking on—and slaughtering—all comers. The fierce opening ceremony you Maori players, all big, husky brutes with tattooed faces, perform before a match in itself usually intimidates the opponent teams so much that they melt in the actual match. The Maoris are naturally powerful, regular muscle machines, and once they'd learned to play rugby, there was practically no beating them. Hats off to you for bringing yourselves into the public eye.

Rod, an Aussie from Perth, and I were old fuck buddies from our days in Hawaii, where we studied physical therapy together at the university. I went back to the States and worked in the NFL, where I gained a taste for big bruiser football players. I loved how they took me and overpowered me and fucked me anyway they liked, with no thought to what I liked—without knowing that I liked to be taken brutally and totally. But years of pounding by them have left me craving even more.

Rod went back down under, and once he'd landed a job with you lot in Napier, he coaxed me to come on down, knowing that you Maoris could give me just the cocking I'd go half way around the world to get.

You remember me. I know you do. I was on the bench for your home matches against Auckland and Dunedin, where you wiped the field with the other teams and sent nearly half of their squads to the hospital.

I was there on the bench with Rod, and you kept eyeing me. Giving me that look that is universal for those with monster cocks who know how to use them on other men—the look that I'd seen from many a fullback in the American football leagues before they trapped me in the showers and fucked the stuffing out of me. I knew you wanted me. And Rod assured me that you fucked men; he'd seen you do it, and seen you leaving them sucking air and moaning and not able to close their legs and shitting bricks for weeks because their channels wouldn't close up after you'd reamed them. Rod knew that's what I wanted too—that I'd toughened so much that prime American football hunk cock no longer mastered me.

So, yes, you remember me, and I'm here again for your home game with Wellington, and I was out on the field again tonight and you gave me that look and pointed at me, letting me know you were singling me out. You gave me that big smile when I signaled my agreement. I've heard how you Maoris like to take your revenge on white men for the years of suppression. You think I'm going to be surprised and beaten. But the surprise is going to be on you.

You probably think I'll be waiting for you at the players' exit, all randy and naïve, thinking it will be a lark, something to write home to boast about, just a novelty: "Hey guys, I fucked a Maori today." And that you'll bundle me into your car, drive me to the other end of the parking lot and stop in the shadows and make me suck you off—unhinging my jaw in the futile attempt to stuff you all in—and then pull me into your backseat and cock me so deep and thick and hard that it will make me beg for the mercy you won't give me. And that after you've brutalized me, you then will just push me out onto the pavement, used up, exhausted, moaning—unable to close my legs—and will have taught the rough lesson that Maoris aren't normal men, aren't a force to be taken for granted or dismissed or "handled" as the white man has attempted to do to them for nearly two centuries. Another Maori victory over the invading, grasping Caucasians.

I'm sure you think I don't know that you have a killing cock and leave any but your rugged Maori lovers rebored into puddles of jelly. But I know what you can do, and it's what I want—and I'm not unprepared for it, no matter how tame I look. And I won't be panting at the players' exit. You'll see me before then.

Rod, knowing both that I have a hard on for you and that you will ball at the drop of a jock strap—or loin cloth, I guess for you Maoris—has arranged for me to give you your massage after you've torn the Wellington team apart. I'm waiting, trembling in anticipation in the massage cubicle beyond the shower room, listening for the final roar of the crowd when you've done your worst to the other team and you've taken your victory lap and hung the heads of your opponents on your belts.

I hear you and your mates streaming into the locker room and to the showers. Your raunchy, prideful banter is making me hard and making me shudder in anticipation of the tension of that first look, when you see that it's me who is going to rub you down and that I'm going to give you that look of acceptance of anything you want to do to me.

And there you are in the doorway, holding a towel around your waist, looking magnificent and fierce in your bulky muscles and warlike tattooing. I give you that look, and your smile broadens, and you drop your towel and stand squarely in the doorway, giving a statement without words that there's "no turning back" and "you'll never ever be the same again." I gasp at the sight of what's swinging between your legs, and that amuses you—you assuming that I'm in over my head and that you are going to split me in two and use the cocky little Caucasian all up—and I see flames in your eyes and your cock begin to engorge for me.

I know I wouldn't leave this room unravished now even if I wanted to. But I don't want to. And I know that look I'm giving you tells you I don't want to—not that I challenge you but that I surrender to you and that I'm worth the ravishing. That I'm something special just as you are someone special.

Once alone with your hard, muscled nakedness in the massage room outside the steamy showers, all it takes is that exchange of looks when you stretch out on the board for your massage. You lift your hips off the board as my hand glides up inside your meaty thighs, possessing your cock, and you laugh low down in your throat and then grunt in pleasure and satisfaction—and knowing what comes next—as I pull on your thick dick and work it with one fist while I rub your tight, hard-played muscles with the other hand. You grunt as my mouth goes down over your bulging cock head, and you jerk and tremble and open your eyes wide with astonishment as I slowly swallow you down to the quick and close my teeth over the root of your throbbing tool.

With a guttural animal sound, you bound off the table and grab me up in your arms just as if you were still in the scrum out on the field—wanting to take immediate charge, to teach me my place. You are tearing off my shorts, and I am winded but laughing when you slam me down on my back on the board. But by the time you've scrambled up onto the board over me, I've spread my legs and lifted my pelvis to you, clutching your firm, round buttocks as you thrust brutally inside me. Your eyes go wide again and you gasp yourself when you realize giant cocks have been there before—that you glide in easily and that my cries are of passion, not of unbearable pain. I feel you trembling, awakening to the realization as I close my channel walls on your cock and make my internal muscles start to ripple across your invading piece that I'm going to give you the fuck of your life as well.

You are looking down into my face with that fierce, tongue-hanging-out stance you Maoris have used for years just before tearing your enemies apart. I take your stare, though, and give you my "I'm open to you; do your worst" look, and I feel the arousal that gives you all the way down into your thickening and throbbing cock that has split me like a mighty war club.

I want to die impaled on your bludgeon of a cock. Philosophers say that orgasm is the ultimate death experience, and I want to die a thousand times on your plunging cock.

94

The extraordinary strength and length and hardness and endurance of you makes me arch my back and moan to the ceiling as you fuck on and on and on—trying to make me beg for mercy. But your pistoning is spurred to higher velocity as I cry out, rather, for more, more, more. You let loose with a joyous Maori war cry, being taken to heights of passion and ecstasy in your cocking that no previous Caucasian lover has endured.

I squeeze your butt cheeks hard, white nails dug into chocolate-brown flesh, pulling you tight to me with each forward thrust, as the power of your thrusts pushes me up the board. My head drops over the end of the board, and I hear the intake of breath of another monstrously huge Maori rugby player coming out of the shower and into the massage room, where he was scheduled to follow you on the table. You have overused your time, however, just as you are overusing my channel in your never-ending fuck—your unrewarded attempt to hear my death rattle and watch my eyes roll back into my head in mortal surrender of weak Caucasian to unconquerable Maori.

The other Maori's thick, bulbous cock briefly comes into view as he positions himself at my head. As I take him inside my mouth, he leans over my heaving chest, his fingers digging at my nipples, his cock pumping deep into the back of my throat as his lips meet yours. I feel the pleasure of your shared kiss in the throbbing of both of your cocks pounding inside me.

And I die a thousand deaths and am transported to a ninth heaven under the pounding, pounding, pounding of the mighty Maori clubs inside me.

Cairo Captive

He had his dick inside me a half hour after we'd met. Jorgen was that good, he was. It also was like I was fucking myself. Almost a mirror image, which was no less surprising because he was Scandinavian and I'm an American—never knowing before then that my ancestry might have been Scandinavian too.

Granted I'd entered the beach bar in Brindisi, Italy, to get pretty much what I got. But I had no idea it would happen so fast—or that it would lead to what it did.

I had come to Rome as international financier Theo Gamboni's boy toy, having picked him up in New York City when he was slumming in a gay bar. Gave him such a good ride in his hotel room, making all of those noises and responses that made him feel like he was my first and had the world's most potent tool, that he asked me to stick around. That surprised me. I'd gone with him because I'd seen the wad of bills he was flashing and I figured I'd lift it off of him sometime during the night. That was what I usually did. I primarily was a pickpocket; and I was really good at it. And I'd found a good angle on it. Most marks were too embarrassed to contact the police after I'd fucked them and fleeced them; most didn't want to explain the circumstances to the police or their families.

Theo couldn't get enough of me. He'd attend all of those nerve-wracking meetings on Wall Street and come back to his hotel room all keyed up—and there I'd be. On the edge of the bed, or in a chair, or leaning against the frame of the sliding glass door out to the balcony, naked and posed for him. He'd drop what he was carrying and start stripping as he moved to me. And I'd get all "Daddy, yes, yes" and spread my legs for him and cry out like it was the first time—each time—as he thrust inside me.

It worked a charm. If I'd known being taken care of was this easy, maybe I wouldn't have become a pickpocket in the first place. Maybe not—but, again, maybe I still would have. It was like a compulsion with me.

Theo Gamboni so much couldn't get enough of me that he invited—no, begged—me to go back to Rome with him. Which, I did, not having anything to speak of holding me to New York.

For a couple of weeks that worked out all right. Until two things happened. Theo started sharing me with his friends, and I started picking their pockets.

The first time was rather a surprise. Theo and I were having dinner in a swank Rome restaurant and one of his business associates, older, bulkier, and uglier than Theo, joined us. I gathered from what they were talking about that Theo was trying to get the other guy, name of Aldo, I think, to come in on a business deal. Ugly Aldo kept eying me and saying maybe, and Theo got the message long before I did. Aldo said he wanted to see Theo's new apartment. And when we got there, I didn't have a chance. Aldo knew how to control and to undress and to fuck. He might have been ugly, but his cock was long and thick, and he knew what to do with it. Theo watched. And after Aldo had left, Theo fucked me too—and the ardor with which he did it told me he had found a whole new game he liked to play.

There were other "chance" encounters after that with other men who also wanted to see Theo's apartment. And Theo always watched while they fucked me and then took me with added lust himself afterward. After the second one, I decided I needed to be recompensed over and above what I was getting from Theo. So, I put my pickpocketing talents to work and relieved these men who just had to see Theo's new apartment of some of their wallet cash—not all of it, but enough to make me feel this was worth my while.

This, of course, could not go on forever, so I left Rome before Theo and the Italian police could catch on to what I was doing. And not really knowing all that much about Europe, I headed south, down the boot of Italy, rather than north up into Europe proper, and wound up on the Adriatic Sea at the port city of Brindisi.

I nosed around when I got there and found out where the best place was to pick up middle-aged men, the ones likely to have enough money to make it worth my while, and that's how I ended up at the beach bar overlooking the Adriatic at the edge of the city.

There was a fairly good crowd in the bar when I got there. A lot of good possibilities for getting my fingers into their wallets. I was a fool, I guess, for letting Jorgen take me.

He stood out in the crowd. A tall, well-muscled blond with blue eyes and a smile that drew me right in. I guess I first latched on to him because of the striking resemblance between us, but the more I looked, the more I decided that he had more than I did. The facial expressions he used were manipulative in the most arousing of ways. He drew me in just with that smile of his—a knowing smile, knowing that within a half hour he'd be fucking me—if that was what he wanted. And somehow this message was conveyed to me and I didn't fight it. I didn't care. The middle-aged men would wait, I was sure. If he motioned to me, I knew I'd follow him.

He did motion, and as I passed him, he turned and placed the palm of his hand on my butt and guided me out onto the deck of the bar, facing the sea. We weren't alone. A couple of men were in a deck chair in the shadows, one lapped by the other, slowly and silently fucking. They might not have actually been silent, but whatever they were voicing was lost in the screaming of the surf reaching out for high tide not far from the railed edge of the deck. It was windy too, which also would snatch words out of one's mouth and scatter them to the elements.

Jorgen guided me over to the railing, facing me out to the sea, and covered me closely from behind, his hands gripping the railing hard on either side of me, imprisoning me there at the rail.

He kissed me in the hollow of my neck and then on the cheek, and then he took an ear lobe into his mouth and put pressure on it with his teeth. I sighed and turned my face to his, and we kissed. He unbuttoned my shirt and let his hands glide all over my chest and belly. He whispered in my ear how nice I was. And I believed him.

He murmured what he wanted to do with me as he was unbuckling my belt, lowering my zipper, and pushing my jeans and briefs down off my hips. I believed him and turned my face to his again, giving him a kiss of acquiescence.

I felt an engorged cock rubbing up and down inside my crease, across my hole. He whispered then that he was going to do it, that he was going to fuck me there and then. And I moaned and said nothing to disagree with him.

He flashed a condom packet in front of my face, still covering me close from behind, against the railing, and said I would have to tear it open if I wanted him. No problem—other than the trembling of my hands.

And he fucked me there, from close behind me, taking me in long, deep strokes, nibbling on my ear, whispering what a good fuck I was, me gripping the railing for dear life, him stroking my cock with a fist until I spouted off in long arcs toward the pounding surf—all within the first half hour of walking into the bar. I didn't even know his name until afterward.

After, when I asked if I'd see him again, him still holding me prisoner against the railing, his cock still buried deep inside me, he said I could see him every day if I wished.

"See that sailboat out there?" he asked. "The one anchored off the pier over there?"

"Yes."

"That's mine. I sail for Alexandria tonight. I live in Egypt. You can come with me if you want."

* * * *

The journey across the Mediterranean to North Africa, first across the Adriatic Sea to the Dalmatian coast and then down the coast of Greece, along the southern stretch of Crete, and then the dash across the Mediterranean to the Nile delta, was a progression of five things: trim the sails, fuck, eat, fuck, and sleep, with little time available for eat and sleep.

I learned little about Jorgen other than his first name and that he owned a dive of a gay bar in Giza, outside of Cairo and near the pyramids, which he had to keep on a very low profile because of the supposed Egyptian taboos about homosexuality, a taboo many of them paid no heed to in their private lives. The bar was named Amr's, and Jorgen said he thought I'd like it there. I didn't tell him much about myself, either—certainly not about my pickpocketing proclivities. I wondered if the middle-aged men of Cairo had wallets as thick as those of Rome.

Off of Alexandria, within sight of land, Jorgen hove to and anchored. It was twilight. He said that I should go ahead and sleep, that he'd take the dingy into the harbor and smooth our entry into Egypt—that after his trip into harbor, we wouldn't have to worry about Customs, that he'd be back by sunrise. He floated off into the night toward the lights of Alexandria, and I went to our berth below, nagged suddenly by the question of whether we were transporting—or had just finished transporting—something Jorgen didn't want to declare to Customs the normal way. I hadn't asked what Jorgen was doing in Italy; perhaps that was a mistake. Not that he would have told me the truth if he was smuggling something one way or the other—or both.

I woke with a jolt— the slamming of the side of one boat against another. And my first thought was that it was the authorities, having caught onto whatever Jorgen was up to—and me being left here holding the bag. And it occurred to me as well that I looked enough like Jorgen that they might think I was him if they were looking for him in particular.

I only made it to the hatch leading onto the deck before hands grabbed me and a cloth bag was pulled down over my head. I was bound and gagged, and I realized that I was being transferred from one boat to another and that we were casting off and moving under the power of a muffled motor.

Was I Jorgen now? What had Jorgen done for this to be happening?

I started to squirm and then I felt a tight grip on my arm and the prick of a needle, and I was dead to the world.

* * * *

When I came to, I thought I'd been dropped into an Arabian nights film set, if a rather seedy one. The room was stone-walled, with a vaulted ceiling and high-off-the-floor, heavily barred arched windows. Although the furnishings, such as they were, were composed entirely of oriental carpets and a scattering of large, damask-covered pillows, the Arabian nights theme hit me because I had been bathed and powdered and perfumed and was only wearing diaphanous, billowy harem pants and lace-up sandals. I also had gold serpent bracelets banded around above each of my biceps and around my ankles.

I wasn't alone. There were three other good-looking guys, all of Middle Eastern extraction, lying around on the pillows too, each with the same wary, scared expression I knew I had, and each dressed, or, should I say, undressed, in the same manner as I was. And at the four corners of the room stood four guys looking like thugs and wearing Egyptian robes, which I learned were called thawbs. All were muscle men. Three were obviously Mideasterners; the fourth looked European. The European stepped forward and addressed me.

"Good. You're back with us. Good timing. They will send for you soon."

"They?" I asked. "Where am I and what am I doing here?"

"You're here for the auction," he said, and then he gave me a sardonic little smile.

"What? What the hell?" I asked. "I'm not interested in any auction . . . what's being auctioned?"

"You're not a buyer," he answered, and I thought he'd break out into a laugh. "You're what's being auctioned."

"Good joke," I responded. "Now, really, what's going on? People can't be auctioned in this day and age. Slavery's dead. Haven't you heard?"

"It isn't dead here in Egypt. You're in Cairo. And, Caucasian to Caucasian, let me strongly suggest that you convince the auctioneer he wants to keep you. I can guarantee you won't want to go with any of the other men who are at today's auction."

The European briefly explained while we were being herded down the narrow, stone-walled passageway what was going to happen now. We would be sent in, one by one, into an entertainment room, where we would see five men spread in a semicircle around a small platform stage, reclining on pillows. There would be music and we were to dance for them. If we danced well, one of the men might bid on us. If we didn't, we possibly were living our last day. The men could take their purchases away and do whatever they wished with them.

A small, lithe, but well-built Lebanese young man was sent in first. We all stood out in the corridor, waiting our turn, as we heard the music begin. Shortly, we heard the raised voices of men, bidding enthusiastically. Then a period of silence.

I was the second one to be sent in. Four men were sitting in a semicircle around the spotlighted platform I was led to and made to stand on. I had been told that there would be five, but as my eyes adjusted to the contrast of the spotlight in which I stood and shadowy, smoke-filled edges around the platform, I saw that buyer number five was already trying out his purchase over on a pillow-strewn divan at the side of the room. The young Lebanese man who had preceded me was on his belly on the divan, half on and half off it. A large-bellied, middle-aged Egyptian, thawb lifted up around his armpits, was crouched between the young man's legs, already ready to mount him.

I tore my eyes away from that scene and looked back at the four remaining men. Three of them were pretty gross, fat and middle-aged and ugly. The fourth one was younger and more comely and well-muscled. He showed that he was in charge by gesturing for the music to start.

This was where I was supposed to dance and, the European captor's warning ringing in my ears, convince the auctioneer, obviously the younger, more presentable of the men, that he wanted to keep me. I started to undulate with the music, never having been a dancer before, but being a dancer now for dear life.

I was egged on by the cries from the side of the room, where the older man was slapping the young Lebanese man hard now, on face, arms, legs, and buttocks, while he drove his cock inside a barely ready hole. The older man had the younger man by the hair with one fist, and he reached for a riding crop with the other. The cries from the younger man rose and the expressions of the three older men watching me dance—whose eyes were flicking at the fucking at the side and then back at me—left no doubt of how this combination aroused them. They all had hands inside their thawbs.

I could see interest in the eyes of the younger man, but not yet a "sold" sign.

In panic, I pulled out all of the stops. I danced, but I danced only for this younger man, the man holding all of the power. While I danced, I traced my cock through the diaphanous fabric, leaving little to the imagination of what I had in there and that it was getting hard, hard for the younger man among the bidders. I had had much practice in getting hard for men I didn't desire, and I brought all of that art to play here. By the time I had pushed the front of the harem pants below my ball sack and shown what I had and was stroking it, I could tell I had sold the younger man. He had his thawb open, his hand was in his lap, and he was stroking himself too.

I heard him cry out one word in Arabic. He had raised a hand—the one not teasing his cock—in the air, and the music stopped immediately.

The other three had been no less impressed and aroused with my dance as he was. The fifth bidder was much too busy ravishing his purchase off to the side to care what was happening in the center of the room. And the young Lebanese man's cries and screams had decreased to whimpers and groans as his new master continued to beat and to fuck him roughly.

There was a cacophony of sound as the three older bidders went into overdrive, trying to assert their bid for me over all others. But the younger man cut them all off, and I discerned, to my temporary, partial relief, that he had withdrawn me from the bidding. I was led over to the side of the chamber and chained with metal cuffs to a ring in the stone wall.

I watched then as the two remaining captives were auctioned off. The one loser of all bids stood in a semi huff, a sour expression on his face, and left through a doorway behind a tapestry hanging. One of the other bidders led off his new slave through that door as well. But the last one started enjoying his purchase on the pillows on which he had been sitting. And I could see that he was going to be as cruel as the first master, who was still enjoying himself at that other side of the room.

The younger man, the auctioneer, walked over to me, undid the chains that had attached me to the wall, and, with me still handcuffed, led me through yet a different doorway behind a tapestry that led directly into an opulently furnished Oriental-style chamber with stone walls, high clerestory windows that let in filtered sunlight, and a gurgling pool in the center, complete with central fountain of a young boy pissing water into the pool. It was quite an unusual fountain, though. The rump of the statue of the young boy was attached to the crotch of a standing statue of a naked man. The man statue had his arms bent and spread out before him, and the young boy's legs were draped over these.

The man released me from handcuffs, then disrobed, showing a magnificent body and good-sized cock, and sank down into the pool. He waved to me, and I stripped down my harem pants and unlaced my sandals, which apparently was what he wanted me to do, and also slipped into the pool. The man had lifted himself to a sitting position on the side of the pool and I swam to him and took his cock in my mouth and started working all of the wiles I could think of on him. I was fully in his control now. I knew it and he knew it, and I wanted him to want me—for him to always want for there to be a next time. No matter how long it took. No matter how much time it took me to escape from here.

I could tell that my willingness and the mastery of my attentions were very arousing to him. He came almost immediately after becoming rock hard.

He lifted me out of the pool with the strength of his arms then and guided me over to a nearby pillow-strewn divan and laid me down on my back. Then he showed me that he was a master of lovemaking too. He handcuffed me again to rings at the side of the head of the divan on each side. Putting his knees between my spread thighs, he lowered his face onto my torso and tongued and kissed all over my body. And I sighed and moaned for him, not all of it being an act, but all of it focused on pleasing him.

I was laying there, on my back, my legs spread and him sitting on the edge of the divan between my legs. The touching had stopped, and I looked up to see that he had a huge ivory phallus in his hand. He was rubbing oil all over it. And then there were oiled fingers at my hole too, opening me up. I whimpered as I saw that phallus descend, and the bulbous cap of it was at my hole. I cried out and arched my back as the bulb invaded my canal, stretching me wide. He put a palm on my belly and pressed down as he pushed the oiled phallus in another couple of inches. I widened my stance as much as I could and lifted one of my legs to hook on his shoulder at the ankle. He turned his face to the muscle of my calf and kissed and licked me there . . . as the phallus sank in a couple of more inches.

I was panting and moaning and the phallus kept creeping up into me. When it had bottomed, perhaps nearly a foot inside me, the man lowered his mouth onto my cock and started to suck me, pushing his tongue as far as he could into my piss slit. He also slowly pumped me with the ivory phallus, keeping up the same rhythm he was using with his lips on my cock. It didn't take me long to come.

Then he removed the phallus, uncuffed me, turned me, forced a couple of pillows under my belly to raise my buttocks to me, and fucked me long and slowly with his own cock until he had ejaculated.

Leaving me and rising off the divan, he clapped his hands and two of the thug guards entered and bundled me back to the room I had started in, which was now deserted. There was a dinner tray waiting for me, and then the guards left and I was alone, counting myself lucky. I decided I must thank the European for the advice he had given me if he ever showed up again—and perhaps if I could weave my thanks around him, I could find some means of escape through him.

* * * *

The European captor did reappear. He apparently was the one who was assigned to watch over me for my new master. On each succeeding day, I was brought to the master's chamber. And each time I was fucked in a different way. And each time the master seemed to want to go a little farther, seemed to be working his way in the direction of the point at which the other bidders at his auction had started off.

During my second visit to him, he used an even bigger phallus on me than the first time before he fucked him, this time with me bound to the divan even when he was fucking me. And on the third visit, I was chained to the wall of his chamber, closely attached at spread wrists and ankles, while he swished, with increasing force, a many-thonged hand whip against the tender flesh of my back, buttocks, and thighs. That he then had me taken down and licked my wounds and lap fucked me in the cooling pool did not go far in mitigating my fear of what was to come. The fourth visit I was cuffed, straddling the divan on my belly, on all four corners, and the whip cut deeper as he rode me hard.

Near the end of that session, an attendant came into the chamber and placed a wooden box down on a table near us. He opened it to revealed a set of sharp knives. My master shook his head and waved the box away with a muttered, "No, not today." I knew then, though, where all of this was headed.

That evening I stopped the European captor after he had placed my dinner tray in my chamber and before he left by means of the locked door on the opposite wall of the door to the passageway that led me to my daily taking.

"Tell me, lesser master," this being what I had been told to call the European, "If this is an auction house, where are the new slaves?"

"New slaves are not needed until the old ones have been used up," he answered. And then I saw the expression on his face, an expression of dismay, as if he had revealed some secret to me. And there was little doubt that he had. Perhaps it wasn't that my master was less cruel than the others who had been at

107

the auction. Perhaps he just took longer in using up his slaves. It was obvious to me now that time was of the essence.

"I have never thanked you properly for your advice that first day, lesser master." I told him, and I turned my body—naked other than the gold serpent bracelets at biceps and ankles—and a new one that had been added, winding around my cock—in as provocative a pose as I could. "If only there was some way I could show my appreciation. But I have so little. There is only my body—and it withers with each passing day." At that I lifted up my cock, which, in fact, hadn't withered a bit.

This more than gave the European pause. I knew he wanted me. He hadn't been able to hide that from me, not since that first moment when I had come out of my drugged state and had seen him looking at my body.

But he hesitated. At least he was calculating.

"I'm not sure how long I can go and still properly show my appreciation, either," I then said. Shooting home the reality that we both knew, but that neither one of us had been able to give voice to.

"What lies beyond the door you come through?" I asked. It wasn't all that innocent of a question. I had seen him go out that door and come in from the other passageway. Whatever was through that door also had access to other parts of whatever building we were in—and, conceivably to the outside world.

"My chamber," he whispered.

"Your bed chamber?" I asked.

"Yes," he answered in a husky voice.

* * * *

I had gauged the European rightly. He didn't want to take me. He wanted to be ridden. And that worked perfectly with my plan. I prepared him on the bed of his in the chamber beyond my prison, sucking his cock to his creaming and letting him suck mine big. And then he was wholly mine. I turned him on his belly on the bed and crouched between his spread thighs, and, leveraging the balls of my feet off his stone floor, plowed him until he begged alternately for mercy and for deeper penetration.

After I had come, I turned him on his back on the bed and stretched out on top of him, assuring him that I would not leave, that he would be fucked royally that night.

He was dozing off in a satiated reverie as I started to make love again to his cheeks, ears, the hollow of his neck, his nipples, the pits of his underarms with my tongue and lips. He was fully relaxed. I started teasing him, saying he needed a reward for his sweet channel and expert receiving. He laughed and reminded me that I had no rewards to give other than my body, although he was quick to say that my body was enough reward.

As if just thinking about it, I unwound the gold serpent bracelets at my biceps and, lifting his arms above his head, one at a time, began winding them back around his wrists. He was so besotted with me and off guard, that I was nearly finished when he realized that his wrists were now bound to the corners of the railings at the head of his bed, imprisoning him there as neatly and tightly as any metal handcuffs.

He started to bellow when he saw me searching around for clothes to put on my naked body and was cursing me when I was standing at the other door of the chamber, the one leading to a deserted courtyard where I could see an open gate out into a busy Cairo street. My last cheery gift to him was to remind him that he still had a royal fucking to come—and I assured him that, as far as I could see, he now was truly and royally fucked.

* * * *

It took me a couple of days to make my way across the Nile and to Giza. I took furtive tricks off the street to get enough for food; jeans, a T-shirt, and some sandals; and somewhere I could take a sponge bath from a tap that did no more than drizzle. I had remembered what Jorgen had said about owning a gay dive there named Amr's, and I slowly worked my way in the direction of the section of the Giza he'd said it was in. If Jorgen was OK, if he hadn't somehow been captured as well or taken by the Egyptian police for whatever he was doing, he most likely could be found at Amr's. At least this would be my best bet for getting out of Cairo and somewhere where they didn't trade in human bodies.

I was in luck, I found Amr's and Jorgen was there. He seemed delighted to see me and pulled me over into a relatively quiet section of the room. He was doing good business. Mostly Egyptians, I thought, but an American or European here and there. Mostly middle-aged businessmen types, but enough of the younger crowd there to keep the middle-aged ones circling and hoping.

Jorgen settled me down in a banquette and wanted to hear all of what had happened to me. He said when he'd returned to the sailboat, near dawn, as he had promised, our entry into Alexandria all worked out, he'd found evidence that the boat had been boarded and I was missing.

He said he'd been looking frantically for me ever sense. This was the first discordant note I heard. He looked anything but frantic when I entered. He did look relieved when he saw me enter Amr's, but there was a hint of something else. It was almost as if he wasn't surprised to see me.

I stumbled through my story, while Jorgen, sitting close beside me, encircled me with his arms and clucked at me like an old mother hen, occasionally taking my lips in his and calming me down with his attentions. Men swirled around us, and several showed interest in us—but none intruded. We could be fucking, naked, in the banquette and none would have taken that as unusual. All the time Jorgen was cuddling me, he also was twisting one of the red cloth napkins on the banquette table around his fingers.

My story stumbled out. Jorgen then said he had to go to the gents' and that he'd return in a moment and would order drinks for us at the bar on his way back. He stood, still fingering the napkin in his hand, and headed for the back of the room and into a corridor. I'd already been to the gents', however, and I thought the door to it was off to the right of the corridor. But Jorgen went straight back and entered a door at the end of the short hall.

Order the drinks on the way back, I thought. Why didn't he order the drinks on the way to the gents' and bring them back with him when he returned?

110

When he returned, having stopped, as he said he would do, and ordered drinks at the bar, Jorgen was all sympathy and gliding hands again. He hadn't brought drinks back with him. He wanted me to start going over my story again, slowly, with him asking questions as I went. At one point I looked down at the space between us, and I saw that the red napkin he had been fingering was now in my side pocket, half in and half out.

I had wondered how this was going to work.

I took a deep breath and pulled away from Jorgen, saying I thought I saw that our drinks were ready and I'd go get them. He thought that was a fine idea. They were, in fact, sitting on the bar. When I got there, I saw the three thugs—the European noticeably absent—from the "master's" auction house come through the front door of Amr's. I called over to Jorgen and motioned for him to come to me. Instinctively, obviously not having given it enough thought, he did stand and move toward me.

The red napkin was now hanging out of Jorgen's side pocket—the Jorgen who was a spitting image of me. I took the drinks and scooted into the shadows of the corridor back to the toilets and, obviously, Jorgen's office with its telephone, and watched, sipping on one of the drinks, as the eyes of the thugs honed into the red napkin in Jorgen's pocket, and he was dragged kicking and screaming out of Amr's.

I reached down and took Jorgen's wallet out of my pocket. I had lifted it while I was moving the red napkin from my pocket to his. Enough documentation—even his passport. This should be enough to get me out of the country. Not quite enough money though.

I downed one of the drinks, and took a swig out of the other. Then I took a deep breath, walked back into the bar room, all smiles, scanning the room for the wealthiest looking middle-aged businessman here.

Career Guidance

"What is this shit?" Bernie Wasserman grabbed up tabloids in both fists and threw them across his desk at his client, who sat slouched and defiant in a club chair on the other side of the big mahogany desk.

"Those stories are exaggerated. I didn't know she was a man."

"Good god, Danny," Wasserman continued to bluster. "You are playing parts of a sixteen-year-old still. Caught being fucked by a transvestite in the back of your Hummer. What were you thinking? And a Hummer, god almighty. Who told you you could buy a Hummer? Your fans think you're riding bicycles. I didn't sign off on any of those bills."

"I'm almost nineteen," Danny blustered defiantly. "I don't have to tell you about every job I go out on anymore."

"You sure as hell do, Danny Delmonte," Wasserman yelled. "I've got your contract. I've represented you since you were ten. I own your ass."

"That's it, isn't it?" Danny shot back. "This is all because I moved out when I was eighteen. You'd convinced my folks to let me live with you and you were just licking your lips, playing it safe and waiting to fuck me when I turned eighteen—and I moved out instead."

"No, Danny," Wasserman said in a carefully controlled tone after taking a minute to pull himself together. "This is about your life. I've been lenient with you—and you've lived high on the hog. You've been spending it as fast as you make it. You've got maybe two more good years left in your category and then it's iffy if you can transition to anything from the child roles. Very few are able to. And whoring around and getting high and making a fool of yourself in public isn't going to get you there. You need to come back under control. You need to move back in with me."

"No. You just want to get me in bed," Danny spat back. "And I'm going to beat that drug rap. The lawyer you got for me says it's a slam dunk."

"And what are you going to say about being caught in the backseat of a vehicle with a male prostitute in a car you weren't supposed to be driving as a condition of your release on the drug charges? Tell me about that. Tell me how happy the Children's Express Theater is going to be with this now if you sign this contract." Wasserman was waving a thick sheaf of paper that constituted a contract for three high school musicals.

"Fuck that. Fuck you. Fuck it all," Danny muttered as he sank down into his chair.

"This is your future," Wasserman said, his voice ominous and full of venom. "This is the only contract we have on the table. You already were aging out of these roles and now you've really fucked yourself with this stuff you are feeding to the tabloids. You are out of control. Do I tear up this contract and show you the door, or do we start this conversation all over again with you saying 'yes, sir' to me?"

Silence for a long minute with Danny looking at the floor. But his eyes came up fast enough at the sound of the tearing paper. Wasserman had torn apart one of the tabloid newspapers, though, instead of the contract.

"That got your attention, didn't it?"

Danny mumbled something into his chest.

"What? I didn't hear you."

"Yes." Just getting that word out seemed to be torture for Danny.

"Yes, what?"

Another moment of silence and then a muttered "Yes, sir."

"Stand up."

Danny looked up, he eyes showing confusion.

"I said stand up. And strip."

"What?" Now Danny was shocked.

"You said you were off the drugs. I don't know if I believe you."

"I never was on drugs—well not that kind," Danny said, his voice still showing his shock. And maybe a bit of fear now too.

"If not, then I won't find any marks on your body, will I?" Wasserman declared. "I can maybe clear this up—but only this last time—if you haven't fucked up your life more than just what's in these tabloids. If you're shooting up, you won't pass the studio tests and it doesn't matter if you sign these contracts or not. If not—and if I'm convinced you're not shooting up—I can get a doctor to say you were on prescription medicine because you were overworked and headed for a breakdown and that this is what has caused your behavior—but that you are back on the road to full recovery now. That always goes down OK in this town for at least the first time. So, if you want this contract, strip now and I'll check you out."

Danny looked all of the vulnerable sixteen-year-old role that he played so well as he meekly stripped down and stood there, naked, shivering slightly. He was a beautifully well-formed man—but still boyish looking, still able to pass as a teenager.

Wasserman sat behind his desk and looked Danny up and down as Danny's head hung in embarrassment and his hands crossed over his privates.

Wasserman opened a drawer in his desk and took out a couple of items and then, on his way around the desk, he dragged over a Chippendale straight-back dining room chair and plopped it down between where Danny was standing and trembling a bit, as if it was cold in Wasserman's office—which it wasn't—and his desk.

"Here. Sit," Wasserman commanded.

Danny looked up in confusion and just stood there.

"I said sit. And what do you say?"

Danny mumbled something, and Wasserman pushed the young actor down on his bare butt on the chair cushion. "What? I didn't hear you."

"Yes, yes, sir," Danny muttered. There were tears in his eyes now.

"This is all for your own good, Danny. You've gotten very cocky and beyond yourself. And you've lost control and you are this close to losing everything. And not just for you but for me too. I have given representation and career guidance priority to you for nearly ten years now. You need to learn control and discipline. You're fucking this up for both of us."

While he was saying this, Wasserman placed a wooden box and a couple of more items on a small cigarette table between the club chair and where he'd plopped the straight chair down.

To Danny's consternation and confusion, he was then strapping Danny's ankles to the front legs of the straight chair and pulling Danny's arms behind his back and tying off his wrists together.

"What the . . . ?"

"Just shut up, Danny. You've been building up to this. It's time you understood who's the boss around here."

"God, Bernie, what . . . ?" The exclamation was set off because Wasserman was stripping off his own clothes now.

And then Wasserman, naked, was pushing himself in under Danny's buttocks and thighs and onto the seat of the straight chair. Danny was blustering and objecting in words that no child star even should know how to pronounce and then whimpering and pleading as Wasserman got his body below Danny's and Danny was lapped.

After he had lapped Danny and his engorging cock was running up the small of Danny's back, Wasserman reached over to the adjacent table and retrieved a condom packet, which he tore open, and a tube of lubricant. He rolled the condom on his cock and began to diddle lube into Danny's asshole with one hand palmed under the young actor's butt and, after lubing up his own crowned cock, slicking up Danny's cock as well.

Danny was moaning and pleading and cussing up a storm.

116

"Your trannie do this for you in the back of the Hummer, smart ass?" Wasserman asked darkly. "How many other cocks have you had up there? Ones I didn't know about. Ones before me. Oh, yes I waited. But who didn't wait? Tell me, Danny?"

"Oh, God, Bernie, no. No, not many. None before I left your house. Oh, don't do this, Bernie. I'll behave."

"Who's the boss, Danny?" Bernie said.

"You are; you are the boss, Bernie . . . just don't . . ."

Bernie was lifting Danny's buttocks and hovering it over his erect phallus, the bulb of which was touching the rim of Danny's hole. Danny was panting and whimpering. "Who's your daddy, Danny?"

"What?"

"Who's your daddy, I said."

"You. You. You, sir."

"No 'sir' now, Danny. Say it. Call me Daddy."

"Daddy. Daddy. Oh, no . . . oh my god, noooooo."

Wasserman was pulling the younger man down onto his cock, slowly bringing him down, as Danny groaned and moaned and writhed within the close embrace Wasserman had him in. At length, he was bottomed—fully skewered—and defeated. He just sat there in Wasserman's lap, fully impaled, moaning softly, tears streaming down his cheeks, collapsed.

But he had taken all of Wasserman with a minimum of effort. Danny wasn't anything close to a virgin—and this ticked Wasserman off. He had wanted to be the first and had waited and schemed for it for years.

"Who was the first, Danny? Who? Tell me."

Danny was moaning but Wasserman lifted the young actor's buttocks half way off his cock and slammed him back down, and Danny yelped and struggled out an answer. "Sid, Sid Soltan."

"Soltan? The director of your last movie. When? When, Danny? And where?"

"My eighteenth birthday. In his studio trailer."

Now Wasserman was upset—really upset. Why that old fart, he thought. All of my plans and he sweeps in with a trump card.

117

Wasserman sat up very straight in the chair, forcing Danny to arch back into his chest and Wasserman's cock to be driven deeper into him. Danny groaned. "It's all for our own good," Wasserman was growling in Danny's ear. "You were running away. Weren't paying attention. Completely out of control. You need discipline. You need control. You need to be dominated. Is that right, Danny?"

Danny was sobbing quietly.

"I said, is that right Danny? Aren't I right?"

"Yes . . . yes, Daddy," Danny murmured through his tears.

"You've been ass fucked before," Wasserman said, "enough to make the papers. There has to be something else, something more, to impress on you who is the boss here, who dominates."

"Please . . . please, Daddy," Danny muttered.

Then his eyes got really big and his body tensed and went rigid as he watched Wasserman open the wooden box on the table to reveal a series of size-graduated silver medical instruments—wands with slight bulbing at the tips—long, thin phalluses—arranged neatly in indentations in a blue-velvet foundation.

"What? What?" Danny's voice was filled with question and fear.

"The instruments of discipline . . . of ultimate domination, Danny," Wasserman said in a low, hoarse voice. "I want you to understand. I don't want to ever have to do this again—not as long as you have a career. Consider this career guidance. The best lesson you will ever learn from me; your salvation in being able to prolong your career. Your utter understanding of who is in charge here."

"No, please . . . don't, Daddy. I'll be good. I'll . . . Oh, noooo."

"Hold still. Hold perfectly still. But not rigid. It will be much easier if you are relaxed. But very still. Very, very still."

Danny was whimpering again and Wasserman couldn't feel him breathing he was holding so still. Wasserman had taken one of the smaller wands out of the box and was holding it in front of Danny's terrified eyes.

"Breathe," Wasserman commanded. "Don't hold your breath. You won't be able to do so. We will be at this for a while."

"Noooooo," Danny whimpered.

When Wasserman had come under Danny, he had lifted the young man's arms over his head, so that Danny was stretched out against Wasserman's chest, his tied wrists at the back of Wasserman's neck. With his ankles shackled to the chair legs and his ass fully impaled on Wasserman's cock, Danny was sitting close in Wasserman's lap with little or no room to wiggle.

"Oh, nooooo, pleeaasee," he cried out as Wasserman ran the tip of the wand down Danny's belly, toward his crotch. He cupped Danny's cock in the other hand, holding it at an angle jutting up from Danny's belly.

Danny began to pant and moan and sob for mercy as soon as Wasserman maneuvered the tip of the wand to Danny's piss slit and began to carefully insert it, sounding the young man's urethra in possibly the most intimate and dominating sex act one man can perform on another.

His cock deeply impaling Danny's ass, Wasserman was, in effect, fucking Danny's piss slit as well—or at least he was fully doing this when, after running the wand into the urethra channel nearly three inches, he began to slowly push it in and out.

Danny was moaning for real. Gurgling sounds were coming up from deep inside him, and he was holding very still but trembling and gasping and noisily taking in huge breaths of air.

"Who's the boss, Danny?" Wasserman asked in a low tone.

"You. You are, Daddy," Danny answered in a gaspy voice.

"And when I say you are to do something, what will you do?"

"Oh, god, oh god. Please stop. I think I'm going to come."

"No, no, you're not going to come, Danny. Daddy will tell you when you can come."

119

Wasserman slowly extracted the wand and laid it back in the case and picked another one of a larger size, and, ignoring Danny's pleas, began fucking the young man's piss slit with it in the same manner as he had done with the thinner wand.

"What will you do if I tell you to do it, Danny?"

"I'll . . . I'll . . . do it . . . Daddy. Ohhhhhhhh."

Wasserman brought his free hand up and cupped Danny's chin, arching the young man's head back into the hollow of his neck. He reached up with his thumb and pushed it between Danny's lips. "Suck this," he commanded. And Danny pulled the thumb into his mouth and gave it suck.

"This is it. This is how much I dominate you, Danny. Fucking you in all three orifices. No one owns you like I do, do they?"

"No . . . no, Daddy," Danny murmured in a thumb-strangled voice.

"And you will come home with me now—after we have signed these contracts—and I will fuck you whenever I want. And only me. And you will act the perfectly behaved, chaste child actor to the world. Right?"

"Yes . . . yes, Daddy . . . Oh. Ohhhh. I can't hold on any longer. I have to . . . come."

"Yes, you may come now, Danny," Wasserman said. And as he pulled the wand out of Danny's piss slit, the young man's cock burbled up in white fluid and he came in four jerks.

Danny was panting hard and Wasserman felt him relaxing and collapsing on his body.

Wasserman reached over and exchanged the wand for a larger-sized one.

Danny cried out in fear and frustration, knowing now that the ordeal was not over, but he was reduced to soft whimpering and shallow pants as Wasserman moved through two more sizes of wands and a second coming by Danny and until he felt there was no resistance in Danny at all anymore.

"I think we've made our point now," Wasserman said at length.

"Yes, Daddy," Danny murmured.

"OK, I'm going to unbind you now and I want you to reverse on my cock and face me and I want you to fuck yourself on my cock. Of your free will. You do that and we'll sign those contracts and get on with our life—together. If not, your career is over. Do you understand?"

"Yes, Daddy," Danny whispered in a voice of resignation.

And then, after he was unbound and turned himself in Wasserman's lap, Danny proved what a good actor he was by fucking himself to Wasserman's ejaculation—and giving an Academy Award performance on selling that he couldn't get enough of his master's cocking.

Chain Gangbanged

I was only in for thirty days, and then not because of something I'd actually done. My buddy Phil had left drugs in my car, and the cops found them when they stopped me because I was driving a little too fast when I pulled away from a country beer hall they were staking out. I should have known better. I was only nineteen, and I shouldn't have been in that beer hall at all, let alone drinking. But I'd just finished my first year up north at Yale, and I was on the top of the world.

Thirty days in a county lockup had been my sentence. And not a lockup in a suburban county like the one I lived in but in a county back in the hills, where life is a lot rougher than where I came from.

I stopped going to the workout room because the guys there were giving me looks I didn't like, but the inaction was making me so jumpy that I volunteered to go out on work details. This proved to be a big mistake.

On my seventh day, my first work detail came up. We were going out to a rural spot to clear brush from the side of a road running through a heavily forested and hilly area. It was with great dismay that when I jumped up into the back of the van, I saw both Bobby Joe and Maurice, trustees who had eyed me weirdly in the workout room, among those who were going

123

out on the detail. When you got to trustee status in this workhouse, you were almost on the level of a guard and could come and go as you pleased.

It was a hot day and the work was hard. We had small saws and machetes and were clearing brush and saplings back some twenty minutes from the road. There were six inmates and three guards. Maurice clearly was in charge and everyone there, including the two other guards, were afraid of him. Everyone, of course, except Bobby Joe, who seemed to be a special friend of Maurice's.

Bobby Joe was probably the best and fastest worker among us. It wasn't long until he was so heated up that he stripped off his shirt and undershirt and was swinging away, covered with sweat that matted the thick, black hair on his chest and arms into swirls and made his undulating muscles gleam in the sunlight. The other inmates quickly followed suit in stripping down to their waists—all except for me.

"Take off that shirt," Maurice called out to me in a booming voice. "Can't you see it's too hot to work in?"

I pretended that I hadn't heard him.

"Take off the shirt, I said," Maurice boomed again.

"I'm okay the way I am," I answered in the most pleasant voice I could muster. "But thanks, anyway."

Maurice stomped over to me, and all of the other inmates stopped to watch us.

"I said for you to take off that shirt, son, and I meant what I said."

"Sure thing, sir," I said and I stripped my shirt and undershirt off. My eyes flicked over to Bobby Joe, and I could see a wide smile of appreciation on his face.

"And because you didn't do what I asked, you can go ahead and strip all your other clothes off too and work that way for a while."

I was dumbfounded. "But, sir, this is a public road."

"Good point," Maurice said with a big smile. "You can go on into the woods there a bit and clear brush over by the picnic area. We'll see that no one goes in there, but not much of a chance they will. Not many want to picnic next to where a chain gang is working."

124

I started to argue, but I could see that this would just get me into more trouble, so I started to move off toward the picnic area.

"No. You can strip here," Maurice said. "The clothes will still be here when you get back."

So, I stripped all the way down to my work boots and could see that this gave both Maurice and Bobby Joe a little thrill. I was in very good shape and was better hung than the average.

"Okay, now go on over into the picnic area and start working," Maurice said. "You can't go there alone, and if a guard goes, that will leave too few guards here, so . . . Bobby Joe, you come on over there with us. The rest of you go back to what you're doing here."

"Oh, God," I thought, as I stumbled off into the brush, trailed by Maurice and Bobby Joe. The very worst situation I could think of.

Maurice and Bobby Joe watched me work for a while, and the first thing I knew they both had their dongs out of their pants and were working them. Bobby Joe had one of those championship dicks in length and Maurice's was regular length but was extra thick, and his balls hung low out of his fly.

I tried to make a break for it then and run back to the road, where maybe I could get some help from the other trustees. But Bobby Joe lashed out with a hand and caught me as I ran past him and slammed me up against a tree. The blow caused me to sink to my knees, my back to the tree, and Bobby Joe was standing up against me, his pelvis pushed into my face.

"Suck me," Bobby Joe commanded in a husky voice.

"Maurice," I called out plaintively, begging for help.

"Maurice ain't going to help you none, pretty college boy. Open those lips and suck my dick. And don't do nothin' funny while you're about it."

He grabbed my hair with one hand and his dick with the other and forced his tool into my mouth. I gagged as he filled my mouth cavity.

"Ain't done this before, have you, pretty boy? Well, you're going to get real good at it in days to come. Open wider and get your teeth out of the way and your tongue runnin' under my dick. There, that's good. Now let it slide in and out. There, yes, like that. Ahhh, such a sweet, soft mouth."

I felt tears coming to my eyes, and I was having trouble not gagging. His dick was getting bigger and harder as he slowly worked it back and forth in my mouth.

"Now, I'm going to pull out," Bobby Joe said, "and I want you to suck on the head like a lollipop and to work your tongue around it. Ahh, yes, I like that. You're going to be a good bitch."

His dick head was big and the pisshole was leaking precum. It tasted salty. The sweat of his groin was giving off a strong musky smell. These were entirely new sensations for me, and they were not all that unpleasant. I admit that when I was being propositioned in high school, I let my imagination play with the possibilities, and I could feel my own tool coming to life under these new sensations. I also admit that being forced took much of the guilt away and was also turning me on.

"There, that's good," Bobby was saying after he'd pushed his dick back in and had pumped my mouth for a couple of more minutes. "Stand up."

I did so, and he pulled away from me a bit. I was trembling there, close to him. He held my head between his hands and came in for a kiss. I struggled with him, holding my lips together hard, straining to create a solid barrier to him, my arms went between us, and I tried to elbow him away from me. He brought his chest in hard against mine and lashed out with one of his hands, backhanding me hard across the mouth. Then he brutally kissed me again, this time working his tongue into my mouth and causing me to gag as his dick had already done. My jaw came unhinged and I just let him have his way.

The next thing I knew, Maurice was next to us and was digging my arms out and swinging them up and around the tree, where he used handcuffs swung over a branch above my head on the other side of the tree to suspend my arms over my head.

Bobby Joe continued his long kiss, as his hands flew over my naked torso and explored my balls and cock, which started to engorge at his touch.

"Whooie!" Bobby Joe exclaimed, as he broke away from my lips and started to wander down my body with his lips. "You're one fine bitch. Candy, candy. How sweet."

My lips now free, I started to yell, trying to get help from anywhere it might come. The ever-helpful Maurice whipped a dirty handkerchief and a roll of duct tape out of his pocket and had me quickly gagged.

All I could do was tear up in frustration and make muffled sounds of objection as Bobby Joe tongued and teethed my nipples and continued working his mouth down across my belly and taking possession of my dick, which responded to his attention, and my balls. In no time, he had his strong hands under my thighs and jackknifed my legs up and off the ground and swung my ass up to his waiting lips and tongue.

I was being penetrated and wetted with his tongue, which dug ever deeper, widening and lubricating my hole.

"Ah a really tight ass," Bobby Joe was saying as he dropped my legs and stood and turned toward Maurice. "We got ourselves a virgin, Maurice. Young meat. Yum, yum. Can I have him? Can I get firsties on a fuck?"

"Yeah, fine," Maurice answered. "But then you gotta do me, Bobby Joe. I'm dying here. And you gotta go easy with the kid. You've got a real club. The damage can't show when we get back."

So this was how it was between the two of them.

"Thanks, Maurice. You got a rubber and some lube? He's gotta be open a lot more if I'm goin' get up in there."

Maurice, the walking supply closet, produced a small tube of lubricant and a condom in a packet.

"Now, let's get him turned around and hangin' on a lower branch," Bobby Joe said.

The two of them manhandled me while Maurice released the handcuffs and got me turned facing the tree. Then he handcuffed my arms again around the tree on a somewhat lower branch than before. Bobby Joe pulled my legs away from the tree by the hips and his lips went to my asshole again. Maurice slipped up between my legs and hunched in front of me, with his back to the base of the tree. He proceeded to take my cock in his mouth and give me head, while Bobby Joe was lubricating my

127

ass, first with his tongue again and then with his fingers, heavily laced with lubricant.

I grunted in pain as he worked first one finger, and eventually three, into my ass, probing ever deeper and opening me up. The pad of a finger found my prostate, and, under the spell of circular rubbings on that, I ejaculated down Maurice's throat.

Then both Bobby Joe and Maurice rose and stood near me, where I could clearly watch, as Maurice opened the condom packet and rolled a condom onto Bobby Joe's huge tool. The two of them hugged and kissed deeply and worked each other's tools until both were fully hard again. Then Maurice stood in front of me, his eyes glued on mine, his hands wrapped around his dick, as Bobby Joe got behind me, pulled my hips back again, positioned his dick head at the entrance of my asshole, and slowly worked the head in.

I was screaming in pain and shock behind my gag, and my eyes were tearing up again. Bobby Joe pushed in a couple of more inches and then his hands went to my butt cheeks, encasing them and squeezing them and pulling them apart, giving him as bigger opening. I lifted my hips as best I could and arched my back, trying myself to widen the opening, knowing that all was lost now and no fight was possible.

At the same time, a little guilty thrill ran through me. All of that dick was going to be inside me. I was turning this dude on. I was being forced, raped, and none of this was my fault. I was both in control of being the object of his lust and being controlled by a hot stud. All of my "what if" fantasies were being brought to life, and no one could blame me for what was happening.

I gulped for breath, pulling as much air as I could through my nose. Maurice saw that I was in distress and said that he'd pull the gag out if I promised to be quiet. I nodded my head in assent, and he ripped the gag off. My mouth now free, I couldn't help but grunt and whimper at the four inches of dick pulsating inside me. Bobby Joe was going slow. When he sensed my canal opening to him, he pushed in another couple of inches. Six inches in now, and he went into a slow pump, two inches out and then back in two inches. After a couple of minutes of this, though, he came in another inch when he pushed back in; seven inches up my ass now. I yelped when he did this, and his hands went to my pecs.

He stroked my nipples, and I began to tremble and sigh for him, not wanting to do so, but my anger at being violated was being overcome with a new sense of pleasure mixed with the pain. He took his dick in one hand and revolved it in my ass. My ass walls responded by widening to him, and he pushed in another inch. I flinched, but I was managing him now.

"That's so nice," he whispered as he brought his mouth to the side of my neck and nuzzled me there. "Don't you feel it? Don't you feel yourself opening to me?"

"Yes," I whimpered softly. "But please, please stop." But I grunted in vain, as he went in another inch; nine inches now. But of course I didn't know how far he was in me. All I knew is that I felt totally stuffed and stretched, and my ass walls began to tremble under the strain. I also didn't know how long that was for any normal person to take until he whispered it to me. "God, I'm almost all the way in, son. Do you know there aren't many that can take this much of me even after a long time of trying? You're one sweet bitch."

I was panting and giving little yelps and grunts with the progress of the last inch he had to give. He had his chest pushed into my back now, and I could feel the wet hairs of his pelt on my shoulder blades. He was giving off a sweaty, musky scent that I found heady.

When I felt his curly pubic hairs tickling my butt cheeks, I knew he was in all the way and assumed that this torture was close to the end. But the ordeal had just begun. He started to stroke me deep then, pulling the head of his cock back to where it rubbed across my prostate and then, slowly at first, and then ever quicker, stroking back into me to the hilt.

No more gentleness now, and Bobby Joe himself was no longer in control. Instinct took over, and he went into a primordial fuck, no longer being sensitive to how new I was to this. But by now, my body had adjusted to him, and the pain was tolerable. At length, I felt him tense and the bulb of the condom fill up, and he just more or less collapsed against me.

After Bobby Joe had fucked me up against a tree, he and Maurice went over to a picnic table, and I just watched as Maurice rolled another condom on Bobby Joe's rising cock and they slowly aroused each other to the point where Bobby Joe laid Maurice on his back on the picnic table and held his legs up and out from his body, as he pumped away inside the trustee's ass.

Maurice laid there on the picnic table, his arms stretched out and his eyes hooded, swimming in Bobby Joe's semen, and holding my own eyes by the intensity of his gaze, his desire palpable. His thick cock bounced around on his flat belly, maintaining its erection.

When they were done, Maurice handed Bobby Joe a third condom, and this time Bobby Joe rolled it on Maurice's thick cock. Maurice waltzed back to me and before I had a chance to even figure out what was happening, he lifted my legs off the ground and crouched under me and plunged that big, thick sausage of a cock up into me. My ass walls complained at the new challenge to their capacities, but Maurice was quicker at jacking off than Bobby Joe had been and couldn't go nearly as deep. By this time, though, I was too worn out and defeated to struggle.

Bobby Joe and Maurice dressed and I was freed and we returned to the van and the inmate crew, which had worked its way several hundred yards up the road by now. I quickly and silently dressed and just laid there on the ground as the others finished up what they were doing.

Only Bobby Joe and Maurice could keep their eyes on me while the van jostled us back to the jail, searing pain jabbing my ass with every jolt in the road. There was no question, though, that the other inmates and guards knew what had happened to me. I still had three weeks to go on my sentence, however, so everyone, including me, knew that I was going to keep quiet about this.

The next day was a rest day, and I managed to stay in my cell and to rest my body as well as to try to avoid Bobby Joe and the rest of the inmates. The following day, I went out on work detail with an entirely different set of men, and I began to build hope that my sexual abusing had been a one-time event and that I'd manage to serve the rest of my time without incident.

But late that night, my hopes were dashed. I was sleeping in the lower bunk of my cell. That morning, the other inmate they'd had in my cell disappeared and he wasn't replaced. At the time, I'd thought that was a stroke of luck. I was skittish now about being locked up with anyone else. But, of course, luck had had nothing to do with me now being alone in my cell. Deep in the night, I was rudely awakened by two figures grabbing my wrists and spinning me around in my bed and handcuffing my hands to the middle of the inner side of the rails of the bunk above me.

Bobby Joe and Maurice were in the cell with me, and Maurice stood beside the closed door as Bobby Joe tore off my clothes and roughly lifted my legs out and above me, with my feet wedged in the springs of the upper bunk. He lifted my hips and plunged his dick inside me and pumped me for several minutes, swinging my body back and forth on his pulsing skewer. Then he stood, and Maurice was inside me, forcing that thick cock in where Bobby Joe had just been. Bobby Joe moved in behind Maurice and fucked him while Maurice was fucking me. After they were done, Bobby Joe kissed me on the mouth and offered to protect me if I'd be his bitch for the rest of the time I was there. I refused, saying I wouldn't willingly submit to anyone. And Bobby Joe just laughed and said to let him know when I'd changed my mind, while Maurice uncuffed me and let me collapse on my bed.

Two nights after that, I woke as the door to my cell opened. A hulking blond guy loomed in the doorway for a second and then came barreling into the room, as the door clanged shut. I rose off my bed, groggily stumbling into him as he reached me. I threw a punch that went wild, while he connected with my chin with one fist, followed by a blow to my midsection. I reeled around and he got me with a upper cut to the eye.

I dropped to the floor of the cell on my belly like a rock, and me was sitting on my back, pulling my shorts down. His arms went around my armpits and neck in a full nelson, and I screamed in pain and surprise as his engorged dick found my asshole and pushed into me. He pumped me there relentlessly, and I tried my best to relax and accommodate him. He pulled me up to my knees and got up on his feet, crouching behind me, and pushed deeper into me.

He was barebacking me, and I had the fleeting thought that I hoped he was clean, as I felt the new sensation of unsheathed cock inside me. He must have been uncut, because his skin seemed loose, and I'm ashamed to say that my ass walls were intrigued by this loose friction. He spun me around and pushed me on my back, and I tried to rise again. He backhanded me across the face and wishboned my legs and pushed in to the hilt of his dick again. His mouth and teeth went to my nipples, and I grabbed his shoulders and tried to push him off me, but he was too strong for me, and the beating he had given me had weakened me. I dug my fingernails into his shoulders and he grunted and caught me in the chin again with his fist.

I must have blacked out then, because when I woke, he was under me, the full length of my body running along his, his strong arms wrapped around my chest and his cock still buried in me from the rear. We were hit with a square of light, as the door opened, and another man entered. He was tall and thin and was pulling off his clothes as the door shut. His cock was thin, but it was unusually long, and it was pointed out from his body, hard and ready to go.

He gave me a big grin as he dropped ·to his knees, pushing my legs out so that his legs were between mine and those of the blond below me. He then lifted and wishboned my legs, and, as I watch in horror as he moved up toward us, his long thin cock pushing into me and along the blond's cock that was inside me. I was being double fucked. The blond underneath me came to life in pleasure, as he felt the cock sliding in alongside his, and the two of them began to play me like a calliope. The door opened again, and Bobby Joe and Maurice entered, closed it behind them, and watched as I was being double boned.

I passed out again.

The following night, one of the guards took a turn. He pulled me out of my sleep, stripped me down, and handcuffed me to the bars of the window, facing them. He pushed a gag into my mouth, which filled my mouth with a hard, rubber plug. He stripped down to where he was wearing only a studded leather harness, a studded leather cock sheath, and shiny black boots. He was completely hairless, all bullet head, muscle, and bulging cock and balls. He had a leather riding crop at the end of a billy club, and he used both ends on me, first flicking the leather whip across my shoulders, on my back and legs, and against my butt cheeks.

And then, when those were red and slightly welted, he invaded my ass with the billy end of the club. The club was replaced with his studded cock, which caused my ass passage walls to scream with dueling pain and pleasure as they rubbed back and forth with his relentless pumping. The studs on his chest harness dragged back and forth on the welts on my back, heightening both my pain and the sensations inside me. He sank his teeth into my shoulders, neck, and back as he fucked me, and he pinched my nipples and raked my chest and belly with sharp fingernails.

When he was finished, spurting semen deep inside me in several thrusting fountains, he ripped off my gag and released my hands. I just sank to the floor of the cell in sobs of pain as he slipped outside the door. I looked around, as he left, to see that, once again, Bobby Joe and Maurice had observed my ordeal.

For two days after that, I received no visitors. But I also was left alone in my cell, with my meals deliver in a slot at the bottom of the door.

Then on the next night, the door opened, and the biggest and fattest of the guards was standing in the opening. I shrank back into the corner of my bed. The guard moved aside and Bobby Joe entered the room. The door clanged shut behind him. He came over and sat down on the bed beside me.

We just sat there for several moments, staring at each other. And then he spoke. "There's no need for you to have to go through all this, you know. All you have to do is to say that you'll be my bitch and the others will leave you alone."

I just sat there rocking back and forth, not knowing what to say.

"I'm here to fuck you either way," Bobby Joe said with a slow smile. "I can do it brutally, or we can become lovers for the rest of the time you're here, and I can make the others leave you alone. Even Maurice."

I mulled that one over, my arms embracing my chest tightly.

"Ten inches. I'm going to give you ten inches again. You came to like it last time. I could tell. It can be even better than that, or you can keep fighting me, and be visited by friends of mine every night. Which is it to be?"

I let my arms fall beside me in defeat, but I didn't look up.

"Here, give us a kiss," he said gently, and he lifted my chin with his hand.

He brought his mouth to mine and gave me a kiss. I didn't respond.

"You can do better than that," he said. "I know you can. Should I call Chad in? You know, the one who used you as a punching bag before double fucking you."

This time when he approached me, I opened my mouth to him in resignation, and we entered into a long, tonguing kiss.

"There. That's better," he said. "Here, stand up."

I rose from the bed and he undressed me and then guided me in undressing him and we stood there, belly to belly, his hands exploring my body and, at his urging, my hands exploring him as well. His cock was already fully engorged and mine was coming to life as well. His mouth went down to my nipples and I arched my back away from him, while he played there with his lips and teeth. He pulled me back up so that we were chest to chest. He wasn't sweaty now, and his curly chest hair tingled on my smooth skin. His hands went to my butt cheeks, and then a finger of each of his hands entered my asshole and opened me.

We rocked back and forth in a close embrace, me panting, as he fingered deeper into me. I melted to him as he found my prostate and brought my cock to life. I was sighing and groaning as he laid me on the bed and then stretched his body along mine, head to toe.

"Follow my lead," he said. "Do what I'm doing." Then he took my cock in his mouth and sucked me off. I did the same to him. But I came after several minutes and he was able to hold off. He turned me on my back with him above me, still head to toe, and he then reached down and brought a condom packet and a tube of lube from his pants pocket. He went up on his knees above me. His dong was brushing against my face.

"Here," he said, as he handed me the condom. "Sheath me with this and then find something else other than my cock to play with while I'm busy down here."

I got the packet open and was rolling the condom on his cock while he rotated my hips until he could get his lips on my asshole, which he gave considerable attention to with a wet, long tongue. Meanwhile, I sucked on his heavy balls. I lurched as the cold lubricant was spread around on my asshole, but it quickly warmed as he worked it into me with his fingers.

Then he turned me back around so that my back was nuzzled into his front along the bed. I felt his cock running up the small of my back and felt a guilty pleasure at the thought of all that length inside me. I was laying on my right side, and he lifted my left leg above us and slowly but relentless side split me with that battering ram of his and ran his cock up inside me, reaching for the very core of me.

I didn't fight him but matched my rhythm to his, and the pleasure of this fuck far overshadowed the pain. He turned my head, and we kissed, this time with a far more enthusiastic response from me than I had managed before. He ran his fingers on the hand of the arm that was wrapped around me around a nipple and slowly pumped me off to a second ejaculation with his other hand encasing my cock.

"Ah, that's my sweet little bitch," he murmured in my ear after we had ended our kiss. "How much longer are you going to be in here?"

"Two weeks," I whispered back.

"Sweet," he said. "By the time you leave here, you are going to be begging for this cock."

I didn't believe him yet that night. But by the time my sentence was up, he proved to be right. I was hooked.

Fireplugged

I awakened with my butt spooned into Jesse's groin, both of us on our sides, his placid cock inside me, me encased in his arms, his strong hands fanned out over my pecs. I felt for the ring. It was still there. I didn't care what the courts had said, Jesse and I were married. One unit. As solidly linked as we now were in one body, linked irrevocably by that cock now at gentle rest inside me.

Jesse felt me stir and kissed my ear and nibbled at my neck, while his fingers started to make little swirling movements in the curly, downy hair around my nipples. I felt his cock stirring, that long, slender rod with the upturn that caused his dick head to drag along my inner walls maddingly as he stroked me. I pushed back into him with my butt. His mouth started to suck on my neck, more insistently, more awake. One of his hands dug into a nipple; the other fanned out over my belly, holding me there, while his hips began a rhythm. The rhythm of the early-morning deep, slow, languid, sensual fuck. I lifted a thigh over his, giving him deeper access. I sighed and moaned for him.

But he wanted more. He was fully awake, fully reinvigorated. He wanted to fuck me wildly. He always wanted to fuck me like a wild man. We didn't really have time for this; I wasn't really in the mood for this. But he was my partner. He wanted me, and I loved him for that.

I allowed him to pull me up onto my knees, and I widened the stance of my legs, opening wide to him. My chest was flat against the sheets, and my arms were flung out wide, my fists gathering and releasing bunches of bedspread and sheeting in rhythm with the furious stroking that he, on his knees between my legs, was applying with that long, draggy cock of his inside me. As I knew it would, that cock of his was putting me in the mood for him. I cried out for him, loving those long, deep strokes. I writhed underneath him, as he plowed me hard and long. I loved the feel of the sliding uncut cock inside me.

With a cry of exultation, he came inside me, flooding me, no need for any protection between us now beyond the rings of pledge on our fingers.

We collapsed on the bed, and he stroked me off to an ejaculation with his hand. The loving, caring partner. I could feel him stirring again, and he wanted more, but one of us had to be sensible. He had a class to go teach and I needed to get to work on the new chapter of my novel.

Stolid against all of his protestations, teasings, and attempts to arouse me, I forced him out of the bed and lay there, half asleep, contentment filled, as I heard him patter about the apartment and then leave for the university. I would not make the mistake of stirring before he was gone. The last time I had done that, he had taken me, roughly and wildly on the kitchen counter and almost not made his class.

I waited until I was well sure that Jesse was on his way, and then I groaned my way out of the bed, showered, threw my favorite white, diaphanous caftan over my head, and padded out to the kitchen. Immediately, my mind became lost in thoughts of where to pick up the threads of my writing for the morning. I put the coffee on and wolfed down some cereal in milk while my mind was a thousand miles away. The coffee brewed, I poured a cup and moved out to the balcony overlooking the back garden. I just stood in the doorway there, breathing in the clean air through the aroma of the rich coffee. Not seeing the garden, but my mind calming down, preparing itself for what I had to write this morning, the mere presence of the garden helping me to focus inwardly.

I loved a morning fuck from Jesse, of course, but I still wasn't fully satisfied. I had begged him to enter this monogamous relationship, I know, but I had no idea how hard it would be for me. He tended to be the one who had gone from one long-term relationship to another in a consecutive stream, never overlapping his lovers. I had been the one who sought variety—who fed off that variety to enrich, I had thought, each of them. My insistence on a more permanent arrangement with Jesse was really my struggle with myself to settle down, now that I had found the right man.

But this wasn't getting me anywhere on my novel, I thought. I shook my head, sipped at the coffee, and tried to pull myself back into what I had to write today.

"You know that when you stand with the light to your back in that white thing you're wearing, I can see every contour of your body, don't you?"

My head snapped around. I had no idea I wasn't alone on the balcony. I'd been so lost in my thoughts when I'd come out here that I hadn't even bothered to check. The apartment that shared the balcony had been vacant for months. I vaguely knew that someone was rumored to have moved in—a young fireman, I'd been told—but I'd forgotten. I instinctively wrapped my arms around my chest, trying to withdraw into myself.

"No, don't bother with that," the bronze god, who evidently had been doing his morning stretches, said with a laugh. "I've seen it all now, and it's much too nice to cover."

"Uh, umm," I stammered as much lost for words because he was a hulking beauty, all hard-packed muscle, with massive chest and arms tapering down to a divine six-pack and, from what I could see below the gym shorts he was wearing—the only thing he was wearing—massive thigh and calf muscles as well. And his face—a regular poster model. He no doubt posed for those sexy calendars fire stations put out to help pay for their wild parties.

"You're Jesse's partner, aren't you?"

"Ummm, yes," I managed to dumbly mutter. He was beautiful. He was all I looked for in a man before I had decided to settle down. Gorgeous, smiling, and gregarious.

"I've met Jesse already. He told me about you."

"Uh, he did?" I said, not yet together enough for intelligent conversation. Jesse, I thought, was possibly gossiping a bit too much with strangers.

"Yeah, he told me you were a sweet fuck."

Lost for words altogether now. Jesse had, indeed, been saying entirely too much around the neighborhood. But had he used that bald language?

"Here, come here," he said with a big smile, as he moved around to an iron patio chair with arms on it that sat on his side of the balcony and settled himself in it. "I'd like to get to know you better."

"I'm sorry, Mr. Mr. . . .," I said, trying to keep this on a civilized basis, although my knees were knocking and my hands were trembling to the point of slooshing coffee out of my cup and onto the front of my caftan.

"Ah, you've spilled that on yourself, come on over here and I'll lick it off for you. Chet, you can call me Chet. And I'd like to fuck you. Come on over here."

"Well, excuse ME . . . Chet," I almost bellowed. "But that's just a bit forward. I have a partner and we are loyal to each other."

"Ah, it's just a little fuck," Chet was saying, still dazzling me with that smile. "I don't want to marry you, I just want to fuck you. And there, I can see you want it too. Your cock is at attention under that tent of yours, and you are trembling so badly you're spilling that coffee all over and I think you're about ready to buckle at the knees. At least put the coffee down. It's very hot . . . just like you."

His first good idea. I managed to get the coffee cup over to the table on our side of the balcony and set it down. But I went much farther than that. I also slipped my ring—my partnership ring pledging me to Jesse and only to Jesse—off my finger and laid it beside the coffee cup. I knew, of course, what that meant. He was just so beautiful and hulky and hunky and forceful. If I couldn't resist a muscled hunk, I simply melted at a cocky dominator.

I turned toward him, he put out his hand to me and simply said, one more time, "Come," and my feet betrayed me and my pledge of fidelity to Jesse. Even with the rationalization that it was all Jesse's fault anyway—he and his big mouth about my being a bottom—the guilt at what I was doing flooded me.

The guilt kept me silent, as he pulled me into him on the chair, my knees between his thighs and the chair arms, and began sucking on the coffee stains on my caftan. The guilt kept me silent as his lips found my nipples through the diaphanous material and sucked on them too. The guilt kept me silent as his lips found mine and searched and possessed. The silence turned to moans, however, when his hand went under the hem of the caftan and found my alert cock—aching for the touch and stroking that he was giving it.

Strong hands pulled the caftan over my head and discarded it to the side. And warm, moist lips went to my nipples, buried themselves alternately in my bushy pits, taking in the clean, postshower man smell of me, and worked their way down my sternum. He lifted my body up under my armpits and my knees found the arms of the chair.

All the time, I was whimpering and whispering pleadings for him to stop, that I couldn't, that we mustn't, that it wasn't right. But all the time sighing and moaning for him, not wanting him to stop. Hardening for him; melting for him. My plaintive "nos" became compliant "yeses," as I let him know in murmurings and body responses what he was doing was driving me crazy.

His hands were dancing on my cock and balls, and I was hugging his searching lips to my chest, burying my fingers in his fine, blond hair. He put his hands under my butt cheeks and brought my body up to him. I instinctively reached up and found a couple of chains hanging from the balcony ceilings, chains that could hold flower pots for the more fussy tenants, and I hung on tight with them with my hands. The tenant before the fireman had had a veritable jungle of hanging pots out here.

I arched my back and cried out an "Oh, Gawd!" as he swallowed my cock and started working it with his mouth. He was relentless and didn't stop working me until I had come and collapsed into the chair, my hands losing hold on the chains, and my knees slipping down off the chair arms and back down between the arms and his thighs.

He took one of my hands then and placed it on his basket, letting me feel the strength of him there. He felt massive, even there. He freed the monster with one of his hands, and brought my hand back to it. He wasn't particularly long, but he was thickest I'd ever seen and felt—he had a regular fireplug between his legs.

"Do you like my club?" he asked in a hoarse whisper. "All of this goes inside you. I'm going to fuck you good."

"No, noooo," I whimpered. "I don't think I can."

"Sure you can," he said. "You just have to be loosened up a bit."

With that he turned me and brought my knees back up onto the arms of the chair. I grabbed for the chains again, as he buried his face between my butt cheeks and wettened and tongued, and widened, and ate my ass out until I was a burbling mass of jelly under his talented attentions. I don't know how good he was at putting fires out, but he was the tops at starting them and making them rage.

He must have had a tube of lube nearby, because he was now lathering my ass up and sliding his fat fingers in and out of me, checking me, preparing me.

I panicked when he turned me and I could see that he was about to set me down on that greased up monster cock of his.

"No, oh no. A condom. Gotta be sheathed." This was one pledge to Jesse I couldn't give up. We had foregone condoms ourselves, both loving the feel of skin on skin, as the reward for only having sex with each other. This would have been the final betrayal. I could not have returned to Jesse if I had gone back to multiple bareback partners.

The hunky fireman gave me a pained look, but he dutifully reached around and fished out a condom packet from somewhere, a bit too conveniently at hand, I later thought. He made me roll the condom on his cock, which was no easy chore, even though he had the largest size made. His cock was just gigantic in circumference.

I had been well prepared and had a long history of taking cock, but, even so, I howled to the breezes crossing the balcony as he rolled that massive mushroom cap around the rim of my hole and forced himself into me. A few excruciatingly painful moments, and my ass decided it would take him—in fact, that it had to have this fireplug inside it, and my muscles gripped his club and pulled it inside me, with me groaning and grunting deeply to stretch for him and him laughing his delight at splitting me asunder. He soon had my butt cheeks nestled into the tops of his thighs, and that giant cock grinding around inside me and stretching my walls almost beyond the limit.

I moaned and writhed for him. I arched my back way back so that I was draped down his legs and hanging onto the legs of the iron chair with my hands. One of my legs was running up his torso and the other one hung out over the chair arm. And all the while, with those big, strong hands on my hips, he was stroking me back and forth on his fireplug. When he got tired of that, he lifted me and set my butt down on his monster cock in an ever-faster rhythm.

He was a virile stud, fast to reload, and he took me twice more, once with my knees on the chair arms and the back of the chair biting into my chest, and him standing, straddling the chair and fucking me from behind and, at last, down on all fours on the steel grated floor of the balcony, me huffing and puffing and staring down three flights of balconies to the ground and him covering me from behind and making magic between my legs.

At last, we collapsed in a heap on the balcony floor. I was breathing hard and moaning from the exertion and the stretching of my ass. He had hardly broken a sweat.

"Jesse was right," he muttered at last. "You are one sweet fuck."

I was feeling totally guilty all over again. Mostly because I had betrayed Jesse and gone with another man. Partly, though, because if I was going to go with another man, and a hunk like this didn't want to use a condom, I was not taking full advantage of the sin. "I'm sorry about the condom," I murmured back to him. "It's just that . . ."

"Oh, that's OK," the fireman hunk responded with a little laugh. "Your Jesse made me use a condom when I fucked him too."

Friday Night Football

They had told me that it would be just a matter of time. That I needed to adjust to being out of the battle zone and back in civilization—just to take life at a low key for a while and be happy to hold down a low-stress job for a while and enjoy TV and playing videogames at night. But I couldn't tell them what all of the stressors were in coming home to a completely different environment.

It hadn't been something I'd volunteered for, but I'd been the smallest guy in the unit out there in the isolated outpost, and it had just happened. And it had become part of me. But it had happened to me; I hadn't gone looking for it. I didn't really know how to look for it. But it had become part of me—and a great deal of my stress was that it had just stopped. It had stopped the day before I left Iraq.

How does a guy go cold turkey on something like that? Maybe he can't. Maybe that's why I said what I did when Wayne called the next week after that Friday-night high school football game we'd gone to.

"Jack, it's me, Wayne. Uh, you OK? You didn't say much when I took you home last Friday night. I wondered if you're OK."

"It's been three days now, Wayne. It's kinda late to be asking me if Friday night was OK, isn't it?"

"Yeah, well. You know. It's hard to call on that. I didn't know, man. I swear."

"You didn't? It seemed it was OK with you at the time."

"Well, you know . . . you told me, and—"

"I had to tell someone, Wayne. You're my uncle. There isn't anyone else around here really I could talk to. And I was thinkin' I'd explode or something."

"But it seemed it was OK . . . you seemed to get into it."

I didn't answer for several seconds. I couldn't really deny honestly that I hadn't gotten into it. I know I'd been thinking about looking for it myself, and it was just there. I hadn't a clue really on finding it myself.

"Well, I'm doin' OK, Wayne. Is that the only reason you called? To check on whether I've gone crazy or something? Or if am going to tell anyone about it? 'Cause if that's why you called—"

"It's not, Jack. It's not why I called. I called, because the guys want . . . well, Wayne junior's team has another football game this Friday night, and we thought . . . if you were OK and all . . . that . . ."

"You want me to go to the game again? Like last Friday night?"

"Yeah. If you're OK with it. Just if you're OK with it. And if you're interested. I could pick you up again. I know you don't have a car yet."

"I don't know, Wayne. I just don't know." I was trembling, knowing what I should say and also knowing what I wanted to say.

"Well, you could think about it. I thought . . . well, that the way you took it . . . that you were OK with it. More than OK. So, then, you think about it. And give me a call. If you don't call, I'll figure–"

"OK, Wayne."

"OK what? You'll call?"

"No, OK, I'll go to the game."

My hand was shaking so bad when he rang off that I almost couldn't hit the button to turn my cell phone off.

* * * *

It was a close game. The second half had just started, and the score was tied. Wayne's son's team was moving the ball pretty well down the field, though. And Wayne's son was catching passes left and right—the real star of the team.

Wayne leaned over to me in the bleachers and whispered, "Got the signal. They want us down there now."

"Now?" I asked incredulously. "Wayne Junior is burning up the field. I bet he takes it in. You don't want to see that?"

"They've signaled. It's time to go. Wayne Junior will do what he's going to do whether or not I'm in the stands."

There were four of them standing between the side of the bleachers and the refreshment stand, looking a little bit nervous. They were smoking or drinking cans of coke—obviously wishing it was beer, but this was a high school event. Last Friday there'd only been three of them. All dads of football players on Wayne Junior's team and all gym buddies of Wayne's. Big bruisers, who obviously spent most of their time in the gym bulking up. I was a midget in their midst when Wayne and I got down there. Even Wayne was a good foot taller than I was and all bulked up like Mr. Atlas or something.

They watched Wayne and me as we came down from the stands, and I was watching them too. I knew that look. I'd seen that look on lots of occasions in the isolated outpost in Iraq

One of the guys had some sort of black strap contraption with handles, which he had doubled over and was nervously slapping slowly on his calf.

"He OK with this?" one of the guys asked Wayne as we approached their tight little circle. He was speaking to Wayne but looking at me. And I knew the question was about me.

"Yeah, he's cool," Wayne answered.

"Same as last time. $30 apiece. That OK?" This was spoken to Wayne again, like I wasn't even there or something.

"Yeah, that's good," Wayne said. He said it like he was the one who had to do something for it.

"OK, then let's go on under," the spokesman of the group, a sandy-haired tower of a guy—the father of the quarterback, I thought—said. "No more than two at a time, though. Don't want anyone noticing."

I went under with Wayne, after two other guys had looked around to see if they'd be noticed and then sauntered in under the bleachers. We went at least half the distance under the bleachers. The stands were wide and it was dark where we ended up, coming up to the two guys who'd gone in first. For some reason it made me think of a prison. I think that's because the light, such as it was, came into the space under the bleachers in thin horizontal stripes. The stands were almost completely closed. There was a strip just maybe four inches at the base of the seats, where they met the standing boards, that was open—mostly to let water run off when it rained. The light that came through in strips came from the banks of strong light from the stadium lights.

"OK, me first," one of the guys who had preceded us under the bleachers said. He had his hands on my shoulders and pushed me down on my knees in front of him.

I worked his zipper down. There was a roar from the crowd on the bleachers, like something had gone wrong for the home team. A muffled announcement indicated that maybe there'd been an interception or a fumble and the other team had the ball.

I was sucking the guy's cock when the other two men showed up and a circle formed around me. Wayne was in the circle. He hadn't been there the last Friday night. He'd stood off then, asking the guys in a rather plaintive voice to not push me and to be less rough, not knowing whether I'd let them fuck me regardless of what I'd told him had happened to me in Iraq and how conflicted I was over that. But I had let them fuck me during last Friday's game under these stands.

There were three of them then. Now there were five. Wayne obviously was in on it now.

The spent condoms from last Friday were still here—and maybe more from some other encounters that had happened under here in the last week. It had been right here where they'd done it—and I'd let them do it and then just walked away when they were finished. I was kneeling on top of the used condoms now—letting them do it again.

I felt hands on my hips and another set of hands was unbuttoning my shirt and struggling it off my back. I momentarily had to take my mouth off the first guy's cock, but after the shirt was off, he put his hands on the back of my head and guided me back to trying to deep throat him. The hands on my hips were lifting me off my knees, so I was standing, half crouched, and bent over. Those hands then went to my belt buckle and undid that, and my trousers and briefs were stripped off my legs.

I was naked now. The guys circling me were still dressed, but they all had their flies open and were handling their cocks with their hands.

The first guy came in my mouth as a cheer was going up in the stands. There had been another fumble or interception and the ball was back in the home team's possession. I heard Wayne's son's number called, and I looked at Wayne, who was smiling and pumping his fist in the air. But he also had his cock out and was pumping it just like the other guys were. I suppose I should have felt sorry for him in his conflict of interests here. But I didn't. He was just another guy wanting tail now and willing to take sloppy thirds or fourths to get it.

I had another guy's cock in my mouth and someone was knelt behind me, palms on my butt cheeks, spreading them. His tongue went to my ass.

I moaned and closed my eyes, thinking of Alphonse, in Iraq. The big, black stud who fucked us all. His tonguing had been like that—bigger than some guy's cocks. And his cock had been the biggest of the unit.

I should be all tensed up and worried and not OK with this, I knew. But the more this brought my mind back to that outpost in Iraq and how we'd all fight our fears and uncertainty by fucking—and I was finding this soothing. At least it took up time in which I had no part of any decision. These guys were big and motivated now. I was going to be fucked now one way or the other.

Once the serious fucking started, I just relaxed and went with it. I closed my eyes and thought about all those guys I lived with in danger and intimacy in Iraq, and I just went with the flow.

Five guys. Five guys, including Wayne, although I have no idea where he was in the line, fucked me in succession. The first one started about the time the roar of the crowd went up as the home time scored a touchdown—Wayne Junior's number was called out once more.

With the first one, I found out what the black strap was. The first guy, standing behind me, his cock already worked up into my channel, flipped the strap over my head and laid the center, thick, padded section of the strap against my lower belly. He had his fists in handles at each end.

He then jerked it up into my belly, lifting my feet off the ground and doubling me forward. Then, using the muscle power he'd developed in the gym and his significant size over mine, he just raised and lowered me on his cock at the rhythm and speed he desired, with me just hanging in front of him like a rag doll, moaning and groaning at the churning of his cock inside me.

That's how they all took me. All five of them. Thick, long, thin, curved up, curved down, deep thrusting, prostate punishing, churning, thrusting, rotating, fast, slow, caressing, cruel. It took them all well into the fourth quarter of the game to finish with me.

I lay on the ground, amid both new and old used condoms, panting and still moaning as they all zipped up and the four guys dug $30 each out of their pockets and handed the money to Wayne.

"Away game next Friday," the sandy-haired brute said, "But another home game the Friday after that. Will he come to that game?"

I wanted to scream that I most certainly would not—that I couldn't be treated this way. But who was I kidding? I loved the cocking. I'd go another round now, if the game wasn't running down.

"Yeah, he can be here," Wayne said.

I said nothing.

As Wayne helped me up and found my clothes and helped me get those back on, he murmured, "You did great, Jack. You OK? You're sure you're OK with this?"

"Yeah," I answered. "I'm OK with this."

"Great. Here's $50. You sure you're OK about being fucked? You like it, right?"

"Yeah, I like it," I answered. And that wasn't a lie. That's what I was missing since coming home from Iraq—what I'd been initiated in there and that, if I was honest with myself, I didn't want to give up.

"That's great, 'cause there's something I've been meaning to ask you. Wayne Junior's eighteenth birthday is coming up week after next, and he tells me he fancies you—has this idea about the ideal birthday gift. And, Jack, I gotta tell you, this kid's got a cock on him you wouldn't believe."

Gotta Keep This Job

I had been summoned to the medical suite at my office at the end of the Friday dayshift of my second week on the job, and I showed up with a great sense of trepidation. It had been hard finding this job, and I just had to keep it. But I'd scored drugs for a short time when I'd been in college, and I knew this company had a strict drug policy. I hoped that they hadn't found out about that—or that they wouldn't find out about it in this surprise appointment. I'd given them up now, of course. I just didn't want my youthful adventures to spoil the rest of my life.

"Come in here, take off all your clothes, and sit up on that table," a perky young nurse told me. "The doctor will be in to see you in a minute."

"Take off all my clothes?" I asked dubiously.

"Yes. Don't worry. I go off shift now. It will be just you and the doctor." She gave me a saucy little look like she was sorry she wouldn't be around for the show.

"Great," I thought, as I followed her direction. I didn't know why I felt self-conscious. I was in great shape and wouldn't have minded the cute little nurse knowing just how great shape I was in and how well hung I was.

But I was in shock when the doctor walked in. It was Larry, my boss, the owner of the company.

"Mr. Sturgis," I stammered. "What . . .?"

"Oh, didn't you know?" the handsome young redhead said, "I'm the company doctor too. It saves a lot on the medical bills. Now, let's see what we have here. Everything seems to be in order and in good shape. Yes, in very good shape, I'd say. Here, put this in your mouth and cough for me."

He stuck a wooden tongue depressor in my mouth, and I coughed for him. He ran long, elegant fingers up and down the sides of my neck and prodded around the top of my breast bone. Then, in turn, he lifted my arms, pushed a finger up into my arm pits, and gave my arm muscles a good feel.

"OK, very good there," he said. He whipped out a stethoscope and listened to my chest.

"Take deep breaths and hold them," he said. His stethoscope went to one nipple, and he laid his hand over the other one.

"Cough," he commanded. I obliged.

Then after a long time, he reversed the stethoscope and the hand over the other nipple and commanded me to cough again. I obliged again, hoping he hadn't noticed that my nipples were hardening up from the attention.

"Good, full chest," he said. "Lungs seem fine. Not a smoker, are you?"

"No," I answered too quickly. That had been another one of my vices in college. But I'd also been on the swim team and had developed a deep chest and lungs.

"Been an athlete requiring good breath control?"

"Yes . . . yes, I was a competitive swimmer in college."

His hands glided down the sides of my torso, and he put one palm over my belly and left it there for a minute. I had no idea what sort of new examination technique this was, but I was mortified that it was causing me to have a half-hard on.

He had a hand on my balls, and I flinched as he rolled them.

"Cough," he commanded, and I did so.

"Everything seems in fine shape here," he said. "In fine shape."

He had his hand on my dick and was flopping it around gently. "Get it off regularly?" he asked.

"Uh, yes, regularly enough," I answered. "Uh, Mr. Sturgis. I mean Dr. Sturgis . . ."

"Would have liked to stick it to that cute little nurse who was just in here, would you?" he continued.

"Well, yes. Wouldn't anyone?" I responded, embarrassed. I was doubly embarrassed, because my cock had thickened and lengthened significantly at this suggestion.

"Sorry about that," he said with a laugh. "I was just checking to see if everything was in working order down here. It sure seems to be. That's good news. Now, I want you to lay back on the table and draw your knees up to your chest. I need to check your prostate."

He was putting a glove on his hand and dipping his fingers into a jar of lubricant.

"But, shouldn't I stand and lean over for . . .?"

"Naw," he answered. "I have my own procedure for this. It's less painful this way. You'll be more relaxed."

So, I laid back on the table and drew my knees up to my chest. It seemed like quite a while before I felt anything else, but then there was his cold and wet gloved finger working its way into my asshole. I knew when it had reached my prostate, because he was rubbing me there, sending strokes of pleasure through my balls and dick, and I felt precum forming on my cock helmet. A moan escaped my lips.

He withdrew his finger, but I heard him mutter something about thinking he'd felt something odd in there and needing to probe farther.

And then he was probing farther, but it seemed like he was probing with a bigger finger, and then I realized that he had both hands on my knees, squeezing them.

I lurched up in pain and surprise, but he already had his dick far enough inside me to maintain leverage, and he just kept unwinding his hose up my ass chute. My legs shot down and my torso came up, and I flailed around as his strong hands grabbed my shoulder blades. His long, slender hands wrapped around the sides of my pecs, and his thumbs landed on my nipples. His white doctor's coat was open and he otherwise was naked. He had a good build, and there was fluffy red hair covering his pecs and working its way down to and beyond his belly.

155

I cried out in pain and frustration as his cock continued its journey up my ass canal until I felt his pubic hair tickling the insides of my thighs.

"Oh, God. Sturgis. Don't . . ."

"I already did, Mark. You're already split and filled. Can't go back now. Just calm down and enjoy it."

"Enjoy it?" I screamed. "Get off me, you . . ."

"Get off you, or what?" Sturgis asked with a heavy laugh. "I'm already in you, and I'm going to fuck you regardless. You can either enjoy it or fight it, but you are already fucked. I've had my eye on you since we interviewed you for the job. Why do you think you got the job over all those others?"

I was fighting him now, but he was too strong, and every time I tried to move, his dick went a little deeper into my ass.

"Stop fighting for a minute and listen to me," he commanded. I stopped moving. He moved his torso into mine, and his chest hair felt silky against my bare skin. My cock was throbbing against his belly. "Do you think you were picked because you were the most qualified? No, you were picked because you were the most desirable. And do you think you were picked only because you are a stud?"

"I don't understand. Why . . .?"

"You were also picked because you had a drug history. You were picked because if you want to keep this job, you are going to let me fuck you now. And you are going to let me fuck you again and again, if I want to. Do you understand?"

"But, but . . ." I whimpered.

"How badly do you want this job, Mark?"

A long moment of silence and then I whispered, "Badly."

"I didn't hear you, Mark. How badly do you want this job?"

"Badly," I almost screamed back at him. "I gotta keep this job."

"And what do you want me to do to you so you can keep this job, Mark?"

"Whatever you want," I whimpered after a moment of contemplation.

"Tell me you want me to make love to you, Mark."

"I want you to make love to me, Larry."

"Like this?" Sturgis asked, and his lips went to my nipples, which he started to ravish with his tongue and teeth.

"Yes, like that," I moaned.

"And, perhaps more crudely, but more succinctly, tell me you want me to fuck you."

"I want you to fuck, me?" I whimpered.

"Like this?" he asked as he set his cock in action. Stroking me, first shallow and deep and then in longer strokes that brought his cock helmet almost to the rim of my asshole and then glided in again down to the hilt.

My cries of "Oh, god, no, you're splitting me," turned to moans of pleasure and "Yes, yes," as my ass passage calibrated to the size of his rocket and ripples of pleasure ran around my ass walls.

"I asked you if you wanted it like that," he said in a hoarse voice.

"Yes, yes, like that."

"Deeper and harder?" he asked.

"Yes, yes, deeper and harder. Plow me. Fuck me."

I no longer was thinking just of the job. I was thinking of having a piston alive inside me, filling me and stroking me in waves of pleasure.

His lips went to mine, and I opened to his tongue. I was gasping for breath and groaning and moaning. He was completely turned on by my compliance. He turned me on the table and pumped me in a side split while he stroked my cock with his hand. In my excitement and nervousness at the newness of all this, I came quickly, which set off his ejaculation as well.

He pulled out of me, buttoned up his coat, swept his pants off of the floor, and turned toward the door.

"Let's see how well you can do with a blow job tomorrow. Say ten in the morning in my office? We'll see how permanent we can make your job from there. If you can learn to suck as well as you take a fuck, I see a quick promotion in your future."

And then he was gone. I lay there and collected myself and tried to pull the shreds of my pride back together again.

But what was I to do. I gotta keep this job. And truth be known, I was looking forward to my next session with Larry.

Gustaf's Castle

"Oh, come on, Rob. Come with me," Josh had said. "What's the worst that could happen? You could get laid. So what? It's about time. We've never been to a gay bar before—at least I haven't. And I hear Gustaf's is a gas. All made up in Transylvania style and everything."

No, I'd never been to a gay bar before. In fact, I hadn't been to anything gay—that I knew of—or had even thought of doing so until Josh and I had drawn each other as college roomies. I think being around him for three months so far had bent me. I was beginning to have strange thoughts and urges—ones I'd never had before. All because of how Josh looked and what he did with girls and guys alike.

"Aren't you worn out from the football scrimmages today?" I asked. "Don't you have too much studying to do?"

He was standing at the sink in the bathroom, with only a towel draped around him, having just showered. He was leaning into the mirror, using short scissors to trim his eyebrows. He always wanted to look good. And he always did look good. Two hundred and twenty pounds and nearly six and a half feet of solid fullback muscle; built like a tank.

"Naw. Tonight I feel like something new; something a little wild. You know, give the girlie boys something to gawk at."

"I don't know," I mumbled. I liked him like this, though. He got my juices going when he was being a bit wild. But I really didn't know. Being in a gay bar with him when he was in this mood. Who knew where it would lead to? I was scared and jacked up at the same time.

"Is OK," Josh was saying. "If you don't want to go, I'm sure Scott will go with me."

And that pushed me over the edge. Scott would go with him for sure, and Scott would probably wind up doing things with him after going to the gay bar that I'd only dreamed of doing with Josh myself. Scott had hit on me more than once. I couldn't think of anything worse than Scott getting something on with Josh that I was too shy and scared to attempt myself.

"OK, then," I said. "I'll go with you."

"Great. And wear that black net muscle shirt you have and the tight black jeans. You'll be a smash there. We'll really knock 'em dead."

Gustaf's—really Gustaf's Castle—was all it was rumored to be. The entrance foyer was five steps down, under the stoop of a massive brownstone townhouse in a quiet street off the main drag in Old Town.

The bouncer who answered the door was a regular Egor right out of a Dracula movie, and after giving both Josh and me the once over and being satisfied, he opened a heavy, steel-spike-studded door in the stone-floored foyer we first entered, and we were descending again into a dimly lit, rock-walled, cool, subterranean chamber, complete with vaulted ceiling, thick cobwebs, an armory of medieval weapons and chains hung on the walls, and raucous male noise rising above the eerie sounds coming from a small band. I couldn't tell what instruments were being played or even what style of music; I just know it sounded a little creepy and dissonant.

The room wasn't all that big and the temperature increased as Josh and I descended the curved stone staircase into the pit, no doubt heated up by the tightly encased swirl of man flesh in high heat.

I immediately felt out of my element and sensed my throat constricting, and all I wanted to do was turn and flee back up the stairs and out into the night. But Josh didn't seem to be perturbed at all. He just kept walking—no, strutting—down the stairs, as faces lifted to take in our arrival and opened up into wide smiles. Cat calls and whistles floated above the sounds of a male crowd on the make, and a corridor was opened between Josh and me and the bar.

Everyone made way as I followed Josh into the crowd and places opened up in the center of the long bar, with men pulling off to the side to give Josh and me space—all except for one man, who would have stood out from all the rest even in the center of the crowd.

He was well over six and a half feet tall and had a dark, glowering aspect about him that exuded domination and control. As tall as he was, he was also a mass of muscle, which made Josh look almost stunted as we approached. He had marble-white skin and black, piercing eyes that both repelled and enticed me as they took both Josh and me in in one, long, languid sweep from toe to head. It was impossible to determine his age. I would have gauged him at more than fifty if it hadn't been for his excellent muscle tone. His face had the craggy appearance of long years of experience without making him any less handsome and arresting in appearance. His silky silver hair stood out wide from his angular face and tumbled down to his shoulders. He was holding up a glass of red wine in long, elegant, strong fingers, the backs of which were covered with curly black and gray-peppered hair.

He was dressed for the locale, tight, fawn colored britches rising out of high-top black leather boots, stretching over heavily muscled legs, and ending in a low-rise waistband, with a pouch for his privates jutting out provocatively at his basket. A white, diaphanous cotton shirt floated above the tight riding pants. This was open at the neck and half-way down his sternum, to reveal a gold medallion on a thick gold chain nestled in a matting of silver and black curly hair. All very B horror movieish, but on him, very arousing.

"Ah, fresh prey," he said in a rich, silky baritone as we approached. His broad smile was one of simultaneously open and challenging welcome. "My name is Gustaf. Welcome to my castle. I don't think you have been here before, so please accept the first drink as my guests."

161

Somehow the way he said "prey" sent shivers up my spine. I maneuvered so that Josh was between me and this very disturbing man. For the second time, all I wanted to do was leave—but Josh was already deep in conversation with the bar's owner.

Standing there, watching them, I couldn't help but be taken with the contrast between the two men. It was the personification of good and evil in my mind, although I chastised myself for rushing to this conclusion. It probably was only their coloring. They were both magnificently built, although the much older Gustaf was an exaggeration of power and manhood that eclipsed young Josh in size and presence, even though Josh was no slouch in that department himself. But Josh's Nordic blondness, with his blue eyes and a body that I knew was smooth and hairless and only lightly tanned, contrasted starkly with the dark, mysterious, almost gypsy-like presence of Gustaf. And Josh's smile was entirely open, honest, and fun-loving. Gustaf smiled, but it went to something like a sneer at the corners, and his eyes blazed and darted in a way that you felt was penetrating to the very center of you and pulling at every evil and dark thought that you had.

One drink led to another, and I found myself in a close encounter with a shirtless Hispanic construction worker type who was making no bones about wanting to get to know me better—and intimately. He had wandering arms like an octopus and, while being quite complimentary and full of humorous good will, also seemed quite adept at moving into me and crowding me against the bar.

He was copping a feel of my basket, holding the outline of my cock through the material of my jeans with two beefy fingers and suggesting that we "take a walk for a few minutes"— and then laughing and saying it might take more than a couple of minutes, when I decided enough was enough and turned to tell Josh it was definitely time to leave. That this hadn't been such a hot idea to begin with. All the time feeling guilty, because I was enjoying what the construction worker was saying to me and, more disturbing, what he was doing to me. And I was shocked that this was so. I needed to get out of here.

But when I swiveled to get Josh's attention, he was gone. And so was Gustaf. I turned to the barman even as the construction worker was pulling my buns back into the hard on I could feel through the material of both of our jeans.

"Where—?" I called out over the din.

"Eh, what?" he called back.

"Where did they—?"

"Gustaf and your friend? Back to the back. Back there." He was pointing toward the back right edge of the bar.

I struggled to move in that direction, but the construction worker gathered me back into his lap with strong arms and turned me, and then he took my lips in his. I was taken by surprise and by shock and before I could react rationally, I was kissing him back passionately.

He was holding me to him, as he sort of perched on a barstool, my rump against his pelvis, and my torso twisted around so that our mouths met. I felt the palm of a hand glide down my belly, and my zipper was being worked down, and he had a hand inside my jeans, pushing up to the waistband of my brief and then down under. And then he was fisting my cock, skin on skin. And I was moaning and writhing and engorging under his touch.

His mouth was becoming more insistent, more possessing. His tongue was probing deep inside me. My ears were buzzing, and my mouth was melting to him as I felt myself hardening under his attentions. My mind was racing and screaming "No, no, no," but in an ever-fading roar. My reason was numbing, but my senses were heightening. I raised one hand to behind his head, holding his mouth to mine, and ran the other one down to cover the fist that he was now slowly, but relentlessly pumping my cock with.

I briefly panicked at the thought of being taken like this in a crowded bar, but I'd seen all of the fucking that was going on as we descended the stairs, so I hardly thought I was the center of attention—and right at this moment, I guessed I really didn't give a fuck what anyone else was seeing.

At the point of being lost to him, though, my mind came screaming back and, with a jerk, I pulled away from him in one swift movement.

"Sorry. So sorry," I muttered. "Gotta find Josh."

And without even looking around to see what effect this had had on the construction worker, I stumbled toward the side of the bar where the barman had said led to the back. To where Josh and Gustaf had gone. As I stumbled, I pulled up my zipper, requiring both of my trembling hands to get the job done.

* * * *

The corridor is dark, black-painted rock walls, oozing moisture. And it seems endless. Doors off to either side here and there, but all locked. No sound from the other side. My head is still buzzing. Completely out of my element here. But gotta find Josh. Where is Josh?

At the end of the corridor is an open doorway, covered by a black, beaded curtain. I hear whimpering and murmuring as I get closer. Groans and moans and sighs. And another sound, a more ominous sound—a sound I can't quite identify. Almost a sucking—or maybe a slapping—sound. Both, really. Quite unreal, echoing.

The room—a stone-walled chamber—is nearly pitch black when I stumble into it and off to the right of the opening my shoulder blades pressed against cold, moist rock.

I can see them only in outline at first, but as my eyes adjust to the darkness, I can clearly take in the mesmerizing, enticing horror of it.

They are both naked now. The young, blond, tanned, hairless hunk and the older, marble-white, silver-haired, hirsute dominating master.

There is some sort of black-cloth-draped dais in the center of the room. Josh is at the edge of this, on both of his knees, undulating torso upright and arched back into the hairy, heaving chest of the other figure, arms hanging listlessly down at his sides.

Gustaf is behind him, but close, one leg flexed and leveraging with the ball of his foot off the floor beside the platform, and the other leg kneeling on the edge of the platform, his thigh insinuated between Josh's spread legs, crotch to ass. The hand of the Gustaf's arm away from me is lifted to Josh's

164

cheek, cupping and holding the younger man's jaw, raising it at an angle, stretching the veins in his neck so that they pop out, fully accessible, vulnerable.

Gustaf has his mouth pressed to these stressed veins, sharp fangs incising into them, gurgling his pleasure in that sucking noise I heard as he drinks Josh's blood deeply, with a slurping sound.

Gustaf's inhumanly thick and long cock is moving, rhythmically, now shallow and fast, now deep and languidly, slapping in and out of Josh's ass canal, the slapping noise reverberating off of the stone walls of the chamber. Gustaf's other hand has snaked around to Josh's flat, ripped belly, and he's slowly pumping Josh's fully engorged cock with his fist.

Josh is whimpering and sighing and groaning and murmuring his pain-pleasure at the testing and full mastering of all of his senses and desires—and fears. There is no struggle in him. His body is slowly swaying back and forth, the expression on his face beatific, his plump butt cheeks slowly moving back and forth, up and down, opening in full acceptance and making love to the gigantic cock that is splitting and mining him deep. Slap, slap, slapping.

As I watch, Josh cries out in passion and twitches hard, and his cock spouts out semen in three strong arcs. But nothing changes. Gustaf continues to suck and to fuck and to pump Josh's still-hard cock.

I whimper and involuntarily work at my belt buckle. Without losing purchase on Josh's throbbing vein with his incisors, Gustaf turns his eyes to me, although I know, instinctively that he has always known I am here, that he heard me stumbling down the long corridor, willing me to continue toward him, to be here to see this—to be part of this.

The power of his eyes—now golden yellow and luminescent in the dim light—pins my shoulder blades to the wall. And the eyes continue to hold me there, not interfering in any way with his sucking teeth, fucking cock, or pumping fist, as my jeans and briefs hit the floor and I begin to work my lengthening, thickening, leaking cock with shaky fist, my ragged breathing and moans merging with Josh's.

Gustaf turns his head and smiles to me, a sneering, knowing smile. He moves his pelvis back, pulling out of Josh's ass, showing me a foot or more of hard, thick, jet-black, throbbing-veined cock. The black cock in stark contrast to the marble-white of the rest of his skin, slowly turning blush now as he feeds. Never dislodged, though, no hint how much is still buried there. I watch as he carefully, almost teasingly, removes his hand from Josh's cock and spreads the hairy-backed palm on Josh's lower belly. Suspended there for the longest time. One more look directly into my eyes and then he licks the jagged wound at Josh's neck and I see his teeth sink in one more time. Eyes back to mine, then descending to my crotch, causing me to look at his as well.

Heavy panting and little cries of the taking from Josh, slipping into a long, drawn-out moan, as Gustaf's palm applies pressure to Josh's belly and slowly, relentlessly pulls his channel back along the gigantic foot-long cock. Until all I see are two hairy, lemon-sized balls hanging down from Josh's entrance. Gustaf's eyes back on mine, now, as I shudder and ejaculate and Josh's voice starts in a whimper and crescendos into a cry out, punctuating his spouting once more in three strong arcs, and then collapses into himself with another whimper—still being held in place by Gustaf's strong arms, deeply embedded cock, and sucking teeth.

Horrified at what I am watching, at what he is doing to Josh. Terrified that he might soon be doing the same thing to me. Hardening and leaking because I know he will be—and trembling in anticipation because that's what I want too.

* * * *

Me lying on the dais now, on my back, one leg dangling off the end and the other being held up and spread by a strong hand with long, sharp fingernails. Looking down, seeing Josh—or what is left of Josh—lying crumpled at the side of the dais. Looking down my belly and seeing the black cock—seemingly only at my entrance but already buried deeper in me than I ever thought possible. Pulsating, causing the muscles of my stretched channel to ripple around it. Moving in and out, penetrating me ever deeper with each inward glide.

Looking at Josh again. Strangely not caring. Wanting what Josh experienced. Black cock sinking ever deeper. Moaning, groaning, wanting more of it.

Looking up into its eyes. Golden glowing eyes. Loving me. Caressing my body with its eyes. The eyes asking for acceptance. I smile. And the beautiful face smiles back at. The thick, ruby-red lips open to a broad smile. Fangs. Dripping blood. Josh's blood. But I don't care. I want it too. I want to be completely taken, possessed.

All sensation going to my stretching channel as the black cock sinks deeper into me and begins to pump. Slap . . . slap . . . slap, slap, slap. The sound of fucking reverberating off of the stone walls. Inside me. The . . . thing . . . fucking me. But I don't care. I want it.

The face disappears, descending below my cheek. The sharp, quick pain at my throbbing vein, and I turn my head away from it, stretching out my neck, making my vein bulge. It is holding my hands in each of its large hands—away from my body, fingers intertwining mine. Intimate, loving. I feel warmth at my neck and a pleasant pulsing sensation. The sucking noise. The same sucking noise I'd heard upon entering the chamber— echoing off the stone walls. Someone in the camber is groaning and sighing. I slowly become aware that it is me.

Everything joining in one rhythm: the slap, slap of the fuck, the throbs of the deep-digging cock and the answering ripples of my channel muscles, the sucking sensation at my neck and the responding pulsing of my life's blood to the point of giving, the rhythmic changing of pressure of its fingers interlaced with mine. Even my sighs and moans are joining in harmony with the ultimate taking. It is humming to me—letting me know that it is enthralled in its feeding. The supreme compliment. I am found acceptable. I am ecstatic, but in a warm, increasingly detached way. Everything is getting hazy—except for the reverberating sound of the slap, slap, slapping and the rhythmic suck.

A great sense of peace and deep pleasure is drifting in. The cock is reaching up, grabbing for my stomach, becoming one with me. I am whimpering my love for the mingling of my now-trickle of blood with the numbing saliva of my master. My master's humming tells me it is well pleased and accepts my offering.

My ears, already having started a soft ringing, reverberate with the primeval cry of the master bouncing all around the stone walls as I feel the fountaining deep inside me. Warm, flowing to my very quick. The slap of the cock holds in suspension as does the outflow of my blood, as for one, panicked moment, I feel like I have not been worthy. But then the huge black cock comes back to life inside me again and the slapping and sucking resume, as I . . . grow . . . progressively more lethargic . . . and the ringing in my ears . . . increases to blot out the slapping and sucking . . . and, with an ultimate feeling of bliss, I . . . drift . . .awa . . .

Halloween Filmfest Conversion

The champion soccer player for the night, all decked out in his silks and his team-color knee-high socks, left his basement apartment in the old row house and strutted down St. Phillip and across Basin Street and North Rampart, into New Orleans' French Quarter. He held his head high, his chest out, his tight butt tucked in, and his basket thrusting out in front of him. He earned most of his money in porn movies now over in the second-floor walkup studio on Burgundy, and because of this, he'd been invited to the Halloween film fest at the gay porno movie house just inside the Quarter on Barracks. He would have devised a more complex costume for the party, but he felt tense and hyper tonight. He knew what he needed; he needed a blow job, and he'd dressed for ready access in the steamy dark theater. He also needed to do some work on what new twist he'd put into the movie they were doing next Tuesday night, so he's probably stay in the theater after being sucked off and collect his thoughts, keep an eye on the positions being used in the films, and not drift into the party room.

He spent most of his time at the gym, building his body to perfection. He was one ripped dude; hard as steel everywhere. So hard that his veins had nowhere to go other than to pop out on his body and flow across it. He liked that. All men of steel had that. He'd worked hard to get here. Big veins, pumping rich blood throughout a young, virile body.

The bodybuilder entered the theater and sat in one of the back rows, away from the doors. He knew it wouldn't be long now. He'd seen the movie they were showing already and thought it was a bit pedestrian, but it was a costume piece in keeping with the Halloween theme of the evening. That's probably why it was being shown. Happily, it was nearly finished—the one guy, some sort of big muscle Mongol invader, was yelling loud as he thrust his man sword into the ass of some hapless young peasant, whose village was burning around him. The bodybuilder hoped the next one would be more interesting. He also hoped it wouldn't be long until some dude with a talented mouth showed up to relieve this pain in his nuts.

He looked around the dimly lit theater. Everyone was in costume; they had to be to get into the place tonight. Most had a sameness to them, however. They either were dressed in rags as flood victims, which he thought was a bit tasteless, or they were cowboys in various stages of undress, which he thought lacked imagination in view of a recent major movie with a gay cowboy theme. Some of the cowpokes were pretty hot, however, and he hoped one of those would sit down beside him.

This was not to be, however. It wasn't long before a middle-aged man draped in a black cape sat in the seat next to the bodybuilder. The bodybuilder looked over at him in the dim light. He obviously was decked out as some sort of ghoul of the night. At least the costume was different from most of the rest. Not the greatest of catches, with that craggy face, but it probably had been handsome once, and there was something about the eyes. The way he was wrapped in the cape, though, suggested a beer belly and a tiny penis. Oh, well, he was only here for a soft mouth and a deep throat anyway.

And that's what the bodybuilder got in short order. The man's arm extended within the folds of the cape and a long, slender hand landed on the bodybuilder's basket. The bodybuilder didn't know if he liked those long, sharp nails at the end of the fingers, but he did like Pop's directness and the way those fingers were finding and measuring his cock through the

170

layers of soccer shorts material. He was hardening up pretty quickly under the attention of those long, slender fingers.

The man's fingers went to the waistband of the bodybuilder's shorts and he pulled the shorts down and off the bodybuilder's legs, followed by his thong briefs. The bodybuilder wasn't sure he liked being stripped down completely like this, but he didn't raise any objections, because Pops was already stroking his cock and kneading its knob in a highly experienced fashion. Within minutes, the man had lowered his mouth onto the bodybuilder's cock and was giving him efficient and tantalizing head. Prime physical specimen that he was, the bodybuilder came in three strong spasms that hit the back of the man's throat. The man licked the cock dry, and the bodybuilder assumed that that was that and his attention went to the new movie showing on the screen.

He laughed, because he himself was in the movie now showing, one themed on a Halloween costume party in a haunted house, where he was dressed in Roman military gear and was pursued around the house, caught, and fucked by a guy in a vampire costume.

The bodybuilder wanted to concentrate on the movie, and to admire his own Oscar-quality acting. But the older man didn't leave. He leaned into the bodybuilder, obviously wanting a kiss for a job well done. The bodybuilder took pity on Pops and gave him a short brush of the lips. Or at least that's what he intended to do. But the older man surprised him by forcing his lips open in a wet kiss. The bodybuilder was caught completely off guard, and an intoxicating wash of the man's saliva was swirling around in the bodybuilder's mouth before he knew what was happening. He immediately became woozy and lost much of the sensation in his body. He certainly found that his limbs wouldn't fully respond to his commands, and he fought hard, and unsuccessfully to put two thoughts together.

The man turned out of his seat and knelt in front the bodybuilder. His cape opened and swirled around the two of them, and the bodybuilder got a glimpse that made him think the older man was naked to the waist and seemed to be in pretty good shape for a man pushing fifty.

While the man was pulling the bodybuilder's soccer jersey off, leaving him naked down to his sneakers and knee-high socks, the bodybuilder was trying to form the thought of why this wasn't disturbing him.

Under the enveloping cloak, the man was sitting on the bodybuilder's thighs, facing him, and his lips and tongue were exploring the bodybuilder's torso. The bodybuilder reached down and felt something gigantic between the older man's legs. Must have brought along a super-sized rubber dildo, the bodybuilder was thinking. That didn't scare him though, he'd taken eleven inches and been double fucked in his movie career. He probably had the slackest hole in the business. In fact, in this movie now on the screen, if he remembered rightly, he'd taken a full ten inches.

Meanwhile, the man's tongue was tracing the popped out veins crisscrossing the bodybuilder's chest. The man must have found one he really liked; because the bodybuilder felt a pricking sensation and then began to feel like he was being sucked.

Hokay, he thought. It didn't hurt—much—and there was a real interesting segment playing on the screen just now— where he'd been stripped of his armor down to his cute little Roman skirt and was sucking the ten-inch cock of the actor in the vampire costume, about ready to be topped by him—and the bodybuilder was feeling lightheaded and disjointed anyway, so he just turned his attention to the screen. Pops was stroking his cock again now anyway, and that was a more interesting place for him to focus his attention.

At length, the vein the man was working on dried up and collapsed, and he moved to another, and then another.

The bodybuilder's cock was fully engorged again now, so the man slipped down on his knees and sucked him off again, taking in all of the semen for a second time. After having done this, he rose up on his knees and fluffed out the cape. The bodybuilder's eyes wandered down to take a look at him and he went into shock. The guy wasn't old at all. He was very well cut and was nearly as hard bodied as the bodybuilder himself.

But the bodybuilder had only gotten a quick look, and his mind seemed confused, so he wasn't all that sure what he saw. The man had quickly swirled the cape over both of their torsos again, and his tongue and lips were moving around on the bodybuilder's belly. There, at the edge of the bodybuilder's flat belly was another throbbing vein, running from somewhere near his navel down into the pubic hair of his groin. The man traced the line of the flow and sank his teeth into a likely spot and fed with little mewing and gurgling sounds.

The bodybuilder was feeling increasingly tired, he had developed a slight headache, and there was a quiet buzzing in his ears. He continued watching the movie screen, having a hard time focusing on it.

When the vein down into the groin collapsed, the man worked his thighs under the bodybuilder's butt, which was jutting out over the end of the seat. This tilted the bodybuilder's pelvis up. the man took the bodybuilder's legs and draped them over the back of the seats in the row in front of them. The bodybuilder just watched him doing this, wondering a bit about what was going on down there.

The man raised his chest to the chest of the bodybuilder, and now the bodybuilder felt that the man seemed younger than ever and he also had pecs of steel, with veins popping out. What the bodybuilder didn't comprehend, however, was that his own chest veins now were collapsed and his thinned blood was madly dashing about in his body, searching for open passages.

The man moved his lips to those of the bodybuilder, and they engaged in a passionate kiss that stifled the bodybuilder's reaction to the man's engorged monster cock sliding, with some difficulty, into the bodybuilder's slack-jawed asshole. With effort, the bodybuilder moved his hands to the man's cock and realized that this was no rubber super-sized dildo. This was a living cock and it was larger and thicker than the bodybuilder could ever imagined a human cock could be. What a porn movie this fucker could make. It seemed like what—twelve inches by two and a half? This was a challenge, and the bodybuilder was game for such challenges.

His eyes went to the screen, and just as he was being slowly entered here in the dim theater, there was a big close-up on the screen of the horse-hung, ten-inch vampire-costumed dude slowly entering the Roman-costumed him on the screen from the rear. On the screen, the Roman soldier him raised his pelvis to welcome the entry, and then the bodybuilder him did the same down here in the theater seats for the caped man's ass splitter. The bodybuilder was getting skewered massively in two dimensions—both on film and in real life.

The bodybuilder returned the man's kiss. This master fucker no longer was to be considered Pops, as the bodybuilder could tell by moving his hands languidly around the man's chest, down his abs, and to his hard, flat belly. This had to be another bodybuilder, and maybe even younger than he himself. This man could be a star.

The man continued to work his cock into the bodybuilder, who was taking him in pretty good stride.

The man disengaged from the kiss and let his tongue work its way down the bodybuilder's throbbing neck on the right side and to his arms. He located a vein standing out near the bicep and sank his teeth into it. His cock had now homed to the root at nearly twelve inches. The bodybuilder was groaning and moaning quietly, loving the cock this far up his ass, proud that he was managing more here than his Roman soldier persona was sheathing up on the screen. He did a little constricting of his ass muscles, a trick he'd learned on the movie set, thinking that this would get the man's rocks off in short order, but the man's cock responded to that—and to the blood being drawn out of the bodybuilder's arm—by stretching out to immobilize the bodybuilder's ass muscles and by lengthening to thirteen inches. This was farther in than anyone had pushed into the bodybuilder, and he was doing a little huffing and puffing.

The vein in the right arm collapsed, as did the bodybuilder's right arm, and the lips and teeth moved onto the chest and buried themselves around the rim of the aureole of the bodybuilder's right nipple; a little blood able to flow there and also from the left nipple, serving to push the caped man's cock to fourteen inches. And it went to fifteen inches before the vein into the bodybuilder's left arm—and the arm itself—gave out.

The man moved up and on to one of the carotid arteries in the bodybuilder's neck, which was still weakly throbbing, and the man sank his teeth into that and sucked. The bodybuilder's head lolled back and his eyes rolled up into his head. He was very nearly dead now to the world he had known.

On the screen, the top in the vampire costume pulled his long cock out of the Roman soldier bottom and shoot off on his prey's back, and both the top and bottom shouted for joy. In the theater seat, at sixteen inches in, the bodybuilder was releasing everything he was—young, assured, vital, resilient, perfectly formed, alive—to revitalize the man of the black cape and the monster cock for yet another week. And, in his confused and intoxicated state, the bodybuilder had no regrets. He was having the most fantastic fuck of his whole life.

At seventeen inches in, the caped man of the night achieved a thunderous ejaculation deep inside the withered shell of the bodybuilder, their vital body fluids mixing, and a new life, albeit a far different life than he had previously known, started seeping back into the bodybuilder.

The caped man rested and then, reloaded, pumped his prey with renewed vigor and, at length, ejaculated yet again into the very center of the bodybuilder, bathing the insides of the barely breathing convert once more with life-giving, magic potion in floods of semen that welled up inside the young man's canal and burbled out over his balls. With a swirl of his cape, he withdrew and left his latest lover and convert then; leaving the bodybuilder slumped in the theater seat in the flickering light of a doggy-style fuck a virile Roman soldier was performing on a fluttering wood nymph on screen. Leaving him to be found later by a theater custodian, pumping barely enough blood to sustain himself, but pumping a richly formulated blood that would see that he survived to change his choice of costume to a swirling black cape of the night and his screen persona to the stud with the monster cock and intoxicating love bite.

Heartbreak

I feel like a fool. Many would say I should have seen it coming. But I didn't, and it wasn't something that crept up on me and that I might have adjusted to—although I have no idea what comes after being a stud top. Do you? Still, when it came, it fell on me like a load of bricks, because I didn't see it coming. It's a heartbreak.

The hiatus may have had a lot to do with it. I'd held down the end-of-bar available stud fucker position at a popular gay beachside bar near a major university in Miami throughout my thirties. A former Marine, however, I jumped at the opportunity to go to Iraq with a private security firm to work as a protection unit scheduler. I worked at that for six years before returning to Miami. It wasn't only because the money was phenomenal but also because I wanted to do something for the effort and I was years past being able to go in on the ground as a grunt. That probably should have clued me in on what was happening. But it didn't.

And maybe it didn't because there was no change in position on the sexual chain throughout my Iraq duty. There's a whole lot of tension and need there to be served in a warfront situation. And although the need hasn't lessened in the Iraq action world, it's gotten increasingly difficult for the soldiers to

177

relieve each other in their own environment. My situation was ideal. I had a storefront office in the Green Zone and my living quarters were right behind the office, complete with vibrating queen-sized bed. The young soldiers would stop in when they could to shoot the bull and drop the hints about how keyed up they were and what they wanted to do to relieve that, and I'd usher them through the door into my bedroom. They would strip and open their legs to me, and I'd fuck all of the tension out of them. And they kept coming back. No one complained that I was getting too old to make them moan and groan and to fuck the stuffing out of them.

I knew my body was changing. I still had the bulging biceps and pecs, but I knew the midsection was thickening. Not to any significant degree, though. My stomach was still flat in spite of the military grub and beer—thanks to spending a good fifth of my life in the weight room—where my dicking was quite popular in the shower room. I may not be an Apollo—in fact, I never was—but I was a perfect Zeus now. And there is no end of young men, I don't think, who melt at being manhandled by a beefcake Zeus. And my sideburns may have gone gray in my years in Iraq—but, then, whose haven't? Iraq does that to a man—or at least to a man who manages to keep his hair.

And significantly, a man's dick—as long as nothing happens to keep him from getting it up—doesn't change in size and his balls are as heavy as ever. And most important, a man gains in knowing just what to do with that dick as he gets older. I won't mention that a man looses endurance and recharge powers over time. And I won't mention it because I still haven't fucked a man who I couldn't power drill to exhaustion.

So, it was without a single twinge of fear or self-doubt that, within days of returning to Miami from Iraq, I stood in front of my full-length mirror and studied my body in a Speedo—not one of the Speedos I'd worn when I worked this bar before, because I'd lost my narrow waist—but one that showed off my beefcake muscling up from the Baghdad Green Zone weight training to good effect. I'd been very careful to tan up all over on the flat roof of an American State Department official's residence, while enjoying myself in working his asshole while his wife sat and watched us—and then doing her. I am happy to say I'm an equal opportunity fucker.

Satisfied—falsely it seems—with what I saw, I tucked my car keys, a credit card, and a couple of condoms under my waistband and drove my Sebring convertible down to the beach.

As in days before, I went straight into the surf to slick myself down and swam over to the beach right off the bar. Looking into the bar from out beyond the surf line, I saw that it was as crowded as it had been six years earlier and that most were young, snotty chicken types from the nearby university. I enjoyed fucking twinks. I liked to hear them squeak when they realized they were getting a bigger and more vigorous dick then they dreamed of and when I was only beginning when they thought they were already at their limit. And I had learned a trick or two with the toughened soldiers in Iraq that probably would make these little tight asses faint. And even more, I liked fucking the snot out of the snotty ones. I liked leaving them sobbing and unable to close their legs. And they liked it too, because they had always come back for more—just as soon as they recovered from the first dicking. I was giving them more of an education than their university did, I think.

Then, like before, I slowly walked out of the surf and onto the beach, posing all of the time, and padded into the open-walled bar, drawing the attention of all, as I knew I would. I got the same little thrill I always had as I heard the raucous conversation die out under the thatched roof as I approached. I entered under the roof and walked down to the end of the bar to find my spot occupied by a late twentysomething dangerous-looking Hispanic hunk.

I stared at him, but he didn't move—at least not until I'd given up and taken another stool, where I perched, facing the table area and spreading my legs and letting the edge of the stool seat push up my package.

I could have moved into my old place within a couple of minutes, but by then I was in shock. While I watched, one of the university twinks, a dirty blond, thin guy, with an almost too-pretty face, had come up to the hunk and backed his butt into the hunk's package, and the two had done a dry-fuck lap dance to the rhythm of the rock music coming out of the speakers up in the rafters.

What changes had six years brought, I thought. We couldn't have gotten away with being that overt about sex the last time I was here. But then I looked around and saw that there were others in here well beyond the boundaries of suggestive too.

I went into a slow burn when the two guys moved over to a thick palm and fern fringe at one of the side the wings off the bar, which, however, wasn't so thick that I couldn't, in short order, discern the soles of pale-white feet set wide apart and waving in the air and the hint of a moving brown bare ass between them, the toes of the feet scrunching up in rhythm with the movement of the butt cheeks. This was a location I'd used hundreds of times myself to draw attention and advertise my wares. How dare he, I thought. He'd not only ruined my entrance but stolen my turf and had upped my moves at the same time. All eyes would now be on the greenery until they saw the final curling of the toes on the feet and the jerk on the brown buns and heard the cries of release.

But that wasn't really true. The twinks huddled around several of the tables were actually watching me. But they were whispering among themselves and smirking and laughing and pointing while trying not to make too obvious that they were pointing at me.

At me!

My world collapsed in that instant. And I could feel my heart breaking into a hundred pieces.

I looked around the bar area. Realization set in that everyone there was at least twenty years younger than I was. Even the bartenders. All except one, though. There was a guy, probably in his late thirties, trim and ivy league-looking even in his baggy orange swimming trunks, sitting at a table by himself at the outer edge of the bar area. One of the twinks had approached him as he caught my eye. He waved the student away, though. He had his eyes trained on me.

If my tan wasn't so good, everyone there could have seen that I had turned red as a beet. I'd always been a little older than the clientele. That had been part of my package. The twinks liked getting laid by someone obviously a little more experienced than they were. Most of these kids wanted a dominating daddy fucker. Many the time it had been my buns undulating between those spread twink legs until toes curled and some young university snot felt the filling out of the bulb of my condom deep inside his ass.

But a twenty year difference between me and all but one other? And I had about ten years on him even. Why hadn't I seen it coming?

My hope now was that the rustling of the palms and the moans increasing in volume from that direction would galvanize all of the attention under the thatched roof there and I could pick the pieces of my heart off the floor and quietly melt away.

But the thirtysomething guy was rising from the table and walking in my direction. When he reached me, he smiled and leaned over and whispered to me, "You got a car and a location and want to ride me?"

Grateful for any sense of an honorable exit, I croaked, "Out on the curb; the silver Sebring convertible."

I drove to a secluded spot just short of rocks and surf at the back of a burned out mansion down the coast toward the keys, while the hole—that's how I thought of all the guys committed to getting fucked, because by this point I was only focused on getting my dick sheathed someplace warm and tight and shuddering and backed up by moaning and begs for mercy—rolled the waistband of my Speedo down under my nuts and expertly sucked me off, time after time bringing me to the brink and then backing me off and, when the ejaculation finally came, swallowing me and holding me inside him until I'd softened.

I'd checked the location out beforehand and it was still available and private. So many of my favorite places had changed and lost their usefulness in the six years I'd been gone.

Once in place, I turned to the hole and took his mouth with mine and swabbed his inner cheeks, tasting the essence of what I'd deposited there while we were moving down the ocean highway. I didn't usually do much kissy face; my technique was based on taking the hole's breath away and making him immediately lose control and either go frenetically wild in surrender or beg for his life in the face of fast-developing power drilling. But I'll have to admit that I needed some time to recharge from the hole's surprisingly expert blow job.

I made the hole strip his trunks off. Then I spread an extra-large terrycloth beach towel on the rear decking of the convertible and pushed the hole down on his back on the towel, with his legs hanging down into the backseat compartment.

Then I overpowered him with my body, still stinging from the revelation at the twink bar, angry and, for the first time, thinking I had something to prove to the world. Panicked, because, as I've already asked, where does an aged-out fuck stud go from there that isn't humiliating?

I knew I could dick him into melting submission, but I wanted to prove there was more to me than that—especially since he had sucked me better than I knew I could do. And he was a little smirky at how well he'd held me in check during the blow job and had made me want it.

Having him on his back on the trunk of the Sebring, I covered his body with mine, one arm laced around his back and holding his chest tight to mine. I outweighed him by quite a bit and outmuscled him by even more. Pushing my thighs between his, I reached down with the other hand and grabbed his balls and squeezed.

His eyes bugged out and he yelped. This had been completely unexpected, as I meant for it to be.

"You came out here to be fucked, good buddy. But you are going to be fucked with a big F. You understand that? You want to back out?"

His eyes were watering, and I knew he was having difficulty forming the words because all of his attention was centered on his aching balls.

"Uhhh."

"No need to answer, because you aren't getting out of this. You are going to feel fucked before I even dick you—and then you are going to feel fucked with a capital F."

Holding him close just like that and staring down into his face to savor every tortured and impassioned expression there as he writhed under me and shuddered and trembled and shot off twice before I even got my dick in him. I'd brought a month's supply of lube and used it liberally with my free hand to slowly open and spread his ass. His hole was slack, which fit my plan perfectly. I worked it with my fingers until I could get my fist in, him screaming and groaning and moaning as I stretched his ass channel as he'd never been stretched before. And then the surprise on his face when he realized that my fist was in him and he'd taken it.

I fist-fucked him—something the real macho types in Iraq had loved and that I had sorta looked forward to surprising some snotty college twink with—while he went from yowling and writhing and panting and struggling against me to softly moaning and whimpering and just laying there, his eyes glazing over, all of the fight out of him. Then I withdrew my fist but left my fingers in and spread them and inserted my hard dick between them and slowly withdrew them as my dick plowed deeper inside him.

The cocking, when it came, came in a flood of relief to him, even as big and thick as I was, and he was pushed over the edge of lust and passion—paradise so much closer now after having gone through hell. He wrapped his legs around my hips and started going with the plowing. We were moving as one, ultimate fucking unit. We came simultaneously and then I turned him on his belly and we fucked on and on and came almost simultaneously once again.

My spirits soared. I hadn't lost it. He was putty around my pistoning dick.

He begged me for more, and I turned him on his side and side-split him back into paradise.

Spent, we both lay there, arms entwined, staring up into the sun, our chests heaving from the effort.

And then he calmly told me the fuck would cost me $100 and he could take credit cards.

He was just another prostitute scoring off a john. My heart broke into a million and one pieces.

Hello Good-Bye

Herb went to Baltimore's Mount Vernon Stable and Saloon on North Charles Street several blocks up from the inner harbor fairly often for lunch. He didn't go there for the food, although it was good. He went there, first, because he didn't want to see any of his coworkers at Dunstan and Dunstan outside of the nearby office at Franklin and West Liberty and the Mount Vernon S and S was just edgy enough that none of the stuffed shirts in Dunstan and Dunstan were likely to come in here. And second, he came here for lunch exactly for its edginess. This was a gay- and lesbian-friendly establishment, but it was also popular enough with straights that you wouldn't be categorized if you were seen eating lunch here.

And Herb Dunstan didn't want to be categorized—at least in that way. And he'd been very careful not to reveal that he had preferences in that direction. He lived the perfect advertising firm vice president life (with every hope of being president when his father kicked off): a trophy wife; two glowing, bright children—the requisite older boy and younger girl; a big house in the planned community of Colombia, located half way between Baltimore and the nation's capital; a Lexus SUV for her and Mercedes sedan for him; a floppy dog of indeterminate breeding;

and one and a half cats. (No one was really sure that their family could lay full claim to the roving tom, Luther.)

But Luther wasn't the only roving tom in the Dunstan family. Herb was a cruiser, and he had done most of his cruising while out of town on business trips. But there hadn't been a business trip in some months now, and he found himself looking over the clientele of the downstairs bar at the Mount Vernon with more speculation and anticipation than usual.

The ham and rye sandwich was history and the ash tray in front of him at the bar was four butts deep when his attention was arrested by the inviting visage of a young man entering the bar and ordering up a beer.

He was Hispanic and carried himself with confidence. A little on the thin side, at least through the hips, but with a pretty deep chest and strong thighs. He was in well-pressed jeans and a plaid flannel shirt. He looked like he worked with his hands, though, so Herb decided he had slicked himself up to come into the Mount Vernon. All alone and taking a good look around him at the pickings. His eyes met Herb's and he smiled. Herb smiled back and the young man was beside him at the bar.

Herb's glass was empty when the bartender turned and set the Hispanic's beer down in front of him—and now beside Herb.

"I'll take another Coke, and this will cover that and my friend here's beer," Herb said, laying a twenty down on the top of the bar.

"Thanks, man," the Hispanic said to him with a big smile. "But you're drinking Coke, man? That ain't no man's drink."

"I'm plenty man enough," Herb said, going straight for the opening. "But I haven't had a hard drink in two years."

"Health?" the Hispanic responded, trying to show interest and concerned together in light of the free beer.

"In a way," Herb answered. "I'm an alcoholic. My wife says I'm so obsessive about everything that I'm not really addicted to alcohol; I'm addicted to addiction."

"Your wife?" the Hispanic said, his eyes already starting to shop the room again.

186

"Yes, I'm married," Herb responded in a steady voice. "But I won't let that bother me if you won't let it bother you." Once again getting right down to business. If the young man wasn't interested, Herb would move on. He might even go back to work, although he was hoping that he wouldn't be returning to the office this afternoon.

"Hey, OK with me," the young man answered, still feeling beholden for the free beer. "My name's Manuel, but you can call me Manny."

Manuel sat there, expecting a name in return from Herb. It wasn't forthcoming.

"Hello, Manny. You've just about polished off that beer. Ready for another one?"

Manuel was ready for another one. He was a little nervous. The Mount Vernon was a little upscale for him.

Herb quickly ordered another beer and slapped another twenty down on the bar. He lit up another cigarette off of the previous one as the bartender took the empty beer stein away and scooped up the twenty. The twenties weren't really for the bartender, though. They were for Manuel to see and absorb, and he was quick enough to get the point.

Manuel looked at the quickly filling ash tray. "Did you smoke all of those?" he asked nervously, not knowing where to take the conversation from here. Just saying the first thing that came into his mind.

"Yeah. I guess you can say that's the habit I moved to from the liquor. I need to kick that as well. But I can quit anytime I want to."

Manuel gave Herb a searching look. If he could go cold turkey on liquor, maybe he could do that with cigarettes to. Manuel could sense the steeliness in Herb.

Herb moved right on with his plan for the day. He didn't have all day to set this up. "Work nearby, do you, Manny?"

"Not too far," Manuel responded. "Down in the harbor. I work the docks, helping to unload whatever comes into the harbor this far."

"Done that for long, have you? You look like you've muscled up a good bit." Always the "get to it" edge in Herb's approach to projects.

"Yeah. All over the world. I was working in Turkey recently. I got this puzzle ring there. Do you like it?"

"Yes, I like everything I see, Manny."

Somewhat nonplused at Herb's innuendos, Manuel took the ring off his finger, and jangled its segments apart. It came apart in six strands that were still connected at the base.

"Watch this. I can put it back together real quick." Manuel concentrated hard on manipulating the strands of the ring back in place, while Herb lit up another cigarette and then concentrated on looking at Manuel's butt and at the young man rippling his muscles as his hands danced on the silver metal of the ring.

When he had the ring back together, Manuel looked up with a grin of triumph.

"There, see, it's easy."

"Yes, I see that," Herb responded. "No, let me slide it back on." And Herb did slide it back on but then, while holding Manuel's palm in one of his own hands, he slid the ring up and down, suggestively, on Manuel's finger. Manuel screwed up his face in embarrassment. But he didn't take his hand away. Herb pushed the ring to the root of the finger and then slid two of his own finger tips back to the tip of Manuel's strong, callused finger.

He then slowly reached into his pocket and took his wallet out again, extracted a fifty, and laid it on the top of the bar, close to Manuel.

"Umm, I'm not sure I need another beer, at least not yet," Manuel stammered.

"The fifty's not for the bartender, Manny. Are you a top or a bottom?"

Manuel looked a little shocked, but then he looked hard at that fifty. "Umm, either . . . sometimes . . . I guess." He was fishing for the answer Herb might want.

"Well, I'm a top, Manny. The fifty's for you if you'll take what I give without question and you do it right now, this afternoon."

Herb had already booked a room at the Galaxy Hotel just up the street, which rented rooms by the hour. He had rented a room there on three previous occasions but hadn't had a lunch turn out like this before and had yet to need the hotel room. And, of course, he didn't get back to the office that afternoon.

They were barely inside the door to the small hotel room, when Herb kicked it shut and had his hands all over Manuel, busily stripping Manuel down to the skin. Then he had Manuel down on the floor in all fours just there between the bed and the door and he had his tongue in the young man's butt cleavage and a hand milking a nice brown dong to the tune of Manuel's grunts and moans. Manuel heard the scrunch of a zipper being lowered and then his moans turned into cries of surprise and initial pain as Herb covered Manuel's back with his chest—the brown dock worker fully naked; the advertising executive still nearly fully clothed—and took him hard and deep right there on the floor with a thick, throbbing rod. Herb was filling Manuel almost beyond capacity before he was fully prepared. He cried out, initially in pain, and then in passion, as Herb stroked him hard and fast, finding every sensitive inch of the younger man's passage walls, fucking him with obsession and a fury of pent-up need.

At first Manuel endured because of the fifty already lying on top of the night stand, waiting for him to earn it. But after a while, he began to love Herb's cock for itself and for the passion it brought out of him and the release it brought him as he had never felt with a woman. The fifty was still an incentive to take the pounding, but it increasingly wasn't what was holding him here—and that would bring him back if he pleased Herb.

After Herb had pumped Manuel's ass to frenzied completion and stroked the young man to his own finish, Herb took his own clothes off and the two of them removed themselves to the bed for a slower, more languid side-splitting fuck, with the finish coming with Manuel on his back, holding onto the headboard slots for dear life, as Herb, his thighs under the young's man's butt cheeks, stroked relentless in and out of Manuel's stretched ass chute.

When Herb had had his fill, he lay there on the bed, smoking, while he watched Manuel put his clothes back on, make sure he had the fifty in his pocket, and respond affirmatively to Herb's offer—more a near demand—of a follow-up meeting the next week.

For the next several months, this was to be the routine. They would meet in the hotel room, and Herb would ravish Manuel on the floor, up against the wall, on the straight chair, bent over the bed, or in the shower, and then they would go to the bed for a slower, more spun-out fuck showing that Herb was a champion at endurance and vigor. At first it was once a week, but it soon became twice a week, and then three times. And Manuel slowly noticed that Herb no longer was smoking as much and then that he had given it up altogether.

Herb also showed a continuing interest in Manuel's Turkish puzzle ring. Manuel would take it off his finger and jangle it loose and Herb would almost compulsively try to put it back together again while Manuel was dressing to leave. Manuel never showed Herb the solution to the problem, though, even though Herb asked him to. In all else, Herb dominated Manuel; but Manuel held out on the issue of the ring. He would show Herb what he was doing but would quickly move through the strategic step that brought all six of the strands back into an alignment that made the ring a ring. And then he wouldn't give Herb sufficient direction to figure it out. The puzzle of the ring became almost an obsession with Herb. And after a few months it seemed as if Herb was spending more time struggling with the ring than he was fucking Manuel.

It was Herb's wife, however, who brought the liaison to a conclusion. Herb was spending more and more time away from home, and more and more of their money was going unaccounted for. Herb's wife assumed it must be another woman. Herb was very attractive and a great lover—and he was a good catch. He'd inherit the presidency of Dunstan and Dunstan some day, and there obviously was some bimbo at the office who had decided to cash in on him. Herb's wife could come to this conclusion because that's exactly how she had gotten Herb away from his first wife.

Herb had always wanted a sailboat and had a fantasy of sailing the length and breadth of the nearby Chesapeake Bay. Herb's wife splurged and bought him a sailboat for his next birthday. They berthed it in Easton, Maryland, and, increasingly,

Herb could be found away from the office and on the bay in his sailboat. Sailing became his new obsession.

Manuel was no dummy. He sensed weeks before Herb said a final good-bye to him that the "fifties" money tree was about to tumble. Herb cut their meetings to twice weekly and than once and then only every other week. And increasingly Herb talked about sailing on the Chesapeake Bay as he was trawling Manuel's ass with his cock.

On their last day together, Herb was running at the mouth, his eyes sparkling, about the new sail he'd gotten for his boat and how this meant he could sail farther down the Chesapeake.

When Manuel had dressed and looked regretfully at what undoubtedly was the last easy fifty he was to receive from Herb, he just blew Herb a kiss and left the room, leaving Herb still naked and stretched out on the bed.

Herb looked over and saw that Manuel had forgotten his Turkish puzzle ring. It was lying on the nightstand all jangled out. Herb picked it up and started working it, trying to get it to fit together, obsessively lost in a puzzle he could not solve, working up to a headache.

As Manuel walked down five flights of stairs to the seedy lobby of the Galaxy Hotel and out toward the docks of Baltimore's harbor, he smiled to himself. He hadn't forgotten the ring. And he must certainly hadn't forgotten not to tell Herb how to put it together.

Helpful Hiker

I will always remember the barn. How could I ever forget it? It was a big, corrugated iron one, dull with age and with no windows on the lower level and just one at each end high up in the gable. Tall narrow windows that let light into the loft, while below the barn was dark and silent, cluttered and filled with dust. But I didn't know that when I first saw it.

I came upon it slowly as I emerged onto the top of the mountain after a climb up through untouched forest from the bay below. And I came at it from the rear, seeing the high window lit with the full afternoon sun, and I saw him there caught in the sun, naked and golden, like some lost angel. Perched up there on the windowsill looking down at me. And he is the reason I remember the barn so well.

By the time I looked up, I wasn't surprised to see him there. I had tracked him here, by the ruts made in the mud by the wheels of the motorbike he'd left the clearing on—the marks that the wheels, spinning in his anxiety to escape the clearing, had made in the track up the side of the mountain in earth softened by the rain the previous evening. The motorbike itself was down on its side in front of the yawning door into the dark interior of the barn.

193

I wasn't even all that surprised to see him leaning precariously against the window frame, more outside the barn than in, looking so confused and sober—and forlorn. But, God was he beautiful. A young god, perfectly formed, curly golden locks framing his head, pale blue eyes brimming with moist tears. All he lacked was wings. But even without the wings, he appeared ready to take flight at any moment, whenever courage overtook confusion and indecision. Below the window the mountainside tumbled down toward the bay in a cascade of jagged-edge stone outcroppings.

A precarious moment when he saw me looking at him. Surprise swimming into embarrassment and a moment of indecision as he first leaned out over the abyss and then withdrew into the darkness beyond the window. If he thought to wait until I had hiked on by along the mountain ridge, he had another thought coming.

* * * *

I had first spied him down in the clearing in a fold in the mountains where the hiking trail dipped down into the quiet forest before rising again to the ridgeline.

And I first heard him—or, rather, heard the other one, the young god had been silent throughout—before I saw him. He was naked then too, that other one.

I heard the unmistakable sound of lovemaking as I neared the clearing. So, I slowed down and stealthily approached, interested, not wanting to disturb before I had taken in the scene. The woods were dense here all around the clearing except for the track leading into the cleared area, so I could get very close without being detected.

The first thing I saw was an expensive sports car, a sleek Jaguar sedan, I think, although I hardly am an expert in flashy, fast sports cars. And propped up on a stand beside the car was a motorbike that perhaps was flashier than the car, although not in a refined way. It was painted some psychedelic metallic color and had skull and bones-type stickers plastered all over its fenders and gas tank. The seat was some sort of fuzzy black carpeting material.

The presumed owners of the vehicles were on a blanket a bit away from their rides and near the sun-dappled center of the clearing. It wasn't all that hard to match vehicle with owner. The elegant blond god surely belonged to the Jaguar. His legs were hooked on the hips of the other kneeling figure, his feet suspended in air and dangling, with his torso bent back toward the ground, his shoulder blades and a cheek touching the blanket. His face was turned toward me and his eyes had a vacant look. His cheek was tear stained.

Knelt under the suspended pelvis of the blond angel was the dark one. The blond's legs spread and hooked on his hips and his dimpled butt cheeks rested on the thighs of the kneeling dark one, whose naked body was a veritable showcase of punk body piercings and tattoos. A total contrast in the angel's clean-cut blondness and the other one's swarthy darkness. Undoubtedly the owner of the in-your-face motorbike.

The dark one's body rings jangled and his tattoos undulated as his long, thin cock, revealed also to have a ring through the glans when he withdrew completely before plunging back in, fucked inside the blond one's channel in long, sweeping strokes.

The dark one clearly was excited and was having a good time; the blond angel seemed barely there at all mentally and emotionally. A pall of pot smoke hung over the clearing, and my guess was that the blond god was well ahead of the dark punk in drags of that. There were a couple of empty bottles of wine lying around at the edge of the blanket to. Yellowtail Shiraz. I recognized the familiar label. I liked that too; smooth but cheap.

I stood in the shadows of the bush and unzipped myself and shared in the rhythm of the dark one's thrusts inside the blond as well as his stick play with the blond one's cock.

The blond gave a little shudder and twitch, and his cock head bubbled up in whitish cum. The dark one took longer at his pleasure, increasing the pace and intensity of his thrusts as he climaxed in three long strokes that moved the blond's torso up the blanket several inches.

When done, but not withdrawing his cock, the dark one gathered the blond up against his chest and began murmuring in his ear. I couldn't hear what they said, but obviously the dark one was trying to cajole his lover into agreement on some important issue. The blond had his face buried in the dark one's shoulder and seemed to be crying softly. At first he whispered back and shook his head several times, but at length he stopped talking back and nodded a few times.

Having apparently won his point, the dark one turned the blond onto his hands and knees, rose up behind him, crouched over the angel's hips, encircled his thin waist with a dusky, heavily muscled forearm, and dog-fucked his complaisant, nearly comatose lover again in long, hard strokes.

Jeans and T-shirts for both of them were scattered beside the blanket. I saw the dark one whisper something in the blond's ear after he'd finished fucking him a second time—or at least the second time I had viewed the action. The blond answered him and the dark one leaned over and went through the pockets of one of the pair of jeans. He came up with the keys to the Jaguar. Then he grabbed up one of the bottles of Yellowtail, which apparently hadn't been empty, and left the blond, who curled up into something close to the fetal position on the blanket. The dark one went over to the motorbike. He took a long swig of the wine bottle and threw it to the side on the ground. Then he rummaged around in a pack hanging on the back of the motorbike and came up with a long length of flexible hosing.

I watched, fascinated, as the dark one went over to the Jaguar and placed and end of the hosing over the exhaust pipe and then ran the hose up to the back window on the other side of the car from where I was hidden. He opened the car door and rolled the window down a bit and pushed the other end of the hose into the opening. Then he rolled the window back up as far as it would go. He closed the door and opened the driver's seat door and got behind the wheel long enough to turn the engine on. That completed, he got out of the car and shut that door.

He walked back around to the blanket and leaned down and whispered something in the blond's ear. The blond must have heard him, but he said nothing. The dark one tried to lift the blond, but then the blond became animated enough to indicate that he wasn't going to get up just then. I saw him rummage around at the edge of the blanket and come up with a packet of cigarettes. He lit one with a match from a matchbook that had been lodged underneath the cellophane wrapping of the packet. He took a long pull on the cigarette and spoke softly to the dark one, but not so softly that I couldn't hear him.

"Just give me a few minutes. I'll be there."

"We agreed. You'll do it, won't you?" the dark one asked. "Together. We wanted to be together." His voice came out in cajoling velvet, but I could sense the steel behind them too. I could sense that he had some sort of control over the blond angel.

"Yes, yes. Just need to smoke some courage."

With that, the dark one stood over the blond for a few seconds, looking down at him, giving him a stern, searching look. Then he went back to the Jag, opened the back door facing me, climbed in, and closed the door.

I could see him in there, his head reclined back on the seat. And I could hear the car's motor running, and I fancied I could smell the exhaust gas being hosed from the tail pipe directly into the passenger compartment.

I heard something of a sob from the blond one. I looked over at him. He had finished his cigarette. After a moment of stony silence, he uncoiled from the bunched-up position he'd taken on the blanket, stood, and slowly walked over to the Jag. Even in distress, he moved beautifully. He opened the back door and joined the dark one on the back seat.

They were fucking again. The blond was straddling the dark one now, facing him, and, I'm sure, although I couldn't see the point of contact in the closed car, rising and falling on the dark one's cock. The dark one just remained laying back in the seat, his eyes closed, his eyebrow and lip rings glittering in the streaks of sunlight stabbing at the Jaguar through the gaps in the rustling leaves overhead.

It took me several minutes to work my way around the perimeter of the clearing to get behind the car on the other side, but I moved as quickly as I dared. When I got there, I crouched down and slithered as best I could over to the rear end of the car and quietly pulled the end of the hose off the tailpipe.

Then I sat back and watched.

It didn't take all that long after that for the blond to have a change of mind or to decide this wasn't working for him, or maybe that it wasn't working fast enough. The back door of the Jag opened and he stumbled out. Leaving the door ajar, he hobbled over to the blanket, pulled a pair of the jeans on while rummaging around in the pockets of the other pair. I heard the jangle of keys, and the blond, walking a little more steadily now, went over to the motorbike, mounted the bike, revved up the motor, and clumsily rode out of the clearing. The bike turned, its wheels spinning out in his anxiety to leave the clearing, on the uphill track toward the summit of the mountain.

I waited for a few minutes. The dark one wasn't moving, but I thought I was able to detect some sign of breath, a small twitch or something.

I stripped off my clothes, opened the back door of the Jag, and climbed in.

* * * *

After I had seen the angel withdraw from the barn window, I entered into the dark maw of the corrugated iron building and stood just inside the door for a minute or more, waiting for my eyes to adjust to the darkness. It was a good ten degrees hotter in here than outside, no doubt a result of the sun beating on the barn's metal skin. I could smell the hay, and as my eyes reset to the dim light, the atmosphere clouded with swirling dust, I could see that the barn was being used to store bales and bales of it.

A great candidate for an internal combustion fire, I thought. A natural place for the angel to have escaped to— ascend in fiery launch rather than drifting off in a snuff of noxious fumes. That was precisely the impression I'd gotten back in the clearing of his condition—ready to blow at any moment from internal combustion.

I saw the ladder to the loft off to the right, and I climbed it, being sure that I made enough noise that he knew I was coming and that I wasn't trying to sneak up on him. He was like a skittish pony, ready to bolt and do something stupid at the least excuse. I wanted him; I'd wanted him from the first minute

I saw his slender hips suspended over the blanket in the clearing and being fucked by the dark one. And I wanted to help him get to where he wanted to go. I didn't want to spook him at this delicate stage.

He had tugged the tight jeans back on and was leaning his butt against an old wooden table, crackling with the hint of several layers of different-colored paint, that was pushed against the metal wall beside the open window he had just been standing in.

He wasn't looking at me. He was hunched forward, head hanging low over a beautifully formed torso, golden curls cascading down. He held an elbow in the palm of one hand and he was picking at his teeth with the fingers of the other hand. He didn't look at me, but I knew he knew I was there. His body twitched as he hunched there in the silence and I heard a little hiccup or sob, I know not which. My eyes went to his bare feet; beautiful, slender feet, long, perfectly spaced toes.

I wanted him. I wanted to fuck him. And I wanted him to respond as he hadn't responded to the dark one. I wanted to suck on those toes as I drilled him, down to the quick. I wanted to help him get to where he wanted to go.

"Are you OK?"

No response, except, yes, maybe another little dry sob.

"I said, are you OK?" I increased the volume a bit, but I tried to keep my voice calm and silky. These were the worst moments, the most dangerous, delicate moments of the dance. "I saw you from below . . . in the window. And I was afraid—"

"Yes, I'm OK, thanks. I just need to be alone, thanks." The voice, the first time I'd heard anything from him, although I felt I'd known him forever, was a rich, soft baritone. A voice to attract attention, just as his beautiful body did.

"Can I help . . . with anything?"

"No, no, thanks. I'm fine."

I moved slowly and quietly over to the table and pulled the pack off my back and gently lowered it to the floor. I leaned my butt against the table next to him and placed a hand tentatively on his forearm. He twitched once, and there was another slight sob, but I could feel him calm down, tension starting to drain out of him from the mere contact of skin on skin. His head was still hanging down, his eyes cast toward his crotch. My eyes were drifting there too, and I could feel the increasing tightness in my own crotch.

"Fine? I wasn't sure from seeing you in the window that . . . sure you don't want to talk with someone about it . . . whatever it is?"

I moved my arm around his shoulder and he just sort of collapsed into me, his face buried in my chest.

"Vince. Vince and I . . . Vince thought . . . convinced me. . . . Life is such shit."

"There, there," I cooed, and I started an almost imperceptible rocking of our bodies. The young man seemed to like this. I could feel the tension flowing out of him. "A beautiful young man like you? How could life . . . ?"

"Up to our necks in debt, and nothing going right—"

"Vince doesn't take care of you?" My mind was racing. Vince obviously was the key; Vince obviously was the dark one. "You're with Vince? Vince is your lover?"

"Yeah, I'm with Vince. But things aren't going . . . Vince said we had no other choice."

"Vince doesn't take care of you? Who pays?"

"Vince is an artist, a musician," the blond god spoke through quiet snufflings, ". . . there's never enough . . . and what I get from my parents . . . Well, we've come to an end and Vince said it was time."

I had my lips against the golden curls and my free hand was moving on his torso, progressing from tentative touches to light stroking, and now to gentle massaging. He was responding to me. I was hearing more sighs now than sobs.

"Your parents. They don't approve of Vince?" I had my palm on his belly now, down low, my pinky under the low-rise waistband of his jeans.

"No, no, they don't," he whispered. He was slightly shuddering now, responding to my attentions.

I took just a minute away from where my arms and hands were to pull my shirt over my head but then I returned them to where they'd been immediately, not wanting him to realize I'd ever lost the purchase I had attained there.

"And are they wrong about Vince? Really?" I wanted him to think about that, but I didn't want him to say anything, so I turned his face up to mine and took his sweet lips with mine. As I took his breath away with a deep kiss, I moved the palm of my hand down under his waistband, pushing his jeans zipper open as my hand descended. I possessed his cock. He melted to me. Having some idea of the hold that Vince held over him, I rode on that crest of taking charge and showing authority, and the young man put up no resistance to me.

"And is Vince a good lover?" I asked as I released his lips from mine but also released his cock from the restriction of his jeans. I pressed a thumb into his piss slit and slowly worked his tool up and down with my fist, giving it pressure in a slow rhythm. I lowered my head and took one of his nipples between my teeth. He was moaning quietly.

"Does Vince make love to you like this?"

"No," his answered in a small, whispery voice.

I laid him gently back on the table and worked my lips and tongue across his belly and up and encasing his cock. He murmured quietly above me and sighed and moaned as I made love to his cock.

I raised my head and looked up at his golden curls-framed face. "And does Vince make love to you like this?"

"No," he moaned as I returned to sucking on his glans and darting my tongue in out of his piss slit. The fingers of one of my hands was opening up his anal canal and those of the other were playing a concerto on his nipples and belly. He was moving his beautiful body now in languid undulation in concert with the lovemaking I was giving him.

I lifted my head again and said, in a husky voice. "I want to make deep love to you. I want to move inside you."

"Yes, yes," he moaned.

I pulled away from him then stripped off my trousers. I retrieved a condom packet from the pocket of the trousers and held it up for him to see. "If you want it, you have to make a decision, do something decisive. You have to cap me with this." This was a start. I wanted to fuck him, yes, but I wanted to help him to get to where he wanted to go. He had to take some responsibility, show some life.

I tore the packet open as he sat up and then he took the condom out and rolled it onto my cock while I took his lips in mine and we kissed deeply.

Then, with a sigh, he slowly laid back onto the table, scooted his butt to the edge of the table, and lifted and parted his legs and dug his heels into the edge of the table in a wide stance. I went down on my knees between his legs and started tonguing his hole while I stroked my cock to fuller power.

When I stood and entered him, he emitted a little cry and arched his back and grabbed for the side edges of the table with his hands. I took hold of his slim hips and pulled him up to me as my cock slid farther inside of him. He was moving and writhing under me as I bottomed and then started long, powerful strokes inside him. I was panting and breathing heavily at the thrill of fucking such a beautiful, nubile blond body, he was gasping and groaning and giving little yipping sounds at the taking. This was nothing like I'd seen on the blanket in the clearing. He was giving me his all, taking the fuck in the fullness of what I had to offer and to give him.

We were into a rhythm, with his pelvis as fully in motion and revolution as mine was. He came up and threw his arms around me. He buried his face in my chest and teethed on my nipples. And I fucked on and on, in deep, long thrusts of lust.

I looked down into his eyes, which were swimming in passion and want. I wrapped a hand around one of his ankles and brought one of his feet to my lips and I kissed and started sucking on his toes as I stroked away inside him. He was writhing away under me, stroking his own cock, and as I sucked on his big toe his body lurched and he cried out and shot his seed up onto my heaving belly.

"This is life." I cried out in mid thrust. "Do you embrace life?"

"Ohhh," he responded, but then, "But Vince said . . ."

"Fuck Vince," I cried out and thrust deep inside him. He gave a little yelp and dug his nails into my shoulders. "Fuck what Vince said. Think for yourself. I've fucked Vince, and he wasn't half as alive as you are."

The blond arched his back down to the table top and looked at me with a shocked expression in his face. "You know Vince? You couldn't. You couldn't have fuc—"

"Want proof?" I sneered. I'd stopped stroking inside him, but I was still buried deep and had a grip on his hips, holding him to me where we both centered. I released one of his hips and reached down into my backpack and pulled out a golden-yellow T-shirt.

"Yours or Vince's?" I asked as I fisted the shirt over his face.

"Mine. How did you? Where did you . . .?"

"You left it in the clearing. Where I left Vince after I fucked him."

"Vince wanted—"

"Vince is gone," I yelled down into his face. "What is it you want. Vince is gone."

"Vince? Gone?"

I dropped the shirt and got both of my arms around him and lifted him off the table in fury and turned him and forced his chest down on the table top roughly with a fist to the small of his back. He yelped. I thrust my dick brutally inside his canal and he cried out again in pain, Digging a fist in his blond curls, I cruelly pulled his head back toward me as I fucked hard and furiously inside his channel.

"Oww, that hurts. Oh, Gawd, you're splitting me," he cried out.

"Life or death? Which one is it? Which do you want? Vince or life?" I was bending my lips close to his ear and hissing at him.

"I don't . . . Ohhh, ahhhh. Vince says we couldn't . . . Ohhhh. You're killing me."

Fucking away furiously still, I bit his earlobe, drawing blood, and hissed again. "What is it you want? Fuck Vince. Which do you want?"

He was crying out at the hard taking now, not responding with more than groans and yelps.

"I could fuck you to death. I will fuck you to death. Is that what you want? If not, fight for your life, damn it!"

More crying out, writhing under my assault on his body. I wrapped my arms around his waist and lifted him off the table and frog-marched him over the window. I suspended him outside the window over the abyss, my arms wrapped around him, my cock continuing its vicious upward stroking in his ass.

He began to struggle hard against me now. I was too strong for him, but he was struggling against me, and he grabbed the frame on either side with his hands and was holding on for dear life, grunting and gasping in an affirmation now that he wanted to live. Holding on for dear life and struggling to live.

But I was much more powerful than he was and this was the apex moment. I covered his face with one of my hands, the heel of the hand jammed against his mouth and my fingers pinching his nose shut.

I shot my load deep inside him while he was still struggling, but it wasn't long after that that he went limp from lack of oxygen and blacked out.

* * * *

The blond, his spent and battered beautiful body in a heap on the floor by the low-linteled window in the barn's loft, started to stir, and I buried myself deeper in the shadows of stacks of hay bales. He thought he was alone. I couldn't leave him like this, though. I couldn't be sure where this went from here. I needed to know that I'd gotten through to him, and that where he wanted to go wasn't where he had been thinking he wanted to go. He'd been lying to himself. He would never had left the clearing if he wasn't being steamrolled into something he didn't really want by Vince.

I watched him stretch and gingerly uncoil and regretted immediately that I couldn't—or, at least, shouldn't—go back and fuck him all over again.

I heard the burring of the telephone a long time before he seemed to. I panicked at the thought that it could be mine and could give my presence away, but the burring clearly was coming from near the table.

The blond stood slowly, stiffly and then stretched and reached for his jeans. Out came the burring cell phone.

"Hello?" he said in that silky baritone voice of his.

He became more animated. "Vince, Vince. You're alive! I thought." a few moments of silence at this end and then "You were what? Saved and then fucked by a hiker? I don't know. I just don't know what to think . . ." Prolonged silence and the, "I know, I know. I just couldn't . . . can't. Listen, Vince, it's just not going to . . . Yes, I'm sorry I took your motorbike. I'll return it to the apartment, but when I get there, you need to be packed and ready to move on." Another few moments of silence. "No, Vince, no. It's over. I'm making other choices. Just pack and go."

I had the impression Vince was still talking when the blond snapped the cell phone shut and stooped down beside the table and retrieved his clothes and shoes and started to dress.

I waited until I no longer could hear the motor of the motorbike before I climbed down from the loft and walked out into the late afternoon light. I shivered when I walked out of the barn; I hadn't realized how hot it had been in there, how much heat the corrugated iron sheathing captured and held. Once more I thought of the possibility of an internal combustion fire in all of that hay packed into the barn. But I no longer related the blond angel to thoughts of internal combustion. I had hope renewed there.

Before I started out along the ridge of the mountain top, I turned and looked down at the barn, and at that odd window high up on its side, deserted now. No, I wouldn't be forgetting this barn for a good long time.

Highballing

If the CEO of my company hadn't seen me recently in that gay bar over on 12th and Madison, I don't know how long it would have taken me to get invited to the executive floor. But Pete Peterson had seen me, and there I was, in his conference room, sitting in a second-row position in the weekly executive meeting.

I'd been surprised, but pleasantly so, to see Peterson in the bar. He was one of those young, charging CEOs who took real good care of himself and whose movie-star looks popped out of the eminently eligible bachelor stories in the Sunday paper. I'd seen him working out in the office gym over the past several months and had found him to be quite a tasty package. I'd observed him looking me over there, too, but until our across-the-room mutual sighting at Rockies, I'd assumed he had been assessing my management potential—or just wondering who the hell I was and where I fit into his business empire. Now, I thought maybe something else had been going through his mind.

It was a long meeting, I had to take a piss pretty badly when it finally broke up. I asked the man next to me where the men's room was on this floor, and, having overheard me,

Peterson chimed in that I was welcome to use the executive rest room just down the hall from the conference room.

This was quite a snazzy room, all brown marble and expensive fixtures, and mirrors everywhere, including over the two urinals. There was even a convenient place for me to hang my suit coat. I did that and then quickly moved over to the urinal, unzipped my tight-fitting pants, pushed my ultra briefs down to under my balls, and sighed a great sigh, as I let loose with a strong and steady stream into the urinal.

I heard the door open and then the click of a lock, which I thought was a little strange, and, although I expected to have one of the executives belly up to the urinal beside me, I was surprised to feel someone right behind me. Before I could turn around, which would have been a little awkward because I was still pissing out a steady stream, in the mirror I saw Pete Peterson's well-chiseled face appear over my shoulder and heard him speak in a low, husky voice. "Here, let me help you with that."

He came up right against me in back and reached around with his right hand and took my dong in his hand. I could feel his intake of breath when he got the measure of me. His left hand came around and rested on my tightening stomach. I felt myself go a little weak in the knees and reached out with both hands to steady myself against the wall. I looked into the mirror and let my eyes be captured by his. He gave me a movie-star smile of assurance.

I had finished my business, and he shook the last drops into the urinal, but he kept his hand wrapped around my penis, which was steadily growing. "Nice," he whispered in my ear, "Very nice. Bigger than I had thought. That's very nice." He reached down with his left hand and cuddled my balls for a brief moment, and then he moved his hand up my stomach, under my shirt, and found my right nipple and played with that and in my chest hair.

I gasped as the fingers of his right hand went to the tip of my dick and he lightly ran them around the rim of my glans and then put a finger over my piss slit and applied a gentle pressure. He was nibbling on my ear, and I pulled my right arm away from the wall and wrapped it around his head so that I could run my fingers into his hair. I turned my head and found his mouth in a searching kiss. He began to stroke my cock, and I felt my knees go weak again.

His left hand left its exploration of my chest, and I heard the sound of a belt being undone and a zipper being lowered. I then felt my pants and briefs being pulled off my butt, and my pants hit the floor. We were still kissing and he was still stroking my cock, and now his other hand was wandering all over my butt cheeks. He gave a sound of animal pleasure, and broke away from the kiss long enough to whisper, "What a great, round butt. I love good, round butts."

I could feel his engorging penis pressing at my butt, working its way into my crack, and I began to spread my legs to receive him, when he pulled back a little and stopped stroking my cock.

"My limo will be down on the street in fifteen minutes to take me to my country home for the night. May I assume you would be willing to be my guest there for tonight?"

That was a good assumption.

A few minutes later, I was down on the street in front of our office building, where I found a stretch limousine and a big, black, bald body-builder driver holding the back door open. He gave me a smile and motioned toward the door with his head. I only had time enough to register that the back of limousine was roomy and plush, burgundy velour with wood paneling, and some pretty hefty throw pillows around, when Pete Peterson entered the limo and plopped down beside me. The door closed with a good solid sound, and Peterson informed me, with a proud grin, that we could see out of the smoked windows, but no one could see in—including the window to the driver's compartment—and that the car was quite soundproof.

As the limo moved into traffic, Peterson moved to the jump seat facing me and said, "It's a long drive; more than an hour. So, we might as well go ahead and get comfortable."

He flipped a CD into a machine next to him, which introduced a sensuous sound, with a good beat to it into the compartment. Then he proceeded to do a private strip tease for me. First his coat and his tie, which he folded and placed on the other jump seat, then his shirt and his shoes and socks. He was probably in his late thirties, but he was in superb condition. He had sandy-colored hair, tending toward the red and hazel-green eyes that held a smile real well. His chest was well developed, and the hair on his chest was a fine, blond-red color, descending straight down from his neck, flaring out over his chest muscles and then back down to a thin line stopping above his navel. He pulled his pants and briefs off, folded them, and placed them on top of his coat and tie, and there he was in all his glory. His pubic hair was even redder than his head hair, and his overly long, very thick cock stood at attention as if he had not forgotten in the least our recent encounter in the executive men's room. He pointed to a bar between the jump seats and offered me a drink, to which I could only croak a "Thanks, maybe later."

That caused him to smile broadly, and he went down onto his knees and moved to where I was stretched out in a sitting position at one side of the plush bench seat.

"Okay, then we might as well get right to the second round," he said. He tugged at my suit coat, and I slipped it off and gave it to him. He folded it neatly and placed it on top his folded clothes. He loosened my tie, but didn't take it off. Instead, he slowly unbuttoned my shirt and took it off me, adding it to the clothes pile.

"My, my, we're pretty everywhere, aren't we?" he said, and I was happy that he seemed to appreciate someone with darker and more body hair than he had. He leaned in to me and gave me a kiss. My hands went to his waist and then one wandered down and cupped his balls and his dick. He sighed and slowly ran a hand up my thigh and to my crotch, where he found my engorging cock and rubbed it up and down through my pants. He kissed me on the neck and then ran his tongue down through my chest hair to one of my nipples. The nipple puckered right up for him as he tongued and nipped at it. I threw my head back into the seat and moaned quietly, pushing my dick into his hand through the fabric of my pants. I wanted to feel skin on skin there.

"Ah, such nice tits," he whispered, as he slid his tongue over to the other nipple, "and such a sweet, big cock too." He then undid my belt and unzipped my pants and pulled my pants, briefs, shoes, and socks off in one smooth move. He reached over and grabbed a couple of pillows, threw them up to me with a "Here, put these behind your back," and he turned me so I was laying the length of the seat. He took my right leg and placed it along the back of the seat, trapped there by his own body. My left leg jutted out onto the floor of the limo, and there I was, fully open to him. I put the pillows behind me, with my head in the back corner of the limo. I could turn my head and watch the world go by, beyond the smoke glass, while Peterson did me.

And he did do me. Immediately after we had both gotten comfortable, Peterson took my dick in his mouth and started playing with my glans with his tongue. My dick steadily engorged to its full eight inches under his attention. His right hand was running all over my upper body, up and down arms, up to my throat, playing with the hair in my pits, spending extra time on my chest hair and nipples, and trailing down across my washboard abs and into my pubic hair. With the other hand, he massaged my right leg and foot and then my butt cheeks. He pulled away from his sucking long enough to say, "Man, I love your butt. I can't wait to get more of these cheeks." Then we went back to my now-fully stiffened cock and began a rhythm of ever-deeper swallows. I moaned and moved to join his rhythm. My hands went to his head, playing in his hair, and down to massaging his shoulders and reaching down to playing with his nipples.

I was bucking wildly with him now, meeting every deepthroating with a plunge of my own. He had both hands encircling my butt cheeks, and I gasped as his hands pulled the cheeks apart and his thumbs reached for my asshole. He flicked my asshole with both of his thumbs, and I twitched in response, digging my hands in his hair. He was deepthroating me down to the root now.

"Oh, Gawd, I think I'm going to cum," I croaked in warning. But he didn't stop pumping me and took the three separate jerking spurts down his throat with ease. I rolled my head back toward the window, and that's when I noticed that the window between the compartments in the limo was now down, and that the burly limo driver was eyeing the action through the rear-view mirror. All I could think of was that maybe I'd get a piece of that hunk sometime during this adventure as well.

I felt my hips elevating, as Peterson took up another pillow and placed it under my lower back. His hands went back to covering and squeezing my butt cheeks, and his thumbs to gently resting on the rim of my asshole and spreading that entrance. His mouth went to my balls, which he licked and sucked and then gently pulled away from my body and down. I moaned in mixed pleasure and pain. And then his mouth was buried between my butt cheeks, his tongue exploring and moistening my asshole, until I found the hole loosening and opening to him. He came up onto the seat on his knees between my legs, and I felt the head of his cock against the door of my hole. I gulped and gasped, as he entered me a couple of inches.

He held himself there, into me up to the rim of his glans, giving my canal time to adjust to him, rocking his cock head back and forth just inside my entrance. He then took his cock in one hand, sank another inch into me, and rotated it back and forth in my hole, driving me to distraction, and causing me to open even more. I had done this often enough already that I had no trouble opening further to him, and his big, thick cock then just slid right in until a good seven inches of it was buried in my hole.

Once again, he then took his cock in his hand and rotated it within my canal, stretching and adding to the sensation of being properly and fully stuffed. He started a rhythmic pumping action, squeezing my butt cheeks with his hands in syncopation, and it wasn't long until he came with a jerk and collapsed full length on top of me. He found my mouth with his, and we consummated our union with a deep-tongued kiss.

I didn't have to wonder what came next. While he still held me in a lip lock, Peterson slowly withdrew from my anus, and brought his knees up on each side of my waist and lifted his chest off of mine. I could feel him wrapping a hand around my still-engorged cock, as he maneuvered over me. I felt the head of my cock sliding across skin and being positioned at Peterson's asshole. He took his mouth from mine and let out a little whimper of pain as he took the head of my cock into his ass. Then he arched his chest back, taking several inches of my cock into him, and grabbed his ankles. I took his waist in my two hands, as he slowly raised and lowered his buttocks, taking more of me in with each downward slide. He pumped away for what seemed like ages, and after I had cum for the second time, he gave a little sigh and lowered himself unto my chest. Without pulling himself away from my buried cock, he laid his head on my chest and slowly tongued my nipples and chest hair.

I must have gone to sleep soon thereafter, because the first thing I knew was that the car had stopped, the door had opened, and Peterson had gathered his clothes and was exiting the vehicle. I sat up and started gathering my clothes as well, but as I started to exit, I found the door was blocked by the hulky driver.

"Not so fast, Sweet Cheeks," the Hulk said to me with a grin, as he pushed me back onto the floor of the limo with a big mitt. "Someone has to pay the taxi fare," he said. "And Mr. Peterson said that someone might as well be you."

I laid there awestruck, as he pulled his shirt out of his pants, quickly unbuttoned it and drew it off his gigantic, barrel chest. He was magnificent, and I sucked in my breath at his hairless, burly beauty. Just as quickly, off came his pants and shoes, and I sucked even harder for air. His rod was a veritable telephone pole. It wasn't hard to imagine that it must reach almost to his knees when it wasn't hard, but just now it certainly was hard.

I made another dash for freedom past him, but he was too quick for me. Grabbing me around the upper arm, he threw me back into the limo, and, with the momentum of that, came through the door himself. I tried to fight him off, but he must have been a professional wrestler, because in no time he had me flipped across one of the jump seats, and, with my leather belt and his own, he had my wrists tied together and laced up to the anchor of one of the front seats with one of the belts and my left ankle attached to one of the anchors of the driver's seat. Wasting no time at all, he pulled my butt cheeks apart and had his tongue buried in my ass. I tried to raise myself, but he just pushed my back down with one of his big mitts and kept on tonguing me with satisfied gurgling and slurping sounds.

His tongue seemed bigger than some of the dicks I had entertained, and it wasn't long before I was lathered up real good again. I felt his tongue pull out of my ass, but he gave me no time to wonder what came next. The huge knob of his cock was at my asshole, and there was no coyness to his approach at all. He just drilled that telephone pole right on in, spreading my butt cheeks as much as possible. I screamed, and rose up involuntarily, but he only stopped long enough to push me down by the back of the neck.

After he was in a good seven or eight inches, he reached around me with both of his big mitts and started deeply massaging my chest, back, and shoulder muscles while vigorously pumping away, ever deeper and wider up my ass channel. there was pain, to be sure, but the thought of this big, beautiful monster, with what was now ten or more inches of thick black cock stuffed inside me, going wild with lust in my body—and that I was able to take him and give him such a buzz—gave me exquisite pleasure. It wasn't long before I felt him release with a violent jerk, coating my insides with his cum.

Then the lion turned into a lamb. He kissed me on the back of the neck and then returned to slowly and deeply massaging my aching body. One of his huge hands wrapped itself around my cock, and he gave me a slow hand job. After I had cum, he continued to massage my body until a slept. When I awoke, I was free of my bonds and lying across the backseat of the limo. The driver had dressed again and was waiting to show me into Peterson's country home. I pulled my briefs, pants, and loafers back on, stuffed my socks in my pockets and put my arms through my shirt. I didn't have time to dress further, though, before the Hulk had taken up my suit coat and tie, picked up my duffel bag, and was heading for the front door of an ostentatious beach house. Not knowing what else to do, I followed along behind him.

We entered a large foyer with two banks of stairs rising two stories. The Hulk started trudging up the stairs to the second floor, with me trailing behind him, gawking at the undoubtedly expensive erotic art on the stairwell walls. We went down a long corridor and entered a large bedroom, decorated for a gentleman in soft leathers and greens and browns and golds. I heard the water running in a side room, and before I could explore there, a Greek god appeared at the door. He was young, couldn't have been twenty yet, and lithe, with a slim waist and hips, although with well-defined musculature; black curly hair, flopping down into his face and gorgeous light-blue eyes. His welcoming smile showed luminous pearly whites. He was wearing form-fitting white T-shirt, and tight gray slacks that showed a respectable basket at the crouch. Fine, curly black hair laced down his forearms and blossomed from the V neck of his T.

"Hello, there, my name is Salvas. You both look exhausted," he said with a grin. "To the showers with both of you."

Both I and the Hulk stripped down again and padded into the bathroom, which boasted a particularly large shower stall. The water was on from two jets, and the Hulk and I entered. I turned and watched the Greek god pull the T over his head and strip off his trousers. He was wearing a silky thong that left little to the imagination, and he was beautiful—slim, lithe, well-muscled through the chest and arms, and covered with curly hair. He winked at me as he stepped out his thong, showing a good seven inches of fairly thick, uncircumcised dick, picked up a cake of soap and a wash cloth, and entered the shower.

I was the guest, so Salvas soaked me up first, running his soap and wash cloth around my body in a way that made my cock stand at attention again. During this process, the Hulk leaned back in a corner, watched us, and languidly pulled at his dick.

Having soaped me up, Salvas turned to the Hulk, and quickly soaped him up as well. Fascinated by Salvas's pert little butt cheeks, I couldn't help but reach over and run my hands over them and then to continue on around his hips with one hand to explore his cock and through his legs with the other to nuzzle his balls. Salvas stopped his soaping of the Hulk long enough to turn his face to me and part my lips with his. I gasped, as he ran his tongue into my mouth and explored. I ran my fingers down to the tip of his dick and received a little thrill at the feel of the uncut loose skin there as I pulled it back and got my fingers between it and his glans. Salvas shuddered with

215

pleasure, and, leaving the Hulk to wash himself off, put one of his hands over mine and brought my hand up to encase his engorged cock lightly. I kept my thumb on his piss slit. He wrapped his own hand over mine and provided the slow pumping action on his dick. With each downward stroke, I could feel foreskin coming back up onto his glans and touching my thumb. This was a new, very interesting sensation for me. Shortly, with a shudder, Salvas came in my hand, and his cum was washed down into the drain. I looked around and the hulk was gone. It was just me and Salvas now.

I got out of the shower and Salvas dried me off with the towel, making quite sure that all of my private parts were dry and well rubbed. After he finished, he moved around the room, straightening up, but never quite getting around to putting his clothes back on. I sat on the end of the bed and watched him.

"Now, Mr. Peterson told me to tell you that you were expected out on the patio in an hour for drinks with his other guests." Salvas told me as he stood at the door, ready to leave. "He said that dress would be optional, because anything you wore probably wouldn't stay on you very long. Was there anything else before I go?"

"Yes, I think so, I said. Please come over here." He walked over to me and I spun him around and threw him down on the bed. He went down on his side, and I just lifted his leg up and entered him with my engorged cock. He gasped but took me deep without any trouble. After pumping him that way for several minutes, I turned him on his stomach and gave it to him doggy style. I was determined to get a little of my own back after playing bottom on the road trip here. I felt quite sure that it would be bottom for me again when I went downstairs.

I never did make it downstairs for drinks. But when I was missed, Mr. Peterson and his guests came looking for me and, indeed, I spent the rest of the evening being bottom for a variety of men in a variety of positions. I only hoped Peterson and our company were going to be making a whole lot of sweet deals out of this little gift-giving evening, because I was really putting out for the firm.

Hook or Crook

I wanted to fuck Nathan from the moment I saw my son, Seth, fucking him. And I didn't just want to make love to him like Seth was doing, but to really give him a good pounding. I happened upon them in Seth's bedroom. I heard the moaning from the hallway and couldn't resist checking it out. Seth had won the neighbors' new pool boy—a golden blond surfer type with heavenly cut features, brown-tanned as a berry, and unruly curly hair flipping up at his shoulders. This was fast work even for Seth. Nathan had only been working for the Carnadays for two days. I'd seen him too and masturbated to the thought of fucking him twice already. But I'd barely thought of a scheme to get him for myself, and here he was already, on his belly on my son's bed, moaning, and undulating to the fuck my son was giving him.

Seth had the blond's thighs closely encased between his knees and his chest pressing on the pool boy's shoulder blades. He was running the fingers of one hand in the blond's golden mane and kissing him in the hollow of his neck. They could have been resting in postcoital repose, except the hips of both of them were moving like a ship on a rolling sea. Seth was slow fucking Nathan in a rolling undulation and Nathan obviously was enjoying it. His hips were moving in consort with Seth's and he was sighing and moaning.

They were making love, and the coupling made for a beautiful tableau. It got my juices going. Not because I wanted to make love to him like Seth was doing, but because I wanted to enter Nathan like that and make his eyes bug out because I was longer and thicker than Seth, and I wanted to slam my cock up into him again and again and make him groan and grunt rather than sigh, and cry out alternately for me to stop and for me never to stop.

This was not Seth's way, though. He fucked for the intimacy of love. And all these young hunks who gravitated to him left him eventually. He always seemed to be bewildered by not being able to find something permanent—a young man worthy of him who was willing to stick with him. I knew, however, that it was because the young men who gravitated to him really wanted to be fucked to exhaustion. They wanted to be dominated and squeezed to the limit and plumbed to the depths.

That was where I was entering dangerous waters with my son. My son was a romantic; he fell in love with those he was screwing. I just wanted to get my rocks off with a delicious hunk—to fuck the living daylights out of him, to dominate and leave him exhausted and moaning. It was probably my son's bad fortune that he attracted just the sort of young man I wanted to bang the living daylights out of.

The last time I'd taken after someone my son was wooing was that young Israeli Ely on the Elat resort beach. He had been a waiter in our hotel and had his tongue out and panting for my son that first morning on the balcony café overlooking the Red Sea. As he was pouring coffee—almost putting mine in my lap because he couldn't take his eyes off Seth—I asked him if he ever was able to get off work to enjoy the beach himself, and when he said he did and wasn't working that afternoon, in fact, I asked him if he wanted to come out on the beach with Seth and me—that I had a cabana reserved. He didn't hesitate in saying yes.

I could tell that Seth was taken with the dark, hirsute Israeli immediately. But I didn't suggest the assignation for Seth. I knew I wanted to fuck the stuffing out of the Israeli hunk myself. I regret to admit that I often used Seth like this, as bait for my own needs and desires—almost regret, I should say.

And I never took more than the young men wanted. They enjoyed the fuck my son gave them, but I'd leave them with their tongues hanging out, their asses steaming, and a look of total satisfaction on their faces.

I watched from a stretch of sand in front of the cabana as the two played in the water, becoming increasingly frisky and intimate. I could tell the instance that Seth's dick first entered the Israeli, because the Israeli, who was one of those kind of men who always had to be in motion, suddenly went rigid and his eyes took on that "Oh fuck, yes!" expression I so often saw on the young men my Seth was fucking. They were out in the water almost up to their nipples. Seth was close behind Ely, and I could see below the surface of the water well enough to know that Seth's hands were palmed across Ely's lower belly. They were moving with the gently rolling surf, but I could tell that they also were in the rhythm of the fuck, Seth crouched a bit and controlling the rise and fall of Ely on his cock by pushing off from the sandy sea bottom with his heels. I retreated to just inside the cabana, pushed the waistband of my bikini trunks below my balls, and masturbated as I watched Seth and Ely fuck in the gentle surf.

There were few other bathers around, and those that were there seemed focused on enjoying their own time in the sea and on the beach. No one appeared to be paying any attention to the coupling except me. I sat there in the shadows just inside the entrance to the cabana and slowing jacked off to the sight of my son making love to a dark, curly haired Israeli beauty who seemed totally lost to the experience. All the time I was scheming my own taking of him.

The three of us lunched together on the hotel terrace, with Seth and Ely already comfortable with each other, happy and satisfied, and likely to become even closer the longer we stayed in Elat. This was my son's way. Other men were comfortable and immediately smitten with him and prone to dropping their current lives without giving it a second thought and turning themselves over into Seth's hands—willing to rise and fall on his cock forever in some sort of love-filled mystical world. That wasn't my way. My way was fuck 'em hard and leave 'em gasping for air. And few had objected to that.

After lunch, Seth and Ely left me sipping a brandy sour on the terrace and went back to the cabana, closing the entry flap behind them. A half hour later, Seth emerged and came up to the terrace and said he was going up to the room to shower and dress and would be meeting Ely in the hotel lobby—that Ely wanted to show him around the area on his motorbike. I could tell by Seth's contented look that not only had he fucked Ely again in the cabana but also that he was completely smitten with the Israeli.

I waited only long enough for my son to turn toward the door into the hotel and then rose and strode down the beach to the cabana. Ely was still stretched out on the day bed on his belly, his eyes closed and a huge smile on his face. He was naked, having just been loved well, I'm sure. His hole was still puckered and slack from where it had taken Seth's cock, and the small of his back was still splattered with gobs of my son's semen.

Already hard from the anticipation of what I was going to do, I stripped off my bikini, rolled one of the condoms that had been tucked below my waistband onto my cock, swung a leg over his pelvis, and thrust hard between his dark curly-hair covered bubble-butt cheeks, finding the slack and well-lubed hole opening to me immediately.

I had picked up the belt of my terry cloth hotel bathrobe before pinning Ely's belly to the day bed with a deep thrust of my cock, and when Ely's body flopped around from the surprise and pain of the assault, I grabbed for his wrists and got them bound to the railing at the head of the daybed. And then, crouched over his hips with my pelvis and leveraging my feet off the sand of the cabana interior, with my hands pressing down on the small of his back to give me a deep angle inside him, I fucked Ely hard, deep, and brutally. He cried out and cursed and begged for relief at first, but he quickly subsided into groans and whimperings.

When he had quieted down to accepting the fuck, his hips rolling with the rhythm of my plowing and Ely sighing his enjoyment of my technique of rotating my pelvis as I dug in, I moved a hand below his belly and onto his cock. His hips were moving in perfect harmony with mine, and I squeezed his balls and cock and jacked him off, making sure that he had come before I did.

We held there, panting. He was still whimpering, though, when I pulled out of him, felt myself ready to rise again, and changed condoms. Then I turned him over, and ignoring his weak entreaties to leave him be, I straddled the narrow daybed with my thighs again, between his spread legs, and gave him another, even deeper, rapid-pistoning fuck. He flopped around under me until he had come again and then he just lay there, collapsed, his tongue hanging out and a silly grin on his face while I pile drived to my own release.

He was exhausted and semicomatose when I was done this time. I just pulled my bikini trunks back on and turned and went up to the room and showered. Seth returned to the room while I was drying off, a sad expression on his face. He told me that Ely had not shown up in the hotel lobby as arranged, and, like a dutiful father, I clucked my condolences that perhaps Ely had flitted off to somewhere else, having gotten what he wanted from Seth. We never saw Ely again—and although Seth had not said anything to me about it at the time, I couldn't be sure that he didn't suspect some of his boyfriends just disappeared after I gave them a proper fucking. Seth would have to be a dope not to suspect some sort of pattern in play—and my son wasn't a dope.

I had tried to lay off after that and had usually managed to do so—with one or two lapses. I was a highly sexed guy and needed to get my rocks off regularly—in something beyond personal release. I needed the affirmation that I could completely dominate my partner and fuck him to his exhaustion—that I wasn't too old to do that to a younger man. And Seth and I had identical taste in men—we just had different things we wanted to do with those men.

I watched Seth and Nathan making love on Seth's bed. As usual, Seth was the one controlling the fuck, and Nathan was the one loving whatever Seth wanted to do to him—knowing instinctively that Seth would be gentle, would give Nathan time to adjust to him, and would take care of Nathan's needs and desires so that they plateaued and released almost simultaneously. Seth's sex was loving, giving as well as receiving.

Nathan was in ninth heaven, the two moving in perfect harmony and rhythm. After a long, lingering kiss, Seth raised his chest off Nathan's shoulder blades and held Nathan by the hips as Seth moved his own hips in circles—a technique he had inherited from me—making deep cock love to every aspect of Nathan's channel walls. At length Seth raised up and pulled his dick out so that his bulb was just inside Nathan's entrance, rubbing up and down on Nathan's prostate.

Nathan was panting hard and making mewing sounds. His hips lifted up off the bed and one of his hands went and encircled his dick. He was dragging his cock head along the sheets under him, fucking the bed.

Seth pulled all of the way out of Nathan, jerked off his condom, and languidly went into a 69 position with Nathan, with both of them deep throating each other and swallowing each other off in a nearly simultaneous ejaculation. It was like they had been lovers forever, knowing exactly what to do and when, even though they hadn't laid eyes on each other before three days earlier.

I knew three things then—that Seth was really enthralled with this one, that I couldn't keep my hands off this one for however long he would be in our life as Seth's lover, and that I was going to fuck this one hard myself by either hook or crook.

The avenue to my scheme was given to me that evening at dinner. Seth was bubbling over about his new friend, Nathan. It seemed that Nathan wasn't just the neighbor's pool boy. He also was one of those computer technicians who went to people's homes and helped them get their computers set up and troubleshooted.

After dinner I went up to my study and sat down at the computer. I knew the Web sites I wanted to use, and for the next hour I went through them, going to the pages that evoked what I wanted to the most and earmarking them in my favorites list. The next day, when I was sunbathing by my pool in the nude, I watched the Carnadays' yard until I saw that Nathan was out there, dipping leaves out of their pool. I went up on my diving board and did a few expert dives, giving Nathan every opportunity to check out the goods, which, if I must say myself, were plenty good. Then I sauntered over to the fence and called out to Nathan.

"Hi, I'm Seth's dad," I said.

"Yes, I know, Mr. Arrington," Nathan answered. A very nice, tenor voice. Steady. He didn't seem at all nervous talking with the naked, forty-five-year-old father of his new lover. Well, I intended to fuck some fear into him before I was done.

"Seth tells me you work with people's computers . . . sort of work out the kinks. True?"

"That's right. You got kinks in your computer to straighten out, Mr. Arrington?" He was giving me a smile that I couldn't figure out. These open, hunky surf dude types can be hard to read. I didn't know if he was being half snotty or just friendly. But I knew I did have something for him to straighten out. In fact, it was already straight, and if I backed off from this fence between my patio and the neighbors', he could see how straight—and fat and long—my cock could get for him.

"Yes, I can't figure it out. My favorites list is all fucked up," I answered. "When I click on one URL, a different site comes up."

"That's strange," Nathan said. "I've never encountered that." And I could tell by his smile—he was almost salivating—that I'd given him a challenge that no computer geek could resist.

"Do you have anything to do at about eight this evening?" I asked, knowing that Seth planned to be off to the gym then.

"Nope, I can come around then." Nathan answered. I was thinking that both Nathan and I would be "coming" a little later than that, but I just smiled and nodded and turned and walked away from him, giving him a great shot of my still-tight buns.

Nathan arrived promptly at eight and I took him up to my study. He was wearing loose shorts and an athletic T, all of which would be convenient for me and set his blond hunkiness off quite nicely.

I sat him down in my chair and turned the computer on for him, and he was soon working his way through the favorites I had set up the previous evening—all of fuck sites of daddies taking on blond hunks just like him, all earmarked to hot fuck scenes.

He spun through the dials for a while and eventually said, "Umm, I don't find anything wrong, Mr. A. All of the URLs seem to go where they are supposed to go." His voice was husky, though, so I knew he'd been looking at what he'd clicked on.

Time to make a move. Either it worked or it didn't.

I pulled the chair away, forcing him to get up on his feet, crouched over the computer. Then I covered him close from behind, with one hand snaking up under the hem of his T and up to a nipple and the other hand moving around to his basket. He was hard. And so was I.

I pushed the front of my shorts down—that's all I was wearing—and the back of his shorts down, and I had the underside of my cock running up and down along his crack.

"Umm, Mr. A. Ohhh, Mr. A." His voice was cracking.

"Don't speak. I want you. I want you now. You can feel my cock; I plan to slam that as far up your ass as I can. If it's not what you want too, you can just break away and leave. I won't stop you." He stayed put, and that and his ragged breathing told me that he was mine.

I crouched down behind him and went for his hole with my tongue. I kept a hand wrapped around his cock, and he has hardening nicely and panting hard for me as well.

And then, hands grabbing his hips hard, I was standing behind him and fucking him deep—brutally—in a pistoning action that had him yelping and writhing under me.

And then the surprise. He was turning and grabbing me in a wrestler hold—showing that he was a lot stronger than I was and well trained as a wrestler.

Here it came, I thought, he was going to punch me unconscious and leave me unfucked—and I didn't know what disturbed me more: that I would be black and blue or left sexually unsatisfied.

But he wasn't punching me. He was pushing me to the floor on my back and straddling my pelvis with his hips—and bringing his channel down on my erection. And he was fucking himself hard on me. He wasn't rejecting me; he was showing that he liked a rough fuck like I liked—in fact, that he loved it.

We were really going to town when Seth entered the room.

I was momentarily shocked that he'd found me in a compromising position with the young man he was currently wooing. But this didn't seem to be the case. I watched him strip off his shorts, and then he was sitting in the chair from the computer desk and watching Nathan fucking himself wildly on my cock and slowly jacking up his own cock.

When I had come, surprised that Nathan could bring me to the boil so expertly and quickly, the blond hunk pulled off me and then went and sat on Seth's cock and the two of them fucked in slow, sensual undulations that had me hard and masturbating myself again.

Later, on my bed, with Nathan wedged between us and Seth and I sharing him, Seth told me that he had no trouble sharing like this—that it turned him on.

"So, you like it both ways, Nathan?" I asked. "Both the loving Seth can give you and the rough fucking I prefer?"

"No problem. No problem at all, Mr. A." And Nathan was giving me that sunny surfer-boy smile of his. And I was content for the first time in my life and not feeling guilty about my son anymore at all.

"I think we may have found a new high-paid houseboy," I murmured around Nathan's nipples to my son who was sucking on one. "That is, if Nathan feels he can do better here than at the Carnadays,'" I said.

"No problem," Nathan squeaked, whether at the tonguing Seth was given his nipple, or the slow hand job Seth was giving him, or at my dick pumping him deep, or at my hand on his belly, I didn't know—or care.

I Only Wanted to Watch

Brandon had told me that if I wasn't going to move to a new, all-the-way level with him, he was going to a gay bar and would bring someone back to the dorm with him. He said he couldn't take the frustration any longer. I thought he had been joking, that he was as scared about this as I was. But there they were, entering the door from the street and moving toward Brandon's room at the other end of the suite in the middle of the night, having awakened me from a light sleep when Brandon's friend knocked over a lamp and exclaimed a four-letter word.

I had only been dozing, because I had been aroused by Brandon's plan, even though I hadn't really believed he was going to go through with it, and I hadn't been able to keep my hands off my own cock and couldn't go to sleep when I was that hard. I wasn't any less frustrated at the nonmovement in our relationship than Brandon was. If he had been here, we would have just jacked off together, but I just couldn't bring myself to do certain things yet. I was more of a watcher than a doer still.

I thus was quickly out of my bed at the sound of their arrival, and when I'd opened my door a crack and peeked out, I could see that Brandon had brought back a four-letter-word kind of guy. He was decked out in black—black leather vest over a tight black muscle shirt and black jeans, shredded at the knees and also tight on well-muscled legs. He had a square-jawed face, covered in a couple of day's growth of black stubble. His hair was long and tied off in a ponytail, and I wouldn't have doubted a claim that he was a gang banger straight off his motorcycle.

Brandon's friend had almost fallen when he'd run into the lamp, and when Brandon instinctively put out his arms to keep his friend from going down, the friend came up hugging Brandon tight. He was kissing Brandon on the lips and arching him over backward in a possessive stance.

When he broke away from this, I could hear Brandon whisper that they needed to wait until they got in his room, because he didn't want to wake any of his suite mates. And then they were out of my sight and down the hall toward where Brandon's room was.

My dick went hard and I thought I was going to hyperventilate. Brandon had done it. He had said he was so horny for a guy that he was going to go out and pick one up, and he'd done it. I'd thought that was all talk.

I scurried down the hall as quietly as I could and came up real close to Brandon's door. He hadn't gotten the door shut tight, and I pushed it open a smidgen, giving me a full view of the bed in the glaring light of the overhead bulb.

They were both sitting on the opposite side of the bed from me, next to and close to each other. Their shirts were already off, and Brandon's friend had Brandon's smooth, cut torso arched back, with one arm wrapped under Brandon's shoulder blades. The guy's lips were already on Brandon's nipples, and I could tell from the angle of the guy's other arm that he had a hand on Brandon's basket. The expression on Brandon's face told me a lot. I could see apprehension and a little fear, but an overwhelming helping of desire and excitement that were overpowering the other two emotions.

Brandon's friend came up for air from nibbling at Brandon's nipples and loosened the hold of the arm around Brandon's back, permitting Brandon to slowly lower himself on the bed. The friend's torso was turned toward me now, and I could see it clearly. Where Brandon was the blond, smooth-bodied college jock, his visitor was a dark, hirsute gypsy—lithe and sinewy, with a hairy chest and arms, and a look of danger about him. This impression was only enhanced by the two silver rings in his nipples, the stud in one ear, and the crown-of-thorns tattoos around both bulging biceps. Even the expression on his face contrasted perfectly with Brandon's hesitancy and indecision at this point. Full confidence; full control. He conveyed that he knew exactly what he wanted and that he was going to get it.

He placed his thumbs under Brandon's pecs and his fingers around his sides and pushed the blond's body up until it was fully on the bed. And then he came down, full length, on top of Brandon, pecs to pecs, belly to belly, and basket to basket. They were only in their jeans now. They had removed both their shoes and their socks. They kissed deeply, and then the gypsy put his arms on Brandon's upper arms, pinning him to the bed, and raised his chest up, putting the weight of his body on his hips and pelvis. He proceeded to grind his basket into Brandon's while he possessed Brandon's eyes with his own, focusing Brandon on what was happening, forcing Brandon to acknowledge what was going to happen, no matter what simpler, less dangerous ideas Brandon might have had when he brought the man back to the dorm with him. The gypsy reached around and undid his ponytail, and long, silky black hair cascaded down to his shoulders.

Uncertainty and a bit of fear were fighting the lust in Brandon's eyes—and slowly losing the battle. The gypsy had his knees between Brandon's legs, and Brandon slowly opened his stance and then, in resignation, brought his legs around and placed the backs of his calves over those of his new-found friend. The gypsy raised up on his knees then and unbuckled Brandon's jeans, pulled the zipper down, fanned out the two sides of the material, pushed the band on his briefs down to below his balls, and brought out Brandon's rod. Brandon had a very nice dick, rather thin, but of good length. I had admired it often when we were showering. I instinctively pushed my sleeping shorts down to below my own respectable cock, and lightly fingered what had already hardened nicely.

Then I almost audibly gasped when the gypsy proceeded to undo his own belt buckle, unzip himself, and fan out the waist of his jeans. He hadn't been wearing anything under the jeans, and his cock was mammoth—both long and thick, truly horse hung. The bulb of his dick was a dark red and bulbous, and a silver ring piercing it caught the light of the overhead fixture. I could feel my own cock beginning to form precum.

The gypsy came down onto Brandon again and mashed his pelvis into Brandon's, introducing the cocks to each other. Brandon's hands had gone to the slats of the headboard above him, and I could see the whiteness of his knuckles as he held onto the iron rods. The muscles of his arms were bulging under the strain, as the gypsy ground his hot cock into Brandon's pubes. The gypsy was holding Brandon firmly by the wrists with his hands, and he had his lips and teeth buried in the hollow of Brandon's neck. Brandon's back was slightly arched back, and his head was bent back at even a greater angle. His eyes were wildly searching the ceiling, as if he was on the brink of trying to bolt from the room.

But there was no bolting. The gypsy was firmly in control, both physically and psychologically. He was the older of the two by a good ten years, but there appeared to be limitless strength in his body, and he had the manner of a man who knew exactly how to get what he wanted. Brandon was a soft, spoiled college student in comparison, no matter how well built he was. He was probably thinking now that this obsessive lark of his hadn't been such a great idea, but the two were well beyond just calling it a night and going their separate ways.

The gypsy was so fast in stripping them both of the rest of their clothes, that I hardly noticed it had been done. My attention was arrested by that blunderbuss of a cock swinging between the gypsy's legs as he rose up over Brandon. I'd certainly never seen anything this formidable in the dorm shower room. The first I noticed, he was up with his knees on either side of Brandon's pecs, and, while still holding Brandon's wrists at the headboard slats, he was forcing his cock between Brandon's lips and pumping his face slowly. I was getting all of this in a side view, and I couldn't help but start stroking my own cock as the gypsy's eight or nine inches started working their way down Brandon's throat.

Brandon's knuckles were even whiter than before from the pressure on the iron rods of his headboard, and I saw his knees come up and his heels dig into the bedspread under the strain. The muscles of his calves and thighs were popping out, and I could hear him moaning and groaning and gagging under the assault. I tried to see his eyes, but he had them shut tight.

I could almost hear the audible sigh of relief from across the room, as the gypsy pulled out of Brandon's mouth and turned him around until he was laying across the width of the bed on his back, with his butt cheeks at the edge of the bed.

The gypsy was giving Brandon head now. Although I was watching from the angle of the top of Brandon's head, I was standing at the door and looking slightly down on the tableau on the bed, so I could look down Brandon's trembling torso and see the gypsy's head bobbing above his pelvis. The gypsy was running one hand up to Brandon's nipples and then down, fanning out over his flat, pulsating belly. And the other hand was between Brandon's thighs somewhere, probably doing something lustful with Brandon's balls.

Brandon had his head arched back between his arms, which were bent at the elbows close to each side of his head, with his hands bunching up the bedspread above and to the sides of his head. I could tell by the rhythmic bunching of Brandon's fists in the bedspread and the bouncing of his hips that the gypsy was stroking him deeply and fully with his mouth. He was probably an expert at this. I found myself matching the rhythm with the stroking of my own cock, and I was beginning to begrudge Brandon his adventure. He had such a look of pleasure and abandon in his eyes that I envied him that. We had talked about the pleasure of getting good head, and even had done some fumbling experimentation with each other, but I could tell from the expression on Brandon's face that we had never even come close to the real thing.

I realized then that Brandon could see me. His eyes were piercing mine. I could almost tell that he was trying to convey that this could be us—that it might very well be us on another night, if I could suspend my inhibitions as he now had. My cock gave a lurch, and I moved my free hand up and glided up my taut stomach and pecs and squeezed my nipples. I returned his

231

look of expectation and desire as best I could, sealing the unspoken agreement. He seemed almost to be telling me that this whole episode had been constructed to bring me out fully, to make me acknowledge that I wanted him and was willing to go the distance. I lifted my cock and pointed it at him, and he gave me a kissing gesture with his mouth. The agreement was ratified.

I now could see Brandon's cock bouncing on his belly. The gypsy had moved on—and down—with his lips. Brandon sighed and then moaned and then gave little yipping sounds and beat his fists against the bed in ecstasy as the gypsy expertly worked his asshole with his lips and tongue. Brandon raised his legs and then pulled them down onto his chest with his hands under his knees, giving the gypsy the deepest, widest possible access to his ass. All the time, Brandon was holding my eyes in his, conveying the deepest sense of pleasure and desire that he could across the room to me.

With a little cry, Brandon unfolded his legs wide, dug his heels into the edge of the bed. He then wrapped both of his hands around his long, engorged cock and stroked himself to ejaculation. I found that I had been stroking myself along with him, and we shot off together. I had cried out myself upon release, but the gypsy showed no sign of having heard me.

This might have been because he was changing position now. I saw the look of elation on Brandon's face at the prodigious release of his cum up his belly change almost instantly to surprise, pain, and fear upon the realization that his new-found master had come up and had his bludgeon at Brandon's back door. There was little warning and no mercy as the gypsy pushed his humongous cock into Brandon's ass. Brandon first arched back, his heels scrabbling for purchase at the edge of the bed, and showed me a face of deeply wounded pain, his mouth open in a big "O" that somehow couldn't muster a sound, and his eyes rolling back into his head so that about all I could see were the whites. He was clawing at the air with his hands at first. Then he raised his shoulders, and reached for the gypsy, trying to put an end to the relentless plowing up his ass canal. But the gypsy just laughed and pushed Brandon down onto his back on the bed with strong hand in the sternum.

Brandon's hips were briefly rolled up and the gypsy came up onto the edge of the bed with his knees, and I now could see the impossible thickness of his cock buried under Brandon's balls. He was fucking down into Brandon now, with a good four inches of dark cock root still showing against the paleness of Brandon's thighs. I held my breath and pulled at my own, reawakening cock, as I watched those last four, thick inches bury themselves in my classmate. Then the gypsy emitted an evil laugh. The cock came out almost the whole way, and, as Brandon cried out, it slowly started to disappear inside him once more.

The gypsy came back off the bed and onto his feet between Brandon's legs, and the horse-hung cock continued its second, less hampered journey to the center of Brandon, during which Brandon writhed under the gypsy's hand and gulped and gasped for air. Then I could see from my vantage point black silky pubic hair meeting and mingling with the blond down on Brandon's balls again, and the world held still. Brandon's gulping turned to panting and then to just quiet moaning, as his body slowly decreased its trembling and twitching and he accommodated himself to having been so thickly and deeply skewered.

After a short while, the gypsy removed his hand from Brandon's chest and took Brandon's legs in his hands at the ankles and spread-eagled them up and out. I saw the gypsy's hips go into a slight in and out stroking motion. He looked down into Brandon's face and gave him a big, appreciative smile. I couldn't see that Brandon was smiling back, but I could see that the tension had gone out of his body, and his own hips were moving slightly now, in rhythm with the man who was fucking him, the stranger who he had brought back to the dorm, the mysterious gypsy who now had eight or nine inches of pulsating cock up Brandon's undulating ass canal.

I could feel the strain going out of my body now too. I had seen the unknown and it could be conquered. If Brandon could adjust to eight or nine thick, horse-hung inches, I surely could manage Brandon, and he me. Brandon had arched his head back and he was watching me again, his eyes glued to my face, telling me that it was all right; that the pain had been worth the pleasure.

And then his eyes took on a look of pure ecstasy, as the gypsy started pumping him fast and deep. He was rotating his hips as he pumped and his undulating torso was glistening with sweat in the overhead light. I found his hairiness, with the silver nipple rings and bicep tattoos mesmerizing in their exotic dance of lust. His head was moving, and his hair was flipping around in the air. Brandon's hips were meeting his gyrations, and the younger man's legs were now propped on the older man's shoulders and their arms were entwined with the firm grips of their fingers on each other's elbows. They were one now, one pulsating, pumping, fucking machine. One part blond, smooth and all-American; one part dark, hairy, and mysterious—but both united as one, at the pelvis, exchanging pleasure, moans, sighs, and body fluids.

I thought the dance had gone on longer than it actually had. They had stopped before I noticed it, with no sign of the gypsy's release. And they were both looking up, at the door, at me, suspended in time. Waiting for me to realize that there were three of us in this, not just two. Brandon wasn't the only one who had seen me in the shadows just beyond the door.

I have no idea when the gypsy had realized that I was there. But it had been long enough for him to decide what he wanted to do about that.

Through the fog of discovery, I heard him mutter, "Next." And before I knew what was happening, he had me over at the bed, bent over, my legs spread wide, and that big juicy cock of his was probing beyond my protesting sphincter and then, with a bursting of the dam inside me, being pulled in by my undulating ass muscles and making its journey up my ass canal from behind. He had his fingers digging into my nipples, and his cold, nipple rings were sliding around on my shoulder blades. I was writhing and struggling, my fists buried in the bedspread and mounding that up just as I had seen Brandon do under the same circumstances. I had my mouth open to scream, but as with Brandon, my lungs were in shock and I couldn't form the sounds.

Brandon came to my rescue then. He had his knees under me, at my belly. He helped me stretch my arms around him and cup his butt cheeks in my hands for leverage and for some place to put them, and he was gently pushing his rehardened dick between my lips, giving me something pleasant to concentrate on while the gypsy stretched and plowed me deeply from behind, giving me that education I could use for the rest of the semester with Brandon.

The two of them found each other above me with their lips, and I heard Brandon whisper a thank you to the masterful stranger. It occurred to me then that this had all been Brandon's plan, all of it, from the start.

Late Night Workout

I had been going to Gabe and Steve's Gym for a couple of months, and I was quite pleased with the results. I could tell that Gabe and Steve were pleased too, as they'd both been giving me the eye when I was in the shower. I didn't mind all that much; it was a free world and looks didn't cost me anything—or so I thought at the time. I knew that Gabe and Steve were a couple, but that didn't mean much to me either. Somewhat of an odd couple. Both were handsome and well built, to be sure, but Gabe was a bulging Nordic god, while Steve was the lithe and hirsute Mediterranean type.

Everything was going fine until that evening when I'd worked late and didn't arrive at the gym until near closing. No problem, Gabe had said. I could continue working out after they closed, as Steve had to do some paperwork anyway. Gabe could spot me, if I liked for my barbell set. While he was talking to me, he stripped off his shirt. His bulging chest muscles tapering down to washboard abs and strong stomach muscles were an inspiration for me to work harder on my own routines. He was well tanned and hairless; I knew that he shaved all over regularly, as he appeared in many local bodybuilding contests.

When I got around to doing my barbell lifts, I started to settle on my usual bench, when Gabe suggested I try the new bench in the back room. It was a strange contraption, raised higher than the normal bench off the ground and with stirrups for the feet. Gabe told me this was an improvement in two ways, as it prevented the lifter from using his feet so much for traction and put the barbells at a better height for the spotter to work with. I knew little about such things, so I didn't ask any questions and jumped up on the bench and flopped down on my back.

Gabe called Steve in from the office and asked him to help get me settled on the bench. Steve must have been on his way to the showers when Gabe called, because when he entered the room, all he had around him was a skimpy towel that veed in front to below his waistline. Incongruously, though, he was carrying a big pair of scissors. He was deeply tanned and covered in curly black hair that spiraled down the front of him to where the towel was knotted. His muscles didn't bulge like Gabe's, but he was still well muscled and lean, a regular Apollo. He sauntered over to us, gave me a big toothy smile and, flipping my right foot out of my sneaker, began strapping my foot into one of the stirrups. When I was lying flat on the bench, my legs didn't reach the ground, but the stirrups, which were attached to the bench by long leather straps could be adjusted to my leg length. They really were quite comfortable when Steve had gotten my feet strapped into them.

Gabe put a set of bells on the stand, and I took hold of the bar. He wrapped his big fists around mine, but let me provide all of the power in the lifts. I had done a couple of lifts before I even noticed that Steve had his hands on my knees, and I probably wouldn't have noticed even then if he hadn't been working his hands up my thighs.

"What?" I said as I looked up sharply. Steve was still smiling that smile, but he had lost the towel and his prick was standing at attention. I started to lurch up, but Gabe swiftly tied my hands to the ends of the barbell rack with leather straps I hadn't noticed being there before.

Steve's hand went up into the legs of my shorts and stroked my dong through my jock strap. I started to curse them both in a loud voice, but Gabe just laughed and told me to go ahead and yell. No one would hear. I looked back down at Steve, whose hands had withdrawn from my shorts, and my eyes opened wide as I saw him coming at me with that pair of scissors.

"Be still, or you'll get hurt," he said, as he snipped at the hems of my shorts and gym shirt with the scissors. Then, in almost simultaneous motion, he ripped off my shorts and, after cutting the bands on my jock strap, ripped that off as well. At the same time Gabe reached down, took the hem of my gym shirt and just ripped that off my body.

"Hmmm, nice, Steve, said, as he took my now-naked and quivering body in." I gasped, as he took my dick into his mouth, He swallowed it all the way to the root in one gulp, and, I couldn't help myself, it started to engorge.

"There, that's good," Steve said, as he withdrew. "We'll have this stiffened up in no time." He licked down to the root on one side and then back up the head, which he took into his mouth. He rimmed the underside of this with his tongue and then moved the tip of his tongue to my piss slit, which he flicked back and forth while I moaned quietly in guilty ecstasy. His hand went to my balls, which he rolled and pulled gently.

I felt something hard and moist strike my cheek, and I looked up to see, to my horror, Gabe's huge dick and balls suspended above me. He took my head between his two big mitts and positioned my mouth under his dick and commanded me to suck him. I refused indignantly, and suddenly I felt an excruciating pain in my balls, which Steve was crushing.

"Do as he says," Steve commanded, "or you'll be singing soprano tomorrow morning." So I started tentatively giving Gabe head. Meanwhile, I felt my legs being pulled apart and up by some unseen adjustment Steve had made to the stirrups and Steve took hold of me by the hips and slid me until my butt cheeks were off the end of the bench. The next thing I felt down there was Steve's tongue. He started rimming my ass with his wet tongue and flicking his tongue in and out of my ass. I felt myself tighten up down there initially, but as his tongue probed deeper, I felt myself loosening and my ass passage relaxing and widening. I was enjoying this now. I could continue to fight it, but I knew I was beginning to want this.

Gabe took his dong from my mouth and moved around the bench, straddling me above my chest and coming at me again with that big cock of his.

"Rim it," he commanded, and I took the knob of his cock into my mouth again and ran my tongue around where the glans met skin.

"Open wider," he said, and as I did, he pushed his cock farther into my mouth, and I almost gagged on the load.

"Don't fight it," he said. "Stay relaxed and open and you'll manage just fine. This is all quite natural; it just takes some experience."

I tried to do as he said, and I found that I could, indeed, manage the slow pumping action Gabe had set up. After a few minutes, I found, also that, if I brought my tongue into play around his glans, he spent more time right at the entrance of my mouth and less time probing the back of my throat.

Meanwhile, Steve had taken some cool salve of some sort and slapped it on my asshole and was slowly working his fingers into my ass; first one finger and then two, and eventually three. I jerked as he found my prostate. A jolt of sexual arousal and pleasure shot through me.

Gabe reversed above me, taking my cock in his mouth and presenting his cock, balls, and asshole for me to lick and suck.

I gasped and lurched again when Steve entered me. He held his dick just inside my hole until I had adjusted and then just drilled it in deep and plowed me. I began to buck against him in a passionate response to the action of his dick.

All of this was just too much for me, and I shot off in Gabe's mouth, my cum bubbling out of his mouth and down onto my belly. Gabe cleaned me off and then got off me and went behind Steve, where he entered him, and fucked Steve in rhythm with Steve fucking me.

When they had both come, they released me and told me to go off to the showers and then I could dress and leave. They were laughing and joking and saying we'd all gotten a good late-night workout. They acted like they'd done nothing wrong and that I had no reason to be upset. And I went along with them; I certainly didn't want to make them angry. They had the cheapest gym in this part of town, and there was a long waiting list for members. They were nice enough to tell me they'd take the cost of the shredded gym top and shorts off my monthly bill.

But that was all just rationalization on my part. Three nights later I appeared again at closing and they didn't even have to tie me down this time when they ravished me.

Locker Room Revelation

It wasn't a regular day of practice; only Hank and I had come in, and we'd worked out in the gym after we'd done laps on the field. I could tell he was steamed about something, but I didn't ask about what. He had finished first, and it looked like I had the locker room to myself when I came in from the gym. I took a quick shower and pulled on my briefs and some baggy shorts and an athletic T, and there he was, right at my locker before I had gotten around to pulling my sneakers on. There was fire in his eyes, and he slammed my locker closed with his fist.

"What's the matter, Hank?" I didn't want to have Hank upset at me. He was a real hunk of a man and could probably break me in two without raising a sweat.

"I saw you in Hardesties the other night, didn't I?"

Oh God, I was sure I wouldn't be seen going into that gay bar.

"Oh, shit," I said. "Okay, I admit I was there. But you don't have to tell anyone, do you? I was just . . ." If this got out of control and was talked around, I'd be out of a job.

"Tell anyone?" Hank yelled at me. "Don't you get it, I saw in you Hardesties. That means I was in Hardesties. I've wanted you for two years, and I just now find out that you are cruising."

I just stood there, giving him a blank look. And just as I got it, he was on me.

"Hank, I'm not . . ." I started to say, but I got nothing else out, because he came right up to me, wrapped his left hand around the back of my head and pulled me in to a hungry, almost brutal kiss. He had my lips parted with his and was sucking face for all his might. Meanwhile, his right hand had gone to my basket and he was feeling me through the two thin layers of clothing, finding my cock, measuring the whole length of It, and ending by grabbing my balls and almost lifting me off the ground. I groaned, and my cock began to engorge at the assault. While still holding me in a lip lock, his hand traveled up to my belly and then under the rim of my shorts and briefs and dove for my cock. Skin on skin now, and I found I was getting as excited as he was. I lost control. My hands strayed to the hem of his T-shirt and I let my hands slide under and then up his fantastic abs to his bulging pecs. His hands flew to work. He reached down for the hem of my T and pulled it off me and threw it to the side, and in the very next motion, he did the same thing with his. Then he jerked off his shorts, and there he stood, erect and magnificent, and not a little frightening. He jerked my shorts and briefs down in one swift move, going down in front of me, banging me up against my locker and attacking my hardening cock with his mouth.

"Oh, God, you have no idea how I've longed to suck this big prick," he said between licks and swallows. And, he was right. I'd had no idea.

"Straddle the bench with your legs and sit down," he commanded. I did so, rather numbly. I still hadn't gotten adjusted to the sudden assault. He sat down facing me. His big dick running along the bench seat, pointed at me. He scooted up to me, so his knees were pushing mine out and away from the bench, put a big mitt on my chest and said, "Lay back."

I laid back as his hand pushed me down. He leaned in over me, his dick running up beside mine and I gave a little shudder as his mouth went to my nipples. First the right one and then the left. He sucked and nipped and bit, and I squirmed. Not knowing what else to do with them, my hands went to his shoulder and back muscles and I massaged them. He didn't stay at my nipples long with his mouth. He didn't seem to be staying anywhere very long. His tongue and sucking kisses moved to my sternum and then descended as his hands covered my pecs and held me pinned flat to the bench. He was sliding away from me now, and I lost touch with his prick. He was at my navel, tonguing and sucking and then on my flat belly, tonguing through my pubic hair, and he had my rod in his mouth again. He spent a little longer there, as I did some squirming and bucking and trying to reason with him.

"Umm, Hank. Don't you think we should be going slower on this—and maybe somewhere else, if at all?"

"Shut up, stud," was his reply. "I've been building this up for you for two years and I never knew I had a chance. I think I'm going to explode, and when I do, I want it to be in you." That sounded rather ominous, and I started to try to get up, but he pushed me back with his strong arms and latched onto my prick with his teeth. I was hard and panting when he left my rod and moved to my balls. He swallowed those whole and then popped them out and gave them some nibbles. The last few minutes he had my cock in his mouth, he had brought his right hand down and was fingering my asshole. Directly from my balls he moved to my asshole with his lips and tongue and slobbered me up pretty good down there. I was afraid he was going to make do just with that; I knew from his grunting and groaning sounds that he wasn't going to wait long to split me, but he reached down and came up with a little tube of lubricant. He had come prepared. He quickly lathered up my hole and stuck his finger in it, pushing on in past the sphincter and being drawn to my prostate, which he firmly pressed, causing me to almost piss, but quickly making me moan and leak cum.

He rose up on his feet, his erection standing straight out from his body, and lathered his tool up as I watched in awe and fear. He was a wild man. I knew it would be useless even to try to stop him or slow him down.

"Turn over on the bench," he said. And then when I didn't react fast enough. "Turn over, I said," and he reached down and pulled me up and flipped me over. My hard cock was painful lying between my body and the hard, cold bench, but Hank wasn't to be denied. His lubricated fingers went back to my ass, and he inserted them and forced the hole more open, all the time rotating and flipping them up and down, driving me crazy. Then he had his hands on my hips and pulled my butt up in the air.

"Stand where I put you," he directed, and he moved me up to the level of his cock, where he was standing behind me.

"Umm, Hank, I've never really . . ." His answer was a slap across one of my butt cheeks. While holding his left hand to my left hip to show what level he wanted me to maintain, his right hand guided his cock to my hole and he pushed in to the rim of the glans.

"God, Hank, just hold on a minute!" He did hold there several seconds, but then was pushing again. He had trouble getting farther in, and commanded, "Widen your legs. Give me a bigger hole." I wondered really how I was going to manage that, but I did widen my stance. I had one arm between my head and the bench to protect my brains from being banged to death and the other arm was wrapped around the bench to keep me steady. Hank was now using both hands to pull my butt cheeks as far apart as possible. With a grunt, his dong went past the sphincter, which pulled him in a few more inches.

"Ahh," he intoned, as he held there for a few seconds. But then, with another grunt he was pushing right on in. I screamed in pain, but subsided as the pleasure of being wanted this much by another man and of being so intimately stuffed to the fullest turned the pain to pleasure. And then he was pumping, taking slow, long strokes to begin with. Fully encased, He stood, bringing me up with him. He buried his mouth in the side of my neck, finding the throbbing artery there and driving me wild with ecstasy. I arched my chest, pulling my butt up to give him full, close access. I then laced my hands behind his neck, drawing my torso taut. He had his hands on my chest, rubbing my nipples with his thumbs.

Soon after that he lost himself and pushed me back down on the bench, planted a strong hand in the middle of the small of my back, and just pumped wildly away, until with a scream of satisfaction and fulfilled fantasies, he shot his load deep inside me.

Hank collapsed on top of me then, wrapping his arms around me and nuzzling in my neck. "That was the greatest, baby," he cooed in my ear. "You are just the fuck that I imagined."

"Hank," I whispered. "Could I say something now?"

"Shoot."

"When you saw me in Hardesties, I was just trying to pull my kid brother out of there. I'm not really gay. I've never done it with a guy before."

There was a fairly long pause as this sank in.

"Oh, my so sorry," Hank responded, all embarrassed. He started to pull out of me and stand up.

But, I whipped both of my hands back to his butt cheeks and pulled him back into me. "No apologies necessary, Hank. Could you fuck me again, please—just like that last one?"

Loosening Therapy

I was standing in the small room, in front of a curtained window. Paul's hot breath on the back of my neck was doing little to dispel the tension that was tying me in knots, even though that's exactly what we were here for. The room was pretty dreary really; just this curtained window and a padded massage table behind us against the wall. Tired paint on the walls, scuffed tiled floor and ceiling, as if men before us had been walking the ceiling and dragged across the floor, which, for all I knew, was exactly what had caused the scuffing. A set of loudspeakers above and at the corner of the curtained window. Paul's arms came around me, and he started to unbutton my shirt and pull the tail out of my jeans even before he pulled on the curtain cord.

I didn't want to lose Paul, and this might be my last chance to keep him. We'd met at a book event. He was the author, and I was the fascinated reader. We'd talked while he autographed my copy—and I'm afraid I'd gushed about his book. He had taken that in stride and had invited me for coffee after the signing. I was a young, impressionable college student, and he was a good twenty years older than I was—but very distinguished and handsome. Gray at his temples and dancing green eyes that held mine. Thick, sensuous lips, a cleft chin that made him look very urbane, and a well-toned bod. We weren't finished discussing the exotic substory line in his book when the café was closing, so he invited me to his place for a nightcap. His apartment matched my suppositions in sophistication; we kissed on his deeply upholstered couch, and he had my fly open and had sucked me off, with me shooting off quickly, before I managed to escape in embarrassment and confusion.

Two days later, he saw me loitering on the sidewalk in front of his apartment building, and, without words, he came down, took me by the hand, and led me back inside his door. We 69ed on his bed for hours, with him trying to take it farther, and me breaking it off in fear. I'd given and gotten both hand and blow jobs over the past year, but it had never gone beyond that.

Paul wanted to fuck me. He had no interest in me topping him. I wasn't adverse in theory, but I'd tighten right up whenever we got to the brink. He was big and thick and long— and I was terrified of the pain. After our fourth meeting, he was positioned and entered me, but as soon he had, the pain was just too much for me. I tightened right up and screamed for him to stop. His frustration was palpable, and I declared I wanted it but just couldn't do it—that perhaps we needed just to give up on the effort and on any idea of a relationship in the fullest sense. I could tell that he was conflicted, though. He said he was smitten with me, but I knew he couldn't be satisfied with just hand and blow jobs. I cried, and he gently massaged my body and then tried again, but I just couldn't take him; it was just too painful. He then said he had an idea that might help, and so here we were, two days later, in a back room of a men's club, standing in front of a curtained window.

I had to believe that I meant a lot to him for him not just to cast me aside. I cared for him too, so I was trying my best to get over the barrier.

Paul had my shirt open and he was stroking one of my nipples with his hand. He reached over with the other hand and pulled the curtains open, and I let out a shocked gasp.

We were looking through a wide, full-length glass partition into another small room, almost identical to the one we were in. Hung by his wrists from straps only about two and half feet away and facing us on the other side of the window was a young man of only nineteen or twenty, with a thin, twinkish, boyish build. He had a mop of curly red hair that almost came down into his eyes as his head hung down, and, as he was stark naked, I could see a patch of red pubic hair surrounding a smallish, pert cock hanging down between his legs. Despite his thinness, he had good muscle tone and was a handsome lad. He looked like a lad, but I vaguely remembered him from one of my college classes, so I'd say he couldn't be much younger than I was. The pads of his feet barely touched the tiled floor.

I started to say something to Paul, but he told me to hush and just to closely observe what was happening in the other room. One of his hands was still massaging my chest, and the other had moved to undoing my belt buckle.

I heard a hollow sound and looked toward its origin, which was the speakers at the top edge of the window on our side. These were conveying the sound from the other side of the glass. A door had opened in the other room—behind where the young man was hanging—and I let out another gasp when I saw the men who had entered the room. He was massive, but not in any way fat. He was heavily muscled, and sharply defined in every respect. He seemed about the same age as Paul, but he obviously was a fanatical bodybuilder. He was dark to the point of swarthy, with salt and pepper-colored hair that covered his body in short ringlets that kept him from being defined as more than borderline bear. He had a short-cropped beard and mustache and a buzz cut hairstyle. Gold rings gleamed at his left ear and in both of his nipples, and there were barbed-wire tattoos encircling both of his arms across the biceps. The only thing he was wearing was a black leather, studded harness across his chest and leather over-the-ankle boots. What had made me gasp, however, was the horse-hung cock and tennis-ball-sized balls swaying back and forth between his legs as he approached the bound young redhead from the rear.

I felt my pants and briefs hit the floor. Paul had freed them as the dark monster had entered the other room.

The monster stopped and stood very close behind the young redhead. He nuzzled the young man's neck with thick lips in a lingering caress, as his big, thick-fingered hands ran up the sides of the youth from the hips to his elbows. The redhead lifted his head, showing me a frightened expression, and murmured in low tones I could barely hear, but I thought they sounded something like, "No, no, please don't," repeated over and over.

I flinched as I realized that Paul was naked now, his cock running up my back. He pulled my shirt off and nuzzled his lips into my neck and mirrored the hand movements of the monster on the other side of the window.

"Paul?" I asked, a shiver of fear in my voice.

"Hush, hush," we whispered to me. "Just concentrate on the young man on the other side of the window. Watch him carefully, and keep constantly in your mind that he is slighter than you are and that the man behind him is much longer and thicker than I am."

I watched in mixed horror and fascination as the older man on the other side of the window ran his hands all over the body of the redheaded youth, paying particular attention to his nipples and his cock and balls. Paul was doing the same with me, and I found myself moaning in just a slightly lower tone than the youth facing me was. His pert little cock was standing straight out from his red bush, as my longer and thicker one was doing out of my blond bush. Paul turned my face to his, and we lingered in a long, juicy kiss. I was willing myself to loosen up for Paul—but this concerted effort, of course, only kept me tight and fidgety.

When I was able to look back around, the bigger man appeared to have disappeared, but as I focused more closely on what was going on, I could see that the redhead's chest was arched forward and his hips pulled back, and he was standing on his very tiptoes. His tormentor was crouched behind him, his face firmly wedged between the youth's butt cheeks, and his hands wrapped around to the front of the youth's thighs. The redhead was grunting, giving out little yip yip sounds, and writhing his hips back and forth as much as his precarious position would allow.

Paul's lips and tongue were at my asshole as well now. He was forcing my butt cheeks open with the palms of his hands, and I almost lost my balance as my chest arched forward. My hands involuntarily pushed out in front of me to keep myself from falling, and my arms were now widely spread, palms against the window. I pressed my forehead against the glass, my eyes glued on the eyes of the redhead, and groaned and grunted at having my ass wetted and eaten out by the man I idolized.

The redhead couldn't see me—or so I had assumed. Paul had told me he couldn't, but it now occurred to me that that was just part of the illusion obviously being played out for me. By watching the redhead's eyes, which looked directly into mine, I could see his fear and resistance melting and his eyes hooding with desire. And I was going with him on this, moaning and groaning and sighing at Paul's tongue work inside my hole, on my tender inner thighs, and up through my legs on the underside of my cock.

While our asses were being worked, the redhead's cock and balls were getting attention from big, swarthy hands, and so were mine from Paul's long, elegant fingers. I began to move my pelvis in rhythm with Paul's ministrations—and the redhead was moving his as well.

The monster and Paul rose up on their feet behind their objects of desire almost simultaneously, and both produced gobs of lubricant and started to lather up holes and cocks.

The redhead was back to begging for mercy in a low, hoarse voice, and I felt myself getting more tense as well.

One palm on bellies and the other hand loosening and widening up holes with lubricated fingers, both dominators were working their targets.

Paul hissed at me to keep my eyes and senses locked onto the redhead, and I concentrated there as best I could.

I watched in horror and fascination, as the giant in the other room lifted the legs of the redhead and pressed the soles of the younger man's feet wide apart on the window separating us. His feet were precisely on the other side of window from where my hands were pressed. I was closely staring into his face. Paul was pushing my legs wide now, but I was lost in the gaze of the redhead, the intense concentration he was showing. The palpable fear mixed with anticipation. The giant crouched his thighs under the raised thighs of the younger man. When the redhead screamed at the pain of first entry, I screamed too, feeling the cap of Paul's cock rotating around, corkscrewing just

253

inside the rim of my hole. We'd been here before, but I hadn't been able to go any farther.

The redhead was sweating, his muscles knotted tightly, his head thrown back. He was crying and babbling incoherently at the ceiling. having lost eye contact, I looked down between the redhead's legs and I could see the bulky shaft of that horse-hung cock slowly working its way into the young man's hole. An inch in, a half inch withdrawal, and then another inch in. The redhead was taking him; his hole was opening up to the assault. He wasn't being split. The hole was naturally opening to the monster cock.

Paul wasn't *that* massive. If the redhead could take that . . . , I thought.

I felt Paul tugging back on my hips, widening my legs farther and opening my butt cheeks more as he pushed inside me. We had never been this far before. It hurt like hell, but, for the first time in our attempts, his mushroom cap had reached my prostate and he was rotating his cock around inside me with one hand—his other hand still holding me to him with palm on belly—stroking my prostate with it and sending little electric currents of pleasure and engorgement through me that were fighting with the pain.

Panting hard, I persevered. If the redhead could take *that*, surely I could . . .

I heard a scream of "Yes, yes," through the loudspeaker, and looked back up through the mirror, catching sight of the redhead's eyes again. His countenance had completely changed. His eyes were wild and shining with desire now. The monster's cock was completely sheathed inside him and was pumping inside him with little strokes.

The redhead was thrashing his head back and forth, yelling, "Gawd, yes. Gawd, yes. Fuck me. Deep, deep, split me in two." He obviously was enjoying the fuck now, having a huge cock buried inside him. The pleasure and lust in his eyes were revelations to me. This is where Paul had been trying to go. All I needed to do was get past that first pain, and I could have this. I could be crying for it just like the young redhead was. There was no doubt now what he wanted the big monster to do to him.

I laid my head back on Paul's shoulder and whispered to him. "If it could only be like that, Paul. If I could only loosen up enough—get through the pain enough—to get to where that guy is, the pain would be worth it."

"Guess what, sport," Paul whispered back. "I'm in to the root now, and I'm going to pump you deep too, just like that redhead is getting it. You did open to me. You relaxed to me."

I cried out in surprise as I realized that Paul had started churning and throbbing deep inside me—and that I could take it. No, that I loved it. We had done it. I felt the remaining tension draining out of me. My butt cheeks and ass canal were relaxing. I was opening more. Paul felt it to, and I heard the intake of his breath as his cock lengthened and thickened in response and he reached new depths inside me. We were a unit now, moving as one. I had a masterful lover.

I looked at my hands. The fingers were scrunching against the window in rhythm with the stroking of Paul's cock inside me. The redhead's toes were scrunching just on the other side of the window in the same rhythm. He was using his own hip and butt muscles now, rising away from the giant's pelvis as the giant's cock slid out of him and then pistoning back down as the older man plowed back up into him. It was fascinating to watch; nine or ten inches of juicy veined monster cock sliding out of that once impossibly tight, but now perfectly fitting hole and then alternately gliding and plunging back into the root. They were both pounding away furiously now, and I heard the scream of release from both of them as the monster flooded the redhead's insides with his spunk.

I was imagining Paul's cock doing the same thing in my hole, and I trembled and moaned at the feeling of finally being totally fucked. Paul was going wild at my back door, yelling at how sweet my ass was and how he'd never had such a glorious fuck.

After coming, the giant was holding there, jerking the redhead to ejaculation with his big mitts, as Paul pulled me away from the window, backed up to the massage table at the rear of our room, and turned me on his cock until my back was on the surface of the table and he was between my legs. He held my legs up and out then and pumped me in long, slow strokes, until he brought his mouth down to my nipples and tongued them and nipped them. I sighed and moaned deeply for him, begging him never to stop, to ride me and ride me. I never thought I could want it this bad, to open this wide and unconditionally to a man standing between my legs, churning his cock inside me.

I felt him tighten up, ready to shoot, but he buried his cock deep inside me then, and held himself very still, while he draped my legs on his shoulders and both of his hands went to my cock and balls. With him still rigid against me, I writhed all over the table in never-before-imagined pleasure while he beat my cock and squeezed and pulled my balls until I shot up his belly in three fountains. Then, with a grin, he wishboned my legs again with his hands and fucked me in short, rapid, deep strokes until he unloaded inside me.

He then came up on the table, laying beside me and cuddling me in his arms, as he roamed my body with his hand. I looked through the window into the other room, but the other men were gone now.

"Don't worry about them," he cooed to me in a whisper. "They were there just to help you get beyond your fear; to show you what was beyond the brief pain—why getting beyond the pain was worth the slight inconvenience."

"But he was so big and the redhead was so small," I murmured, still concerned about the physics of it all.

"Oh, don't worry," Paul snorted. "They're a team; they do that a couple of times a night. Very good at it too."

We were silent for several minutes, while we kissed and cooled down.

"What now?" Paul asked. "Shall I drive you back to the dorm?"

"Hell, no," was my spirited reply. "Take me back to your apartment and fuck my brains out again. I want to work some more on this therapy thing."

Malta Intervention

It was Giorgio's own fault. Really. Sandy and I were quite happy to do our part. But if Giorgio hadn't been such a snotty little bitch, we would have never done him that way.

For three glorious years Sandy and I had thought we'd found paradise on the Mediterranean island of Malta. We'd managed to live well on his stipend from the British Royal Navy and were quite pleased with our pleasant little art gallery on the St. Julian's waterfront. And we were more than pleased with our association with Rocco and Sebastien, both professionally and as partners in bridge, travels, and just sitting in the cafés on the promenades of whatever quaint Maltese seaside town or village we were exploring on any given day and making catty remarks about the passing tourists. Sandy and Rocco were of an "age" that neither wanted to discuss any more and Sebastien and I were much younger but fully satisfied by our respective "daddies." We were still somewhat different, however, because Sebastien enjoyed serving under his master whereas Sandy preferred me riding his waves. The differences all made for conviviality and some very torrid and amusing conversation.

From the beginning Sandy told me that we were destined to last longer than Rocco and Sebastien and to lose them as friends and coconspirators—and he was right. But he wasn't right for the reasons he supposed. He continually told me that when the top was older, the fire would burn out quicker; that as long as I was young and vigorous, however, we could fuck until Sandy was senile and incontinent. But Rocco and Sebastien had their break a long time before reaching that stage. Both Sandy and I felt the loss greatly when our little foursome broke up. And the split came on artistic differences, of all things, rather than any diminishing of their sex drive or ability to perform.

Rocco was the fine artist. We met him when we started to fill our gallery with his charcoal pastels. And we had started carrying his art before we realized that he lived in the old stone villa high on the hill on the road from St. Julian's to the capital city, Valletta. Sandy and I had often remarked on how intriguing was the villa's blood-red double-entry door and garage door set in a solid wall of ancient gray stone broken only by a curly-rodded black iron balcony over the door guarding a single French window in the second story.

The front of the house was right up against a curve in the road, and once you cleared that wall on your way back to the sea, the east coast of Malta opened up in a breathtaking view. Until we met Rocco we never could discern how good the view was from the side of the old house that faced the sea. And after we met him we fully understood what inspired his art as he worked in the room behind that French door to the street, but with broad windows open to the view of St. Julian's harbor.

When we were first invited to enjoy that view and he introduced us to his "other," we realized that we had known his resident lover, Sebastien, even before we ever heard of Rocco or his art. Young Sebastien, at once sensual and high strung, was the art critic for two Valletta newspapers, the *It Torca* in Maltese and the *Malta Today* in English. He had the best of art credentials from the Sorbonne and had even worked at the Louvre for a couple of years despite his young age. He had come to the Mediterranean for his health and had hooked up with the best artist he could find who was inclined in his direction.

It seemed an arrangement made in heaven, but it proved to be their downfall. Just when Sandy and I thought that our foursome could not get any better, there was a bitter battle royal in the old villa above St. Julian's that we could hear down at the art gallery in the harbor. Sandy and I made a mad dash up the hill in his Alpha Romeo, but we were too late. When we got there, Sebastien had already packed up and was gone.

Rocco met us in the doorway waving a copy of *It Torca* in his hand.

"Did you see what that little turd did?" he yelled at Sandy.

"Could I have been knifed in the heart by any greater treachery?" he turned and yelled at me.

Sandy and I were both mystified. Neither of us spoke Maltese, so there wasn't a prayer we could read the paper he was waving at us—and we were quick to remind Rocco of that.

"No problem," Rocco yelled again, and he disappeared into what functioned as his main-floor parlor, a particularly nice, warm-colored room overlooking a hillside terrace and a small, but inviting swimming pool. We could barely see the rim of the St. Julian's coast beyond the boxwood hedge marking the lip of the hill.

"No problem," Rocco screamed again, as he rushed from a back room with yet another newspaper, this time the English-language *Malta Today*.

"It wasn't enough for him to have stabbed me in Maltese; he did it in English as well."

Sandy and I gathered around and read the article in the newspaper, as a steaming Rocco fiddled around behind his bar, looking for some scotch to douse on the flames.

I could see Rocco's point and said so, in a way. Knowing something of art by now, I could also see Sebastien's point. I didn't want to see this break, though, so I tempered my comment. "I'm sure he didn't . . ."

"No, I'm sure the little prick didn't give two thoughts to my feelings, either," Rocco said as he moved back from behind the bar, scotch sloshing out of a glass far too large for anyone's safety.

That wasn't quite what I meant to say, but I let it ride. Sebastien's article praised Rocco's work but suggested that his talents were wasted on charcoal pastels—that he would develop his skills much farther by moving to colorful acrylics and that a place like Malta was just begging for him to do so.

"I don't think . . ." I started. Sebastien had been unthinking and not a little disloyal, I had to agree, to put that in print, but . . .

I didn't get any farther. Rocco gave me a murderous look and sank down into an overstuffed chair and began to blubber. The glass of scotch, still largely untouched, teetered on the edge of a glass-topped coffee table.

Sandy leaned down, moved the scotch to safer ground, and put his hand on Rocco's shoulder. Rocco huddled even more into himself, however.

"We can stay if you like," Sandy said. "Whatever you like. If you'd like to be alone, however, we'll return to the gallery and wait for you to call us. Whatever you like. You know we will be here for you when you need us."

Rocco continued to sob, but he did mutter his thanks and say that, yes, he didn't like for us to see him this way and it would be best for him to be alone for a while.

As we shut the blood-red double doors behind us and climbed into the Alpha Romeo, I whispered, "Is it really safe to leave him like this? Do you really think it's good of us to?"

"We had to leave just now," Sandy answered grimly. "You were tipping over the edge of saying the wrong things, and if I had remarked, I most surely would have said the wrong things too. It was disastrous for Sebastien to write that, but he's been trying to tell that to Rocco to his face for months now, and he's absolutely right. Rocco is limiting himself with the pastels. And they aren't selling well—or at least as well as his work should sell. His talent goes beyond that. Sebastien was right; he was just a stupid prig about it. And I didn't want to join him in that. And neither did I want to lie to Rocco."

That night, after the gallery closed, Sandy and I went up to the roof of the gallery with a futon and a triangular bolster, and we made wild, exhausting love under the stars and clear skies. In grief, I know, from the breakup of our erstwhile very congenial friends, Sandy, for assurance, wanted me rough and hard and deep inside him, repeatedly. And I obliged, pushing him first belly over the bolster and fucking hard down into him from the rear and then turning him with his back on the broad side of the bolster and rocking him on my cock back and forth on the edge of the triangle until we collapsed in a satiated heap. We fucked as if it was our last time, both of us thinking of the unfortunate split between Rocco and Sebastien—and feeling very vulnerable and sorry for ourselves as well. We kept looking up the hill to the old stone villa that was usually fully lit up at this time of night and alive with the sound of conviviality. But tonight it was dark and brooding. And then with nothing else I could do, I centered my frustration on twisting and turning and churning my cock inside Sandy until his cries for more subsided into whimperings of being well and completely undone.

The situation remained dark and brooding for weeks, as Rocco sank deeper in his depression. And often he was not there when we went up the hill to check on him. When he was there, we saw that he wasn't working on anything in his studio. He didn't even have his charcoals out and set up. But there was a mounting collection of empty scotch bottles lined up on and behind his bar. He was polite and welcoming to our presence, but in a absent, quiet way he had never displayed before.

For a brief time then we thought that he was coming out of his depression. There were signs that he was painting again. And when his first post-Sebastien work was delivered down the hill to be hung in our gallery, Sandy's eyes flashed with pleasure. It was an acrylic painting; it caught the gaiety of St. Julian's harbor and the separate blues of the Mediterranean and the bright sky perfectly, and it was far better than the charcoals Rocco had been doing before. And, justifying much, it was snapped up at the asking price by an oohing and ahhing buyer within days.

But then no more paintings came down the hill and we saw little of Rocco for two weeks. It wasn't long after that before we heard where he was going most evenings and what was absorbing his time. There was a new bartender from Venice at Tom's Bar in Floriana. Sandy dragged me over there one night just to check the rumor out and it was confirmed and we were totally distressed. Rocco was sitting there at the bar mooning over a swishy little transvestite who was serving him scotches. Giorgio was a cute little trick, but not something that we'd ever seen attract Rocco before—and he certainly wasn't any Sebastien. Sebastien was elegant and glib and had a great sense of humor. This Giorgio was pretty all right, but he was also coarse and a little piggish and reminded me of a ferret searching for food to steal.

Rocco saw Sandy and me lurking in the shadows of the club. He called us over, and we tried to be polite and inviting, but it was obvious that Giorgio saw us instantly as an intrusion and a threat.

Rocco suggested that we all meet at a seaside café over in St. George's the next day for one of our "catty gatherings," as we called them. He said he had missed our outings, and we readily—and genuinely with pleasure—agreed. We had sorely missed the outings as well. It was, of course, a disaster. Whereas the delicate balance of Rocco, Sebastien, Sandy, and Hank had been a perfect, made-in-heaven meringue, the replacement of Sebastien with Giorgio was a flopped soufflé. Giorgio resented every word spoken by Rocco to either Sandy or me; he was crudely vocal while saying he failed to see the humor in any of the well-crafted digs we made about passersby; and his own contributions were consistently dumb and off key. Rocco didn't seem to notice, but the rest of us certainly did. As stupid as he was, the odd-transvestite-out message certainly wasn't lost on Giorgio.

This being the case, and Giorgio being Giorgio, and Giorgio already having learned what a good deal living under Rocco's roof was, it was obvious to Sandy and me where this was heading.

The declaration of war came within a week. We had included Rocco's pastels we still had on hand in a gallery opening cocktail party when a cruise ship ripe with rich Americans was scheduled to dock at St. Julian's. We sent Rocco an invitation to be present and to use his abundant charm to help flog his work to the tourists. He didn't answer the invitation; but, then, he never had before and still he'd always shown up. This time he didn't materialize. At the height of the opening, when it was evident that Rocco could sell some of his pieces if he only was there, Sandy suggested I take the Alpha Romeo and zip up the hill and bring him down.

No one answered the door, so I pushed it open, as we had been given permission to do, and went in. I was about to

262

mount the stairs to the studio when I heard low moaning coming from the terrace. I went over to the French window to discover that it was Rocco who was doing the moaning. He was sitting, naked in a chair by the pool, his back to me. Giorgio, in full dress, was straddling his lap, facing him. Giorgio's face was fully made up with a vivid slash of red lipstick across his face. He was wearing a wig of long, black hair, which he was swishing around on Rocco's knees with his head thrown back. The bodice of his dress was pulled down to his waist and his black, lacy brassiere was hanging open. His skirt was also hiked up to his waist and he was waving two, thin, shapely legs on either side of the back of the chair. His legs were encased in long black stockings, and he was pointing the toes of stiletto heels at me. Giorgio was in motion, his answer for a pussy being moved back and forth on Rocco's cock. The transvestite was mewing softly, and Rocco was moaning and grunting at the effort of the fuck.

Giorgio lifted his head and saw me standing inside the French window. He gave me a languid, self-satisfied stare with mascaraed slitted eyelids. With one hand, he pulled Rocco's face into his chest, and I heard the suckling sounds of lips on a nipple. And with the other hand Giorgio, slowly lifted his palm and gave me a distinct, universally understood one-finger salute.

There was no doubt in my mind that the invitation to the gallery opening had never been brought to Rocco's attention.

When we had last met at the café in St. George's we had set the next gathering date in the harbor at St. Julian's. At the appointed date and time, Sandy and I were at the café, willing to try our best to make this work, both for Rocco's sake and for our own. A half hour after we were supposed to meet, we saw Rocco and Giorgio strolling on the other side of the harbor. Giorgio, a shapely and saucy blonde this time in a smart morning dress, was compelling Rocco to look at the displays in the shop windows, turned away from the harbor. Giorgio was giving Sandy and me looks, however. They were looks of hostility and triumph. And once again there was that raised one-finger salute out of Rocco's view before the two turned into a street running up the hill from the harbor and disappeared.

If Rocco were happy and if he was making the most of his art, Sandy and I would just have left him alone. But even though Rocco thought he was happy, we could see that he was growing older by the moment and losing his health. He had bags under his eyes whenever we saw him and seemed a little dazed. We decided that Giorgio must be giving him drugs. And there were no artworks coming down the hill, either pastels or acrylics.

We achingly missed the company of Rocco and Sebastien together. We even briefly considered selling the gallery and moving on to someplace else. But then we got angry. We didn't think we were wrong that Rocco was coming out of his depression before he was taken over by Giorgio and even was coming around to a reconciliation with Sebastien. Premier in our thinking in this direction was that he had painted an acrylic masterpiece, as Sebastien had been after him to do, and that he couldn't have been unaware that the acrylic was far superior to the pastels—that Sebastien had been right and had been trying to help make him the best artist and happiest lover that he could be.

Sandy and I decided to save Rocco from himself—and for us. That meant Giorgio had to go. No guilt there; he had declared war first, and had conducted dirty maneuvers. We would have made room for him even if the quality of the foursome obviously was going to make a nosedive. He was the one who had struck first and hardest. We had to intervene.

It turned out quite simple really. We arranged for a cousin Rocco cared for who lived on the sister island of Gozo, in Victoria, to be conveniently indisposed and needing to see Rocco just in case this was "it." Then we arranged for another friend to pick Giorgio up at Tom's Bar in Floriana, near Valletta after closing for a well-paid fuck. We were sure that Giorgio was still taking tricks on the side when he could, and we weren't wrong. We even had the friend specify that Giorgio would probably be servicing several men that evening—and Giorgio hadn't blinked an eye at the prospect.

The friend brought Giorgio in through the back of a leather bar in Valetta, to a private pool room, where we had gathered a smattering of leather-swathed toughies.

While Giorgio screamed out his indignation—presumably wholly because he spied Sandy and me—we laid him flat on his back on the pool table. Sandy held his arms and our friend and one of the leathermen each held a leg wide with strong fists around his dainty ankles. I then slowly unbuttoned his blouse and his bra and pulled them open and hiked up his skirt, all the time telling him that Sandy and I just wanted to become better acquainted with him. He had black silk stockings attached to a garter belt, but he wasn't wearing any panties, no doubt ready for the after-hours extra money he planned to make.

To bring home our regard for him, I took my wallet out and fished out a few lira and flipped them on the table beside where he was laying. I told him that Sandy and I would certainly pay him for his time, just as he had expected would happen— just as we would make sure that Rocco heard was happening— but that I thought a few lira was all a whore like him was worth.

Then I stripped; rolled on a condom that had been proffered to me; got up on the table, my knees under his butt cheeks; and in front of a cheering audience, I began to work my tool inside the writhing body underneath me. I had learned to be very good at what I did, and it wasn't long before Giorgio's curses of indignation turned into more passioned pleas to ride him hard and deeper. Sandy, still standing above him, let others hold Giorgio's arms and unzipped himself and presented his cock for sucking, and Giorgio readily serviced him with his mouth and his ruby-red lips. Giorgio didn't seem to mind now at all that Sandy and I were involved in his taking.

Giorgio's cock was getting bigger and bigger and he begged to have a hand released so he could pleasure himself. When we refused him, he begged for one of the spectators to oblige, but we refused that too. I just kept pumping and pumping him at one end, as Sandy was doing at the other.

When it looked like Giorgio's cock was about to explode, Sandy gave a command and I stopped pumping, Sandy withdrew his cock from Giorgio's mouth, and the other handlers held Giorgio very still, not letting him move a muscle until the surge toward ejaculation had subsided. We then started working him again, and, each time he was about to come, we stopped and held him off from release. He was whimpering and moaning now, begging us to finish him, crying that his balls were aching from the built up, unspilled seed. But we didn't allow him to release.

After the fourth standoff, I pulled out of Giorgio and Sandy joined me on top of the adjacent pool table, and we made Giorgio watch as I turned Sandy, stretched out, onto his belly, pulled his hips up with my hands, positioned myself between his thighs on my knees, and fucked him deeply and vigorously to our shared, lust-filled release.

Then, giving Giorgio a contemptuous look, we had him released, and we all just filed out of the room.

Needless to say, we never saw Giorgio again. He left Malta the next day, having cleared out of Rocco's villa that night before Rocco returned from Gozo.

We went to see Rocco the next day, and although he seemed sad and distracted, as well as we knew Rocco we could also see the underlying, unspoken relief. We found him sitting on the terrace, clothed and in front of an easel.

After we'd said our good mornings, Sandy, the cleverer and more sensitive conversationalist of the two of us, said, "What are those paints in your paint kit, Rocco?"

"Acrylics," Rocco said simply, offering no further explanation.

Not needing any, Sandy merely said, "Good. You know the one you did more than a month ago sold quickly at the gallery."

"Indeed?" Rocco said. He returned to dabbing his fast-drying paint on the canvas. But he was smiling.

"We found a telephone number for Sebastien in Nice," Sandy then said. "Hank and I miss him and are thinking of inviting him over for a weekend for a café crawl. Would you mind terribly if we did that? Of course, we won't if you mind."

Silence for a few seconds, and then Rocco said, "No, no, I wouldn't mind that at all." He was still stroking his painting on the canvas and looking squarely at what he was creating there. But he also was still smiling.

Master of the Boardroom

The reports of the week were winding down, and I looked around the table, only half conscious of what was being reported. The three older guys at the table would take care of all that for me. I was sizing up all of the young and beautiful people I'd stocked the board with. The power to do this was the joy of heading a robust family business; I could stock the board with the pick of the crop, and as long as I paid them top dollar, they'd all lay down for me. They'd stay with me through thick and thin—actually, thick and long in my case. Now who would it be this morning?

I had faced my seat at the boardroom table toward the big picture window looking out on the other big skyscrapers of Manhattan. This view gave me a sense of comfort and of power. I could feel the sense of power coursing through my veins now as I contemplated who it would be; hard and young and ambitious, cynical, and compliant. That seemed to suit me this morning.

"Chas," I said, as everyone was rising from their seats and shuffling their papers at the end of the meeting. "Could you stay for a few minutes, please?" A command rather than a request, which he very well understood.

"Yes, of course, JR," Chas responded. And the look he gave me of pleasure and anticipation made my cock stand at attention. I'd made the right choice.

I glanced around at the others I had been considering. Candice looked disappointed. Good. There was always this afternoon. Joe, however, looked relieved. I filed that in the back of my mind; maybe something really special for Joe when his next time came.

I walked around to the side of the table and pushed Chas's chair back as I heard the solid click sound of the door being shut behind the last departing board member. Chas was standing there, facing the table. I came up close behind him, a young, solid, blond hunk. I could smell his aftershave, a musky, inviting smell.

I brought my arms around him, under his arms, and started unbuttoning his shirt, leaving his tie in place. He brought one hand around to the small of my back and the other went to the back of my head and buried itself in my hair, a signal of acceptance and compliance.

I had my hands on his pecs now—a hard bodybuilder. His pecs jutted out and his nipples were already hard. I loved big, firm tits—on both a woman and a man. Surprisingly, arousingly, he had little rings pierced into the aureoles of his nipples, and I played with those briefly as I buried my mouth and nose in the side of his neck and enjoyed the musk of his body. He was even more a player than I had assumed.

I stripped both him and myself of our shirts and threw them to the side. I pulled him close to me and enjoyed the feel of skin on skin as I returned to playing with his nipples and pecs and then slowly worked my way down his belly and to the bulge at his crotch. After tracing his rising cock there, I started working at his belt and the buttons and zipper of his pants. He arched his back to me and turned his head so that we could go into a long, lingering kiss.

He had his hands at my belt and zipper as I found his half-engorged cock and pulled it out and started stroking it. He was sighing and moaning for me now, being able to tell that I liked that.

He had my cock out. I heard him gasp and felt him tremble, as he discovered how thick and long I was. He fondled it lovingly with both of his hands, holding the shaft at the bottom with one hand and running the fingers of the other hand around on the cock helmet, moistening every part of the helmet with my precum.

He arched his back to me as his cock hardened under my stroking. We kissed again, tongues searching tongues, before I pushed him down onto his belly among the papers on the top of the boardroom table.

I pulled his pants down and off and then started stroking his big, firm butt cheeks and his heavily muscled thighs, working my way to playing with his balls and dick from the rear, which he let me know he was enjoying immensely. My fingers went to his butt crack and I stroked him there to his audible sighs. His arms are flung out from his body on the tabletop, and his fists scrunched up sheets of paper in rhythm to my strokes, which became ever more penetrating at his asshole.

I opened a drawer and extracted a bottle of lube, flicked off the top, and dribbled liquid into his crack to the tune of his purrs.

I positioned my hardened cock so that it lay up his butt crack and I stroked up and down there. I could tell I was sending chills of pleasure through his body. I took my cock in my hand and slapped it around his butt cheeks, dribbling more lube on that on in his crack, until he began revolving his hips, anxious for my entry. And then I teased him by moving my hips in and out, poking at his hole with the head of my dick, pushing against his hole with him trembling with the expectation that at any moment I was going to penetrate him and thrust deeply up his passage.

I reached into the pocket of my pants, which were still hugging my hips and buttocks, and fished out a condom. I lubed up his ass real well and then opened the condom packet with my teeth and rolled the condom onto my throbbing shaft.

Pulling apart his butt checks with my hands, I moved the head of my cock to position at his hole. He shuddered when he felt the head of my cock at the door to his ass once more, knowing that this was going to be the moment of penetration. I took the cock in one of my hands and moved it around his hole, rimming him and seeking the best angle of entry. When I felt I had found it, I gently pushed the cock head into him. The bulb just plopped inside. He grunted in pain, though, and I heard the crackling of paper as he bunched up his fists ever tighter. But he didn't tell me to stop. I pushed in farther, beyond the sphincter, and I could tell I was rubbing against his prostate because his body twitched and lurched and he let out a breathy groan. I held at that level, rocking back and forth gently, rubbing my cock head on his prostate, waiting for him to open fully to me, waiting for him to beg me to fuck him.

"Oh, God; Oh, God," he was moaning softly to himself. "Fuck me, please, fuck me good," he murmured. I felt his ass walls loosening, and I slid in a good six inches.

"Oh, oh, awwww," he responded, and he arched his back up to me, raising his head to mine again, and we kissed. My hands went to those taunt ringed nipples and thrusting pecs again and dug in.

I stroked him at that depth for a few minutes. In, out. In, out; at first slowly and than a little faster, and finally pushing in those last two inches and a third that I'd gained since entering him until I could feel the skin of his butt cheeks being tickled by my pubic hair.

"Awwww, Shit! Awwww, Shit!" Chas screamed, as his chest fell hard on the table top and his fists beat against the crumpled stack of paper.

"Too much?" I asked in a voice of concern. "Should I pull out some?" I had no intention of pulling back on this marvelous fuck, of course. But then I knew that Chas was too much of an ambitious prick to show any sign of weakness or unwillingness.

"Hell, no, boss. Fuck me. Fuck me hard and deep. God, it feels so good. You're so good. You're the best."

Just as I had thought, and so I did as he asked—with extra zest because of his vaunting ambition and my own undaunted cynicism. I fucked him hard and deep, with short, slow strokes, gradually moving to longer deeper strokes, pulling out to where my cock head rubbed across his prostate and then a deep thrust into the center of him.

"Oh, baby, yes, oh, baby, yes," he kept muttering. He was telling me how much he loved it and to ride him harder and harder. I grabbed his tie and pulled it around to the back and held his body arched half up toward me with those reins, as I slapped his butt cheeks with the other hand, riding his ass hard.

When my legs got tired, I pulled him back toward me and collapsed into my desk chair, my cock still buried nine inches in him.

"Now fuck yourself for a while," I said, as I grabbed his torso to me with my hands buried in his pecs and my mouth buried in his neck. He grabbed the arms of the chair with his hands and used his strong leg muscles to fuck himself, both shallow and deep, on my shaft and to rotate his twitching ass around my cock. One of my hands traveled down his abs and into his curly blond pubic hair and grasped his cock and stroked hard.

At length, with a spasm and scream of pleasure, Chas's arm and leg muscles gave out and he collapsed back on me in a fountain of his cum squirting up and onto the very carefully crafted monthly company report on the table in front of us. His mouth found mine, and he offered his thanks, feigned or not—I didn't really care which—in the form of a bruising kiss.

With renewed strength, I lifted Chas and myself up out of the chair, turned him, laid him down on his back on the top of the table, and side splitted him until I had come myself in a scream of power and release. Even while I was spasming inside the luscious, compliant blond hunk, I was thinking of what I would be doing to the lithe, dark and hairy, but apparently not fully willing Joe after the next meeting of the board.

My Lover's Stepfather

This must be it; this must be when Shawn finally takes me.

That thought raced through my mind as Shawn brutally attacked my lips with his. We were stretched out on my dorm bed, me on my back and him covering my body with his. His tanned and muscular body, a gymnast's perfectly chiseled body, was undulating full length on mine. He held my arms above my head, his strong hands wrapped around my wrists, as I gripped the slats of the headboard and arched my pelvis up to him, willing his hard cock, stroking across my belly, to move down between my legs. I wanted him inside me so badly. I moaned for him and was begging for him to take me at last when he shut off my pleas with his lips and searching tongue.

His tongue invaded my mouth just as his hard, thick cock had done before he pushed me back on the bed.

I had never done this with anyone before. He was my lover. My first. He had come after me. I'd been reluctant at first. But he was just too beautiful, too persistent, too arousing. He had told me we wouldn't go all of the way—him fucking me— until he knew that I really wanted it.

Well, I had really wanted it for weeks now. I had told him so; I had done everything I could to show him it was what I wanted. But it hadn't happened.

Maybe it would happen now, though. I had brought him to the brink when I had given him suck. I could tell that he was about to explode. But he didn't. He withdrew and pushed me down full length on the bed on my back and made full-body love to me. I was the one about to explode now.

Shawn rose off me and turned me on my stomach, and he held me close, still trapping my arms above my head with the strong grip of his hands holding my wrists. I felt his cock move down the small of my back. I cried out for joy and turned my face to his, and he was deep kissing me again. His hard cock was between my ass cheeks, in my crack, rubbing across my hole as he stroked up and down across my hole.

I lifted my pelvis to him, willing the cock to enter me on an upward thrust. Not caring that I wasn't prepared to receive him, not caring that he was barebacking me, that he hadn't used lube yet, only his spit. Beyond caring for anything but for that last barrier to be crossed, for my lover to totally possess me.

I felt him shudder, and I felt the wetness of his ejaculate spinning up the small of my back, and he collapsed on me with a long sigh of satisfaction. His lips went to the hollow of my neck, as my hopes collapsed in another night of "almost," and not quite enough.

Shawn sucked on my neck, marking me as his—to take whenever he wanted, but not before—while I tried to suppress my own shudder. Mine not the product of release but of frustration and disappointment. When I was able to control myself, not wanting to whine or start an argument, or in any way move back from the brink we had almost crossed, I whispered the question I knew he'd understand, because I had asked it before.

"Why? Why not, Shawn? I've said I was ready."

"Not here, baby," Shawn whispered back. "Not here in this room. I want the first time to be special. Don't you?"

"The first time will be special, Shawn. I've told you that. All it needs to be special is that it needs to be you. You've overcome all my inhibitions. I surrender. But to you; only to you."

"Soon, love. Just not here. Not in a college dorm room. The place needs to be memorable—and separate from our everyday lives. Soon. Very soon. Give us a kiss."

* * * *

Soon came three weeks later, at spring break. Most of the guys were going to Daytona Beach. But Shawn and I were going to his family's remote house near Oriental, North Carolina, on the inland waterway inside the Carolina Outer Banks. It really wasn't all that far a drive for Shawn and me down Route 17 from Old Dominion University in Norfolk in his new Thunderbird, but his family was coming down from New York and Boston. Oriental was really remote, far out on a peninsula with only one road in from New Bern. Shawn said they had the house there because of the good duck hunting in the marshlands on the fringes of the Pamlico Peninsula.

"My stepfather is an avid game hunter," Shawn said. "Nothing he likes better than bagging fresh game."

"Your stepfather?" I asked. "Your father, then, is—"

"Dead, yes," Shawn said. "He shot himself right after my mother divorced my stepfather. I don't see much of her. She lives in Europe somewhere or in South America. Who knows from moment to moment?"

"Your father shot himself after your mother divorced his replacement?"

"Yeah," Shawn said. "It's not all that complicated. My father and stepfather were in business together. Their company builds skyscrapers across the Northeast. My mother went from one to the other—to my father's best friend and partner, and my father didn't get around to making a statement about that until after my mother dumped my stepfather."

"And you stuck with your stepfather rather than your mother?"

"He's the one with the money. So, of course I did," Shawn said with a mischievous smile. "Now, enough of that. You haven't noticed that Willy is taking in the sights."

Actually, I had noticed that Shawn had pulled his dick out of his pants and was driving down Route 17 with one hand on the wheel and the other stroking his cock.

"I really shouldn't be driving with one hand, Gabe. Help me out so we don't get a ticket." And with a grin, he pulled my face down to his lap, and I gave him head at 60 miles an hour down the East Coast.

"Take good care of it now, and it will take especially good care of you tonight, Gabe."

At last, I thought, as I took very special care of him in the North Carolina sunshine while cruising down Route 17.

* * * *

The Morton's house just a couple of miles outside Oriental must have been the seat of an early plantation on the inland waterway. The main house was an imposing, if not an oversized wooden structure with a southern colonial portico and six thick white-plastered columns holding up a full-length porch over the front verandah. The room Shawn led me to was large and grand, one of the corner rooms with French doors out to the second-floor porch. From these I could see down to the water and could make out pleasure craft taking the inland passage back up the coast from Florida to summer quarters in New England.

The bed was a huge, dark-wood four poster, whose highly polished corner columns were crowned with wooden pineapples, which Shawn was quick to tell me was the southern symbol of hospitality.

"I've wrangled you one of the best rooms, Gabe," he said, brushing the back of his hand up and down my arm and giving me goose bumps of arousal. "This is where your desires will be fulfilled, if you are as welcoming as these pineapples symbolize."

"Of course," I whispered in a hoarse, desire-filled voice. "Now?"

"No, not now. Joe wants us to picnic with him down by the water now. And what Joe wants, Joe gets. He's in the mood to bag some game and wants company before he sets forth. This room is for later. For you to experience an initiation beyond your wildest dreams. Now, isn't this better than our dingy little dorm room?"

"Yes," I answered in a small, thick voice. "But, Joe?"

"Oh, Joe's my stepfather. The others aren't getting here until late this afternoon."

"Others?"

"Yes. His three brothers. The rest of the firm of Morton and Stabler. The Morton brothers. I'm afraid I have to hold up the Stabler part all on my own now."

Our discussion was interrupted by a bellow from out on the lawn. "Hey, you comin' or not?"

The voice was gruff, deep, an edge of impatience. A voice not to be denied. Shawn had a hand on my arm, and I felt him give a little shudder. There was something in his face, something that I couldn't categorize. Just the sound of the voice appeared to have subdued him, changed him somehow. He wasn't as brash and expressive as he had always been in my presence.

"Stepfather Joe calls. Our's is to obey," Shawn said with a sigh. He took my arm and pulled me out through the French doors and to the edge of the porch.

We looked down onto the fore lawn of the house, and I saw him.

Joe Morton was obviously a formidable man. A king of industries who went straight for what he wanted and usually got what he went for. He was wearing camouflaged hunting gear with high rubber wading boots, obviously prepared to chase down whatever game he shot down over the marshlands. A heavy shotgun rested comfortably in the crook of a brawny arm that handled the weight with ease.

He was a good six and a half feet tall and was, by no means, a small-boned man. Plenty of meat on this man, most of it gristle. It was obvious that he didn't run his empire from behind a desk but with constant supervision at the top of unfinished skyscrapers. He had a rough-looking, squarish, florid face that probably had seen more of its share of barroom brawls, and he was bald, although the thick, dark hair on his forearms suggested that only his head was hairless.

"You comin' or not? Is that him then?" Joe Morton had turned his gaze on me, and I felt myself shuddering at the power in his voice and gaze.

"Yes, Joe. We'll be right out as soon as I swing by the kitchen and get the cooler. And yes, this is Gabe. I told you I'd bring him. Gabe, my stepfather, Joe. It's all fine, Joe. It's a go, we'll be right down."

I helped Shawn carry the cooler, which was pretty heavy with beer bottles in addition to a picnic lunch, down to the water. Joe had picked out a grassy place under trees with broadly reaching branches overhanging the water, where there was little verge between land and water, just a drop of a couple of inches. Not much in the way of sea vegetation on the margin right here either, although not far in either direction, tall grasses and cattails marked a transition zone of marshy land. There was a pier going a good fifty feet out into the water from here too, with a fair-sized boat house at the end, so it appeared that this was where the family moored their boats and they probably periodically had the water dredged in this strip of land. We were just around a bend of trees from a line of sight from the house.

We might as well have been the only three people on earth in this isolated spot on the remote Pamlico Peninsula. It was the height of the afternoon, and I could see sails far out in the Pamlico Sound, but certainly no one was able to see us.

We were shaded here under the low branches of the trees. The ground was mossy and soft. Shawn threw out a large blanket, plunked the large cooler in the middle of that, and started pulling out sandwiches and beer. The sandwiches were great, but the free-flowing beer was even better. Shawn and Joe were drinking Bud, but Shawn insisted that I drink my favorite, Corona, which he said he'd brought especially for me.

Eventually, Joe went off to do his hunting, and Shawn and I began to make out on the blanket.

The beer was going to my head. I must have drunk more of them than I thought I was. It wasn't long before I was pretty woozy and everything seemed to be happening in slow motion and in a blue haze.

Shawn was being unusually amorous, and I did nothing to stop him. He'd said we'd finally fuck for the first time in my room in the house, but if he took me here and now, that certainly was fine with me.

We were naked and Shawn was sitting on the blanket, facing the water. He had pulled me down to where I was sitting, facing him, on his thighs, with my legs straddling his hips. We were kissing and he had a hand wrapped around both of our dicks, holding them together, and was stroking them slowly. We were both hard as a rock and I was panting for him, pining for him to take me at long last.

We'd never done this before, and I loved it. I loved it even more when he pushed me down on my back along his legs and lifted my pelvis up to his face and was giving me head. I moaned and groaned for him, and he kept playing my cock until I spouted for him too. We'd certainly never done that before.

I was in a daze. I had no idea how we had changed position so that I was bent over the cooler on my belly, my buttocks presenting, ready for the plowing, but there we were. And Shawn was on his knees behind me, and his hands were spreading my cheeks and his tongue was at my asshole.

I writhed and sighed and grunted for him. He was going to do it. He finally was going to take me. I only wished I wasn't so drunk. Why was I so out of it? I'd never gotten this drunk before in my life. I was at the moment of fully coupling with my lover, and I was too drunk to do anything but lay there and take whatever he gave me.

Shawn moved around to in front of me. He went down on his knees and took my head in his hands and guided my lips to his cock and slowly slid into my mouth.

But what was that? Shawn was at my head, but I also had hands on my hips. Big, strong, callused hands.

I was almost lifted off the cooler in shock and surprise and pain, as I felt a bulbous pressure at my asshole—a club pushing to enter my virginal ass. I tried to retreat from the assault, but the hands were holding me fast at the hips and Shawn was now pinning my biceps in a vice grip, holding me down, belly plastered to the plastic top of the cooler, butt waving in the air.

I wildly pulled my head away from Shawn's cock and looked around to behind me, as best I could. I opened my mouth in a primeval cry that caused a flutter in the cattails nearby, and a covey of ducks took to the air, as Stepfather Joe's thick cock breached my sphincter and rose inside me, grabbing for the very center of me, possessing me, taking my virginity.

He was still wearing his camouflaged vest and those high-topped rubber boots, but he was otherwise naked. Big, heavily muscled, hairy, powerful, filling and stretching me to the limit.

And unrelenting in his deflowering of me. Together, the two men were just too strong for me, and I was too far gone from the beer—and not just from the beer, I groggily realized, but also from whatever they had put in the beer.

Joe was virile and strong and long-lasting and hard and thick and long. He fucked and fucked, while I weakly writhed and took him long and deep in relentless thrustings. It wasn't long before I gave over to the pleasure enveloping the pain. What was gone was gone. At this point, any release from the frustration was freeing. I still wanted Shawn; it would just now have to be later rather than sooner. Shawn pulled my face back down to his cock and I sucked him to completion, trying to convey to him that he still was my lover, and had spilled my seed myself before Joe was finished with me.

The haze overpowered me before Joe had withdrawn, but when next I returned to some semblance of consciousness, I was stretched out on my belly on the moss beside the blanket and Joe now was fucking Shawn. Shawn was on his back, with his legs spread, and Joe was crouched between Shawn's legs and pumping away inside his hole. Now that I could see the power of what Joe had between his legs, I almost swooned at what I had taken from him. Shawn's head was lolled to the side, facing me, and I could tell by the expression on his face that he loved this congress with his stepfather. Even in my groggy state, the truth of who was whose lover here and why Shawn hadn't taken me before now seeped into my brain.

After they were finished, Shawn helped me up to the house and upstairs and sat me down on the bed. He brought out another Corona and forced the cool beer down my throat. I was zoning out again as he took my head in his hands and guided my mouth to his invading cock, face fucking me to his completion.

He stretched me out on the bed on my back and was tying off my wrists above my head at the headboard.

Then he turned and walked out of the room. Still not taking me properly and fully.

My mind swam around with no focused thoughts until I fixated on the sensation of being penetrated again. I opened my eyes, or at least thought I did, and all was dark. Still, I thought I got some sense of being in that large bedroom on the second floor of the Oriental house. My legs were being spread by brawny hands, and I could make out a big, barrel chest hovering over me. Neither Shawn's young, sculpted muscles, nor Joe's hairy chest. Definitely not Joe—a full head of hair. Older than Shawn. I was being plowed, filled and pumped. I whimpered and protested, but I was too weak and groggy to put up any sort of resistance and I was bound. I heard a groan and felt a shudder and then relief as the pressure in my bowels lessened.

I drifted off to sleep only to partially awaken, on my side this time, to being encased by strong arms by a body stretched behind me. My leg was being lifted, and I almost was startled into full consciousness as a club thrust itself into my channel and began churning away. I started to scream out in indignation and surprise and pain, but a hand went over my mouth and pinched my nose, and I couldn't breathe. I was fighting for breath and unsuccessfully trying to pull away from the hot rod rising up my channel, only serving to pull a throbbing tool deeper inside me, when I blacked out.

The dream was so vivid that I could have sworn I was completely awake while I was being fucked a third time in that dark room. This time I was on my belly, apparently turned and retied at the headboard, and there was a heavy weight on my hips and hands holding down my upper arms, as again a hard tool was plowing my channel in long, deep strokes.

* * * *

The click of the bedroom door woke me the next morning. I was stretched out on the bed, naked and sore. Sore of muscles, but mostly sore inside my channel. I had no illusion that I had finally been fucked. But everything was hazy. Had

Shawn and I made love? It seemed like I had been fucked repeatedly, but somehow I didn't feel Shawn had been doing any of it. I was confused. But I no longer was tense from the frustration of not being fucked, because I definitely could feel that it had happened.

I looked over to where there was a wing-back chair in front of a fireplace. There was a small side table next to the chair and a breakfast tray on top of the table. I decided that was why I had heard the door click. I'd received breakfast.

I had to admit I was hungry. I painfully pulled myself off the bed, took a pair of jeans from my suitcase, pulled them gingerly on, and went over to the tray. I was pouring a cup of coffee, when I heard the braying of more than one dog out on the front lawn. Taking the coffee with me, and sipping as I went, I went out on the porch and over to the railing.

I arrived there just in time to see five men striding down the lawn toward the water, with three hounds nipping merrily at their heels. Four of the men were dressed as Joe was the previous day, prepared for a day of hunting. One of them was Joe Morton and three of them were almost carbon copies of him—undoubtedly the remaining Morton brothers. The head of hair on one of them brought back a painful memory. They must have arrived yesterday while Joe was fucking me down by the pier. I wasn't all that dumb. The "nightmare" of the previous night was getting a lot less hazy. I'd been drugged and bagged by the Morton brothers. It wasn't only ducks they hunted down on the remote Pamlico Peninsula.

The fifth figure, dressed in khaki slacks and a red T, was Shawn. Shawn, my erstwhile lover. A procurer of virgins for Joe and his brothers. Joe his real lover. Shawn broke away from the other four and headed around to the side of the house as the four brothers jauntily walked toward the marshlands, their shotguns slung over their broad shoulders, ready to continue bagging game.

I ate and dressed and slowly descended the broad staircase to the first floor, bowlegged and fighting the pains deep inside me that screamed at each step—pains not only inside me but also in my conflicted emotions. I should be angry and indignant, but I had wanted to be fucked—and now I certainly had been.

An elderly black man, dressed in a black suit, was waiting for me at the bottom of the stairs.

"Good morning, sir," he said. "Mr. Morton told me to drive you back to Norfolk this morning, sir. He and the other gentlemen will be out hunting all day."

"But Shawn—" I started to say. I had quite a bit to say to my college roommate.

"Young Mr. Stabler is already gone, sir. He drove out just a while ago."

Gone? Shawn gone? "But I came down here with him. We came together." I was having trouble processing. This was all just too much for me to process.

"Mr. Stabler isn't going back to Norfolk, sir. He's transferred elsewhere. He won't be going back to Old Dominion."

So much for all of my dreams of a first time with Shawn.

New Man at the Village Café

Me, trembling. I'd just noticed you watching me at the café in the square. I was sitting where the young men displayed themselves for the tourists, but I was new to this. More curious than anything else. Sure I could handle one of those paunchy, cigar-chewing, middle-aged American tourists—just a surreptitious suck—usually him sucking me—in the alley nearby and a quick 20 pesos and then maybe an East European. But I was told to look out for those. They'd pay for a suck—almost always them—but then take you deep in the alley and ass fuck you rough and hard. The advice was to stay near the mouth of the alley with those East Europeans.

You were watching me from where you were standing at the doorway of the café. I was sitting where we were told to sit, so I didn't know why you were watching me like that. You owned the café, but you made more off of the percentages young men like me slipped you to be able to display here than you made on selling thick coffee to rude foreign tourists.

You scared me a bit. Twice my size and a cruel look about you. Maybe it was the red-welted rapier scar that extended down your cheek from your ear lobe. Maybe that's what made you seem dangerous, dangerous in a swarthy, handsome, mysterious way. Rumors were that you had been a pirate off the

285

Colombian coast before buying this café—that this was where the money for the café had come from. And there were other rumors too.

Walking my way now, your eyes blazing, staring at me. Surely you weren't coming to me. I was sitting in the right place. You'd get your percentage. You were twice my size and so strong; you had nothing to worry about from me.

Bending your lips down to my ear. "In the alley. 50 pesos for a suck."

Shuffling toward the alley, the two of us. Me having second thoughts. More dangerous than an East European, I was thinking. I started to walk faster. You picked up the pace and grabbed on to the tail of my shirt, which I had been wearing open, an advertisement for the tourist clients. My shirt coming away in your hands as you did. You laughing; me beginning to pant a bit. Everything moving too fast. Your arm around my shoulder, as you guided me into the mouth of the alley, slipping a hand in my pocket, moving it to cup me and feel me and play with me while you found a place behind trash barrels near the mouth of the alley. Stay near the mouth of the alley, I was thinking, hoping, praying.

Pushing me against the dirty stuccoed wall and down on my knees between your thighs. Unzipping yourself and pulling out a huge, half-ready tool. I gurgled and you hummed as I sucked you. You giving me little time to adjust, thrusting and thrusting at me.

You dragged me up and pulled me toward the back of the alley. No, not back there, I screamed in my head. I resisted, but what resistance is possible to one such as you? And you own the café; if I wanted the easy money, I would need to keep you well pleased.

"Stop your struggling," you hissed in my ear. "200 pesos for your ass. If willing. Otherwise, who knows? Maybe you can find another café. Maybe I'll take you anyway—for free."

I stopped struggling and let you drag me to the darkness at the back of the alley. But what use the struggle anyway? You could have me if you wanted me now without the threat of banishment from the café. And 200 pesos was so much more than I dreamed of making today.

You impatient and cruel and thick and long, all of what I had been warned of the East European tourists and more. And overarching that, you were masterful, and I flowed and moaned and cried out for you, as I lay back over the bales of used paper and you crouched between my thighs and fed me fast and hard and deep. Passion and cruelty combining to lust—and not just yours but mine as well. And all good steeling for the future, I had to admit to myself.

"That was very pleasant," you muttered as you finished. "Well worth the 200 pesos; well worth more time and attention."

I didn't know what you meant, until after you had guided me back to the café, through the café, to the stairs in the dimly lit hallway beside the café's indoor room, now deserted because the warm weather had beckoned all out to the tables rimming the square.

The room above that you manhandled me to had a single iron-railed bed in the center. Ochre paint, probably once white, blistered off of the barren walls in tatters. Unvarnished, stained wood-planked flooring underneath. A scarlet scarf and a violet scarf draped over the headboard, the only adornment in the room.

Soon adorning me, the scarlet scarf wound around my wrists and tied off at the headboard rails, the violet scarf stuffed in my mouth.

Your cock stuffed once again inside me, thrusting, thrusting, thrusting, as I writhed underneath you. Overtaken in exhaustion by sleep while you were still riding me hard. Waking up, alone, if only briefly. The room dimmer in the late afternoon. The sound of your footsteps on the stairs. Your cock stuffed once again inside me . . .

Next!

I couldn't be there. I couldn't stay there. I didn't know what came next. I hadn't looked at the script. I just knew I couldn't be there.

I tripped down the stairs of brownstone and out onto the sidewalk of Richmond's Fan District. It was dark already. I instinctively turned left, toward the downtown area, and shuffled along with my hands in the pockets of my jacket. At least I had my jeans jacket. The weather had turned nippy. It had been much warmer just a few minutes earlier, when I'd gotten back. I just had on a T and my jeans, though, having pulled them on quickly at his command. It wasn't cold when he'd sent me out. But I was cold now. I was shivering. I don't know if that was from the cold, though.

Nick had sent me out for cigarettes. I didn't even notice until I got back that he had almost a full carton right there on the nightstand.

He'd sent me away so I wouldn't see.

Where was I heading. I didn't know. But, yes I did. I was so keyed up, there was only one place for me to go when I was in this state. Nick had denied himself to me for so long. It was driving me crazy. I'd never gone this long without it before. He was so controlling. And to come home, after a fool's errand, and to find him . . . .

I had to let off steam before whatever came next. There was only one place. Davey's Locker. I hadn't been in there for ages, and I'd heard it had gotten a lot rougher. And it was Saturday night. High party night. But for how I felt, the release I needed, it was the only place I could walk to. And my body already knew that, because that's where it was leading me. Right out of the Fan District and into the seedy tenderloin underbelly of Richmond's downtown.

Davey's Locker was right there where I'd last seen it. Even more rundown than before, but it was a Saturday night, and it had a good crowd and a noisy band giving off a frenetic, insistent, intoxicating beat. There were guys stripping down already and dancing on the bar—although it was a little hard to see them through the smoke clouding the room. The floor was littered with used condoms. It was going to be one of those nights.

I found a place at the bar in the wake of a Hispanic delivery guy being guided toward the rooms in the back of the bar by a big black dude.

I plopped down on the barstool, ordered a bottle of beer, and swiveled around to face the room. A blond college guy was dancing just to the left of me on top of the bar. He still had his briefs on, but a clutch of construction workers were zeroed in close to him, stuffing bills in his waistband and making offers, so I doubted he'd be up there very much longer. He seemed spaced out. Well, he shouldn't have come in here if he wasn't able to take care of himself.

I was beginning to feel better already. Fuck Nick, I thought. Fuck, fuck, fuck. To go and do that to me. Well, I'd show him. All these months. I had time to make up for. When I wasn't so keyed up . . . when I'd taken care of that . . . then I'd figure out what came next.

I watched a couple of well-muscled shirtless black guys dancing real close together right at the edge of the dance floor. Practically making sex with each other right there in the middle of the crowd. But not like they were the only ones. And they were making me forget already. My eyes were slitted, watching them, and I was running my hand down my sides and felt myself hardening up inside my tight jeans. I took a couple of quick swigs of the beer to cool down. But that didn't make me feel cooler.

The black dancers were pelvis to pelvis and were undulating suggestively against each other to the rhythm of the music. The taller, thinner one, was moving a big hand, with long, sensuous fingers, around the waist of the other one, and I saw it disappear below the waistband of the other dancer's low-slung jeans right where I could see his butt cheeks parted in the middle, and I saw the hand dig lower and lower. I could tell when the guy's fingers had found the other dude's rim, because the other dude went up on his toes and took the taller guy's face in his hands and went into a deep kiss. And he was shuddering the "finger fuck" shudder.

Then something, a big bulky something, with heavily muscled arms and blue, red, and green tattooing spilling out of the arm and neck holes of his white T, was standing between me and the two black guys.

"Hey," he said. Another construction worker. One that I'm sure the others didn't mess with, though. Solidly built. Some sort of mixed breed. Maybe Caucasian and Vietnamese. Or Hawaiian. But something built like a Mack truck. Black hair in a pony tail; it probably came down to his shoulders when he let it down. Square jaw, a serious body builder; barrel chest, tiny waist, a six-pack to moan for. Low-slung faded jeans with construction dust on them. Construction dust on the boots too. But he'd pulled on a clean white T before coming in here. I gave him extra points for that. Slit armholes; silky black pit hair. My cock told me I was interested. Was he next?

"Hey," I said back. I took another swig of the beer. I was probably drinking it too fast. But with what I'd just seen at Nick's, I'd be doing a lot more drinking tonight.

"Mind? You're clogging the scenery," I then said. He didn't move. He just stood there, swaying with the music a bit, giving me a sloppy grin. That's when I realized I had my hand on my piece. He seemed to enjoy the sight. If he wasn't next, I will have done something really stupid. But I wasn't in a hurry.

"I know you, don't I?" he asked, not moving—or at least not moving out of the way. He had actually moved in closer to me, jostled there by the slow swirling bodies of man meat on the make within the cloud of smoke.

I barely heard him. The band seemed to have gotten louder and to have put more of a thumping beat into the bass notes.

"What was that?" I nearly shouted.

"I said I think I know you," he repeated in a louder voice than before. "You used to come in here a lot. But then I heard you'd become Nick Jordan's punch. Nick Jordan, the movie star. You're his fuck toy, aren't you?"

"Yeah, was. Not anymore." I was too much into the beer to either take umbrage or to lie.

"Not anymore what?" He shot back.

"Not Nick Jordan's punch anymore. Looking for what's next, I guess." I gave him an "are you next?" smile.

He said something, but I didn't catch it, because I'd been thrown off balance. The blond college guy had lost his briefs and was being pulled off the bar by the construction workers. They brushed against me as he came off in their arms, and I almost lost the beer bottle. I chugged what was left and turned and plunked the bottle down on the bar top. The replacement was already there, and I took a long pull from that before I turned back to the room. The tank was still there, even closer to me, and still with that sloppy grin on his face.

"Next up!" yelled the barkeep. "Who's next up?"

"You were wondering what's next," the big guy said to me through his big grin. "That could be you. Dancin' on the bar top. I'd like to see that."

This wasn't like me. But I'd come here to be plastered and plowed into oblivion, so why the hell not?

Another swig on the beer. Then I peeled my T off and finished the beer in one long pull. I handled the bottle to the grinning tank and hopped up on top of the bar. I was greeted with whistles and catcalls all across the room. They wanted me.

The barkeep handed another bottle of beer to me as I kicked off my shoes—I wasn't wearing socks—and balanced on the top of the cold bar on the balls of my feet. I took a drag on

292

the bottle and then began melding to the beat of the music, letting my body go with the flow of the rhythm. The whistles and catcalls increased in volume, and I heard several voices trying to cut through the din in the room, trying to tell me something, to give me instructions. But I couldn't pick out what they were saying, and I'd never needed instructions on how to dance for the men. I'd done that in here a lot—before Nick.

It wasn't just the noise in the room; the booze was beginning to get to me. My ears were beginning to buzz. That was exactly what I wanted to happen. It had been too long. I had to punish Nick somehow. I took another pull on the beer and began to sway my torso to the flow of the music. I was running my free hand over my chest and belly . . . and lower. The hunky construction worker who had encouraged me to dance was still there right in front of me, closer to me, leaning into the stool. He had his crotch perched on the barstool and I could see that he had quite a package on him. And it was hard.

His was the first bill in my waistband. A twenty. Soon there were others; nothing less than a ten spot.

The barkeep was keeping a close watch, and when I'd topped $100 in bills, he yelled. Jeans! Jeans next! Lose the jeans.

I was a little reluctant to do that so soon, so I just moved the dance up a notch. I pushed the jeans far down on my hips, but I got more expressive in my dance.

What I could see from my vantage point was helping me perform, was loosening me up and giving me incentive. The pair of black dancers were still there, but their positioning had changed. The taller one was now behind the other guy, very close behind. He was leaning against one of the tables and his partner had his butt wedged into his lap and was doing something of a lap dance for him. The taller guy had one hand cupping one of his partner's pecs and the other fanned out on his belly. If they hadn't both still had their jeans on, they'd be fucking—still to the rhythm of the band music.

The construction workers who had taken the blond college guy off the bar top weren't nearly as subtle. They had the college guy's belly laid on top of one of the tables and his legs spread, and they were standing in line, rolling on condoms, handling their meat, ready to take turns in fucking him. The first of the construction workers was already plowing away and well on his journey to paradise. The blond was laying there with a silly grin on his face, his mouth bubbling, obviously either very drunk or drugged out. But with it enough to be yelling out "yeah, yeah," which took him off the endangered innocent list.

More money was being jammed into the waistband of my jeans, and the barkeep was yelling for me to get on to the next step.

A roar went up from the crowd, "Next! Next! Next!"

My own personal encourager leaned in to me and unbuttoned my fly and started peeling the jeans down off my legs. A roar of approval went up in the room. I'd been holding off because there were no briefs to display for the next phase.

The tank encased my cock in his hand and I continued dancing to the beat. He held his hand loose, so that I was fucking into it as I swayed with the music.

The first construction worker was finished with the blond college guy and drifted over to join the crowd gathering in front of me while the second worker in line thrust himself inside the blond. The blond gripped the edges of the table top, and I could tell he was moaning and groaning, but I couldn't hear him over the crowd and band noise.

The tank's hand was replaced with his mouth, and he was giving me head while I danced to the band. Money was piling up on top of my crumpled jeans. I downed the beer, and the barkeep sent up another bottle. I was feeling a little hazy, which was exactly what I wanted to be feeling, and it was getting a little blurry at the edges of my eyes.

I heard a cheer in the room as the third construction worker finished with a shout inside the blond college guy, and this caused me to shoot my load, which led to an even louder cheer—and more bills.

I wasn't sure exactly when the tank lost his clothes and moved up behind me on the bar, but about the time my beer was renewed, I felt his big, hard cock throbbing against the small of my back, and he was swaying with me to the rhythm of the band, which had added an even louder thumping of the low bass.

I turned my eyes on the black dancing couple. They had lost their jeans and the tall guy, without a doubt, had his cock deep inside his partner's channel, as they performed a writhing lap dance.

I had my eyes plastered on them and the rhythm of their fuck, timed perfectly to the beat of the music, as the tank split me from the rear. He took me down on my knees, and the crowd surged toward us so as not to miss a single stroke. He had his arms wrapped around me and I dully looked down at the undulating tattoos on his bulging forearms as he moved my body to him and away from him, holding his cock steady inside me and letting his manipulation of my body create the friction of the fuck. He was filling me and stretching me. Nick hadn't done this much, hadn't possessed me so fully and deeply. I was trembling and moaning, and gulping in smoke-laced air in heavy gasps. I was completely fucked.

The construction workers were finished with the college student now, turning their bulging eyes to me and the tank, and the blond was gingerly pulling himself off the table top and hobbling over to collapse in a nearby chair. He had his arms akimbo and his head lolled back and he didn't even seem to notice when another guy came over and fed a fat cock into his gaping mouth.

The black dancers were watching me watch them, and the rest of the room disappeared for me and for them for several moments as we became one rhythmic fucking movement. The four of us as one, perfectly syncopated group fuck. A ballet of plowing. The tall black guy and my own personal tank ejaculated at almost the same moment with a long, harmonious sigh that seemed to echo all over the room, experienced by a whole crowd of men lost in the incredible sexual experience.

There seemed to be a long interval of near silence, as the ringing in my ears pushed the sound of the crowd and the band into the background. If everything had been a blur before, it was twice as murky now.

I felt the hollow, cacophonous noise of the crowd and band music reasserting itself and the strong hands of the construction workers pulling me off the bar top and carrying me over to the table, where they had gang fucked the blond.

The barkeep was yelling, "Next! Next up!" and the crowd was beginning to take up the chant of "Next! Next! Next!" I took no notice of who replaced me on the bar top.

I was pushed flat on my belly on the tabletop, and the first in line of the construction workers was spreading my legs wide and pushing his cock at my hole. The rest of the gang was standing around me, licking their chops, tearing open condoms packets, and pulling on their meat. I looked wildly around for the black dancer pair I had briefly united with, but they were nowhere to be seen. I groaned and moaned as the construction worker split me and began to stroke inside me, holding me down roughly to the surface of the table with a fist in the small of my back. I wasn't going to complain. This is what I'd come for.

* * * *

When I awoke, at least enough to take stock, I was on a double bed in a room not much larger than the surface of the bed itself. I was on my side, naked, looking up at a window almost touching my nose. The panes hadn't been washed in a decade, a hole—maybe a bullet hole?—had been covered with a criss-cross of masking tape. Not much of a view. The side of a dingy red-brick building that went up higher than the window would let me see. Gauzy mismatched curtains hung limping off a white plastic rod at the sides of the window. Not long enough to reach the sill or wide enough to cover the window if closed. Paint was peeling off the walls, and there were cracks in the plaster.

Nothing like Nick Jordan's bedroom, with its mottled-paint burgundy walls and the king-sized four-poster bed in the center of the room, with silk drapes and satin sheets. French doors on one side of the room overlooking a terrace and lap pool and two silk-draped windows on the opposite wall overlooking the tops of Japanese maples planted out on the curb of the avenue running down the center spine of the Fan District.

Gentle snoring brought me back to the present. A beefy tattooed arm was slung over my side, and a thumb and forefinger were stroking one of my nipples gently. My back was wedged into the firm muscles of the tank's chest and flat belly, and my butt was firmly skewered into his crotch by a tumescent, but still deeply digging cock up my channel. I could feel the strong heartbeat against my shoulder blades and he had his lips implanted in the hollow of my neck. His sighing, even in half sleep, told me that whatever we'd done here was certainly good for him and that he planned to do it again and again before I would be let off the bed.

Was this my next?

Or should what I do next be to gingerly retreat from him without awakening him and return to the brownstone in the Fan District and call 911 and have them come attend to the AIDS-ravished body of Nick Jordan, the movie star. The man who had not let me touch him in months, even though we'd been oh so careful. The lover who had left me when he said he would never do that—who had sent me out for cigarettes when he didn't need them because he didn't want me to see him die. The life's companion who had sent me stumbling into the street to try to cover my grief and pain in an orgy of forgetting.

Next. What was next?

No More Evening Shifts

There were four of them who entered the store close to closing time, all muscled punks decked out in black leather. I owned the small convenience store but found myself behind the counter this evening because my regular night clerk called in sick.

The hulkiest of the four came up to the counter and puckered his lips and tossed me an air kiss. He asked me where Jake, my regular evening clerk, was. When I answered, he told me that I was cuter than Jake and that I turned him on. He asked if I wanted to join the group for a good time after closing. He didn't mince any words on what a good time would constitute. I knew Jake swung that way, which had never bothered me, but I told this guy as politely as I could that I didn't. But he kept right on sweet-talking me. I figuring he was just trying to keep my attention while the other three picked out some presents off my shelves for themselves, and this assumption proved to be correct.

I looked past the guy who was harassing me and saw one of his friends, a big black dude, heading for the door with a six pack of beer.

I brought my handgun up from under the counter where everyone could see it and, as confidently as I could, said in a loud voice, "I think you might want to put that back unless you are going to pay for it. And I have to close up now, so perhaps you guys need to go on to your party."

They left, but not without giving me meaningful looks and a few sniggers. Their bikes were gone from in front when I locked up and walked around to the back of the store to my car, and my mind was so full of business matters that I wasn't even thinking about them. But as I got out my keys to open my car door, there they were—all four of them.

Two of them had me in their powerful grip as the blond hunk that had harassed me and the black dude who had tried to make off with the beer stripped down. They both had strongly muscled bodies and were horse hung. They pulled at their cocks as the other two roughly stripped off my clothes.

The blond broadcast that he liked what he saw—better than the Jake he had expected to find here this evening. One of the guys who had stripped me waved my key ring in the air, and the blond hunk told him to go back into the store and get that beer they had wanted.

The other guy and the black dude slammed me down onto the hood of my car, and the black dude mounted my chest. He was holding my arms against the hood of the car with his knees, and he pulled my head up by the hair so that my mouth was touching the big glob of penis helmet dangling from his loins. He directed me to suck him and to be good at it, or I'd regret it. I took his dick into my mouth and did what I thought would please him with my tongue on his glans and piss slit, and he did indeed seem to be pleased. His dick began to thicken and harden. I could hardly get it into my mouth.

Meanwhile, the blond dude had gotten his hand under my butt and was assailing my ass with his spit-coated fingers. First one, then two, and then three. And he was finger fucking me. I couldn't help it; he was turning me on. My own dick began to harden, and the third guy swallowed it and began sucking me off as he rolled my balls with his fingers.

The fourth guy returned with several six packs of cold beer and a handful of condoms, and they all paused to drink a bottle off. I was in no position to say anything, though, as the black dude was rotating his cock around in my mouth, rubbing his helmet against the inside of one cheek and then moving it to the other.

The blond hunk took one of the condom packets and held it up to make sure that I could see that it was a Golden Ticket Magnum. Then he opened it and slowly rolled the condom onto his huge cock.

"Sure hope you stand behind your products," he said with a laugh. "Cause I'm going to stand behind you and test this fucker out. You'd better hope your goods hold up to the test."

He opened a bottle of beer, held it up, and said, "Think I'll try both of your products out on you. I couldn't find no lube in your store." He passed out of my view behind me and gave a command, and the other two guys were grabbing my ankles and wishboning my legs. I felt the cold neck of a beer bottle being pushed into my ass, and then, at another command from the blond hunk, my legs were being pulled up toward the windshield, my ass was rotating up toward the sky, the bottle was tilting up, and cold beer was gushing down my insides. I heard the blond hunk and his cohorts laughing at this trick. And then the blond hunk's mouth was at my asshole. He was slurping beer and pushing his tongue into my channel.

The black dude was right over my face now, pushing his dick deeper into my mouth. I felt cold beer being sloshed over my chest, belly, and cock and balls, and one of the other guys, whose hands were still holding my leg up at the thigh, was tonguing the beer off me. He was driving me wild with his nipping and sucking at my nipples.

The blond hunk stopped slurping and tonguing my ass, and I felt his bulbous cock head at my hole. He entered me and I lurched, forcing the black dude's cock down my throat and causing me to gag. The blond guy kept his cock helmet just inside my ass opening for a few minutes, rotating it around, encouraging me to open to him—which, luckily, I was doing. When he was satisfied, he started slowly but relentlessly to feed his long, thick hose into me, stretching me to the edge of endurance.

The pain and sense of being filled to the limit was excruciating, but I couldn't scream, as the black dude was now face fucking me deeply, and it was all I could do to keep from gagging and to try to catch my breath. I could moan, though, and I was doing plenty of that. And the blond dude said he loved my moaning and that I should do it louder for him. He also said he loved my tight ass, and that he knew the others would love it to. The others? I moaned louder.

The fourth guy swallowed my cock with his mouth, and my cock betrayed me, showing that it enjoyed the attention.

The blond hunk was in to the root now, and he started a slow, steady pumping action, which started off deep and shallow and slowly lengthened. The pain was subsiding, and, as it did, I found a sense of pleasure increasing. My cock felt like it was going to explode. And then it did, and the guy who was giving me head took the full wad and licked me off before pulling away.

"Liked that, didn't you sport?" The blond said. "Hardened up and came real nice. I knew you wanted to party with us."

Shortly thereafter, the blond hunk pulled out of me and shot his jism up my belly. In a loud voice, he proclaimed it was the black dude's turn, and my jaws were given relief as the black dude withdrew from my mouth, still kneeling above me, although his knees were now off my arms. He barked a command and one of the guys threw him a condom packet, which he neatly pulled out of the air.

"Cap me, bitch," the black dude said, as he put the condom packet in my hand. Once again a Golden Ticket Magnum.

My hands trembled as I fumbled with getting the packet open and then rolling it onto his giant tool. He then pulled my mouth back up to his dick and forced himself back into my mouth.

"Get it nice and wet," he commanded, and I felt the acrid taste of the condom in my mouth. When he was satisfied, he hopped off my chest. The other two guys let loose of my legs and the black dude had me flipped onto my belly and his cock moving up my ass chute before I had time to react. He was holding my torso down on the hood of the car with one beefy arm. His efforts to bury his enormous dick in me were causing him to grunt with frustration, and he commanded me to widen my legs. I did, and this helped him bury himself to the hilt. He got his big mitts under my chest and grabbed me by the pecs and arched my back up to him. He had me in a lip lock, and his tongue was now deeply probing my mouth just as his dick had been doing shortly before. He pumped his cock in and out of me like a piston and soon came in a big gush of semen that filled the head of the condom and made me pray that the condom would hold. He then let me fall in an exhausted heap on the hood of the car and pulled away from me.

I lay there, panting, unable to move, as the blond dude signaled to the other two guys and they stripped. They were both thinner and wirier than the blond and black guys, but they quite clearly were strongly muscled as well. They also didn't have the monster cocks of their cohorts. They weren't all that thick, but both were long and one had an unusual crook in it that brought the head up toward the guy's belly when it was erect. Both cocks were very much erect. The blond flipped them a couple of condoms—regulars this time—and they took their time, standing very close together and facing each other, in getting a condom rolled onto the other's cock.

The blond pointed to one guy and said "bottom" and to the other and said "top," and the bottom, the one with the straighter cock, came over to me, pulled me up off the hood of the car, got behind me, and pulled me back down on top of him. He got his feet on the inside of my ankles and pulled my legs wide apart. And his powerful arms held me in a full nelson hold, with my arms above my head. Thereupon, the top guy walked between my legs, spread my aching asshole with two fingers and helped the bottom insert his cock and run it up my canal.

I twitched and grunted, but this cock didn't compare to what I'd already taken in, so I wasn't all that much alarmed. But then alarm started to set in, as the "top" moved into me and started to push his own dick in above that of the bottom. I suddenly realized what the bottom and top business was all about. I was being sandwiched.

I screamed as my ass canal was being stretched and nearly split, and the blond and black dudes answered with gales of laughter as they finished off another round of beer.

The top, the one with the crooked cock, pushed into where the helmet of his cock was positioned directly on top of my prostate, and he rubbed me there until I was in a sexual frenzy and my cock was oozing precum once more. Then he pushed right on in, and the two of them started a counterpiston action that played my ass passage like a calliope. The hands of the top were wandering all over the bodies of both the bottom and me, and all three of us were alternating kisses. The top's mouth went to my nipples while I was in the lip lock with the bottom, and I just relaxed and gave up my inhibitions. I became adjusted to the action and went with the flow. My cock was rubbing up and down the top's belly, and all three of us came almost in succession—and my cry of enthusiasm was no less heartfelt than theirs.

The top and bottom disentangled themselves, and the black dude picked up my clothes and threw them at me, while the blond hunk opened the driver's door of my car and waved me in.

Relieved that they weren't going to worse with me, I headed for the door. I wouldn't stop to put my clothes back on; I'd wait until I had driven out of danger before I did that. As I got to the door, however, the blond hunk roughly pushed me down on my side across the seat and center console with his hand, lifted my leg over his shoulder, and fucked me in a side split one last time. Skin on skin. No condom this time. Deep strokes, in which he fully withdrew and then power-drived back into me and up to the hilt. I was moaning and sobbing, which he seemed to be enjoying a lot. And then I was enjoying it too. I had to admit to myself that I loved this hunk's cock up my ass. I started to go with his rhythm, and the blond sensed that I had given in to him at last.

"What do you think now, stud? Want me to pull out of you now?"

"No," I reluctantly moaned, "Don't stop now. I think I'm going to come."

"Tell me you like it," he commanded after a particularly long stroke that had me gasping.

"Oh God, yes, plow me. Plow me deeper." I felt shame, but the sexual charge had taken me over.

Satisfied, he continued pumping me. He wrapped his hand around my cock and milked me until I came in a splat on the pavement below the door sill. And this time he came in an explosion and a cry of pleasure deep inside me, bathing my insides with his semen.

He leaned over and whispered in my ear. "There, I own you now, you muthafucker—just leaving you a little something to remember me by until the next time. It was a nice party; thanks for providing both the refreshments and the entertainment."

And then they were gone. I just lay there, until I was sure I was alone. And then I pulled myself out of the car, dressed, went back to make sure the door to the store was locked, and drove on home and took a long shower, ashamed that I had enjoyed much of the evening.

However, this was the last evening shift I ever worked in my store. But it was not because I didn't want to; it was because I couldn't trust myself.

Oilman Jim's Blog

Mr. LaFleur was much more magnanimous about my leaving than I thought he would be. If I'd known he would take it so well—and not only that but help me find another position, albeit temporary—I would have built up the courage to part with him months earlier.

It was the morning that he flogged me while riding me like a horse that I decided I could stay no longer. It was the twenty-first century and yet he ran his Louisiana plantation as if the Civil War and emancipation had never happened. I had come from Jamaica with my family, drawn by his promises of good housing and income if my father would improve the quality of the rum he produced on his plantation. But Mr. LaFleur had been taken with me unnaturally—drawn, he said, by my small stature, well-formed body, and a face that many told me was more pretty than handsome. And perhaps my one vanity contributed to the androgynous look that attracted Mr. LaFleur so—as I also like to wear my hair long in dreadlocks.

When I was eighteen and could work to help my family, Mr. LaFleur took me into his big plantation house as a house servant. I helped in the kitchen and the laundry, and I served in the formal dinner parties Mr. LaFleur held for New Orleans society—at least one per season—and I drove guests of Mr.

LaFleur in his big shiny Rolls Royce. And I valeted for Mr. LaFleur, and at night after the household had retired, Mr. and Mrs. LaFleur to their separate bedrooms, Mr. LaFleur would call me to his room to help prepare him for the night.

Part of Mr. LaFleur's preparation for the night was to fuck me in that big four-poster bed of his. And he was a cruel lover. He would beat me if I was slow to open my legs for him or if I resisted any of his demands. And he liked to use the riding crop and beat my flanks as he fucked me from behind and used my dreadlocks as reins. He treated me just like his black slave.

I was only able to endure this for a few months, and then I had to tell him that I must leave, that I didn't want to work on the plantation anymore. My father was so important to the rum distillery that Mr. LaFleur didn't make a fuss or try to hold me against my will.

"But where will you go?" he asked.

"I am not sure," I answered. I was from Jamaica and had been brought directly to Mr. LaFleur's plantation as a child. I had no skills beyond the keeping of a large house—and the skills Mr. LaFleur had taught me of taking a cock. In my desperation to get out of his bed and away from his cruel riding crop, I had even contemplated offering myself into service in a male brothel up in New Orleans. I knew I was of a type that excited some men. I might as well be paid good money for what Mr. LaFleur was taking from me for free.

"Perhaps I can be of assistance," Mr. LaFleur had said. And then he had given me the benign smile that he turned on the public to maintain his status as one of the first citizens of Louisiana. "It may be only for a few weeks, but you are trained to house service and I have a share in an offshore oil operation. How would you like serving on an oil rig out in the Gulf as a house boy—temporarily? I know they are short of staff. If you do well and like it, perhaps you can be taken on more permanently."

I was very grateful for Mr. LaFleur's help, appreciating the chance to have a job while I tried to gather my thoughts about what I wanted to do—no, that I might be able to do—next in life. This unusual consideration Mr. LaFleur was showing to me, though, did not extend to his bed. That night, the last one

308

I spent at the plantation, he nearly choked me to death by squeezing his hands around my neck as he pushed his pelvis between my thighs and relentless thrust his cock in and out of me until I had fainted.

I was so anxious to get as far away from Mr. LaFleur's plantation as possible—with an oil platform isolated in the Gulf of Mexico waters seeming an ideal escape—that I paid little attention to what the oil drilling company personnel man said after declaring that I could be taken on temporarily as a houseboy on one of the platforms.

Immediately upon being tendered out to the platform on its regular supply boat, I was taken under the wing of a man named Pete, who was head of housekeeping and the kitchen.

"Ah, you'll be popular here, Mano," he said as he was showing me around the kitchen and laundry. "But perhaps not in the way you might wish. My first advice to you—and probably my best advice to you—is to have as little to do with Oilman Jim, the head of the pumping crew, as possible."

"OK," I responded. I was responding to an agreeable OK to anything Pete was saying, so happy was I to be here and not back on the plantation.

"You didn't ask, but you'd best check out Oilman Jim's Internet Web site and blog. It's so lonely out here that Internet blogs have become quite popular and some are very elaborate and full of activities. You really should check out Oilman Jim's Web site before he catches sight of you."

"OK, I will," I chirped back at him. But, of course, I was only half listening to what he was saying.

The next night I was helping to serve dinner for the men who had worked a hard day on the oil rig. They were a rowdy crew, which I expected, and they also were a hearty crew, with hard, bulky bodies, which was also to be expected. Pumping oil up from under the Gulf floor literally was back-breaking work for a man who didn't develop the muscles for it quickly.

When I came back in the kitchen after making a round with a towering platter of biscuits that disappeared when I was no more than half way through the dining room, Pete came up to me with a worried expression.

"You've caught his eye. Oilman Jim's. That isn't good. I've told personnel more than once not to send me a pretty boy like you, but they never seem to pay attention to me. Listen, stay away from the half of the room you haven't served. I'll serve them myself."

"OK, thanks, Pete," I said. I still had no idea who he was talking about—who I should stay away from.

"And for god's sake, look at that Web site I gave you the URL for. I don't think you understand what I'm talking about yet."

"Yes, thanks, Pete. I'll do that. Soon as I go off duty tonight." How was I to tell Pete that I didn't own a computer and had little notion what a Web site or URL were?

My shift finished, I headed for the lowest level of crew quarters on the oil platform superstructure, when one of the men I'd seen in the dining hall—one who seemed to have the respect and attention of all the rest—stopped me in the passageway. He, in fact, clogged up the passageway so effectively that I couldn't have passed him if I'd wanted to. He was a monster of a man—arms like tree trunks and bulging biceps and chest muscles, although tapering down significantly in the waist. Bulging thighs, hardly contained in his jeans—and that big mound at his crotch too. I could well understand why the men working the rig gave him respect and attention. He commanded it by his sheer bulk.

"So, you're the new service guy," he said.

"Yes. Yes, sir, that's me," I answered. His voice was a deep bass, and I felt like I might crumble as he put a big mitt on my shoulder.

"Well, I didn't get my bed changed yesterday—or the clean towels I should have," He said. "Room 219. Bring me some. And just use your service key. I'll be taking a shower."

"Yes, sir. Right away, sir."

I watched him turn and move down the hall. He was quite agile for a man his size, and he had firm but bulbous buttocks.

"Towels in here," He called from his bathroom when I'd come into the room and made the bed. His room was strange— or seemed so. It was the first of the oil rig crew rooms I'd been

310

in. A living area and a bedroom L, with the bath and a closet setting the L off from the rest of the space. That wasn't what was strange. What was strange was that it was pretty brightly lit and there seemed to a pulsating light going on. He had a desk at one end of the room with quite an elaborate computer setup on it.

That reminded me that Pete was urging me to check up on that Oilman Jim's blog and Web site, which I decided to do on the kitchen computer as soon as I was finished in here. I was pretty sure I could figure out how to work the computer; I had seen my younger brother playing with the one in Mr. LaFleur's office. The mere thought of that made my stomach lurch, though. My younger brother. Chances were good he had replaced me in Mr. LaFleur's bed. The unnerving thought of that—which had just occurred to me—occupied my thoughts as I remade the bed in room 219 with clean sheets.

I picked up the towels and went over to the bathroom door. It was open, and steam from the shower was wafting into the living area. He was in the shower, naked, facing me. And as I had surmised from seeing him in the hall, he was hung particularly heavy—certainly longer and thicker than Mr. LaFleur was. And he was one solid, perfectly proportioned, if thickly built, muscle flowing into the next muscle from neck down to his calves.

"Strip unless you want to get that uniform wet," he demanded.

"What?" The surprise hit me like a bolt of lightning. It's not that I didn't fail to understand what this meant; it was that I was in shock that I hadn't seen it coming.

"I said strip or I'll come out there and help you."

I turned, willing my feet to flee the room, but he stuck a meaty arm out of the shower and pushed the bathroom door firmly shut, trapping me inside with him. I noticed that there was the same bright and almost pulsating light in here as in the living area and bedroom L.

With a sigh, I stripped down and folded my uniform neatly and placed it on the toilet. I was playing for time, but I knew that I had no time. I knew what was going to happen. I'd been through this many times with Mr. LaFleur. And I knew I wasn't going to escape it.

When I was naked, the man grabbed me by my dreadlocks and pulled me into the shower stall. There was no fighting him. He was three times my size; I had the body of a mere child compared to him. I was familiar with—and resigned to—this treatment, having endured it for months from Mr. LaFleur.

He forced me down on my knees in front of him.

"Suck it. And make it a good job or I'll split your tonsils with my dick."

I had done this for Mr. LaFleur, and he was quite demanding in how I did it, so I reached up and cupped the man's balls with one hand and fisted the root of his cock with the other and began working his dick bulb with my tongue and lips.

He made me deep throat him, me gagging all the way, until he was hard and then he hauled me out of the shower, both of us dripping wet, and into the center of the living area and forced me down on all fours on the carpet. Straddling my hips and arching my back up to him by pulling on my dreadlocks just as Mr. LaFleur did, he took only a moment to crown his hard, throbbing dick with a condom and then he was fucking me—riding me like I was a horse, just as Mr. LaFleur liked to do.

He rode me to exhaustion until I collapsed on my belly, and then he came down with me and continued to fuck me. My hips found his rhythm, and my own now-hard cock was rubbing along the surface of the carpet. I came first and then, with a yelp of victory, so did he.

We were still wet, but from sweat now rather than the soaking from the shower, and he pulled me up and laid me down at the foot of the bed and spread my legs and thrust inside me again and fucked me to his second ejaculation. I involuntarily made a lot of noise in the taking, which was brutal, especially at first, and which was stretching my channel far in excess of the only man who had fucked me before. The man seemed to enjoy my distress and kept asking if I had been a virgin. He seemed to want me to have been—so I told him yes. After that, he was more sensitive to my need for time to accommodate him, but it didn't stop him from fucking me in long, deep strokes.

He left me after that and went back into the bathroom and showered again. When he came back, he had my folded uniform in his hand and tossed it down on my belly, which was covered in my own cum from my second release.

"These sheets are wet," he said gruffly. "You'll need to bring another set and make the bed again."

I fled the room, intending not to return. But I turned and looked at the nameplate by the door. It said: "Oilman" Jim. I should have known. And now I'd have to return with clean, dry sheets. Pete had made quite clear that, although I should try to avoid Oilman Jim, I should, under no circumstances, cross him.

I was trembling when I returned. Oilman Jim was sitting at his computer, still fully nude, and fiddling with it.

I shivered in consternation as I remade the bed, and just as I feared, when I finished, two beefy arms surrounded my small waist and lifted me, while scrabbling at my trousers and shirt until they were stripped off me and thrown on a heap on the floor, and dropped me on my belly on the bed. Oilman Jim came down onto the bed behind me, gathered me in his arms, lifted one of my legs up, and strongly entered me again in a side-splitting fuck that lasted almost forever.

It was more than an hour before he let me get off the bed and redress and hobble out of the room, so bowlegged from the size and pistoning of his dick inside me that I could barely walk. Snuffling and whimpering, I went straight back to my room and curled up on my bed. It wasn't until morning, shortly before my early call to help in the kitchen for the crew's crack-of-dawn breakfast, that I showered the musky smell of Oilman Jim off my body and dressed for work.

When I entered the kitchen, Pete moved over to me and lay a hand on my arm and asked me if I was OK—or whether I needed to have the day off.

I had no idea why he knew something was wrong. I had tried my best not to show it, and I certainly hadn't told anyone what had happened to me the previous night. This was my problem, something I had to work through. Although Oilman Jim's tool had been huge and his embraces had left me

313

breathless, he hadn't been as cruel to me as Mr. LaFleur routinely had been. And now that I knew who Oilman Jim was, perhaps I could avoid him for the short time I'd be working on the rig—before I could escape and look for other work.

"No, everything's fine. I'm fine," I said, and before Pete could respond, I picked up a platter of fried eggs rimmed with thick slices of bacon and entered the dining room.

All talk was reduced to whispers when I entered the room, and the eyes of all of the men seemed to be riveted to me. It was very disconcerting. They hadn't eyed me like this at the previous evening's meal. They were smiling—some almost sniggering—and several giving me a look of speculation that I couldn't interpret but that sent chills up my spine.

I looked across the room and saw a beaming Oilman Jim, sitting there as if he were the Emperor of the Holy Roman Empire, and looking very pleased with himself. A blond giant of a Scandinavian was sitting next to him, and as I moved around the room, dispensing eggs and bacon, Oilman Jim and the Scandinavian had their heads together in a quiet discussion, although both had their eyes on me while they talked.

Platter empty, I turned and headed toward the kitchen. Out of the periphery of my vision, I saw the Scandinavian rise and move at an angle toward the door as well. He was right behind me when I pushed on the swinging door into the kitchen. I dropped the empty platter on the steel counter, setting off a ringing tone, over which I could hear Pete call out in a strangled voice, "Bjorn . . . No."

I kept on walking through the swinging door into the pantry area, the Scandinavian still hot on my tail and Pete calling out "Borjn" again.

The Scandinavian hulk—who presumably was Borjn—pushed me belly down on the top of a closed heavy rubber garbage bin, pulled down my pants from behind, and was fucking me hard before I barely was able to take a breath. He wasn't as thick as Oilman Jim had been, but he had a way of rotating his cock inside me while he fucked that made me feel that he stretched me more.

When he was finished, he simply rezipped his pants and turned and walked back through the swinging door into the kitchen.

Pete gave me time to stop sobbing and to pull my pants up, before he came in and told me to go to my room until I could collect myself. He also told me how sorry he was but that the oil operations crew reigned on this rig and that there wasn't a thing he could do about what was happening to me. And then he once again cursed the company personnel department for sending small guys with pretty faces into this hell hole.

I was just as confused as anything else. There was no problem at lunch, if only because the oil crew had a limited time to eat and get back on the job. But after dinner, when I was working in the linen room, the lights went off, and I was sexually assaulted by two men together who pushed me down on my back in a low laundry cart, with one holding my shoulders down while the other was holding my legs open wide and fucking down into me. And then they changed position.

And that evening as I was moving down the hall, on my way to my own room, a door off the corridor opened, and another of the oil crew hulks pulled me into his quarters and fucked me standing up in the center of his quarters, handling me just like I was a floppy rag doll, and pulling me up and down on his cock as he held me suspended in air above the floor.

That night, when I'd finally been able to get to my room, Pete found me. He was carrying his laptop computer.

"You didn't check out Oilman Jim's blog and Web site, did you?" Pete asked, and he held me in his arms and rocked me back and forth as we sat on the edge of my bed.

"No, I haven't had time," I answered. "I was on my way to do that when Oilman Jim got me into his room and assaulted me."

"Ah, yes. In his room. Well, I think you'd best see this," Pete said. And then he put his laptop on the top of my dresser, turned it on and tapped out a URL. "Living and working on an oil rig like this is lonely work—and there are no women out here," Pete said. "Here. Here's Oilman Jim's Web site. This is what all of the men on this rig tuned into last night."

315

I looked into the computer screen with horror. That's why the lights were so bright in Oilman Jim's quarters. He was taping his taking of me from several different angles and had put it right up on his Web site. That's why I had been grabbed and fucked several times today already. I was identified at the oil rig poke of the day.

"Oh, god, when will it stop?" I moaned.

"When someone new and as pretty as you comes along, I suppose," Pete answered in a low voice. "And the supply ship doesn't arrive again for three weeks and even then I doubt anyone will be coming who will appeal to the men as much as you do. Three weeks and then you can leave even if no one new and appropriate arrives."

"Oh, god," I moaned again. And then I froze. Pete had been holding me close and rocking me back and forth—mothering me in my time of distress, or so I thought. But now I realized that he held me firmly with one arm around my shoulder, but that his other hand had been palming my basket. Now I shuddered as he unbuckled my belt and slowly lowered my zipper. He was kissing me in the hollow of my neck and whispering sweet nothings to me.

The graphic scene of Oilman Jim fucking me in his room continued to loop around on the laptop screen that both Pete and I were staring at.

"Pete," I said.

"Sorry, but I can't resist, son," Pete was murmuring. "You are going to know so many dicks in the next three weeks, that what's the harm of one more? And we can go months out here without a woman to fuck."

He stripped off my pants and had done so with his own trousers without me realizing it. He pulled me over into his lap, my buttocks nestled into his crotch, and I groaned and writhed as he pulled my channel down onto his hard cock and began to raise and lower my pelvis in a deep fuck. His arms encircled my waist and a hand went to my nipple. And he resumed kissing the hollow of my neck and telling me how arousing I was. And the scene of Oilman Jim taking me continued to loop around on the flickering laptop.

At least Pete was making love to me. With a sigh of resignation, I took over the rhythm of the fuck, and Pete responded with appreciative sighs and moans that told me that I could count on preferred status in the housekeeping department as long as I put out for him like this.

Later as I lay there in the dark in his arms, almost asleep, I heard Peter mutter, "Whoever sent you here was malicious. Anyone who knows these rigs, knows that this is no place for a pretty boy like you."

And that's when it hit me. Mr. LaFleur had arranged this on purpose. He hadn't let me go easily and with good will. He was having his revenge on me. Three weeks of fucking hell. But what was three weeks anyway? Once the thickness and length of Oilman Jim's cock had rebored my hole, all of the other men were just another furtive fuck in the dark. After this I would be so used that I might as well go to that male brothel in New Orleans. Oh, well, if they paid well . . . . Hadn't I already turned into a prostitute here with Pete, exchanging sexual favors for preferential treatment?

I turned and pushed Pete gently down on his back on my bed, my knees straddling his hips, and started giving him a proper "I am yours" fuck with my undulating pelvis. Pete gazed up into my face with a look of awe and love and deep appreciation. And I began at that moment to learn how to manipulate men to do what I wanted them to do.

On the Dock

I was moving among the containers on the dock, looking for the one that had the goods I'd had shipped from Portugal in it, when I reached a pocket of isolated dock space between the stacks of truck containers and the waterfront. I was about to turn and move back along the row of containers to examine the numbers on the other side of the tight aisle, when I heard moaning.

Thinking that it might be someone who had fallen and hurt himself, I went to the end of the line of containers and was making a turn toward the sound I'd heard when I saw them and drew back into the shadows.

The bigger of the two figures, a muscle-bound dockworker, was on his back on some sort of thick matting. He was wearing a yellow safety hard hat, a denim shirt open to expose a darkly tanned barrel chest, a tool belt around his waist, and heavy workers' boots—and nothing else. The wiry young Hispanic sitting on his hips and fucking himself on the prone figure's thick cock in long strides was only wearing a yellow hard hat and work boots. The Hispanic youth was doing all of the work and most of the moaning. He was leveraging off his knees and calves and holding his ankles with his hands, while the big guy under him was lying steady and holding him on both sides at the waist.

The big guy was smiling and muttering something in Spanish that must have been arousing to the young guy fucking himself on the thick pole, because his eyes were glassy and his jaw slack in the transport of the fuck.

I watched, mesmerized, as I liked to watch and was already guiltily envying the smaller man, as the big guy dug his heels into the matting and slowly pitched the young Hispanic forward over his chest and began taking over the upward stroking, more vigorously, and the young Hispanic groaned and moved his hips in a rotating motion to make love to the cock inside him at all angles. My eyes went to the root of that thick cock and the few inches above that were disappearing and then reappearing again, rhythmically, as the big guy drove his cock. The young man's hole puckered closely around the plowing cylinder, his light brown a stark contrast to the hard-white marbling of the big guy's cock. I felt a gravelly moan building up from deep in my belly.

Although I had my hand on my own engorging cock through the denim of my jeans, I was afraid the fucking couple would hear me groaning my arousal at the sight of their raw coupling. So I drew back—only to find there was no place to go. Thick, hairy arms surrounded me from behind and I was being lifted off the ground by a monster of a man. My clipboard clattered to the ground, and the fucking couple glanced my way. Little surprise was being registered, though. They both gazed at me with hooded eyes that showed they were lost in their own lust—and no doubt that they recognized a comrade, the man holding me, as someone who could easily control the interloper.

An arm crossed up my chest, holding me to a mass of muscle and the other hand was pulling at my belt buckle and my zipper. I cried out, and the sound reverberated down the tiny aisle I had walked up between the containers. But I had little hope of rescue. As my trousers and briefs were being stripped off my legs, I turned my head up to see who was assaulting me, only to see in my confusion and consternation a blur of stubble on a square chin topped by yet another yellow safety helmet.

I struggled—fruitlessly—as the giant of a dockworker turned me and slammed my back against the ribbed steel side of the containers on one side of the aisle. His hips were roughly insinuating themselves between my thighs; he rolled my pelvis up toward his pelvis, and his cock cap was pushing insistently at my asshole. He was a swarthy guy with a profusion of black, curly hair and a sloppy grin that told me that he was going to get what he wanted.

And he did just that. His bulb popped into my entrance to the tune of heavy groans and cries from me. He somehow had gotten a condom on, which sent a flash of relief through me in counterpoise to the knowledge that I most certainly was going to be fucked. He held the bulb there, giving me a chance through groans and panting to open to him. And then with a throaty laugh and a profusion of Spanish mixed with the more understandable "fucks" and "nice," he was splitting me wide with his ravishing cock. Having been fucked thick before, I instinctively widened my stance as best as I could and dug my heels into the containers across the narrow aisle.

As he pumped, the pain slowly filtered into a flowing of a familiar, consuming pleasure deep inside me and a rising of my own fluids. Almost involuntarily but with animal instinct, I took up the rhythm of the fuck with him, leveraging my own thrusts off the wall opposite with the heels of my feet. The tones of my moaning and sighing changed, and the unwilling verbalizing of my "yes, yes, like that, oh yes" caused the man to grin down into my face, knowing I was fully under his control now and wouldn't have stopped what had become a mutual taking even if given the opportunity. My hands clutched his butt cheeks, fingernails digging into flesh and pulling him into me with each thrust. I felt him relax and his lips came down to mine, and I opened to his tongue. When he started to take his tongue out, I closed my mouth over it and sucked it, causing him to moan and shudder—and his cock to increase the rhythm of the fuck.

The aisle was so narrow that my knuckles were getting bruised on the container walls on the other side with the back thrust of his buttocks, so I took them away and listened to the rhythmic thump of his butt cheeks on the metal at the up side of his thrust arc.

We were full partners in the fuck now, and knowing I was going with him, his fucking took on more finesse, as in long-time lovers giving and taking all of the mutual enjoyment they can. For a few moments he stopped the movement of his hips, and I took over the fuck, leveraging off the wall with the balls of my feet. Him resting his buttocks against the wall opposite and me coming to him with my channel thrusts. I released his tongue and he grabbed mine with his lips and gave me the same suck I had been giving him.

With a shudder, he regained control and started a screwing motion with his dick, rotating his hips and moving his cock around in me as my walls stretched to accommodate him—no longer resisting him, making caressing love to his cock. He was hitting and rubbing against all walls inside me, driving me wild in the long strokes as his bulb rubbed across my prostate. I was as lost in the fuck as my assaulter was, and I threw my head back and, with the thought that I had reached the height of passion, ejaculated up my belly between us.

I would have been at least neutral about the forced taking if it had stopped then. But it didn't. The dockworker continued stroking me hard, increasingly roughly, ever faster and deeper, as he lost his own control. I raked his back under his shirt with my fingernails, and I cried out for him to split me asunder—my body telling him what I wanted to convey even if he didn't understand my words—and he lowered his head and ravaged my nipples with his teeth as my chin bounded off his yellow safety helmet. I had been fucked before, but it had not been as primevally animalistic as this surprise, forced fucking. I was transported to new heights of sensation and passion and came again. I wanted him to come in great gushes and with a total loss of his control. I wanted him to be as amazed at and moved by this coupling as I was.

I no longer was neutral. Now I wanted it to go on, pushing me to an even higher level of passion. I wanted a third and a forth creaming. But my body could only take so much pounding, and the dockworker, as young and virile and strong and lusty as he was, could hold his load for only so long. I was exhausted and was just flopping around on his pistoning cock when he finished with me—with the yelp of victory I was seeking from him at his climax.

He let me down to the ground then and I collapsed into a moaning heap, grateful that I had survived the size and power and endurance of him, sorry now that it was over. I nonsensically grabbed for his ankle as he stood over me, panting and muttering in Spanish. I didn't know how I was going to manage it, or how soon he would be capable of delivering it again, but I wanted to be transported back to the heights of that virile, primeval fucking.

His hand was on mine, prying my fingers away from my grip on his ankle.

"No, no," I was moaning softly. "You don't understand. I want it again. Fuck me again." All of my previous experiences with men had been too bland. I had no idea such passion and pleasure could be wrenched from me. I was a slut for him—for that long, thick cock swinging free above my head now. He could do anything with me now. Just as long as he fucked me again—when I'd had a chance to recover myself. Just a bit longer. I had to make him understand.

I have no idea if what I wanted conveyed. But after he'd pried my fingers away from his ankle, he was lifting me up and carrying me out onto the apron of concrete at the edge of the dock. The big dockworker I'd first seen on his back was still there, the younger Hispanic drawn off the side, crouched down on his haunches, pulling at his cock, watching the new activity. As we approached, me being carried under my erstwhile lover's arm at his side like a sack of potatoes, my lover said something in Spanish, and the young guy smiled and scrabbled around in the pocket of jeans lying nearby and fished out a condom packet.

The reclining hulky dockworker's cock was standing up straight and hard and thick, and he had a big grin on his face as the younger Hispanic rolled the condom down over his rod. The grin only broadened as my original assaulter hovered me over his midsecton and spread my thighs and butt cheeks . . . and lowered my channel onto this new, ready cock.

One Way or the Other

It was doomed from the start. We were fucked. Fucked by a cocky new civilian president and his naïve cabinet, fucked by the lack of resolve, and fucked by bad weather. You would have thought that someone would have taken lashing rain into account when putting this stupid invasion plan together.

I was barely into the tree line up from the Bay of Pigs, not seventy-five miles from Havana. It's almost as if they knew we were coming. They were picking our small squads of Cuban exiles off even before most of them reached the beach. We'd trained them hard, but what good is expertise in hand-to-hand combat if you're shot before even reaching the beach, for fuck's sake? And where in the fuck was the air support? We'd just been abandoned here. A doomed operation from the beginning.

But I couldn't think that way. It was one thing for these Cuban exiles to be wrapped up here in the underbelly of Cuba in a failed attempt to depose the Castro regime. It was quite another for me, an American commando, to be caught here.

I'd told them I didn't think any of the American advisers should be in the actual operation, and they'd just brushed that away. They said the operation would be a cake walk. That all our Cuban exiles needed to do was to show up on the beach in force and the Cuban people would rise up and overthrow Castro. Just an afternoon's jaunt, and the threat of the Russians getting a toe into the Western Hemisphere waters would evaporate. Yeah, fat chance of that. That Kennedy bunch should be here with me now.

But I was a trooper and did what I was told to do; and now, for the good of my country, I needed it get back out to the sea. I couldn't be caught here on Cuban soil. The shit would really hit the fan for an American combatant's sorry ass to be captured in this circle jerk.

I heard a metallic click that made the hair stand up at the back of my head. I instinctively dropped while turning to the sound and bringing my pistol up. My training had been true, because the bullet passed by me rather than catching me full force in the chest.

Close onto the tail end of the report from the rifle high up in the branch of the tree came the sound from my answering pistol shot.

I had been luckier and a truer shot than my assailant had been. There was great agitation of leaves and branches above and in front of me, and a body dropped to the ground at the base of the tree.

Either the young man's clothes had been ripped almost to shreds as he fell, or he had been dressed in shredded rags to begin with, because his shirt and trousers were largely torn away from him as he hit the ground.

He was bleeding from the head and his eyes were closed, but I didn't think he was dead. I moved quickly over to him and tore his shirt the rest of the way off and felt his chest. Still breathing. I looked down at him. He was an unearthly handsome young man. He couldn't be more than nineteen or twenty. He was small of stature but very well formed, with the fine facial structure of Spanish stock, just barely mixed with the Mestizo genes, which gave him a milk-chocolate skin coloring that only enhanced his beauty. My bullet had grazed his temple, which, in combination with the fall, had knocked him unconscious. For how long, though, I didn't know. And unconscious wasn't dead. He may have seen me well enough to know that I wasn't a Cuban exile, that I was an honest-to-god American. And having no one who was left here knowing that an American was here was only second in importance to getting back off the island and not being captured here.

Still holding one hand on his chest, I instinctively looked around to ensure he was the only shooter I needed to worry about, and then I holstered the pistol and reached for the knife strapped to my calf. I couldn't chance another gunshot, even though there was shooting aplenty going on down near the waterline. I needed to finish this more quietly and get the hell out of here and try to find a dingy with enough inflation left in it to get me out to the submarine. Who knows whether the submarine would stay around—and for how long? There was supposed to be air support. Where in the crap was the air support?

The young man's eyes slitted open and then opened even wider when he saw me crouched over him. I raised the knife, but he came to life and knocked my arm away, sending the knife flying into the dense growth at the base of the tree.

I stood and stepped several paces away and pulled out my pistol and raised it, aiming for a heart shot.

And then we both froze. He was lying there, staring at me pleadingly, with big, brown eyes, and I couldn't take my eyes off him. He was so young. And I wasn't really at war. And this was his soil, not mine. And he was unarmed and vulnerable now. This had been a fucked-up idea from the beginning. I was only here because I was a "yes, sir" trooper. I wasn't at war with the Cuban people. There wasn't anything about this protected by the Geneva Convention or any other creed of military honor.

I let the arm holding the pistol slowly drop to my side, and we were frozen there for what seemed to be another eternity.

I don't know what would have happened then, if the other soldier hadn't appeared. He moved through the underbrush with a great deal of noise, giving me time enough to crouch behind a nearby tree but not time enough to melt into the surrounding brush.

The soldier wasn't Cuban. I could tell from his fatigues that he was Eastern European or Russian. Probably Russian. So, it was true, I thought. The whole reason we had entered this operation was because of the presence of the Russians, not knowing just how deeply embedded in the Cuban structure they were—but believing from all of our intelligence that they were up to their necks in whatever the Castro regime was doing.

What then transpired showed me in very graphic terms how deeply imbedded they were.

The Russian came over to the Cuban youth and spoke roughly to him in a smattering of Spanish. The young man answered him, haltingly. And although he was taking occasional glances over to where he knew I was trying to hide, he must not have been giving my location away, because all of the Russian's attention was focused on him. Perhaps the young man thought I would and could shoot them both before the Russian could turn and shoot me—and, in that, he was right. But any shooting was a big risk now that the firing was dying down at the waterline.

The Russian's voice turned to something more guttural and hoarse, and the Cuban youth's voice was more pleading now. And I didn't have to wait very long to find out why. The Cuban was still sprawled at the base of the tree, and the Russian was standing over him, big military boots straddling the young man's thighs. The Russian was unbuttoning his fly with one hand and had taken a fistful of the young man's curly black hair and then forced his face toward an extended cock.

The young man grimaced at the pulling of his scalp away from his temple wound, but he was too dazed at that point to struggle.

After a short period of giving the Russian noisy suck punctuated with grunts and groans from them both, the Cuban youth was stripped of what was left of his trousers, and the Russian had come down on his knees between the young man's spread thighs.

I heard the youth cry out in pain and then start moaning and giving little yipping sounds as the Russian soldier skewered his channel roughly and began a staccato rhythm with his pelvis, while pulling the youth's hips back and forth on his engorged cock with strong, calloused hands.

At first when the fucking started the young man tried to struggle against him and attempted to rise, but the Russian just laughed and backhanded him across the mouth and continued to thrust at him.

As dire as my own plight was, I couldn't help myself. I had my fatigues unbuttoned and stroked myself off as the Russian was completing his conquest—or so I thought.

All of the time the Cuban youth was unable to look at the Russian. He was looking off in the brush toward where he knew I was in hiding, his eyes glazed, knowing that there was nothing he could do to save himself from the Russian.

Except, maybe, try to whisper to the Russian of my presence and chance that the Russian would plug me before I could shoot him. And if the Russian was successful, what were the probabilities that the Russian would then leave off his assault? But the young man didn't give me away. Whether it was from fear, or shock, or making a choice between me and the invading Russian, I'll never know. And it doesn't matter.

Whatever it was, it made me pause with the thought of somehow trying to save him.

I had thought the Russian was finished, but he proved me wrong. He barked an order at the youth and pulled him up and pushed him over onto his knees and hands. And then, with one forearm wrapped around the young man's belly, the Russian thrust his cock home again and began to doggyfuck his Cuban "comrade" in long, hard strokes.

I could see that the Russian was lost in the fuck, and I decided to take the risk of trying to escape. His face was turned away from me. If I was going to have any chance of getting the hell off this island without being captured on Cuban soil, this was my opportunity—maybe my only chance.

As I melted into the brush, I briefly regretted leaving the Cuban to his fate, but what the Russian was doing to him was more survivable than what I had almost done to him—or that he had tried to do to me, for that matter. The Cuban was going to be fucked one way or the other—by the Americans, or the Russians, or by his own government. Probably by all three before this story truly was over.

Pecker Order

Some clients thought the "Bull" in the Bull Thorne Financial Services name related to Wall Street symbols, but those who had known Jim "Bull" Thorne the longest knew he had that nickname because he had the longest, thickest dick in Texas. Of course, it could just as well have been an acknowledgment that he also had the biggest pair of balls in Houston, based on the dictatorial and ruthless way he ran his highly successful corporation. Jim Thorne was still ruggedly handsome at fifty, and he surrounded himself with those who were equally ruthless, handsome, and on the make for financial success—at any cost or personal sacrifice. It was all about control, and who controlled who, Thorne always told his subordinates. So the gasp that went around the twenty-sixth floor boardroom when the newest vice president, Keith Turner, challenged Thorne's decision on the Mason account was audible down in the ground-floor lobby. It meant nothing that everyone in the room knew Turner had a good point.

Thorne had closed down the meeting immediately and told Turner he wanted to see him in his office—now.

When Turner arrived at the large, corner office of the corporation president, with its floor-to-ceiling windows on two sides, providing an eagle's view of Texas, Thorne made him stand in front of the mile-wide mahogany desk, while the angry president prowled around him, working himself into a frenzy. Thorne locked the door, came around in front of his desk, and addressed his subordinate through clinched teeth.

"When I made you a vice president, you said you clearly understood who made the decisions around here—who was in control. Right?"

"Right, Bull. But the Mason account—"

"And do you remember what, exactly, I said at the time that you were to do in terms of loyalty?"

"Umm, no, not exactly. But the Mason—"

"Let me refresh your memory, then. I said, in these exact words, 'Don't fuck with me or I'll fuck you.' Now do you remember?"

"Yes, sir," Turner answered weakly.

"And I've made no secret that I fuck men, have I?"

"No, sir." Turner was turning pale now. He knew what the original of "Bull" in Jim Thorne's name meant.

"And I also said at the time that my statement was a literal one. Do you remember that part too?"

"Yes, sir, but, I thought . . ." Turner was speaking in almost a whisper now.

"You didn't think too clearly. Well, you have two choices, Turner. I have to have control and total submission in this office. I've made no secret of that. You can either turn and leave—walk out of your job and this office without so much as a letter of recommendation—or you can give me total control and submission. Which is it?"

A slight pause, and then Turner whispered, "Submission. I will totally submit."

"And you will do so in a way you'll never forget," Thorne said with a sneer.

The Bull was suddenly on the move. "Strip," he commanded.

"But, sir—"

"Strip all the way down, move to the center of the room, and throw your clothes over there." While Turner was complying with a sigh of resignation, Thorne was searching around in his drawer for that tube of lubricant he always kept there. Then, with Turner watching him, his lips trembling and letting out a low moan at the sight of what was between the Bull's thighs, Thorne stripped down as well. He walked over to the pile of Turner's clothes and pulled out the younger man's expensive silk tie, and then he walked back to Turner, tie and lubricant in hand.

"Down on your knees and open your mouth to me," Thorne said.

With a sigh, Turner did so, and reached for that gigantic cock, already mesmerized by it.

"No," Thorne said. "I just said to open to me, not to show any signs of control. Hold perfectly still. And raise your wrists to me."

Thorne used that expensive tie to bind the younger man's wrists behind his back. Thorne then pushed his cock into Turner's mouth with one hand and took his subordinate's head with both of hands.

"A lesson of control," the company president said. "I control everything. You control nothing. All you are is a warm, wet chamber for my cock. Just be warm and wet and open to me. Leave the rest of the control to me."

And although Turner couldn't help gagging a bit, he tried to comply fully with his boss.

"Now go tighter. Touch me closely on all sides." That wasn't at all hard to do, because Thorne was so thick and long, even though he hadn't hardened out yet. Thorne pumped Turner's head back and forth on his cock for a few minutes, trying to demonstrate his obedience, which was total, and getting Thorne's cock real hard.

Then, pulling out of Turner's mouth, the Bull said, "Go down on your back right here." Turner rolled back onto his butt and then on his back without comment or objection. The athletic Thorne went down on his knees between Turner's thighs and pulled the younger man's butt up on his thighs. He also brought Turner's hands over his head and back to his front.

"Now, I'm going to fuck you—unless you've decided you don't want to work for me anymore."

Silence, filled only by the sound of lubricant slapping against tender asshole.

"Good. Now, as I work my way in, I want you to jerk yourself off. And I want you to come when I'm in to the hilt—and not before. Understand?"

Turner nodded, a serious look on his face. Thorne slathered his dick with lube, opened a golden-colored Magnum condom packet, crowned his cock, and then guided it to Turner's asshole and rotated it around, working it in, while Turner began to stroke himself and pulling at his balls with his bound hands. Turner was concentrating hard on how he was going to ejaculate on cue. Thorne was pleased. Turner hadn't questioned the instruction. Turner had been a prime pick for vice president—and, truth be known, Thorne had been planning to pork his young associated for some time—so it was good that Turner was going to submit and be staying with the firm.

Thorne slowly worked his monster cock into his subordinate's ass, as the younger man obediently pulled on his cock. The Bull closely watched the tension build in the man he was fucking and managed to be at eight inches inside him when he yelled "Now" in a raspy voice, and Turner shot his load up Thorne's flat belly. As Turner ejaculated on cue, Thorne pushed his dick in the last half inch. He looked down at the white globs of semen running down his black belly hair and perched on top of Turner's golden-red pubic hairs. He liked what he saw, but this hadn't been enough of a turn-on for the Bull. The display of his control was turning Thorne on, but he needed the closeness the merging of bodies, his fully dominant over the other, before he himself could reach an orgasm.

"You realize this was just for instruction, don't you?" Thorne spoke to Turner as he squeezed his balls and pulled on his spent cock, his own cock still hard and buried to the root in his subordinate's ass. "I was the one who controlled when you had fulfilled this task, not you. Even though you thought this was your responsibility. It wasn't. You realize that now, don't you? You realize that I held off jacking off until you had come."

"Yes, sir." Turner answered meekly.

"And you know now that this isn't all that I want, don't you? How quickly can you learn? Quick enough to save that vice president's salary of yours?"

"I can learn quickly, sir," Turner answered quietly. "I want you inside me. And I know that you want closeness, tightness as well as submission and control. Is that right?"

"Yes, that's right. I'm going to unbind you now, and I'm going to fuck your lights out right here and in this position, and I want you to show that you can handle the tightness and closeness without the bonds. You will know if and when you succeed because, for your total submission, I'm going to bareback you now and your insides will be bathed in my cum. Do you want that?"

"Oh yes, please, sir. Flood me with your cum."

Thorne untied Turner then and enfolded him in his arms, belly to belly and nipples to nipples. Turner's curly red chest hair tickled Thorne's hulking pecs. The Bull wrapped his arms around the younger tightly, holding his back down on the floor. Turner returned the hug, wrapping his arms around his boss as well and holding him tightly, almost taking the breath out of the older man with his strong arms. Turner's strong, swimmers legs wrapped around Thorne below his buttocks, pulling him in close, holding him tight and tightening his ass canal as much as he could around the cock Thorne had reburied after slipping the condom off. The two executives kissed deeply, and then Turner buried his face in Thorne's neck, trying to pull himself into Thorne at every point as much as he could. Turner was surrendering to Thorne entirely, and the older man felt the sexual urge flood into him. He pumped and pumped and pumped at various levels, sometimes pulling out to give Turner's prostate attention. The younger man moaned and trembled at this but continued to hang on to his boss as tightly as he could.

When the Bull came, flooding the very center of the younger man in spasms of semen, Turner ejaculated again himself and collapsed back on the rug, arms and legs askew.

"Sorry," he murmured. "It was just too much. I couldn't hang on any longer. I've been royally fucked. This is the greatest."

"Do you want me to pull out of you now?" Thorne asked.

"Whatever you want," Turner answered quietly. "You are in total control. Do what you want with me."

"Good choice," the Bull answered gruffly. "Remember, if you fuck with me again, I'll fuck you again. And maybe I will even if you don't fuck with me."

* * * *

Keith Turner wasn't all that displeased when he was released from the Bull's office. His ass was sore from the gigantic tool the Bull had, but this had answered a question he'd had since he'd come on board and heard rumors that the boss was horse hung. Yes, he could take almost nine inches of thick cock. He'd had that extension toy in his own desk for weeks, wondering if he could get one of his fuck buddies to try out that length, but now he wouldn't have to experiment with that.

He felt slightly humiliated at having had to give up control like that, though, so he was loaded for bear when he saw the memo on his desk from his own accounting section disallowing that bar tab he'd run up at the convention in Las Vegas the previous month.

Who did this Craig Wilson think he was disallowing whatever tab he, a vice president, chose to charge to the office? Sure, they'd played on the same office football team and had playfully snapped each other with towels in the locker room shower—and Keith had obviously been attracted to the young, studly blond—but, as the Bull said, this office was built on the concept of control and rank, and Craig Wilson would just have to be taught where he ranked in the pecking order.

He made Wilson stand in front of his desk at attention while he dressed him down for questioning his authority and then he came right up behind the trembling accountant and yelled in his ear, Marine sergeant style, "I was just talking with Bull Thorne today, and you know what he said about insubordination like yours?"

"No, sir," Wilson squeaked. "What did he say, sir?"

"He said that anyone who fucked with authority around here would be fucked—literally. Now what do you think about that, Craig?"

"Well, I don't know what to . . ." Wilson stammered. And then he squeaked again as Turner grabbed a butt cheek and squeezed.

"Do you like your job and your generous paycheck, Craig?"

"Yes, sir," Wilson answered.

"And would you do anything to keep them, Craig?"

"Uhh . . . Yes, sir," Wilson answered again.

"Well, you have two choices then. You can walk out of that door and clean out your desk, or you can take a lesson in control and a good fuck. Which is it?"

"You want to fuck me?" Wilson asked in a disbelieving voice.

"Only if you want to continue working here."

Wilson smiled broadly then and answered, "I thought you'd never ask, Keith."

This didn't please Turner all that much. This wasn't asserting control over his subordinate.

"Come here," Turner said gruffly, and he literally pulled Wilson around the desk to where he stood between the desk and Turner's chair.

"Assume the position and strip," Turner commanded, as his eyes darted around the room. They lit on the window blind cords. Turner went over and jerked a couple of them down, causing the blinds to accordion down to the floor with a crash. As soon as Wilson had stripped, Turner tied his wrists with one end of the cord, a cord for each wrist, pulled the cords through the kneehole of the desk, crossed them, and then tied the other end tight above Wilson's knee, pulling the cords taunt so that Wilson was spread-eagled with his belly flat on the top of the desk and securely held in place. Turner ripped Wilson's belt out of his pant loops then and fashioned it around Wilson's neck like a dog leash.

Wilson was totally trussed up now. Turner had physical control. Total control. Wilson wasn't laughing now. Wilson needed to be taught the same lesson Turner had endured under the attention of the Bull's big cock earlier today. But Turner didn't have the length and thickness of Thorne. Or didn't he? Turner reached down and opened the bottom drawer of his desk and buried his hand under a pile of papers. He came up with a leather, studded penis sheath with a three-inch extension capped with an extra large stud-covered bulb he'd bought and had been building up the courage to use.

Turner did some lip and spit and finger work on Wilson's ass as the accountant moaned softly for him. After he was satisfied that he'd opened Wilson up sufficiently, Turner sheathed his cock with the oversized studded harness and positioned himself behind the fully trussed figure. Turner palmed the rounded butt cheeks and pushed his sheathed cock up to the opening of the puckered, lubricant-slathered hole with its circle of curly blond hair. Wilson moaned and groaned.

"Oh, shit. Oh, god, no, nooooo!" he groaned, as Turner rotated the studded sheath head around his ass shunt, relentlessly working it farther into the hole.

"The only way you are going to continue working here under me is by submitting totally to me," Turner said. "Do you submit?"

No answer. Perhaps Craig still seemed to think that since they were buddies on the football field, they somehow were on equal footing.

With a push, Turner had worked the sheath extension and two inches of his own cock into the asshole. Thorne's nearly nine incher had little length on Turner under these circumstances, and the extension made Turner's tool, if anything, thicker than Thorne's natural girth.

Wilson cried out. "Yes, OK, I submit!"

"That sounds good, but I don't believe for a minute that you believe it yet." Turner had no idea if this was true; he was just having too much fun skewering the young blond to end this yet.

Turner was in a good five, very thick inches now. The accountant was trembling under his boss and moaning for him to stop, that he was being split. Several more inches in and he was beginning to really feel those studs. Turner took the unburied part of his dick in his hand and rotated it around in Wilson's canal, coaxing him to open more. Wilson was crying and moaning. The laughter was behind far behind him.

338

He kept screaming that he submitted, that Turner had won, and Turner kept creeping up his canal, trying to wipe out his own humiliation earlier in the day, until only about two inches of Turner's cock root were outside the young blond. With the extension, Turner's rod was in a good eight inches now.

"How? How can I convince you I submit?" he whimpered.

"I'll feel it in your body," Turner answered. "When you've totally submitted, all of the tension will go out of your body, and you'll stop yelling at me. You'll take it silently. You'll be totally mine. And then I'll encase your body with mine, and we'll be one. The submissive you and the dominant me. Only then can you work here with me and be my accountant and an acceptable bottom to my top."

"OK, OK, I'll try," he whimpered. "I want to be here. I want your cock inside me. I submit. Totally."

And Turner did, indeed, feel the tension slowly leaving Wilson's body, and he went silent, except for a few grunts and groans he couldn't suppress, while Turner pushed the last two inches of leather- and stud-augmented penis into the accountant's tightened asshole. He left it in there, all the way in, for several minutes, as he felt the tension and fight draining out of the young accountant—and then Turner rode his ass hard and long.

"Oh, god, yesss," Wilson was whimpering. "Fuck me. Fuck me deep. Like that. Yessss. Don't stop." And Turner didn't stop, at least for several minutes. A few minutes after Wilson had spilled his seed on the carpet behind his boss's desk, Turner shot his load into him.

* * * *

Craig Wilson had enjoyed the session in Keith Turner's office, but he hadn't much cared to have been shown so graphically where he stood in the pecking order in this office. It was just the misfortune of the file clerk, Alphonse Pointer, a saucy young black man of pretty Jamaican features, that he chose to give a flippant reply to one of Craig's instructions later that afternoon. Wilson had just stood up from his desk, taken

Alphonse by the scruff of his collar, and pushed him out a door onto the twelfth-floor landing of a disused stairwell shaft. Alphonse had been swinging his hips and tossing suggestive glances at Craig for weeks, so Craig had little question of what Alphonse would take from him. But he doubted Alphonse expected the mating dance to be ended so abruptly as this.

Listen you little queen, Wilson exploded once the two were out on the landing. You work for me, see. So, you don't talk back to me.

"Uh, what's . . .?" Alphonse spouted, trying to wriggle out of Wilson's powerful grip.

"Listen, you've worked here long enough to know the office motto, haven't you?" Wilson continued.

"Uhh, I'm not—"

"It's fuck with me and you get fucked—literally," Wilson blustered through gritted teeth. He was going to assert some of his own control in this corporation now. He had a certain amount of rank too. Wilson pushed the file clerk down two more flights of stairs, to the level of a floor that was waiting to be refitted and thus where no one worked now.

"Stop and face the banister," Wilson barked.

Alphonse did so without question, fully cowed by this crazed—but delicious—blond stud from accounting.

Wilson came up close behind him, unzipped his fly, and pulled out a respectably sized cock. The accountant then doubled the young file clerk over at the waist on the banister with one hand, so that he was facing down the well from the tenth floor, and worked up his unsheathed cock with the other hand, spitting a few times on his hand to lubricate his tool. When Wilson was satisfied he was at least half hard and able to penetrate the younger man, he pulled Alphonse's pants and briefs down off his buttocks, pushed his legs out to open him up as much as possible under these circumstances, and pushed his dick into Alphonse's gaping, well-used hole.

Alphonse grunted and gritted his teeth as the angry accountant entered him, but he grabbed down for the banister slats with white-knuckled fists and took the blond stud without squeal or objection.

Once in, Wilson tightened the young man up by getting his legs between his own. He draped his chest over the smaller man's back so that they were both folded at the waist over the banister and facing down ten flights of the stairwell. Wilson latched onto one of Alphonse's ear lobes with his teeth and held on gently.

Wilson could feel the file clerk grunting and groaning, and then sighing and moaning in ecstasy as the accountant's cock lengthened and thickened inside him and filled him to capacity.

"Who's the boss?" Wilson breathed into the younger man's ear.

"You're the boss," Alphonse answered.

"Who backtalks me?"

"Not me, boss."

As Wilson filled Alphonse to the end and started to pump, the accountant took one of his fists and pushed down the front of the file clerks pants and the two stroked Alphonse off together, the file clerk's hand under the accountant's, encasing his cock, while Wilson controlled the stroking. As Wilson sensed he was coming, he let loose of Alphonse's earlobe with his teeth and started tongue-fucking his ear. Alphonse held his head closer to Wilson's tongue, loving the sensation. Once more the two managed to cum almost simultaneously, the accountant deep inside the file clerk and the file clerk down those ten floors of stairwell.

"Wow," was all the clerk said when it was over.

"Yes, wow," Wilson responded. "Now, how do you feel about needing control?"

"I love being controlled by you, boss. Yes, I certainly do, and you can control me anytime you want. But who can I control in this big corporation? Does the cum stop here?"

Wilson gave a low laugh. "There's always someone you can control in the pecker order, Alphonse. You might try that Cuban bodybuilder in the mail room. You outrank him here. But if you try him, you might need to make an appointment. If I hear correctly, he's fucking Bull Thorne these days."

Phoned

I should never have been flip when Vincent asked me about that photo of Phil and me I kept on the shelf in my cubicle at work. I didn't really want to talk about Phil. We'd been roommates at the university. He'd been the star athlete and I'd been the quiet, studious geek. Still, we'd gotten along real well. Night and day was what we were called at school. But I'd had no trouble with his color and he'd never expressed having trouble with mine. He'd been destined for the NFL, and I'd been teased I'd have made my first million off of some dot-com enterprise before I was twenty-five.

It hadn't happened that way—for either of us. The dot-com revolution collapsed before I could grab my brass ring, and the best I could do was doing "pretty good" as a stockbroker. Phil decided that a tour in Iraq would toughen him for professional football. But all it did was kill him. That's why I had a picture sitting on the shelf in my work cubicle of the two of us, half looped at a frat party, arms draped around each other, and silly grins on our faces. Sort of a shrine to not taking life for granted, for going with the moment, in case there are no more moments.

But when Vincent, the broker in the cubicle next to me, asked, I was flip. I said the other guy in the photo was my boyfriend.

I have no satisfactory idea why I said that. I think mainly it was because Vincent was so crude at the office, always cracking dirty jokes and making with the sexual innuendo—and I didn't want an intrusion like that in the tragedy I saw in my link to Phil. I just wanted to shock Vincent and make him stop asking about the photo. And especially, maybe I told him that because I had a hard time looking at Vincent and not seeing Phil.

Vincent was a real good looker, just like Phil had been. He said he was Jamaican. And maybe he was. He had a build just like Phil's, and he was always flashing a winsome smile and was so self-assured, just like Phil had been. All the women in the office ate him up despite what any one of them could claim was sexual harassment, if they'd wanted to—if someone not as hunky as him was doing it, maybe.

But I also might have blurted it out with half-way wishful thinking. There had never been anything real between Phil and me, but I'll have to admit that he aroused me and I'd had a crush on him that I never got up the courage to fully acknowledge to myself, let alone to Phil. And now that would never happen. Any possible moment of it happening was gone for good.

From the moment I'd blurted that flippant response out, though, Vincent had turned his innuendo onto me—asking me if I liked him, pointing out that Phil was black too. Asking me if I was especially attracted to black men. And, in time, asking me if Phil and I were still doing it, and, if so, which one of us topped.

Always whispered and in passing, at first covered so that I couldn't tell if he was just joking, trying to get a rise out of me. Maybe baiting me for an office joke. But it continued, and when he moved on to touching me when and as and where he could do it when no one was looking, I knew he wasn't joking. He suggested we go for a drink after work, he complimented me on my clothes, and then on my physique. He even started dropping notes on my desk, asking me to meet him in the men's room, the notes becoming increasingly more explicit. Saying we should compare cocks. Saying he was built especially long and thick.

Asking me what Phil was swinging. Asking me again whether I drove or was driven.

I don't know if I could have stopped it. I just know I didn't try to stop it. I tried to hold back, but it was arousing. I'd never had attention like this before. I could have just told him exactly who Phil was and why that photo was on my cubicle shelf. But I didn't.

He got my home phone number somehow and he began calling me—almost always at about the same time in the evening, so I'd know it was him. One phone call after another, progressively more suggestive, more demanding.

"Hey, Jeff, I'm bored. Let's go play some pool."

"Hey, guy, it's me. What'yer doing? Want to do it together?"

"Thinkin' about you, Jeff. What are you wearing right now? Know what I'm wearing? Nothing."

"Hey, guy. I'm all alone and lonely. I've got something for you. It's long and thick and hard, and it wants you."

A phone call entirely of heavy breathing and the whispering of my name.

"You have it out, don't you? You are stroking it, aren't you." And, of course, I was.

". . . A big black, hard cock churning around in your tight white ass . . ."

It had been weeks. Almost every night. A phone call almost every night at just about the same time. I could have changed numbers, gotten an unlisted one. I could have arranged to be out three evenings in a row and see it if stopped. I didn't. I started clearing everything away so that I could sit by the phone. Waiting for the call. Being disgusted when it came. But disgusted with myself, not with the call. Being frustrated when there was no call that night. Wearing less and less as the calls progressed. Something loose; something that didn't hinder access.

A Saturday night. Just about that time. Me, sitting by the phone. Naked.

It rang.

"Something special tonight, Jeff. I have Manuel here. Say something, Manuel."

345

A groan in the background behind Vincent's smooth, velvety, baritone voice.

"Manuel's nice, Jeff. I met Manuel at the gym. He's cut and oh so nice. And he's a bottom—just like I'll bet you are."

Moaning in the background and a distant voice, "Gawd, Vinny. Oh Gawd. Ahhh."

"You and Mani have something in common, Jeff. You know what that is, Jeff?"

"No," I whispered down the line. I had rarely responded previously, not after my initial attempts to tell him to stop got nowhere. But I was mesmerized. I already had my hand wrapped around my cock and was stroking. This was way beyond any of the previous calls.

"Mani loves black cock, Jeff. Just like you do. I'm fucking Mani now, Jeff. And he loves it. Listen to Mani, Jeff."

The other voice no longer distant. Heavy panting and groaning, "Oh, fuck, Vinny. Oh gawd. Yes, like that. Harder, deeper. Oh Fuccckkkkk."

The phone back to Vincent. "Mani can't stay, Jeff, and I'm still horny. In fact I'm even more horny now. It's time, Jeff; it's time for you to come for your big, black cock. You know where I live. I'm waiting for you now."

The phone clicked off. I was stroking, but not anywhere near completion. This was too much. I let out a long sob.

I knew where this was going. I certainly wasn't fooled. I put on just a loose T and baggy gym shorts. Something had to give here, though. Either it was all a big joke and I'd be the laughing stock of the guys at the office Monday morning, or something would explode. But one way or the other, something was going to happen.

I stood at Vincent's door and knocked.

The door opened to a room that was dark except for strobing lights in blue and red and a blast of sound. Some sort of primeval recording resounding around the room; heavy breathing and panting and moans and groans, evoking high heat and lust. Directly across from the door, hung on the far wall, a giant flat-screen TV, screaming out the image of muscle guys fucking. Between the door and the TV some sort of black vinyl

346

cube, not really a chair, not really anything but a waist-high black vinyl cube.

An overwhelming cacophony of sound and sensations of high heat and lust. No time to think, the images and sounds pushing all reason out of my mind, making my heart pound.

And out of the darkness, a big, black, naked Vincent pulled me into the room, and the door closed behind me as if on a spring. Bulging, shiny muscles. Gorgeous musculature. Everything that was boasted of, promised, swinging between his muscular thighs below and full chest V-ing down to a tiny waist overlaid with a hard slab of belly muscle. The spitting image of Phil in all his athletic glory.

Vincent pulled my T-shirt up and off my torso and, while my arms were lifted for that, another set of arms, behind me, caught me in a full Nelson, trapping my arms above my head.

I flinched and squirmed, trying to pull free.

"Just relax, Jeff," Vincent said in a low, hoarse voice. "It's just Manuel. He decided to stay. Don't fight it. You came to be fucked. You decided. Let's all just enjoy it."

Before I could respond, Vincent had leaned in close and had taken my mouth with his big, thick lips, pushing my lips apart and inserting his tongue. Taking my breath away. The moaning sounds of lust reverberating around me. The flashing lights, the swirling images on the far wall of men fucking.

Vincent's hands were on my hips, insinuating themselves under the waistband of my shorts, hot palms on my hips. Manuel was holding me close from behind. And I knew he was naked too, I could feel the heat of a cock pushing up my lower back, the heavy pectorals against my shoulder blades. His lips and teeth buried in one of my arm pits, licking and nipping and licking.

Vincent slowly kissed and nipped his way down my chest and belly, and he nibbled in my thatch as he slowly pulled the shorts down until my cock popped out—and into his mouth. In one movement, he stripped off my shorts.

I was overwhelmed with sensations as never before. I had no idea that cock sucking could arouse me this way. Manuel pushed his hardening cock down to between my butt cheeks and

I writhed and whimpered. Both wanting it all and being scared shitless at what was happening to me. The sounds and lights and the sudden sexual stimulation was overpowering.

There were three men fucking on the TV. A black and a white and a Hispanic, the black and Hispanic sandwiching the white. This couldn't be some coincidence. I nearly fainted when I realized that this was no professional movie. The black on the screen was Vincent, there was no doubt. And if the Hispanic was Manuel, he was every inch the hunk that Vincent said he was.

It was all just too much too fast for me. I came in a fountain of semen across Vincent's face. He merely laughed and went down deep on me, sucking me dry.

Manuel had forced my head to turn with pressure from his enslaving bicep and his mouth was now attacking mine, possessing me fully. Big brown eyes, what I could see of the face was chiseled and handsome. Straight, silky dark hair of at least shoulder length. The pressure of his cock between my legs had forced me into a wide stance, and he was dry fucking me rapidly across my perineum, pushing my ball sac and the root of my cock up. Vincent was sucking my balls into his mouth and rolling them around against his inner cheeks.

The sounds of the moaning and groaning from the stereo system were becoming more stereo like. Or so I thought, until I realized that it was me who was adding to the moaning and groaning.

Vincent moved from in front of me and Manuel frog marched me forward—onto the vinyl cube. I was pushed over onto the cube on my belly, and Manuel released my arms from the full Nelson. But as quick as he did that, Vincent was grabbing my wrists and tying them off on plush-lined leather restraints at each side of the cube.

On the screen, the white guy was bent over the arm of a sofa. The black guy was on the sofa cushions on his knees and was stuffing his cock into the white guy's mouth. The Hispanic was hunched over the white guy from behind and plowing his ass vigorously.

But that had barely registered with me when my view was blocked by a close up-and-personal of a mammoth black cock, which was forcing itself between my lips. Vincent took my head between his hands and was guiding me on giving his cock a tour of my mouth cavity and the back of my throat.

Manuel was restraining my legs in a wide stance at the base of the back side of the cube, and then I felt the wet roughness of his tongue on the rim of my ass. He was squeezing and lightly slapping my ass cheeks and pulling them apart with his fists and seeing how far, first, his tongue, and eventually, his lubed fingers could get inside my ass.

I was gurgling and sobbing and whimpering at what both of them were doing to me. I was overwhelmed with the surprise and the threat of it. But I also was steeped in the arousal and lust of it all.

I tensed and lifted up as much as the restraints on the cube would allow as Manuel started working his cock inside me. He was murmuring to me, though, advising me to relax and go with the fuck, that I'd enjoy it. When I was able to relax, after Vincent had pulled his cock out of my mouth, I found that it was at least somewhat closer to enjoyment than to intense pain.

Manuel was stroking faster and faster and getting noisier and noisier about his enjoyment of my ass canal. Vincent left, leaving me to watch the white guy on the TV get just about the same thing I was receiving—which, I have to admit, I found to be quite hot.

As Manuel was in the last throes of his fucking, however, Vincent came back into my vision. He stood there, purposely in front of me, giving me that "I got you" smile of his, letting me watch as he split open a condom packet and rolled the transparent film onto his tool. It didn't roll back much more than half onto his cock and it was straining at the thickness of him.

"Manuel's real nice, Jeff," he murmured to me. "But, you know, he's no horse like I am. He fucks, but he doesn't FUCK, If you know what I mean. Is your Phil a stud like me, Jeff? Have you had nine thick inches before? Do you know that I fucked a guy for forty-five minutes once?"

I heard Manuel cry out and felt his condom bubble out inside me, and he bent over and kissed me on the shoulder blade and mumbled something about a nice, tight ride.

And then Vincent disappeared from view, and I felt Manuel sliding out of me. And I watched the Vincent of the TV video slowly working his cock into the white guy bent over the sofa arm. And I saw the white guy on the TV open his mouth wide and yowl to the ceiling, all of his muscles and veins straining hard at the invasion. And I felt the heaviness and thickness of Vincent's cock head at my entrance, and I opened my mouth wide and yowled to the ceiling, all of my muscles and veins straining hard at the invasion, as a far superior club to Manuel's started its digging into me.

The moaning and groaning of the sound system changed to cries of overstretched taking and groans and heavy panting, begging for release, begging for deeper, faster taking. All of which was matched from the TV screen and the vinyl cube.

At length, at great length, I both sensed and heard Vincent tense and give up the rhythmic plowing and a burst of release. I felt him relax down on my back, covering me close, his chest expanding and contracting close against my back, and his hands running down the length of my restrained arms. He kissed me at the nape of my neck and whispered, "You done good, Jeff. That was worth the investment."

My whimpers subsided into sighs, just as what seemed to be happening on the screen flickering in front of me. I'd done it. I'd thought about doing it. I'd worried about doing it. I had fantasized about it—nothing like this, of course—but about doing it. And I let it possess me and control me. But now it was done. I felt slight embarrassment and triumph. Which was disconcerting. I should feel anger. But I didn't. I sighed, in almost contentment under Vincent's trembling, sheltering body.

I sensed a change in the air; a new sound. The ring of a telephone cut through the other sounds still circling around the room.

I heard Manuel answer it. "Yeah. That's right. OK."

Then he came into view in front of me—and I saw for the first time what a hunk he really was.

"That's the other guys. They're on their way up from the lobby."

The OTHER guys?!

350

Please, Daddy, Please

I knew he was the one I wanted as soon as he walked into the bar. Clean cut; maybe mid-to-late thirties; business suit; hiding behind sun glasses in the dimly lit bar; hesitant at the door; picking out a table back in the corner, one with a full sweep of the room. I moved a little to my right at the bar, under a light, well within his vision.

I called Chuck, the bartender, over, and we went into the routine he'd always been agreeable to. Chuck and me got along real good. He'd do me maybe once a week back in the bar's storage room and then he'd help me the rest of the week.

"No beer for you, kid. Whatcha' doin' in here, anyway?" Chuck asked me, raising his voice high enough for the mark to hear. I looked over toward the corner with my peripheral vision to make sure he'd heard. If he hadn't, Chuck and me would have to do it again. But he'd heard. I saw him sit up in his chair, tensed.

"Geez. Am I gonna have to show ID till I'm thirty," I groused back. I pulled out my wallet and laid it on the counter. Flipped out my driver's license and put it under Chuck's nose.

"Those things is a dime a dozen, kid." Chuck puffed out his chin for effect. I brought my other hand up a bit, so's Chuck

351

could move his attention there. I had a greenback clutched in my fist, enough showing for both Chuck and the mark to see.

"Well, OK," Chuck said, noticeably palming the money. "But don't plan on getting' drunk in here or causin' trouble. A beer and then move on, OK?"

The guy at the back table was trying to act like he wasn't looking, but I knew he was. And I knew I was well on my way to hooking him. Size and looks had always been my disadvantage in high school. But I was turning them to my benefit these days. My friends were out workin' the street corners, rain and all, havin' no more than a couple of minutes to size their marks up before gettin' into their cars. Thanks to my size and appearance, I could stay inside, in bars like this, pretending I might just not be legal, which really turned some guys on, and decide who was worth pursuing—and I made about twice the money on half the men that my friends out on the street did.

I hadn't grown much, if at all, since I was fifteen. The doctors had told my folks just to give it time. Now it could take all the time it wanted. My size and young looks were keepin' me alive and ahead of debt. And it told me just exactly the kind of man to go after. Saved a lot of time and energy, and thus far I've picked well enough to avoid a lot of fuss as well. That's because I've picked guys like that one over in the corner. I knew what he wanted—what he really wanted. I could give him the next best thing. And whatever happened afterward, he couldn't squeal about to the cops.

"Hey, guy, you want a drink? The tables are for customers." Chuck was calling past me, over at the guy I'd marked. Chuck and me had this down pat. This type was a runner just as likely as a buyer.

"Umm, yes . . . please. A beer I guess. Whatever you have on tap." Kind of a wavering voice. I knew he was close to bolting. But he hadn't. Sometimes they left at this point. But if we got them this far and we were positioned this way, Chuck and I had worked out the closin' of the trap door.

"Comin' up," Chuck sang out. "And stay put. I'll deliver."

While we were workin' this out, Chuck had sometimes screwed it up by saying either I would bring the drink to the mark or just that it would be brought to him. As long as he didn't have to think about me, Tim, comin' to his table, comin' closer to him—temptation actually approaching—he'd stay put for the drink.

He panicked, as I knew he would, as I started walkin' toward him, both of our drinks in hand. But I did a little maneuvering around the tables, looking natural but putting me between him and the exit. So he stayed put at the table.

"Here ya' go," I said. "Don't mind if I sit, do you?"

Of course he didn't mind/of course he minded.

"'Cause it's just, just that you look sorta' like my dad—just not mean like him. Is it OK if I just sit a while?"

"Yes, yes, of course, sit," he replied. His breath was ragged. I could feel him torn between runnin' and movin' deeper into what he'd come here for—maybe, just maybe, taking a step across the fantasy/reality divide. And it was just talk. Nothing needed to actually happen.

"Hi, I'm Timmy," I said, giving him a smile and extending my hand out after I'd set the two beers down and sank into the chair next to him, where he'd turn away from the bar area to be talkin' to me. "But you could call me Tim, if you wanted to."

"Hi, Timmy," he said and then "My name is Joe . . . Joe Clifton." I knew that was a fake name, of course. But I hadn't missed the preference for "Timmy." That was a good sign.

"I don't usually come into places like this," I said.

"Neither do I," Joe quickly agreed.

"But I wasn't feelin' well, and when I get like this, I start thinkin' about my family—my dad and all—and I need a drink or somethin' to keep me solid."

"Not feeling well?" He was following along just like I wanted him to.

"No. I get these weak sessions. Can't move too well. The doctors tell me just to stay in my room then. But it's almost spot on the time last year that dad left me, and I couldn't just stay cooped up thinkin' about that and all."

"That's really too—" he said in a low, sympathetic voice.

"And then I saw you," I interrupted, workin' to keep him with me and not doin' too much thinking on his own. "And you

353

reminded me of Dad. Sort of. The dad as I liked to think of him, and . . . oh . . . excuse me. I feel a little faint."

"You OK?" Joe asked, his voice full of concern. He'd laid his hand on my arm as I swayed just a bit, and I could feel the heat and tremble in his touch.

"Uhh, yes. Just a passing spell. Do you have family, Joe?"

"Yes, yes, I do," Joe said. And then I drew it out of him. His wife and two daughters and his son Johnny. I heard the extra clutch in his voice when he talked about Johnny. I knew as much as he did what that really meant to him. I knew exactly what he was struggling with. Why he'd come here today. What he'd put himself up against the edge to try to satisfy. I was banking on bein' the scratch for that itch. Which I figured would be a service to him—and his son.

Then I told him about my family and how I worshiped my dad but that he'd turned away from me when he found I had this strange sickness. Didn't stick with me. I spun quite a story but left out the part about the nice suburban home and my mother's Escalade. A lot to swallow, of course, but these guys always believed just what they wanted to believe.

I'd gotten the beer down by the end of the story, and then I went back into the faint routine.

"Here, here, steady, Timmy," Joe said, now holding me up with both hands. "Maybe we should get something more to drink and eat into you."

"No, no," I answered. "Not here. The bartender said I was only welcome for one drink. Maybe you could just help me home. All I need do is lay down for a bit. It's not far."

"Of course," Joe said. Hooked.

"Home" wasn't really home, of course. It was just a room in a gay fleabag nearby that I rented by the half day on working days.

"Hot, so hot," I muttered when Joe had helped me to the bed and I laid down. Taking the hint, he stripped my T-shirt over my head. I knew my hairless Twink torso turned him on. He was sitting on the bed beside me, and I could see his basket tent right up inside his tailored trousers.

I gave him that dreamy, "I'm ever so grateful" expression as I whispered, "Please, Daddy, Please. Don't leave me."

I drew his face down to mine, and despite the shocked expression on his face, he didn't resist me.

His kiss was warm and increasingly passionate. I opened two of the buttons on his shirt and ran my hand in and pinched at his nipples. He was sobbin' and groanin'. Making sounds like we should stop, but not being able to stop. I made sure of that.

Holding the kiss, I twisted down around him and off the bed and down on my knees between his thighs. His kiss became more possessive, more insistent as I unzipped his pants and pulled his half-engorged cock out.

Then we were no longer kissing, I was kissing and licking his cock. Sucking at the head of it. He was panting hard, his breath rasping. I didn't want him to catch his breath. I didn't want him backing away from this. As I sucked, I pulled his unzipped trousers and his briefs over his hips, him raisin' his butt off the bed at the right moment for that, and cleared them away. He was stripping off his suit jacket and tearing at his dress shirt. Within moments all he was wearin' was a tie and socks—and a big hard on.

He was in good shape, nicely muscled, a nice-sized cock. I was going to enjoy this.

When he was stripped down and trembling under my touch, I looked up into his face, and whispered, "Please, Daddy, please. I want your love."

Joe shuddered. "We can't . . . I didn't . . . we musn't . . ."

I smiled, searched on the floor under the edge of the bedspread, and pulled out the condom packet I had hidden there, among others, earlier, and showed it to him. "Please, Daddy, please."

There was a deep rumbling in Joe's throat, and he sat immobilized, slipping irrevocably over into reality from fantasy as I stood and stripped off my pants, straddled him, and held his cock up and steady while I rolled the condom on it and then descended my ass on it. A growl started up from far down inside him as I slowly pumped up and down on his engorged cock, pulling him farther inside me with each descent.

Then he was freed, a wild man, a daddy in full control, taking his pleasure. He came up off the bed, carrying me with him, and stood in the center of the room, crouched slightly, bent at the knees, lapping me, his palms on my buttocks as I locked my fists behind his neck and he pounded me up and down on his cock, endlessly, until his lust was released deep inside me.

I wasn't at all surprised that he was crying out, "Johnny, Johnny, Johnny," as he fucked me in his primeval frenzy. I have no idea, though, if he realized what name he was calling out. If he did, he didn't let on.

Spent and starting to regain control of himself, he turned and gently laid me down on the bed. He was red-faced, nearly overtaken by embarrassment and remorse. I tugged on his arm, bringing him down onto the bed, and, following my guidance, he stretched out beside me. His face was buried in the hollow of my neck and he was sobbing. His body was trembling all over. I took his hand and guided it down to my pert cock and made him fist me. I put my hand over his and guided him in stroking my cock till he was doin' that with his own rhythm. Then I left him to it and moaned and sighed for him. I took his head in my hands and moved his lips to mine, and we kissed. When he melted to me there, I moved his lips down to my nipples and arched my back and moaned deeply for him—and ejaculated for him too. He shuddered then, as if the struggle inside him was over, as if all his secrets were stripped away.

"Please, Timmy. Please . . . I want you again," he murmured in a halting voice.

That's when I told him how worried I was—that I couldn't become involved. That I didn't want to be hurt. That I could barely make ends meet. That I planned to move on to another town where there might be work for me. A hint of him having taken advantage of me—in my weakness. Of how big and powerful his cock was. Of how I melted to havin' him inside me. But, no, that I didn't think I could risk it again. All of the time I was stroking his cock and moving my body against his.

"I have money," Joe croaked. "Lots of it. I'll take care of you. I won't abandon you like your father did."

"Shush, Daddy," I whispered. Then I pretended to realize for the first time that he had a finger at my hole again and was slow-fucking me with it.

"Oh, oh, OH!" I cried out and ground my ass against the palm of his hand. "Please, Daddy, Please. Fuck me again. Now! Be good to me. Take care of me."

Joe lost control again and rolled me onto my stomach on the bed, pulled my belly up with the palm of his hand as he straddled my hips and crouched over my ass cheeks and thrust inside me. Fucking me hard. Just as I wanted. And I moaned and groaned for my daddy.

Hours later, when he had left me, I looked over at the nightstand and saw several more twenties than I had imagined I would end up with. Quite satisfying. And a service, I told myself. Joe would be back. And as long as he—and the others like him—came back to me, I would be financially solvent and his Johnny would be safe.

Or so I told myself.

Resting a Demon

I thought I was going to be sick. His mother asked him to entertain us, to play something for us on the piano, and the pert-butt blond tossed the curl out of his face and flowed over to the piano and started to fill the room with Chopin. I'd had this kid in my craw for a good fifteen years, and all I wanted to do was to slam him to the floor and fuck the stuffing out of him. And that was when he was just a series of pictures and narratives in letters from his mother to mine. And now here he was in the flesh, Mr. Perfect. And, damn if he didn't play Chopin like a concert pianist.

His mother, Belle, and mine had gone to school together—more than that, they'd been in the same little social clique from kindergarten through high school in a very small town. Belle had been told she couldn't have any kids. And she didn't have any kids until very late in life, and then there was Jon; her pride and joy. I was the third of five my mother had birthed and was six years old when Jon was born. Mother hadn't thrown it up to Belle that she could have kids at a drop of a hat and Belle couldn't, but from the moment Jon popped out, Belle thought he was the only kid in the world and had made a career out of pushing that idea with all her friends and one upping any talent or achievement mentioned about any other kid in town.

And I think she called my mother every day of her life and had a camera implanted between her tits, so she—and all of her friends—wouldn't miss any of the wonderful things Jon was doing.

We lived half a continent away from her, but every time I turned around, my mother was reporting the latest trip to the top of Everest that Jon had taken—walked and talked and pooped where he was supposed to months before any other kid. Straight As at school and first prizes in art, and baseball, and football, and archery, and swimming, and, of course, piano and violin and trumpet. Prom king and a child TV model, and he'd almost made the Olympics as a gymnast. Two years ago he'd graduated from high school (valedictorian, of course) and enlisted in the Navy, where he went off for a two-year stint and saved the world.

When I'd agreed to drive my mother for a visit with her friend, Belle, I steeled myself for Belle's litany of Jon's superlatives, but little had I known that he arrived home just a few days before our visit, finished with his naval duty, where he'd risen to officer status faster than any other known sailor but had left the Navy because he'd been accepted at Yale for the coming semester.

I was trying my best to be polite, but I know that if Belle had noticed I was in the room at all while she was talking a mile a minute at my mom, she would have caught my sullen looks and, no doubt, compared them unfavorably with her son's perpetual perfect-teeth smile. As it was, as soon as Jon had finished at the piano, she launched into a glowing review of Jon's life with my mother and lost track of both me and Jon altogether.

This turned out to be a very good idea, because Jon came over and flashed me a very warm smile, told me I looked real hot in my jeans and sport coat, and plopped down very near me on a sofa.

"So, how did you like my rendering of Chopin?" he asked me.

"Sounded great to me," I answered. "But I admit that I'm not much of a piano expert."

"It helps to have good fingers," he said, and held up two hands showing very nice, long fingers. When he brought the hands back down, though, one went to the side of my thigh and fanned out. I felt my cock come to life, and I'm sure he noticed that, because my jeans were pretty tight—and my cock is supersized.

"But I'll bet you're more of a trumpet man," he went on to say. "I blow . . . a pretty mean trumpet too, I'm told."

Yes, that's what I'm told ad nauseam too is what I wanted to say. But, instead, I said, "So, did they let you blow the trumpet in the Navy? I mean, you didn't get out of practice, I hope."

"No I didn't get out of practice in the Navy. I got a lot of practice blowing in the Navy. But I didn't have my trumpet there. It's down in the basement, though. Would you like to see my trumpet while our mothers visit?"

By now, his hand was on my basket, tracing my cock through the tight material, so there was no chance that I was missing his meaning.

"Maybe we could fuck around too."

"Sure, I'd like that," I croaked.

We stood, and Jon told his mother he was taking me down in the basement to show me his naval ship models. But neither she nor my mother even seemed to hear him as engrossed as they were in their discussion.

Down the stairs we went and into some sort of rec room, with models of Navy ships lined up on shelves around the room. Jon closed and locked the door and quickly crossed the carpet to me, shedding his shirt en route. He got me into a lip lock and had me stripped down to the waist in no time flat. I had to admit that Belle was right—this kid was really good.

Really, really good, because he had one arm around me, holding me to him, and his other hand, with those long, sensuous fingers, was playing my nipples and pecs and belly as expertly as he had played Chopin.

"God, you're beautiful, man," we whispered into my neck. "I've lusted after you for years just from those pictures your mother sent."

My mother had sent pictures? I had always assumed that was a one-way street between Belle and my mom.

"But we never got a picture of this," he said with a husky voice. His hand had unbuttoned my jeans and found its way under my briefs and to my engorging cock. "Man oh man, it's huge."

"Not yet, it isn't," I responded with some sense of pride. I was fairly sure he hadn't bested me in that department, at least.

Jon's response was to quickly tongue his way down my torso, pull my jeans down to the floor, and apply his lips to tracing my cock through my briefs. There was a pool table in the center of the room, and I just leaned back on that and sighed and moaned as he pulled my briefs and jeans off and showed me what the Navy had taught him about blowing cocks, which was a lot.

When I couldn't take it anymore, I grabbed hold of his arms, pulled him up to a standing position, and folded him down to where his belly was on the pool table top. I crouched down behind him, pulled his pants and briefs down and off his legs, and went for his asshole with my tongue. It was immediately apparent that he had specialized in bottom while in the Navy, which was just fine with me. In no time, he was wet and open to me, and I had buried my cock eight inches into him and was fucking him just as hard as I had been wanting to do all these years because he and his legend had been such a pain in my ass. And he was loving it. His only complaint was that he wanted to watch me while I fucked him, so I spun him around slowly on my throbbing spit, so that his back was on the top of the pool table, and I came up on the table on my knees with my thighs under his butt cheeks and my cock still buried in his ass.

He didn't just lay there while I fucked him. I was holding his legs out with my hands, but he used his strong back muscles to move his pelvis with me, meeting me thrust for thrust. He was panting and moaning, and his gorgeous, well-muscled torso was writhing under me. He pleaded with me to fuck him deep and hard, which I needed no encouragement to do. I entertained him with a pattern of alternating short and long strokes and fast and slow rhythms that caused him to give out little yelps of delight that I was afraid could be heard upstairs. And his gasps and shudders told me that he really enjoyed it when I rotated my cock around in his hole and gave his ass passage walls some individual attention. He was working his own cock with long, sensuous fingers, and he came before I did. When I felt I was ready to cum, I pulled out of him and shot off across his stomach. He pulled me down to him, and we went into a long, sensuous kiss as our trembling bodies calmed down and cooled off.

We must have been gone for a good half hour, but when we returned to the living room, dressed once again and looking as innocent as possible, I at first thought Belle and my mother hadn't even realized we'd gone. But Belle stopped in midsentence and turned and spoke to us.

"Did you have a nice time showing Carl your models and explaining naval vessels to him, Jon, dear?"

"Yes, Mother," Jon answered contritely, "Although I found that Carl knows a whole lot about submarines—probably more than I do. He took the largest sub down there and showed me some tricks about deep diving."

"Did he?" Belle answered absentmindedly, "Quite impressive."

"Yes, it nearly took my breath away."

But Belle wasn't even listening anymore. She was back into a monologue on how a mutual friend of hers and my mother's had been putting on a lot of weight.

"Yes, well, if you're still visiting, Mother, I thought I'd take Carl up to my room and rummage through my trophy case and show him some of my game balls."

"That's nice, dear. When you come back down, we'll have some cake. I'm sure you'll be hungry then."

"So, would you like to see my balls?" Jon asked me mischievously as we mounted the stairs.

"Sure," I answered. "But I think you might be too full for cake before we come back down." And, as I followed Jon up the stairs, I put my hand through his legs and got a head start on getting the heft of his balls while he jiggled his pert butt for me. I had to admit that there were some talents Jon had that I was growing to appreciate.

363

Restrained Freedom

We sat there sipping coffee and chowing down on donuts in an all-night diner, my new partner Hank and me. I was trying to figure him out. Ever since I'd come out in the department, potential street-duty partners had avoided me like the plague. But here I understood that Hank had asked to be partnered with me. As I drank coffee and listened to him complaining about his wife, Janine, I was wondering if maybe he swung both ways. I certainly wouldn't mind if he did. He was a good ten years older than I was and outweighed me by at least twenty pounds, but he was all muscle and handsome as all get out. Dark complexioned and black curly hair matting his forearms and pushing out at the neck of his blue uniform shirt. Pale blue eyes and a smile to die for. Some kind of Latin. And you know what they say about Latins.

The open neck of his blue uniform shirt. There it was. I thought to myself, "Shit. Nailed it with that swinging both ways supposition."

"Does this mean what I think it means?" I asked, as I moved my hand to under his chin and got the round medallion on a sterling string between two fingers. It was red, white, and black enamel on silver in a design like that Oriental Yin-Yang swirling tear drop pattern, but with three swirls rather than two—the universal sign of BDSM.

"Yeah, that's exactly what it means," Hank said, staring me down real good. He moved his hand to behind his collar and pulled around another silver charm he'd been keeping at that back of his chain. It was a miniature set of handcuffs. When he brought it back around to where I could see it, his fingers lingered on mine at the other medallion.

"Women or men—or both?"

"What do you think? You haven't noticed how I am around you?"

I put my face in my hands then, briefly, and then looked up at the ceiling. When I could look him in the eye again, I was sure he could see right into me.

"Do you mind?" He asked. "What I really mean is are you interested? I maneuvered like hell to get a partnership with you. I've had my eye on you since you were transferred to the squad. I can usually read a man well. I mean, I knew you went with men; I just had to be sure you'd give me what I need. God, you're a man's man."

"Fuck yes, I'm interested," I whispered hoarsely to him under the din of the noise of the civilians around us who either couldn't sleep or were on their way to an early shift or back from a late shift. I raised my foot and forced it between his thighs under the table, crushing the sole of my boot into his crotch to emphasize my interest—and a taste of what I could do. He gave me a surprised, but desired-filled look, gripped the edges of the table with white-knuckled fists, and squeezed my calf tightly between his thighs to confirm his own interest.

"But what about Janine?" I continued nonchalantly. "I'd heard you were happily married and an attentive daddy." I dropped my hand from his medallion, not wanting those around us to get the right idea about what we were discussing.

"Yeah, I am," he answered. "I can't explain it, but I've got these urges that go beyond Janine and the family thing. It is getting a little tedious with Janine. Being with a guy now and then heightens the pleasure for both me and Janine when we fuck."

"But bondage and S&M?" I asked. "That's quite a bit farther along that road. And it can get rough."

"I like it rough," Hank shot back. "And the bondage? Well, I think that helps take the guilt away. If I'm bound, it's like I really am not making the choice, if you know what I mean—restrained but suddenly free to fully enjoy it."

I sat and stared at Hank for a couple of minutes, grabbing the edge of the table hard where his fists had just been to keep my hands off him. But I could feel the juices flowing already.

"Well, when it's convenient, maybe we can hook up and . . ."

"Now," Hank hissed through his teeth in a voice strangled with urgency. "When I saw you in the showers this evening after the squad workout and before we hit the streets, I nearly creamed myself. I wanted you to see my jewelry. I wore these today on purpose. I want you take me someplace right now, tie me up, and fuck me hard."

"Well, if it's a quiet night, I know of some places we can park. The car's not the best place, but . . ."

I felt an insistent buzzing in one of my pockets that had nothing to do with the effect Hank was having on my cock.

"Shit," I exclaimed as I reached for my mobile phone. "It's dispatch."

I listened to the assignment call for a several seconds. Hank was already standing and flipping a couple of bills on the table.

"Trouble?"

"Yeah, I'm afraid so. But not a rush, rush. They caught up with that guy who's been kidnapping and raping those college guys over on the east side. We're to go pat down his pad. Guess our business will have to hold fire for a bit."

"Yeah, I guess you're right," Hank said. I kinda liked the tone of regret in his voice on that one.

Chas Sheldon, a smart-assed cop in our squad who razzed me pretty bad about my preferences was standing at the door of the small, rundown bungalow hidden in the undergrowth of a quiet east side street when we rolled into the driveway. He was giving me a snide stare as Hank and I approached.

"You'll just love this one, Lance," he said to me as we walked up to him. "It's right up your alley." He sniggered at his double entendre. Real genius; I bet he'd been working on that for a half an hour.

"Yeah, well, they couldn't have gotten this guy any too soon in my opinion," I answered brusquely. "Any sign of any of the missing men?"

"Just the one we caught him in the act with," Sheldon smirked. "He was pretty far gone, but they've sent him off to the hospital already, and the perp just left for the department in a squad car. We caught him doin' it and followed the book, so this one should be air tight. The forensics crew has started on the basement, but I think they're about ready to call it a day. We've got a crew starting to dig in the backyard too, but it will be too dark to continue with that for a while. Guess you'll want to see the scene yourself though, to, ya know, get some pointers maybe."

I could have shoved my fist down Sheldon's throat, but that would just make for good conversation and more razzing in the squad room. Hank gave a disgusted sound deep down in his throat and pushed on by Sheldon and into the house. I was senior and hadn't gotten the full assignment pass yet, so I stuck with Sheldon for the moment.

"So, what's the call here?" I asked. Sheldon saw that I wasn't going to rise to the bait, so he got through it quickly with just one more jab.

"I was just to stick around until another set of blues— which would be the two of you, I suppose—showed up. Since they won't be able to process the scene completely until tomorrow, we're to maintain a presence here overnight. I understand you've got the shift for the next four hours and then they'll send someone else. Think you can handle that without messing up the toys in there?"

"Roger, Sergeant," I said, staring right at him, reminding him that I outranked him. "By all means shove off now. Hank and I will hold the place."

He was maybe going to say something else, but then he got a look in my eyes, finally got around to assessing my muscles against his, and considered the rumors of what my interests and abilities were, and then just shut up.

I pushed by him and turned back after I'd gotten inside the door to see that he was already half way across the yard to his ride. I looked around for Hank but didn't see him in the small, drab living or dining rooms. I found him in a back bedroom, just standing there, mesmerized by the trophy photos this perp had papered the wall with of what he'd been doing to his victims. I could see at a glance that the perp had been busy and had quite an imagination. Hank was growling deep down in his throat again and was rubbing a hand up and down on his crotch. No doubt that the photos and the other paraphernalia in the room were turning him on.

I swung on my heels and made tracks to the basement in time to see that the forensics crew was struggling up the steps into the kitchen with their bulky cases banging against the stairwell walls and would be gone for the night within a couple of minutes. I quickly scanned the basement to see what I could see and then followed the technicians back up the dark stairwell. As they left the house, I looked out in the backyard and saw the last of the workers out there leaving as well. I prowled around the house quickly to ensure that Hank and I were alone now and locked the front door from the inside before I returned to the back bedroom.

Hank had his pants down around his ankles, although he still had his equipment belt around his waist, and he was all bug-eyed staring at the photos while he pulled on his good-sized dick.

With a mind to what he'd said he needed to perform, I quickly got him into a pair of cuffs hanging conveniently from the upper wall in front of him, which pulled his arms over his head and trapped him there, facing the wall. Then I stood close behind him, my crotch plastered to his exposed butt cheeks so he could feel me getting bigger down there and wrapped my arms around him. I took over stroking down on his cock and squeezing his hefty balls with one hand, while I unbuttoned his shirt with my other hand. As I went for his nipples, he arched his head back to me and we kissed deeply. There was no doubt that he was ready for this.

I reached down and grabbed his balls again and squeezed hard until he yelped. When I let loose, he was breathing hard but he was giving me a look with his eyes that told me he was up for this.

I broke and looked behind me to see what sorts of toys and aids our perp might have dropped around the room. With little effort, I came up with a leg spreader bar, a ball gag with two nipple clamps hanging from it at the end of small-linked chains, an outlandish-sized flexible dildo, and a tube of lubricant. If Hank needed bondage to get excited, then I'd see just how excited Hank could get.

Coming up behind him, I had the ball gag in his mouth and snugly tied off before he even knew what was happening to him. I then stripped his pants all of the way off his legs and clamped the spreader bar between his thighs, forcing him into a wide stance. He was squirming around now and pulling at his wrist restraints. I moved around to in front of him, between him and the wall, and lifted the long, thick dildo up to his eye level. He went all wild-eyed and backed away from me as far as the restraints would permit, but I had one of my hands wrapped around his dick, so I knew he was finding this very stimulating. I rubbed the dildo around on his cheeks for a short time to let him feel the texture and size of it.

I then slowly started tonguing, kissing, and teething my way down his chest, around his nipples and down his washboard abs. I reached up and applied the nipple clamps hanging down from the ball gag one after the other to his nipples, and I heard stifled screams from him from behind his gag. I brought the tip of the dildo to his navel and rotated it around the rim and pressed it in a bit to give him something to think about for when I moved to behind him. The gurgling sound he now was making around the rubber ball in his mouth told me he got the message. Down his belly and into his pubes my mouth and the twirling dildo moved.

I then played with his dick and balls with my mouth and slid the dildo back across the perineum through his legs and back and forth across his puckered asshole until he melted to me. I was deepthroating him, and he was making very satisfied, if muffled, noises from his mouth and had set up a rhythm with his hips. I didn't want this to get too conventional, though, so I popped his nicely engorged cock out of my mouth and moved through his legs, my tongue tracing the journey from the base of his balls all the way back to his asshole.

I rimmed Hank's ass with my tongue at first, letting my tongue flicker into his hole and pushing his butt cheeks apart with my hands. The leg spreaders helped keep him open to me. He writhed in pleasure above me, obviously enjoying the attention. From time to time, I let a hand stray between his legs to check out his cock to ensure it hadn't lost interest and to squeeze and roll his balls.

I had his asshole well lubricated with my spit now, and it was nicely open to me. I stood up and stripped down and reached for the tube of lubricant and lathered up the dildo real well. I moved behind Hank and slapped my half-hard cock around on his butt cheeks. I'd seen him eyeing me in the showers, so he knew I was horse hung. I wasn't as horse hung as the dildo I'd lubed up, though. After that, he wouldn't have trouble handling me at all.

Hank seemed to like the feel of my cock beating against his butt cheeks. I soon had substituted the dildo though, and I worked it ever closer to his asshole. He arch his back, brought his legs back, and dipped his chest when he felt the head of the dildo gently rimming his asshole. He'd seen it and knew how long and thick it was and was doing all he could to ensure it didn't split him in two when I'd worked it in—which I proceeded to do slowly but relentlessly. I had nearly a foot of thick dildo to work inside him, and I took a long time doing so. It had an extra bulbous mushroom head on it, so there was no buildup of strain as it moved up his canal—the biggest was always right up front.

Hank was straining and grunting and groaning through the experience, but I could tell that he was with me on this, that this was exactly what he wanted and that was keeping him on edge. I was getting excited now too. The way he was straining back, there was a shelf at his waist above his big, round butt cheeks, and when I'd gotten the dildo all the way in, I hiked my right leg up onto this shelf and nestled closely into Hank. My now-engorged cock was rubbing up against his left hip, and I knew he was aware of it there. My right hand held the dildo inside his ass and corkscrewed it inside him and slowly churned it in and out, while I wrapped my other arm around him and my left hand pinched on his nipple clamps and stroked down to his cock and balls and gave them some more attention. I kissed and nuzzled his shoulder blades while he trembled underneath me, a background of pain swept over with intense pleasure.

He came in my hand then in a prodigious fountain of pent-up man juice.

I untied and pulled the gag from his mouth and ripped the clamps off his nipples. Free to speak, he told me through gasps and groans that the dildo was awesome but that he wanted me to fuck him with my own cock, that he had wanted my cock inside him for some time.

But I hadn't ungagged him to hear this. I had wanted him free to scream through the next procedure—to be able to tell me if and when he really couldn't endure any more.

I lifted my leg off the small of his back and slowly pulled the dildo out—but when I could see the rim of the mushroom head, I plunged it back in up to the hilt. Hank threw his head back and screamed at the ceiling, but I covered his mouth in a brutal kiss, as I pumped the dildo deep inside him for another thirty seconds. I could feel his knees going to rubber, and I pulled the dildo all the way out and threw it to the side.

"Now you," Hank gasped. "Now your cock inside me. That ring through the head. I want to feel that ring deep inside me."

"Eventually," I whispered in his ear. "First some police work, though."

He felt me pulling his billy club out of the equipment belt that still encircled his waist, and he started to moan and hiccup in fear.

"No, man. Not that. Please."

I lathered the belly club up and leaned my mouth back to just inches from his ear.

"I've heard you've used this in perps before," I whispered. "Haven't you ever wondered how it felt?"

"No, no, Lance. Not that. NO! A-u-g-g-h!"

The billy club wasn't nearly as thick or as long as the dildo had been, but, although it also was rubberized, it also wasn't as flexible as the dildo, so it could only go straight up his canal.

"Oh Gawd, oh Gawd, Ah, FUCK!"

"Precisely," I said in a deep-throated voice, now on the edge myself. "I wonder if the perp who owns this place ever let his victims scream like you are. I wonder if the neighbors heard nothing—or if they heard and did nothing. If they can hear you, maybe they'll just think it's business as usual in here."

Hank had obviously had enough of this, so I stopped, wiped his billy club off on the edge of the bedspread and sheathed it back on his equipment belt.

"But I want you to fuck me now, Lance. No more of this dildo shit. Get that big prick inside me."

"OK, sure," I said. "But I was kind of wondering what our perp might have down in the basement that the forensics team was so interested in checking out." I, of course, knew precisely what was in the basement awaiting us.

I looked around and found some leg shackles and exchanged these for the leg spreader, clamping them at his ankles. I released his wrists from the wall restraints but quickly had him locked up again with my own handcuffs. I shuffled him through the house and down the basement stairs, and, I quite enjoyed Hank's excitement when we found a black-painted, padded-walled room with a sling on chains hanging from the ceiling in the middle.

I pulled Hank's shirt off his back as I pushed his butt down into the center of the sling. He didn't fight me as I uncuffed his wrists and recuffed them high on the suspending chains running up on either side of his torso and then unshackled his ankles and cuffed those up high on the two suspending chains running up on either side of his butt.

I unpopped the gag then and let him talk—and grunt and pant and moan—me through what he liked and what he really liked—and what sent him over the moon. It turns out he liked ten minutes of tonguing his asshole and fifteen minutes of fingering and nearly fisting his asshole. And he really liked throwing his head back and sucking me off while I pinched his nipples. He also really liked thirty minutes of my cock churning inside him with a string of beads I'd found nearby attached to the silver ring piercing the head of my cock combined with what my hands were doing on his torso and with his dick and balls. But what sent him howling over the moon was the twenty minutes of deep fucking with the electrified cock sheath and extender I'd found that made my cock thicker and longer—and more highly charged—then the dildo had been.

During the two hours we spent in that basement room, we each came two more times and Hank admitted that this session had far surpassed what he had been expecting.

In the time we had left, I smoked a cigarette and tossed off some of the perp's scotch while Hank moved around in the nude, cleaning up after our use of the facilities. When he'd finish, I slammed him down on his back on the kitchen table and scrambled up and crouched on top of his chest, my knees pinning his arms against his sides. I forced him to suck me off one last time, with me bobbing his head back and forth on my cock with my fingers buried in his hair and brutally fucking his mouth and throat. He seemed to enjoy that as much as anything that had gone before and gushed over with the regret that we couldn't have access to the toys in this devil's den any more.

As we were leaving, I assured him that we'd have plenty of opportunity to explore our fetishes and that what I had in my basement made this place look like a nursery school.

Saddled

I was immediately suspicious. Leon was smiling today and talking nice. Just yesterday he'd propositioned me for the hundredth time and I'd turned him down for the hundredth and one times—I'd turned him down before he asked the first time—and then he'd gotten pissy and I'd given him lip back and he'd pulled back a lucrative assignment. A faded, and largely harmless, movie star gig that would have paid my rent for the rest of the month.

And yet he'd called me in again today. Usually after one of these fights with my pimp, I would be left in limbo for a week or more. I decided he must be short of staff.

"You ride a horse, don't you?" he asked, using his fat lips to shift his smoldering cigar from one cheek to the other.

"Yes, of course," I answered, thinking that maybe that's what narrowed down the pickings to me.

"Thought so. Pack your bags for the weekend." And, with that, Leon slapped an airplane ticket folder down on the coffee table. I picked it up. Destination Dulles Airport, the international airport located in northern Virginia that serviced the Washington, D.C., area.

"Where from there?" I asked.

"You'll be picked up. Client doesn't want to say."

"And the driver will know me by . . .?"

"Oh, yeah, you'll be a platinum blond." Leon was smiling. I didn't think this was all he had to say. But I stood and turned for the door. If I had to dye my hair before I had to be at the airport, I'd best get to it.

"All over." Leon said. I turned, and he was grinning. Well, OK, that made sense if the hair color was a fetish of the client's. More time, though. Still Leon seemed entirely too pleased. I stood there, knowing I hadn't heard it all yet.

"Except, there is to be little all over. You're to shave everything but your head and a V at the bush."

"A V at the bush," I said in a deadpanned voice.

"Yes, pointing to the goods."

"Well, OK, I've had to do worse," I said. I took one last look at Leon before I turned and left the room. He still had a sloppy grin on his face. And I still had the uneasy feeling that I didn't know everything he found amusing. But it wasn't my job to know everything. I got paid very well for doing what I did and shutting up about it.

My plane was two hours late landing at Dulles, apparently because bad weather at both the Chicago and Atlanta airports, which were nowhere near was I was traveling, had the jets stacked up in holding patterns across the country. I didn't mind the extra time in the air, though. Our flight wasn't crowded, and I made friends with a distinguished-looking man sitting beside me who I'm sure I recognized from the television as in some sort of political job. We had enough time to chat that the delay earned me an extra $100, when I let him slip into one of the johns with me and give me a blow job, him sitting on the can beating his meat into a paper hand towel and me with my butt perched on the small sink and my heels dug into the floor to counteract the slight pitching of the plane. He seemed turned on by the platinum-blond V and licked it down into swirls of curly waves, so I guess that wasn't such a bad idea after all.

He wanted my number, saying he'd like to see me under less restricted circumstances, and I gave him the card for my services in L.A. He didn't even bat I eyelash when I cited the ballpark figure of what I cost; he just said it shouldn't be that long before he had reason to be on the West Coast. I told him who to ask for, and he wrote it on the card.

I hadn't been standing at the baggage area for long—I didn't have more than I could put in my carry-on, but this was where I was told to stand—before I was approached by an extremely well-turned-out coffee-with-cream young guy, complete with contrasting dark brown chauffeur's livery and a big welcoming smile on his face. He was maybe three or four years younger than me and shorter than I was by a couple of inches and a little stocky—but in a solid, four hours-a-day in the gym sort of way. Bullet headed, totally bald, big hands, big feet in his slicked-up black shiny shoes. All promising.

He seemed to have no question who I was. I was standing in front of the designated pillar just off to the left of the baggage belt—and there was the platinum hair that I had moussed up into slight spikes. The West Coast surfer look to go with the tan I'd worked so hard on. I struck the pose for him, and I could tell in an instant he was interested. I often found the clients barely fuckable, but I occasionally, like now, was able to develop other side prospects while on a job. That gym-muscled look, the big hands and the big feet. And the bald head. Testosterone building up somewhere.

He took my bag, even though we both knew I could handle it without any huffing, and led me up the ramp to where a black Lincoln limo was parked right at the door, its engine idling, daring an airport cop to give it a ticket and find out who he or she had inconvenienced.

Eric wasn't exactly chatty, but he willingly gave me his name as we nosed out of the airport spaghetti pattern of roads and onto Route 28—at least according to the signs—and headed east toward I-95, the main highway running north and south on the East Coast. He didn't ask me my name, however, and he shut down when I asked him the name of the one who had sent for me. Good. Eric didn't fuck and tell.

When he turned west on Route 50 before we got to the intersection with I-95, he was friendly enough to tell me where we were going.

"Middleburg. We'll still be in this suburban congestion for a while, but it won't be much more than half an hour now before we reach Middleburg. Five Oaks. It's just on the other side of Middleburg."

Ah, information. I liked to have my bearings. At least something to process if a client was being too rough and I wanted to head for the exit.

"Middleburg. Middleburg. I've heard of that before, but I don't—"

"Maybe from back in the Kennedy era," Eric said. He had his eyes looking at me in the rearview mirror. He looked very interested. He obviously had been told not to say much, but he wanted to be friendly. He was assessing me just like I was assessing him.

"You may be too young," he continued, "but you may have heard about Jackie Kennedy and her horse riding both when her husband was president and then for years later. They had a retreat out here in Middleburg. They ride to the hounds out here, old Southern style. The closest place to the White House that she could do that."

Ah, yes, I remembered hearing that now. Horse riding. Another piece of the puzzle Leon had tossed out on the coffee table. I was riding to the hounds this weekend, maybe. I wondered if Leon had any idea what the difference was between western saddle riding in California canyons and riding to the hounds in Virginia. Well, I'd cope. I always did.

"Thanks, Eric," I said. "Thanks for the information."

"Don't mention it." He was giving me a big smile in the mirror. Some sort of understanding established. I had a friend here if I needed it—maybe a very friendly friend. I took the plunge.

"Later, maybe, Dude?" I said and flashed him a smile.

He gave me a questioning look.

"A freebie hookup. I like the way you're cut. I assume you know why I'm here. I mean, if you're—"

"I'd like that," Eric answered, the grin I could see in the rearview mirror going from ear to ear.

This must be my generous week, I thought. I'd gotten in the mood because of Leon's shit. I felt the need to give it away to someone. The guy on the plane acted like he would become

378

just another paying customer. That wouldn't be sticking it to Leon.

After driving through Middleburg, one of those "quaint" little country towns that looked like it had barely cleared the eighteenth century and was obviously dripping in both old and new money, we drove for maybe six more miles. The scenery was quite an attractive and calming switch from the frenetic pace and arid conditions I'd left that morning—rolling Virginia countryside of majestic oak trees, well-trimmed pasture land, and endless sweeps of white wood rail fencing set against the backdrop of bluish-shaded mountains to the west. We turned off to the south and drove not more than a half mile more before we turned right between two massive stone columns with marble eagles perched on top of each. A bronze plaque in one of the columns announced we were at Five Oaks.

"The five oaks are all gone now," Eric suddenly piped up from the front seat. He hadn't spoken since we'd struck our unspoken deal. We'd both been sitting and enjoying the scenery—and at least I was contemplating what Eric had to offer under that dark brown chauffeur's livery.

I grunted my acknowledgment that I'd heard what he said and appreciated the bit of conversation. He went on, "There are more like a hundred oaks now. Northern money."

Another piece of proffered information. A client who was rich and on the make in the South while being carpetbagger. Grasping and probably anger issues. I sensed bondage and maybe a bit of SM. Well, with the fees we charged, we did see a bit of that. Leon knew I had my limits. But maybe that was why Leon was so nice all of a sudden after our fight and had that sloppy grin on his face when we parted.

We drove for maybe another quarter mile on a freshly asphalted two-lane road running between some or all of those hundred oaks, which must have been pretty mature when they were planted, because they were quite impressive now.

I heard where we were headed before I saw it. The baying of hounds. We turned a corner and there it was, a massive, stately brick building, a traditional American Georgian four over four over an English basement with wide portico held up by four hefty white columns. Newer, but still old, two-story brick wings jutted out from either flank of the antebellum center structure. And gathered on an oval lawn in front of the house was a swirl of sleek, lean horses; riders in scarlet coats and tan breeches; and an undercurrent of teeming hounds, some black, some brown, but most white with brown splotches on them. Everything was chaos and loud gossiping and obvious preparation for a fox hunt. I thought I'd stumbled onto an MGM set. I expected to see Elizabeth Taylor and Rock Hudson stride down the stairs from the portico and mount their fine fillies at any moment.

I had only a glimpse of this, though, as Eric pulled the limo around the side of the house and wound his way through a sea of Mercedes and Jaguars and BMWs, many with horse trailers attached, all parked willy-nilly around under the trees at the side and back of the house. Eric pulled up to a detached five-car garage, hidden neatly behind huge boxwoods at the back corner of the house. He retrieved my bag from the trunk and ushered me, without a word, as if he sensed we now were being closely monitored, into a side door of the house.

We were in a narrow, oriental-carpeted hallway that split the width of the house. From down the hall, a distant patch of light, I could hear loud conversation and the braying of a loud voice for someone to get out there and get the hunt in order and then we arrived in the broad center hallway of the center structure.

The braying voice belonged to a distinguished-looking, trim, yet solidly built, handsome in a matured way man, carefully barbered hair with graying at the temples, standing at the foot of a sweeping curved staircase rising to the upper story, several paces short of a double door with wide side windows looking out onto the portico. The doors were open, and I once again saw beyond those the swirl of scarlet jackets and fine horse flesh standing in a frenetic swirl of braying hounds. The man, who obviously was in charge—who obviously was in charge no matter where he was—was alone in the foyer by the time Eric and I reached it. He turned and saw us and scowled.

"You're late," he said. "Almost missed it. Eric take him to the scarlet room. Dress quickly and come down. We have a horse ready for you. You should be able to make the last trumpet."

That was it. That was all he said, and then he was out the door. I didn't have much doubt this was the client and that he was the dominating type.

We started up the stairs, Eric ushering me to go first. Half way up we were accosted by another equestrian hurrying down the stairs, pulling on white kid gloves, decked out like the rest, a black velvet-covered helmet already on his head.

The same man who had just walked out the front door onto the portico.

"You're late," he said in the same disapproving, "to be obeyed" voice. "Dress quickly and get out there." He swept by me, brushing against my sleeve. Eric, probably well accustomed to this, deftly turned to let him pass without contact.

Twins. There were two of them. Another possibility for Leon's grin.

Eric escorted me up the stairs and down a long transverse hallway deep into one of the wings. The silence of the house contrasted with the muted sound of the developing hunt filtering through thick brick walls. He stopped at the last door down on the hall at the back of the house, opened the door and set my carry-on inside, and then stepped back to let me enter. When I had moved through the door, it clicked behind me, and I was alone.

Scarlet was a good name for the room. It certainly was scarlet—the carpet, the drapes on the windows, the bedspread and drapery on the solid mahogany four-poster canopy bed set between two windows looking into the back yard. The spines on the books in the bookcases beside the fireplace. A rich-looking oriental rug spread in front of the fireplace had a scarlet background. Even the burnished wood of the walls, and the fireplace mantel and surround were a rich red mahogany.

I could see riding clothes laid out on the bed and a pair of gleaming black leather riding booths at the foot of the bed, with a black leather riding crop balanced on the toes. A riding shirt, a scarlet jacket, a black velvet-covered riding helmet, and a pair of tan breeches that flared at the hips and had leather ovals at the inner thighs—the three-quarter-length breeches that were called jodhpurs. And an athletic supporter with a sturdy cup made out of some sort of hard plastic.

I walked over to the foot of the bed and looked up into the canopy frame. Just as I thought. A steel-cage structure inside the wooden frame that gave the bed stability and would take a lot of weight and movement. And in the upper corners at the top of the pillars at the foot of the bed, leather leads and ankle restraints tucked up into the canopy. I walked around to the head of the bed as I started shedding my clothes. I saw the black leather bands around slats at the headboard and looked between the headboard and the wall. Sure enough, wrist restraints tucked down there. I opened the door of the nightstand beside the bed. Piles of condoms, tubes of lube, a collection of dildos, leather blindfolds, and gags with rubber balls for the mouth to prevent the subject from biting his tongue or pulverizing his teeth by gnashing them.

Scarlet room. A very good name for it. Well, forewarned and all that. At least the fee was appropriately impressive.

I dressed quickly, and all fit well—Leon obviously having given them my measurements—except that the jodhpurs were skin tight, were so low slung the top of my platinum V spilled out in curls over the waistband before I got the shirt and jacket on, and I wasn't so sure that the seams of the jodhpurs would hold under the strain of my thighs and glutes.

The hunt wasn't anything to write home about. It was probably quite exciting, and I'm sure catching glimpses of the fox as she gave us a merry chase across the manicured pastures and through the sylvan glens was thrilling for those who were paying attention. But I was doing everything I could just to stay horsed and not make I fool of myself among all these avid equestrians. This wasn't anything like riding the range in the West.

Luckily, no one noticed what a novice I was. And in the hour of cooling down from the blooded excitement of siccing a pack of frenzied hounds on a tiny red fox, when we were all standing around and stroking the flanks of fine horse flesh on the lawn of Five Oaks, each sipping his or her preferred form of southern comfort, I was amused to see that I had become a center of attention. Several of the women—and men—had taken a fancy to me and were floating around me, trying to solve the mystery of Bob and Bill's houseguest. From the looks that a few of them gave me, I assumed they knew.

I had gleaned during the hunt that my hosts were, indeed, twins named Bob and Bill and were fabulously wealthy and extremely powerful in whatever they did and, other than joining in the hunt, were reclusive and seldom in residence at Five Oaks.

While I was spinning lies about my devised-on-the-fly Kentucky roots and charming the pants and panties off my admirers—or at least so it seemed they wished, as evidenced by the young beauty with the thick southern drawl who tucked a card with her telephone number in my waistband—one of the twins stood off to the aside and assessed my every move through slitted eyes. The other twin had disappeared as soon as the first riders to depart started loading their horse trailers.

Eventually, the crowd was quite thin beyond a hopeful handful clinging to my elbow. At this point, the twin must have had enough, because he rudely cut through the ring around me and took me by the arm and said he wanted to show me something in the barn.

I could hear the something he wanted to show me as we approached the barn, which was set off a good hundred yards from the house.

When we entered the structure and my eyes adjusted to the dimness and the straw chaff floating in the air, I saw that the missing twin had a naked Eric bent over a bale of hay, topped by a horse blanket, and was riding him hard from the rear.

Eric was doing a good deal of grunting and groaning and praising of the twin's performance, but I sort of had the idea that he was doing it to please and because it was expected of him. The glistening of the light sweat on Eric's undulating muscles under the onslaught of "no slouch himself" twin was a real turn on. The twin was holding Eric's cheek down on the horse blanket roughly with a hand spread out on his bald head, and Eric watched me as I entered the barn.

"See you started without me, Bob," the twin who had brought me into the barn said. That cleared up for me who was who.

Then Bill turned to me. "Strip off the jacket and shirt. Leave the jodhpurs and boots on."

I stripped slowly, exhibition style, but I was doing so for Eric, not for the clients. Eric rewarded me by widening his eyes and smiling big as I pulled my shirt off and slitting his eyes in an obvious reverie of lust. He grunted and twitched as Bob pulled back almost full length and jammed his cock back inside the chocolate muscle man with great force.

While I was slowly shedding down to the jodhpurs, Bill had more quickly stripped down and had moved deeper into the dimly lit barn.

"Come over here. Now." There was no question that Bill was to be obeyed.

I moved back into the barn, and my eyes opened wide in surprise. Bill was astride some sort of padded pommel horse contraption supported by a grounded center pole, like they used in gymnastics. It had a saddle strapped to the top, stirrups and all. Bill was in the saddle, completely nude. He was angled up at the back of the saddle and was pulling on his meat. His cock was long, if a bit thinnish. And it already was very hard.

"Climb up, facing away from me," he commanded.

I put a foot in a stirrup and swung my other leg up in front of me as gracefully as I could and over the contraption. Bill held me by the hips as I swung over, helping me to hold steady. I came down wedged in front of him in the saddle, with his long, hard cock throbbing up the small of my back. When I was saddled, Bill reached down at both sides and activated straps across my ankles in the stirrups so that I now was trapped there.

Then he began to make love to me as my butt was firmly wedged against his pelvis. Big beefy, hairy arms encircled me, and he was kissing the back of my neck and running his hands all over my torso, palming at last one hand over one of my nipples and digging below my waistband and inside the supporter cup with the other hand to cover my cock and balls and bring me to the game down there. He was moving his pelvis up and down, dry fucking the small of my back with his dick. He was the client and this was kind of nice anyway, so I moaned for him and moved my body against his. And I turned my lips to his and we kissed deeply.

384

"Raise up in the stirrups," he commanded in a hoarse voice, and I did as he directed.

I felt the back seam of the tight jodhpurs split as his fingers tugged at the edges, and I no longer had to wonder if the seams of the breeches would hold—or worry that they were supposed to hold. He drew a tube of lube out of a side pocket on the pommel horse contraption and palmed my belly with one hand while the lubed fingers of the other hand slid through the slitted seam and worked inside my ass. I heard a condom packet being ripped open and saw it land on the floor of the barn shortly before he was tipping me forward and then pulling me back onto his long, throbbing tool.

As he slid into me, I groaned and grunted for him and gave a little cry of invasion and arched my back and threw my arms and head back, pulling his lips to mine in an "Oh fuck me!" maneuver that I knew worked so well with the clients at this point.

We writhed together for several minutes, with me declaring how good he was, how filling he was, how I'd never had it this good.

And then the surprise was on me. The pommel horse was shuddering and the other twin was now swinging up into the saddle as well. Facing me. Grabbing me by the hips, as Bill palmed my pecs and leaned back, tipping our hips up. Forcing the head of his cock at the entrance of my channel, already stuffed with Bill's cock. Pushing a lever somewhere that caused the stirrups to rise and spread, opening my legs further. Giving Bob's cock room to force itself inside me, on top of Bill's. No more acting at this point. I was double stuffed and stretched to the limit. I cried out and groaned and grunted.

And Bill holding his cock steady and hard and deep inside me, Bob began moving his cock in and out, rubbing against my walls, caressing his brother's cock, moving deeper, ever deeper. I was panting and trying to catch my breath. Hands roaming all over me and over each other, lips kissing me and each other. A cacophony of moaning and groaning and sighing.

I glanced wildly to the side as I sensed movement inside the barn at the periphery of my vision. A chocolate mass of fluid muscle coming into view. Eric approaching closer. Watching the fucking in the saddle on the pommel horse. A magnificently compact body of glistening muscle. Eric was stroking his own, huge, thick cock as he watched the twins double me. He was licking his lips. I had a brief vision of being tripled and almost fainted from the shock of how sensually, if physically impossible, I felt about that.

Another switch was thrown and the pommel horse began to gently rock back and forward on the center pole. A heightening of sensation, an effect on the cocks inside me that went beyond the control of the twins.

Was it me or was the rolling increasing in intensity, becoming bucking? No, it was. Oh Gaaawd. The twins crying out in passion. Me joining them in chorus. Bucking, bucking, bucking. The cocks fucking, fucking, fucking, sent churning by the bucking horse. Oh, Gawwd, oh Gawwd. Losing it. Shoooting Offfff.

Not ending there, however; the mechanical contraption continuing to buck and roll until long after the twins had played my channel like a counterpunching piston engine and made their deposits and finished with their shouts of climaxing lust in two-part harmony.

Off the horse now, unentangled. Bob just grabbed up his clothes and strode out of the barn. Bill motioned to Eric and, between them, they moved me over to the bale of hay with the horse blanket on it and laid me gently down on my back.

"Clean up here and then bring the car around at six," Bill said to Eric in that "to be obeyed" tone both the twins had. "We're going into Middleburg for dinner." And then he was gone as well.

Eric dipped a cloth in a nearby trough of water and came over and started dabbing my face and torso with the cool cloth. I put my hand on the back of his hand and let it slide up his forearm and across his bulging bicep, pulling his face down to mine, taking his lips in mine. I spread my legs and wrapped them around his beefy thighs and pulled him into me. Big hands, big feet, bald head, all panned out in this package. The power of him was swinging like a baseball bat between his legs.

I threw my head back and arched my back and cried out for him as he entered me with the thick, thick dick of his, and I bucked hard against him, riding hard, enjoying him as he was enjoying me in waves and waves of freely offered fucking.

* * * *

I was toweling myself off after a long, languid bath in the well-appointed bathroom off the scarlet room that evening when I heard the soft knock on the door.

When I opened the door, Eric entered with a supper tray for me. I'd been told I had to stay in the room for the remainder of my stay. I moved to embrace him, but he leaned away from me, put a thick finger up to his lips and then, blocking his gesture with the tray, pointed to the corners of the ceiling. I looked up and saw the small flickering of pinpoint lights. Of course. What happened in this room was being video recorded.

I let him go with regret, ate the dinner and put the tray outside the door, and then I unwrapped the towel from my waist and threw it into the bathroom and went back to the canopy bed. Stretching myself out on the bed on my back, I masturbated and writhed sensuously on the bed for the benefit of the camera for a short while and then I went into a semiconscious doze. It had been an exhausting assignment. I couldn't remember whether I had ever been as inventively and fully fucked.

When I woke, the room was dark except for the flickering light from the fire in the fireplace. One of the twins was at the fireplace, perhaps having just lit it. He was naked, facing the fire. His legs were spread and I could see his long cock dangling between his legs, picking up the light coming off the fire. He turned at hearing me stir, and I began to learn that the twins were not identical in their preferences.

He, who I later guessed was Bill, motioned me over to the fireplace.

"Kneel on the oriental carpet here and suck me," He commanded. His voice wasn't as hard edged as it had been earlier that day.

While I sucked on his dick, bringing it to life, and fingered his balls, he poured himself a glass of wine and held the glass in one hand and cupped the back of my head with his other hand. I was pleasing him. I certainly knew how to do that well.

When he was fully engorged, he pulled my head back off his cock with his fingers in my hair. I twitched with surprise as I saw the wine bottle in his hand as I arched back. He tipped it, letting wine spill down over my chest. Then he put the bottle down, came down on his knees in front of me. Wrapping one strong, beefy arm around the small of my back as I was arched back on my knees, my head reaching back almost to the floor, he started to lick the wine down my torso, until his lips reached and swallowed my cock. I just lay back supported by his forearm around the small of my back, my arms hanging at my side and staring into the flickering fire in the fireplace as he sucked me to ejaculation.

Then he turned me onto my knees, my chest flat on the carpet, my eyes still glued to the firelight, as he opened a condom packet and crowned himself. The packet fluttered to the carpet beside my face and then he crouched over my hips and took me doggy style in long, smooth, slow strokes.

While he was fucking me, I heard someone enter the room. Eric, perhaps? And when Bill had ejaculated and pushed me down on the carpet and moved sensuously on my body with his as he kissed my neck and shoulders and we both watched the fire until we had calmed down, he escorted me to the bathroom, where a warm bath had been drawn. We went into the tub, facing each other, and then we both drank wine, while I let my toes bring his cock back to life. With a little cry of passion, he grabbed my butt cheeks and pulled my hips into his pelvis. I let my legs rise out of the tub and planted the soles of my feet on the tiles on either side of his head. He held my hips with his strong hands and I used the leverage of my feet on the walls to fuck myself on his regenerated tool.

One satisfied client.

The other twin, Bob, I'm sure, was a whole other story. He silently entered the room late that night. I was barely awake as he bound my wrists over my head at the headboard. I was quite awake, though, as he was trussing up my legs in the apparatus at the foot of the bed that spread my legs wide and lifted both them and my pelvis.

He roughly gagged me with the rubber ball gag I'd seen in the nightstand drawer earlier. Then he lubed up and used a progression of ever larger, ever more knobbly dildos on my ass channel while I writhed on the bed and tried to scream around the rubber ball filling my mouth and pushing my tongue down.

That little excitement over, he jerked the gag off. He wanted to hear me when he was taking me himself. I watched him take a strap-on cock enlarger out of the drawer. It had suction cup-like knobs running around it in a screw pattern. I watched as he lubed himself, rolled on a condom, and then strapped on the apparatus. I begged him not to do this, just as I knew he wanted me to do. I trembled for him and stammered my fear. And I knew this excited him. He walked over to where I had left my riding clothes and took up the riding crop I'd dropped there.

He was flicking it as he approached me between my spread and raised legs, and I whimpered for him. I cried out as he wanted me to and arched my back up and down on the bed and struggled as best I could as he screwed his enhanced tool inside me. I grunted and groaned for him as he started stroking inside me and flicking my butt cheeks and flanks with the riding crop.

After a while, he pulled out of me, freed his long, hard cock from the enhancer, pulled off the condom, and climbed up on the bed and straddled my chest. He fed his cock into my mouth and I sucked him expertly, as I knew he expected me to. He pulled out of me and shot all over my chest with a throaty cry.

Then he moved to a nearby short-backed boudoir chair and just sat there, watching me naked and all trussed up and fingering and pulling on his cock.

I could see that he was beginning to breathe heavily and getting big again, and I wondered what he had planned for round two.

But, inexplicably, he stood and started releasing me from the bonds.

"You can go clean yourself up now," he said in a low, hoarse voice when I was free.

I stumbled off the bed, sore and exhausted from my full day of making money the old fashioned way, and started to hobble toward the bathroom.

But that was the signal for round two. Bob grabbed me by the hair from the back and propelled me to and astride the chair he'd been sitting in with a fist in the small of my back. The breath went out of me as I fell across the chair. He was at me like a thundering animal in full rut. Yanking my head back with a fist in my hair and thrusting hard between my butt cheeks with his long, hard cock. Fucking me and fucking me and fucking me.

I gave him what he wanted. Complete subservience and cries of being cruelly split asunder—which wasn't all that much off the mark.

Another satisfied client.

The next morning Eric drove me back to the airport in the Lincoln limo. I missed the scheduled flight and had to rebook for later, because Eric stopped the car near the end of the drive and joined me in the backseat, where, first, he pushed my head down between his legs for me to suck him as he sat back in the seat and spread them, and then lifted me and sat my channel down on his thick tool while I rocked back and forth on top of him to our eventual mutual satisfaction.

It was only when the plane was half way back across the continent that I realized why Leon had really been grinning. The twins had first fucked me through a slit in the jodhpurs and had at no point commented on the platinum hair, shaved chest and pits, or the V of the bush. They didn't give a flying fuck about this. Leon had told me to do that just as his own private joke. Well, fuck him—but not in this lifetime.

Scratching the Service Worker Itch

"Bummer," I exclaimed with a pout, as I threw the telephone book half way across the room and collapsed onto the sofa.

"What's up?" Nick asked, looking up from his computer where he was checking out the latest Literotica stories.

"I've got the service worker itch, and they don't list who the hunky, well-hung plumbers and electricians are in the phone book ads."

"Fancy that," Nick said as he turned back to his computer. But then he swiveled back around and gave me a level stare. "And what the fuck is the service worker itch?"

"I've got this itch deep inside me that can only be reached and satisfied by a hardworking muscled hunk with honest-work, callused hands, a big, thick dick, and rough technique."

"Well, between the two of us, I've got the biggest and thickest dick. Let's go back to the bedroom and I'll see what I can do for that itch," Nick said, with a smile.

"I said rough sex and burly handyman hunks, Nick. You don't even come close."

"Thanks loads, Mr. White-collar Picky," Nick retorted.

"You know what I mean, Nick. You're too refined and sensitive to scratch this itch. Sometimes I need someone who will skip the preliminaries and just pork me hard, deep, and quick—wham, bang, thank you, ma'am. It's a fantasy I have occasionally. Just go with me on this."

"Well, OK, if that's what you want," Nick said with a sigh, as he logged off the computer and unfolded himself from his chair. "You're in luck. I happen to have met a couple of construction workers last evening at Club 216 who were quite explicit about what they could do with me if I came over to their construction site. I think they were hunky enough for you. Let's take a ride."

Three guys were standing around a pickup truck at the construction site and taking a smoke break when Nick and I drove up. I could tell at a glance that they'd fit my bill: all big, square-chinned sonovabitches, with big hands, muscles on their muscles, and big broad grins on their faces when they recognized Nick. Nick told them what I wanted, and their grins got even bigger as they circled around me, eyeing me lasciviously and whistling at and talking dirty to me. Just what I'd ordered. My cock began to throb; my ass began to twitch.

They led us into what would be the basement of a half-finished McMansion at the back corner of the construction area, and, at my request, two of them stripped down to just their hard hats, their tool belts, and their boots, as the third one slowly stripped me down, feeling me up as clothing items were shed, and sucking me off. When they'd striped down, the other two construction workers and Nick watched me get a blow job. I was just standing there leaning against what was going to be a load-bearing pole. The one working on me was actually the youngest and best looking by far. He was stripped down to just cutoff jeans, and I didn't at all mind him giving me a slow and easy blow job; I knew there was rough action coming later. The other two construction workers were licking their lips and fondling and pulling on their horse-hung meat as they watched the younger one going down on me.

I enjoyed watching them watching me. They looked real hot in just those construction belts, hard hats, and chunky boots.

When I had shot my load, one of the other construction workers came over and took me roughly by the hand and led me over to a makeshift apparatus that the other one was pulling together. He had taken two low sawhorses and slapped a pine board between them. The first construction worker pushed me over on my belly on top of the board, and the second construction worker spread my legs and lashed them at the ankles to the legs of the sawhorses with rope, while the other one was tying my wrists together in front of me with my own leather belt. Construction worker number one then got between my legs in back and started shoving his big, engorged dick at my asshole, finally managing to push in and, with loud grunts from him and groans from me, plowing me to his root. The tools on his belt made clanging noises and chaffed my inner thighs as they swung back in forth in rhythm to his stroking. I could feel him reach my itch, deep inside, and rub it real hard. He was rough with me, just like I wanted, slapping my butt cheeks, pinching my nipples, and thrusting me hard up the ass.

The other construction worker came around in front of me, grabbed my hair with his hand, shoved his dick in my mouth, and fucked my face. Meanwhile, the worker who had blown me came back under the sawhorse and began licking my balls and cock again. After a good twenty minutes of this, construction worker one unloaded inside me, and the two workers who were stuffing me changed positions. The second dick was even thicker and longer than the first, and it found whole new itches to scratch.

When the one behind me had shot his wad, he withdrew from me, released the ropes at my ankles, and pushed me over to a picnic table that was being used as a work bench. Reinvigorated construction worker number one now came at me from the front, pushing me down on the table on my back, wish-boned my legs, and fucked me hard and furiously from the front, while construction worker number two found a hook to hang my wrist bonds on over my head that stretched my torso tight across the picnic table. My itches were being satisfied nicely. The worker who boned me in the number two spot got up on his knees on the bench seat at my head, held my shoulders down on the table, and took another turn face fucking me. Just before my mouth got turned and stuffed, I looked over and saw that Nick was allowing the younger, better-looking construction worker to plow his ass at the sawhorse position.

Lots of itches got scratched well that afternoon, and everyone left the McMansion basement happy. I never again had to explain to Nick what my periodic service worker itch was all about.

Star Player

John Rivers had worshipped Champ Griffin for years, ever since John had begun devoting every waking moment to soccer—on the field, in his discussions with his friends, and in the décor he picked for his bedroom walls. Champ Griffin, the star player for the Big Chiefs professional soccer team, figured prominently in every single poster John had on his bedroom wall. Champ Griffin's cocky smile and his magnificently developed body had been the last thing John had seen when he turned out his light at night and the first thing he saw when he opened his eyes in the morning. John would have given anything to be like Champ Griffin—almost to be Champ Griffin himself. In his dreams, John became Champ Griffin.

So John worked his butt off on the soccer field to morph into Champ Griffin—and he did his preparation well. He made the all-state soccer team in high school, and when he went off to the university, it was on an athletic scholarship—to play soccer.

And here he was, on the Big Chiefs' practice field, during training camp, fighting with three other guys for a chance to sit on the Big Chiefs' bench for a season and maybe to work his way into the starting team. Alongside his ideal, Champ Griffin.

Champ Griffin's status on the team was no more obvious than that he was standing out there on the field, between the club's coach and owner and three steps in front of its recruiting team, and assessing all of the new prospects as they did their "stuff" in search of a nod to become a Big Chief.

John looked in fear and trepidation as those men put their heads together. He certainly didn't miss that they never looked back on the field until Champ Griffin had had his say.

There wasn't a doubt in John River's mind when the call to training camp for "the team" dropped into his mailbox that Champ Griffin had seen and approved of and chosen him to be on the team. At that moment, John would have done anything Champ Griffin wanted him to do. Champ Griffin was a god to John.

The first practice field workout of what was going to constitute this year's team, John was nearly overwhelmed that Champ seemed to take him under his wing and was giving him pointers and encouragement all through their first practice session. No one even batted an eye when Champ put an arm around John's shoulder and announced that he and John would be going back to the showers early and then going over some team rules and special plays back at the locker room before the rest of the team came in.

If there were sniggers among the rest of the team gathered around Champ at that moment, John didn't notice them. He was still starry eyed at being in the mere presence of his idol.

Back in the clubhouse, Champ sent John off to the locker room showers and said they'd meet up after they'd both cleaned up. Champ had his own shower; in fact he had his own private room with his own bathroom and shower and massage table. He was that much of a star player for the Big Chiefs. Nothing was too good for Champ; Champ got whatever he wanted.

When John padded out of the shower, with just a towel around his waist, Champ was sitting there on the locker room bench in front of John's locker, showered but nude—and holding a supersized cock in his hand and slowly working it up.

John froze in place. Shocked. He'd never thought of his idol this way. Sure, he'd gone to sleep and awakened to the power of Champ's bare chest on one of the posters in his bedroom—but he'd never thought of Champ in the altogether. Not even in his dreams.

"Come over and suck this," Champ said in a low, growly voice. He was smiling at John. The same smile he used when he was giving the rookie pointers out on the playing field.

"What? I don't understand." John wasn't at his most glib when he was caught by surprise.

"I'm tense. The rookies always give me head when I'm tense. That's what they're here for."

"I don't . . . I'm not . . ." John stammered, not yet finding whatever words might make all of this go away.

"Come on; come over here. Suck me," Champ repeated. And he said it as if it was an everyday conversation, as if it was the most natural thing for them to be discussing.

"Hey, you were just one of four guys who could play. You were just the one I wanted the most. Do you want to go home and for me to pick the next-best guy?"

"No." John said it but he took his time agonizing before he said it. This was the life he'd been building to; his had been tunnel vision. He had no idea what he'd do in life if not play professional soccer. And the Big Chiefs. They were the best. And Champ Griffin. He was the best of the best.

John slowly moved to the bench. As he came down, straddling the bench, facing Griffin, who also was straddling the bench, Griffin reached for John's towel and pulled it off him. Now John was naked too.

"Nice. Very nice," Griffin mumbled in a hoarse voice. Then he put a big mitt behind John's neck and pulled John's mouth into his.

John had never kissed a man before. And he'd always played lead. This was a strange sensation, but he let Griffin's lips open his and he let Griffin's tongue invade his mouth cavity. He was kissing another man. But not just another man. Champ Griffin. His idol, Champ Griffin. The man that for years John had said he'd do anything for. And now Champ Griffin was showing John what he wanted from him.

Griffin gently pushed John's head down toward his crotch when they came out of the kiss, and John felt Griffin's cock head slip into his mouth and John was suddenly giving

Griffin inexperienced, but sufficient, under Griffin's direction, head. Meanwhile, Griffin was leaning over John's bent torso with those long arms of his and feeling up John's butt cheeks and playing "find and open the rosebud" with John's ass rim.

When the rest of the team came in from practice to take their showers, John and Champ were in full fuck. John was lying on his back on the bench now, one leg hooked around Champ's hip and the other one being held up and out with Champ's fist wrapped around John's ankle. John's hips were rolled up and Champ's pelvis was hovering just an inch or two off the bench surface, giving his thick cock a good angle as it stroked hard and deep inside John's ass canal.

They were well past the painful moments as Champ worked his cock into the virginal canal and John writhed and mildly objected and begged—which went unheeded—and panted and groaned—and cried out at the first breaching. Then, having made his decision to let nothing stand in his way of becoming a Big Chief—and having already been deflowered now in a maneuver that could never be reversed—John lay back and arched his torso to give them both the most comfortable ride, and just moaned and sighed his way through the fuck. The groans and moans slowly drifted into sighs and murmurs of pleasure and letting Champ know what stroking he was liking the best. This was Champ Griffin, John's idol. And Champ Griffin was enjoying his body and telling him how nice it was and what a sweet ass he had, what a good lay he was. He was pleasing his idol.

At the height of the pain, when Champ's cock was pushing in and digging deep and stretching him to the point where he knew he'd be split in two, John kept playing Champ Griffin's statement over in his head. This was his one shot to make the team. If it wasn't him, it would be one of the other three guys he'd gone up against to get the nod. It was all Champ Griffin's call. Champ Griffin, his idol. The guy John had said he would do anything for.

John was writhing and moaning under the pick up in Champ's cocking rhythm as the rest of the team members flowed into the room, looking at them and muttering dirty words and flashing sneery smiles at Champ as they passed by. But they were just going about their business as if this was an everyday occurrence in the locker room. And maybe, John thought, as Champ dropped his leg and wrapped both hands around John's waist and pulled him in harder to his pelvis and onto his stroking cock with each thrust—maybe this was business as usual.

With a cry of release, aroused and coming quickly because of the surprise and newness of it all, John ejaculated up his torso. A few guys turned and gave a little laugh as they were stripping off their gear. But other than that, they gave the coupling in the middle of their activity scant attention.

One of the veterans did toss a "See you in the showers," over his shoulder and wiggled his buns as he and the others padded off toward the communal shower room.

John lay there, spent and putty in Champ's hands, as the Big Chief's star player grunted and thrust to his own release.

Then Champ rose from the bench and pulled John up and slapped him affectionately on the butt. He then half frog marched John to the shower room. The rest of the team was standing there, in a row, under the water jets, in seniority order, working up their cocks in their fists, big smiles on their faces.

As the veteran who had said "See you in the showers," bent John over at the waist and positioned himself at the head of the line and close in between John's thighs and butt crack, Champ Griffin, star player of the Big Chiefs turned to go back to his own room.

Before he left, though, and as John's eyes went wild at what was invading his ass channel, Champ Griffin leaned down and whispered in John's ear. "Buck up, sport. You give good fuck and there will be a new set of recruits in at midseason." Then he went on. "When you're done here, come on over to my room, and I'll show you why I have my own digs. You'll love the special massage table I've got—and, oh yes, the sling."

Stolen

I had the creepiest feeling I was being watched. I was sitting at the table in the small dining L of my high-rise apartment and diddling through my favorite Web sites. I liked all-male bondage fucking. It certainly wasn't something I admitted to in my day job down on the stock market trading floor, but that's how I unwound. In the evening, after a tough day among the bears and bulls, I retreated to my small seventy-second-story hole in the wall and entertained my sensations and my cock in a solo session with my male bondage sites on the Internet. I had them all booked so that I could quickly run through them, looking for what was new until I found something I wanted to masturbate to—to erase the tension of the day and to entertain a fantasy that I was too shy to bring to reality.

I was sitting, sprawled at my table, naked, and cock in hand. Just beyond the table was a full plateglass window that would probably have a gorgeous view out over Central Park if there wasn't another, taller high-rise apartment building just across a narrow street between my building and the park. So, in essence, I had a full view of three floors of someone else's high rise.

I wouldn't have seen the view when I was at the computer anyway. My nose was in the computer when I was cruising Web sites; the computer screen was turned toward that window.

I stood and moved over to the window and leaned into it to scrutinize the other building. I still had the creepiest feeling of being watched. It was only when I felt the head of my erect cock rub up against the cool pane of glass that I recalled that I was naked—exposed to several stories of the brooding building just across the narrow divide of Colombia Street. Had there been lights on across there earlier? I wondered. Now the windows were either dark or close-draped.

I must try to put the money aside to buy draperies for my own windows, I thought. And the time and effort in getting it done, which was an even greater nuisance for me.

Anyone could be watching me from inside those darkened windows in that other building. My dining L was brightly lit, and I couldn't see into any of those rooms. Wasn't that one just across lit up when I first padded naked into the dining room? That's where that hunk who was always working out, building muscles on his muscles, lived. Boy I'd like to meet him in the back room of one of those gay clubs down near Times Square I'd heard about but never been brave enough to go into. I frequently sat and watched him work out—in the nude—and fantasized having sex with him. He was arousingly hirsute, with black curly hair all over his body.

I moved away from the window and turned off the lights in my living area and settled in front of my computer again. I pulled up URLs with one hand and stroked my cock to the images I found arousing with my other hand. Then I reached for the dildo that was on the table top, lubed it liberally, and scrunched down in my seat, my eyes glued to the computer screen as I held the head of the dildo to my hole—and started to gently press in.

* * * *

I knew I'd been ripped off as soon as I got off the elevator after work. The door to my apartment was ajar.

Someone had jimmied the lock, and they hadn't even bothered to shut the door after them.

Well, they were sure to have been disappointed, I thought bitterly, as I entered the apartment, because I lived quite sparsely. Virtually the only thing of value that I kept in my apartment beyond the TV system that was firmly bolted to the wall was my computer.

And, sure enough, my computer was the only thing that had been taken—although I was somewhat distressed to find that my bureau drawers had been opened and my underwear briefs were strewn on the floor. And then, when I entered the bathroom, I discovered that my dirty clothes hamper had been turned over—and all of my soiled briefs were missing.

How odd, I thought. But a little chill went up my spine that wasn't at all unpleasant, and I had the urge to go to my computer and run through my favorite Web sites. Only I didn't have my computer anymore.

What a bother. I'd have to file a police report—which I knew would go nowhere other than support an insurance claim that would also be almost more of a hassle cashing in on than it was worth. And I'd have to get a new computer. And, oh yes, the lock would need to be fixed on the apartment door. But it was late already. I'd stopped for a couple of beers down at O'Donnell's after work—trying to build up the courage, unsuccessfully, to move on to something real beyond the voyeurism of the rough gay sex Web sites—perhaps to that gay leather bar across the street from the tavern, and it was already dark when I'd returned to my apartment. All of this hassle would have to wait for tomorrow.

So, I just shut the door with the broken lock, with the assurance that lightning didn't strike twice in quick succession and that it was unlikely anyone would be trying the doors on the seventy-second story of my building to see if any opened. I showered, toweled off, and pulled on a pair of the red silk, almost transparent bikini briefs I liked to sleep in and that the intruder somehow had missed, even though they'd been hanging on the back of a chair in my bedroom, not that I remembered having put them there.

As I was sitting at the side of the bed, I had that creepy sensation once again of being watched. There was another full-length uncovered plateglass window beside my bed, just on the other side of the wall from my dining L. I got up from the bed and padded over to the bedroom door and switched off the light. Then I went over to the window and let my eyes travel across the surface of the building across the narrow canyon of Columbus Street.

Nothing was amiss, but the feeling of being watched didn't go away.

* * * *

I was jolted from a deep sleep by a heavy body covering me as I lay on top of the covers on my belly. Swimming up from unconsciousness, I drunkenly tried to turn and push the weight off me, but the sharp crack of a backhand across my cheek snapped my head to the side and brought bright orange stars to my eyes. Before I could recover, my wrists were being bound together and tethered to the rails of the headboard.

I started to cry out in shock and indignation, but my bikini briefs were being stripped off my legs and stuffed in my mouth.

I gagged for breath as I was being forced up to my knees on the bed and I felt the wetness of a tongue at my asshole. I moaned deeply. This had never happened to me before. I had dreamed of it happening to me, but I'd never been brave enough to bring reality to fantasy.

This was no fantasy, though. My cock was being pulled through my legs and was being swallowed and worked and my balls were being licked and fingers were invading my asshole. I squirmed and tried to pull away, but big hands roughly pulled my hips back into position, and my buttocks were slapped hard.

"Stay still," a low growl commanded.

And then I felt him crouching over my hips, his thighs encasing me and a fist between my shoulder blades forcing my chest into the surface of the mattress. And I knew it was a "him," because I felt the cock head at my hole. Moving insistently inside me. Spreading my virginal hole, making me

404

gasp and groan at the thick invasion of him. Until suddenly his bulb was past my sphincter muscle, and I felt my channel drawing him in—different from any of the dildo work I had done on myself: warmer, throbbing, more pliable and filling. And moving with a purpose of its own.

I was grateful that there had been that dildo work, though, because even though I've never had an actual cock inside me, I could take this one. And now I knew that no dildo was a replacement for the real thing. I could never turn to dildo work again with the thought that it was enough—what I really wanted.

I panted hard and moaned deeply as his cock moved deeper into me. And then he began to pump inside me and I writhed under him in agony mixed with ecstasy. I never knew it would be this way. Fully possessed; fully under his control. Whimpering for release but now not wanting him to stop either. A fist on my cock, stroking me. For the first time being stroked by someone else—being worked at someone else's whim and rhythm other than my own. I couldn't help myself. I quickly creamed the sheets beneath my pelvis.

But my tormentor fucked on and on. My knees got weak with the exertion and I collapsed onto the bed, but he just followed me down, straddling my pelvis between his knees, and continued stroking into me in long, deep thrusts. At last I felt him stop abruptly, nails dug into my hips, and then a jerk and a little cry and he was finished.

I felt the weight of him leave me, and then he turned me onto my back on the bed. Even though it was dark, the lights of the city coming through my uncurtained window let me clearly see my attacker. He was a big brute of a fellow, all muscle and dark curly hair. His head was covered with a ski mask, but I had little trouble identifying the rest of his body as the bodybuilder from one of the apartments in the high rise across Columbus Street from me.

No more mystery. He had been watching me just as I had been watching him. And I had little doubt who had burgled my apartment and taken my computer—no doubt wanting to verify in a search of my favorite sites that I was drawn to what he was doing to me.

And I was, in fact, drawn to it. And perhaps he could see that in my eyes, because, as I watched him, he stripped the condom he'd been wearing to fuck me off his cock, which was still half hard, and scrambled back up onto the bed and straddled my chest. He pulled the sleeping briefs out of my mouth and pressed his cock head at my lips. He lifted the briefs to his nose and inhaled deeply. I heard him moan, and then he carefully moved them to the side. I opened my mouth to him, not knowing what to do but, having now been taken over the edge, more than willing to learn. I gagged as he possessed my mouth with a cock that was coming to life again. But he held my head in place with a palm on my cheek and a thumb under my chin and face-fucked me in shallow strokes that weren't too taxing, as I sucked on his cock head. Meanwhile, he raised the other hand, holding my sleeping bikini to his nose again and sniffed the essence of me.

Then he was untying my wrists but rebinding me as I laid on my back, trussing up a wrist to an ankle on either side in a form of hogtying that had me helpless, bent over, and spread wide.

He disappeared for a while, and I heard him rummaging in my refrigerator. He returned, drinking a beer from a bottle—just sauntering into the room as if he possessed it—and me—and at least for now he did possess me. I should have been scared and angry. But I was beyond anger now. He was doing to me just what I had fantasized for months and had been too much of a coward to initiate myself.

He set the beer bottle down on my bureau, and I watched in fascination as he rolled another condom onto his rehardened cock. Then he walked over to the bed and pulled me down to the foot so that my rump was on the edge of the bed. He leaned over and took the beer bottle from the bureau top, tipped me over so that my hole was pointed to the ceiling, and let a stream of the cold liquid tipple into my hole.

Then he was fucking down into me again, lubricated by the cool beer. On and on he stroked inside me—until I was exhausted and had passed out.

When I awoke, he was gone and my wrists and ankles were free of bonds. My bikini sleeping briefs were missing and the fingers of dawn were creeping down the canyon that was Columbus Street.

I rose, sore, but exhilarated and padded into the living area. He wasn't there either, and the door to the apartment was shut. My computer had been returned and was turned on. I keystroked it to life and there on the screen was an e-mail address and the words, "If you liked it. If you want it again."

I sat down at the computer and, with tremulous fingers, opened my e-mail and keyed in the e-mail address. "Yes, yes, yes. Again tonight, please. Or any time you want. Door unlocked. After locked fixed, I can give you a key."

And then I made myself a cup of coffee and sat back in the chair and luxuriated in the hassles that had been removed from me today—no missing computer, no need to file a police report, no immediate need to replace the lock on my door, and no reason to sit for hours in O'Donnell's and try to build up the courage to walk across the street and enter the world of the gay leather bar. And above all else, no need to buy drapes for my windows.

The only thing that had been stolen—other than a few soiled briefs, which I would replace with something like the red silk bikini—was my virginity—spectacularly stolen—and I certainly wouldn't miss that now.

Suits

It was a steamy, smoke-filled night at Hernando's, and I and the other two guys had been dancing to the music on the small stage for twenty minutes. I was already down to the ten-gallon hat, the pinto pony vest, the cowboy boots, and the low-slung belt and six-gun holsters with the even lower-slung eight-inch gun swinging in between and nothing else on when I felt the hand on the ankle of one of my boots.

The dude clinging to my boot looked cooler than a cucumber despite the heat and the indoor smog and even though he was wearing a suit—a finely tailored Brooks Brothers navy-blue pinstripe silk suit that was cut close to his well-cut body. He looked like money all over. His pale-blue dress shirt was as finely and closely cut to the perfect curves and bulges of his body as his suit was, and the gold studs in his shirt cuffs and his Rolex watch sparkled in beams from the strobing lights overhead. He was flashing a set of ultrawhite, perfectly capped teeth at me in a full-lipped, sensuous mouth. He also was flashing a fifty-dollar bill.

Having gotten my attention by grabbing my boot as I was undulating on the stage above him, stroking myself off, not far from giving the crowd the thrill it had come to see, he yelled up to me through the loud music and the din of cat calls and stale suggestions. "You fuck me? More of this if it's good for me."

Fifty dollars? His tie alone was worth four times that. An insult. I was having offers twice that high thrown at me by the plumbers and electricians sitting all around him. I crouched down and shot my load across the nice lapels of his $800 Brooks Brothers suit, and then I went home that night and fucked my bass-voiced boyfriend until he warbled soprano. And I did it for free.

Three nights later I was at my other evening job, the more humbling one, as a car hop at the Honeywell Hotel. They made me wear a monkey suit there; I much prefer my cowboy outfit at Hernando's. It had been air conditioned and I was watched when I wore that one. I liked being watched; I was built to be watched. Here at Honeywells I was invisible; just part of the service in getting into and out of the hotel in a jiff. But at least here I got to jockey Porsche Boxsters—at least as far as the parking lot over in the shadows beside and behind the hotel, when I wasn't on break and then could drive the ride around the block—or several blocks—on the way to the lot.

I was contemplating being invisible when a honey of a silver Maserati Quattoporte drove up to the entrance and out stepped . . . the suit from Hernando's. At least he was still noticing me. He picked up on who I was right off, and I was afraid he might take a swing at me for messing up his Brooks Brothers—but he didn't. He was all flashy smiles and knowing looks. And he had been slumming the other night. Tonight he was wearing a lustrous brown Armani suit, easily worth three times what the blue pinstripe the other night had been worth, and he had on an ochre silk shirt under that, a flashy silk tie, and diamond cufflinks. All just as expensively and closely cut as the suit of the other night was. The man was dripping money. It was almost like I could walk along behind him and pick up gold coins as he shot them out of his ass like a bunny with diarrhea.

Two hours later he reappeared through the hotel entrance. Another one of the car hops reached for his ticket, but he held off from giving it to the guy and looked around until he spotted me. He walked over, flashing that big, "see what I've got and you don't" smile at me and handed me the ticket. But he

410

also had $200 in folded fifties in the hand holding the ticket, and he wouldn't let loose of either of those or my hand as he said in a husky whisper, "Shall we up the ante?"

I was going off duty then anyway. And two hundred bucks meant a lot to me—obviously far more than it meant to him. When I drove the Maserati around to the entrance, I didn't get out of the driver's seat; I just leaned over and flipped open the passenger seat door. This was a signal to him, a gauntlet, so to speak. If we were going to do this thing, I was going to do the driving. I liked the idea of the $200, but if he thought he was going to get off as cheaply as that, he was mistaken. Tonight was going to cost him a whole hell lot more than $200.

He got in the passenger side without hesitation, and I fisted the stick shift and he fisted my stick as I drove him into the parking lot and back to the corner where I had my Chevy van parked. I clicked open the sliding side door to the van, and the suit got in without hesitation and whistled in appreciation. I had it outfitted for love—or something. Smoked windows; floor, sides, and ceiling covered in padded sapphire blue velour; grab straps anchored strategically here and there, and an easily accessible sound system with speakers embedded all around. And that stool. He'd be introduced to the stool later.

I told him to take off his shoes in my home—just like they do in the Orient. And while he docilely did that, I climbed into the van, stripped off the hated car jockey's uniform, clicked the side door shut, and turned on the sound system. I selected Lebanese music with a good strong beat and a tortured-voice singer warbling in a manner that would disguise most any yowling coming from inside the van. I planned on there being some yowling.

First thing I did was tie up the dude's right wrist to a strap in the ceiling of the van, a little behind the front seat. I didn't want him going anywhere or getting the notion he was going to be in charge. He hunched there, in his Armani suit, his free hand searching between my thighs.

I stripped the Rolex from his left wrist and, after entertaining him with how well balanced it was when I hung it on my hard cock and spun it around for him, I tossed it into one of his shoes. I didn't want the reminder of money ticking away while I worked here. Then I got his fist off my cock, where he had found a mushroom cap silver stud that flashed in the overhead bulb just as brightly as his diamond cufflinks did, and strapped his left wrist up to the ceiling.

I unbelted and unzipped him, and I peeled the Armani trousers and Calvin Klein briefs off his legs. And I wasn't delicate about it. I heard a rip and so did he, but neither one of us showed that we cared. I was moving with determination and he was already wide-eyed and giving little panting sounds and murmured moanings. He had seen my eight inches in full erection already. He knew what I was packing for him.

He was crouched there on his knees now, panting, in fine silk socks held up with braces under his knees and above his well-muscled calves, but still fully decked out in suit coat, shirt, and tie. I crouched between his spread knees, letting my cock snake up under the tail of his shirt and bedevil his navel while our lips were heavily engaged in a sloppy kiss. I unbuttoned the two middle buttons of his shirt, just enough so that I could spread the expensive, rustling silk and expose a puffed up nipple. Then I lowered my head and pushed his tie aside with my chin and worked his nipple through the opening of his shirt with my tongue and teeth.

He was moaning for me. Begging to be fucked. "Fuck me hard; punish me," he'd called out. Later he might regret he'd asked for that.

I raised his legs, one at a time, and tied them to straps in the ceiling toward the back of the van. He was trussed up now and hanging like a deer over a campfire, face up to the ceiling. I threw a leg over his belly and put my hands on the back of the front seat on either side of his head and clicked my silver cock stud against his white teeth until he opened for me and gave me head. He gave me good head, moaning and groaning all of the time at the length and width and hardness of me. This is what he was paying for. This is what he was going to get.

When I was bored with this, I pulled my cock out of his mouth and threw my leg back over him. He watched in eye-silted lust and interest as I opened a side glove compartment and took out a handful of condom packets. I opened a packet and rolled a condom onto my cock. Then I extracted a leather-studded cock ring and wrapped that around the base of my cock. The last item I pulled out of the compartment was a small bottle of KY. All the time he was whimpering for me, begging for me to get inside him.

He did look a little concerned then, though, when I reached up and undid the cuffs on his shirt on both sides and extracted his diamond cufflinks and then tied them with string to my cock ring. I was chuckling about him getting his money's worth out of this fuck. But he didn't seem all that amused.

He probably thought I was going to take my time and open him up real well for the fuck. But he was wrong there. I soaked down my cock with the KY and squirted enough into his hole for it to be beneficial for me. But then I was rimming him with my bulbous mushroom cap and pressuring his hole and making little forced entries and pulling back a little and then worrying the tight, unready hole again. And then, when I'd gotten the cap all the way in, I just thrust in and bottomed with one lunge. And he yowled to the velour ceiling, hitting a high A even stronger and truer than the Lebanese musician was doing on the background music. And he continued to yowl, first in pain and then in consuming desire, as I picked up the beat of the music and fucked him and fucked and fucked him.

As I fucked him, I bunched up that silk ochre-colored shirt of his in my fists and literally ripped it off his body, pulling the shreds of it from underneath his tie and the brown Armani suit coat. The dude didn't seem to care; he was swinging his body against my plunging cock with the beat of the music and warbling right along with the Lebanese singer. He came in great spoutings long before I did.

Sometime during the fucking, I felt the diamond cufflinks come loose and work themselves up the dude's passage with the thrustings of my cock. The dude gave little yipping sounds at this added fiber to his ass's diet, but he made no objection. He wasn't objecting to anything now except to the possibility that I might stop stroking his ass. I almost went on a laughing jag mid fuck at the image of how he'd be shitting diamonds for the next day or so. Thinking about that being close to the meaning of being filthy rich.

When I was spent, I leaned into him and encircled his torso with my arms and felt the fast beating of his heart next to mine through the shredded ochre silk until he had calmed down and I had started to reload. He was sighing and whispering endearments to me, telling me how good I was and hoping I wasn't finished taking him.

I wasn't finished. Not by a long shot. This wasn't nearly expensive enough of a fuck for this dude yet.

I released both his legs and arms, but I immediately turned him and reattached his wrists to straps at the base of the front seat on either side. He didn't object. He was licking his lips. I was giving him exactly what he was seeking from me. I pulled over a low, velour-covered stool with a hole in the seat and forced the dude down on top of it on his lower belly. His cock and balls were poked through the hole and he found that he was encased in a sleeve around his cock and sacks around his balls, which were the business end of a cock milking machine. I strapped his hips to the stool so he couldn't extract his cock and then turned on the machine. The machine started to slowly contract the sleeve around his cock and undulate over it, teasing his cock to engorge and discharge. And the sacks around his balls also contracted and squeezed in a fascinating rhythm. He seemed to like this, and began moaning almost immediately. He'd maybe have second thoughts after he'd shot off the first time and found the machine wasn't satisfied with that.

I crouched up where he could see me and changed the spent condom for a fresh one and lathered it down with KY. And then I was behind him, making him push his knees wide, his butt waving in the air. I straddled him, my thighs on either side of his waist, above his stretched thighs, my hands on his shoulder blades. And then I reared my hips back and thrust my sheathed cock inside him and pumped hard and fast.

He was singing a loud duet again with the Lebanese singer to the heavy beat of the music.

I tore the coat off his back while I was fucking him and the stool was milking him, and I put it in front of his face and tore the lining out. He didn't care. He was going over the moon with what I and the stool were doing to him. I pulled the expensive silk necktie around his neck to his back and used it as

414

reins as I did a bull bucking rodeo exhibit on his buttocks. I could feel the diamond cufflinks churning around inside him and he could too. I could tell that by the screams of passion he was making. The Lebanese singer was reaching a climax in his yowling and so were the dude and I. The dude shuddered and came, and then moaned as he discovered yet again that the stool wasn't finished with him. And then I gave a cowboy whoop and came as well.

After a second and then a third ride, and continuous attention from the stool, I was finished with him. I turned off the stool and untied him and he just huddled there in thank-you whimpers. As a parting gesture, I untied his necktie, rolled the spent condom off my dick, and wiped my dick and then his asshole with the silk tie and stuffed it in his mouth. His gaze told me that he was still in love. It didn't seem like anything I was going to do was going to tell this guy where he could stuff all his money, as far as I was concerned. Still, I figured when the semen had drained out of his eyes, he'd come to his senses and survey the damage I had done to all his expensive stuff and get a little mad.

I put my car jockey duds back on and made sure he could see where I was leaving the keys to his Maserati. And then I left him there, in the back of my Chevy van, and walked back over to the entrance of the hotel. Within minutes a studly black guy gave me a ticket and a look, and, when I'd driven around his shiny black Mercedes CLS55 AMG, we were driving off to his up-town penthouse apartment, where I fucked him silly and he fed me breakfast, begged for and received my bone a second time, and then brought me back to the hotel for my now-deserted Chevy van.

Two days later, I was dancing on the stage of Hernando's when I felt a fist wrap around the ankle of my boot. There, gazing up at me with love-struck eyes was the suit, now outfitted in a black sharkskin $3,000-plus Valentino, diamond cufflinks cleaned and polished and gleaming in beams from the overhead strobe lights—holding a wad of hundred-dollar bills in his other fist. Wanting me again.

Temptation's Web

I hadn't decided to spend the day exploring the Frank Lloyd Wright houses in Oak Park until I saw Heidi Hines getting "the stare" from my wife while Heidi had her toes half way up my calf under the table at Riva's. It seemed a brilliant fix at the time.

My wife is a fascinating and powerful woman—all sliver blondeness, razor thinness and sharpness, and glittery silver nails flashing and fingers snapping and minions scattering to the winds. She runs the internationally acclaimed lifestyle magazine, *Peak Today* magazine, like a general determined and capable of taking and holding Moscow and of laughing in the faces of all those who never were able to do so. I love that name, *Peak Today*, with its in-your-face double entendre references. Not only does each issue define the new peak of fashion, vacation destination, trend, and latest celebrity, but it is also a play on her daddy's name—a reminder that the media mogul Clifford Peak will always be there to back up his daughter's decisions and to keep her magazine solvent and in distribution.

Not that Clifford will always be there in reality, of course; he is old as dirt and propped up by a bevy of specialists. But his daughter, Claudia, is loaded and primed and primped and ever ready to slide into his Manhattan corner office. She is ever

417

timeless too. Few know just how well preserved she herself was—even I, who saw the marriage license, assumed her dates were lies. But I do know that somehow money and modern science have kept her supple and in fine shape indeed . . . for her age, whatever that is.

I was modeling for *Peak Today* when she "found" me. And I was well bought. But I don't mind. She treats me like I have a mind to pay attention to in the midst of all that is thrown at her, and she is fun and . . . of course, very generous.

The Heidi pass, served up at Riva's on Chicago's Navy Pier while we were at a Chicago office strategy session, was something I was used to, and I didn't, for a minute, believe that Claudia felt the least bit threatened. It was more Heidi I was worried for. For all I knew, *Peak Today* would have a branch office in Botswana as well. And, glancing to my left and catching the come-on stare of the statuesque, highly photogenic Sandra— no last name; just known by every fashion photographer alive as Sandra—I could see that I needed to beg out of further business "meetings" with the magazine's Chicago staff, or Claudia would be shopping for a whole new crew there.

And Heidi was barking up the wrong tree altogether. While she was playing footsie and, probably mellowed by entirely too much good wine, starting to move into groping under the table cloth, I was stealthily eyeing the butts and baskets of the waiters gliding between the tables. God, Chicago had some hot men. I'd been very good about that in New York. But I'd probably had entirely too much wine at Riva's too—and there was something freeing about the whole Chicago magic mile "thing." Brisk breeze coming off the lake and wafting through the avenue tunnels lined with skyscrapers of such breathtaking beauty and ingenuity and style that they made Manhattan seem drab. Such a "high" for me that I almost wasn't aware it had happened when Heidi's hand gently fell on my inner thigh. Almost.

She was intoning in a throaty voice that perhaps she wasn't needed at the office tomorrow and could show me the view from the top of the John Hancock tower, completely ignoring the intensity of Claudia's stare, when I came to her rescue, although she'd never know how close she'd come to seeing a Botswana chief's hut and mighty member up close and personal.

"Great idea," I said smoothly, as I reached under the table and brushed Heidi's hand off my thigh. "But I wouldn't think of taking anyone away from the strategy session tomorrow. I'm not needed there. But an architectural exploration is a great idea. I think I'll take the El out to Oak Park and check out all of the early Frank Lloyd Wright houses out there."

I could sense Claudia uncoiling from the end of the table. The perfect parry. I'd recently let Claudia know that what I'd really like to do was study architecture. I could model forever, I suppose, especially as long as Claudia and her magazine was there. But it was such work keeping in camera trim, and I wasn't dumb enough to think Claudia would always be there for me. I'd gone cold turkey on temptation the moment I realized that she had designs on me. Another man in my bed was certainly something her carefully maintained preservation would never tolerate. In fact, I had deftly managed for her to take me out of the bed of one of her best, much younger girlfriends, which covered all sorts of bases in that particular mating game.

"Brilliant idea, Travis," Claudia twittered from the other end of the dinner table. "I will indeed require Heidi's full attendance tomorrow. In fact, I think I would like to go over the boards for the 'Chicago Scene' column for the rest of the year. Unless you aren't prepared—"

"But of course, they are all ready for you," Heidi said sweetly. Claudia was too far away to see it, but I could see the light beads of perspiration forming on Heidi's expertly powdered upper lip. I had no doubt she'd be working all night. Better than Botswana, though.

I had already lost interest in this particular game, one I'd played so many times before. A luscious tush in tight white trousers was wiggling its way through the narrow gap between our table and the next. I felt myself going hard. I could only have been happier if he'd been turned toward our table for his passage. I was much more interested in the working end of a man's anatomy. Ah, the temptation. But then a bit of panic, and I looked back at Claudia. Good, she was all business talk; she hadn't seen me take that look. It was so much easier in New York, where I was left pretty much alone except when she needed some arm candy for an event or those nights she summoned me to her bedroom—after having adjusted the lighting down low and just so.

* * * *

The trip out to Oak Park from the loop on the El Green Line was a real lesson in urban design—a negative lesson. Within just a few blocks off the lake, the fabulous skyscraper architecture turned abruptly into a thick band of scudsy urban blight. Ash-covered tenements and abandoned mid-rise buildings screaming of poverty and decay. But it wasn't long until we were entering into suburbia, and when I got off at the Oak Park station and started following my guidebook to Chicago Avenue and the early home and studio of the architectural great, Frank Lloyd Wright, the developer of the Prairie Style, I was exhilarated. I loved his suggestively oriental motifs and his use of wood and shingles and sharp angles here in Oak Park. Within a few square blocks, a large collection of houses were built on designs he'd developed through exploration and adaptation. Many of the houses were moonlight designs, sold under the table when his work was fully employed by an architectural firm. I saw so many examples of his work as I made my way to Chicago Avenue that I marveled that his employers didn't find him out. But then, of course, they did in the end and canned him for his dishonesty. They must have been livid when they saw work that was obviously his start to go up in his very neighborhood—that they did only illustrated Wright's egocentric gall.

The young man looked familiar. When I had turned to admire the Egyptian-like columns high up on Wright's Unitarian church design, Unity Temple, I caught sight of a young man who had followed along behind me from the El station. I wondered why he'd come from the El station too, but then it dawned on me that I'd seen him on the station platform at the Loop in downtown Chicago and then fancied I'd glimpsed him on the train as well. And even at the Loop platform, I had the impression of familiarity, although I hadn't thought about it at the time.

Ah, well, I thought. Probably just my mind playing tricks on me. But he wasn't exactly forgettable. Rather the Marlin Brando-in-his-wild-boy-days look. Or James Dean. Dark and glowering in a pouty, pretty boy-covered-in-black leather fashion. Sort of rough. A vision of Jimbo floated across my mind. God, that had been a good run. My danger period. Motorcycles and black leather. About as far away from modeling Calvin Klein for *Peak Today* as you could get. In the past now, though.

I turned and, finding Chicago Avenue, had no trouble in the least deciding which of the buildings was the Wright house and studio. I spent a fascinating hour touring the house and steeping in the brilliant—but sometimes nonfunctional—design world of a major architect who spun his magic in one unified concept from the outer shell of the space down to the furniture and the dishes in the cabinets—always dominating his own tastes over those paying big bucks to live in one of his houses. But not always remembering something as mundane as running wiring where you ever could get at it again or making hallways big enough to get mattresses and bathtub replacements through them.

I was almost so overwhelmed and preoccupied by what I'd seen when I walked back out onto the raised terrace at the entry into the house that I didn't see him. He was lounging languidly on top of the wide stone wall, one leg raised challenging with black jack boot grinding into the aging cement of the wall ledge as if dismissing the scene and era that Wright had so painstakingly painted.

"You must have liked that. You spent more time in there than anyone else, I think."

"Excuse me?" I asked. He'd addressed me like we knew each other well and had just suspended a conversation we were having before I'd entered the museum. "Have we—?"

"Met?" he finished for me. He swung his leg down and moved his elbows to his knees, his legs in wide stance. A lock of curly hair dropped onto his forehead.

James Dean, I thought. Very James Dean. Maybe a model I've met somewhere?

"No, we've never met," he continued, "But I know you. I know you very well." He'd had a cigarette lit and he just flicked it into the shrubbery on the other side of the retaining wall. He could start a fire like that. I didn't think that Chicago had suffered the drought we were still having in on the East Coast. But a lit cigarette anywhere . . .

"Excuse me," I said again. "I don't follow. How——?"

"I work at Riva's. I saw you eyeing the waiters last night. You eyed me even, but I was just the hired help—and it wasn't my face you were looking at—so of course you don't recognize me. I'm interested. I followed you from town. My name is Colt. You wanna go somewhere? You obviously were dying for a fuck last night."

I was speechless. No, of course I didn't want to "go somewhere." The nerve. But, speaking of nerves, I suddenly wasn't in full control of mine. Nor was I in full control of my bodily responses. He was direct and brutal. Jimbo surfaced in my mind again. Temptation. A web of temptation. I'd been so careful.

"I'm sorry. I . . . I came to see the Wright houses."

A nonsensical answer. Completely flummoxed. But it got me off the terrace and propelled along the walking route around the neighborhood that would bring me by the best examples of Wright's work.

Colt gracefully unfolded himself in a fluid motion and fell into step beside me as I strode out in what I hoped was a determined and controlled manner.

"I give good fuck," he said. "I know of a nearby——"

"Please, I just came to see the houses. I'm a student of architecture. I came to see the houses." It was pushing it a lot to claim I already was studying architecture, but this wasn't a time for sense. I was completely flustered.

"And a hoity-toity male model, too," Colt muttered. "I've seen your pictures in those magazines. And hot for men too. I saw the way you looked at the waiters—at me even And especially at Jim."

"Jim?" I blurted. Did he know about Jimbo too? How could he know all of this.

"Did you also notice that I was married—to the woman hosting the party?"

"I could tell that she owned you, yes, but that doesn't necessarily mean that she satisfies you in every way. She's, what, fifty years older than you?"

"I am not interested, I said." I tried to sound authoritative. But my voice was quaking. Ah the temptation. I knew it wasn't true that I wasn't interested. He seemed to know it too. "I am just going to walk around and look at some houses and then I'm getting back on the train and going back to the loop. You're wasting your time."

"I don't really think so," Colt said in a quiet voice. "But I'll just walk with you. I lived here for a couple of years. I can tell you more about these houses then that guidebook can."

And he was right. He did know interesting things about the houses that at least added to what the guidebook told me. By the time we got to the Robbie House, I had stopped trembling and felt the tension start to drain out of me.

But then he put his hand on one of my butt cheeks as we were walking and leaned over and told me he knew of a secluded garden just down that street over there, and I abruptly cut short my Oak Park visit.

"Please. You've got to leave me alone. I'm not interested. I'm going back to the El now, and if you don't just stay here, I'm going to go into one of those stores over there and call the police."

He just stood on the corner then as I strode indignantly off toward Oak Park Avenue. I'd seen enough of the houses anyway. The day wasn't a loss. Certainly a minor victory. I'd faced temptation and overcome it. All to the good.

The train car I picked at the Green Line station was almost deserted. That is, until Colt sauntered down the aisle and sat down in the seat facing mine. The train had already started up, so I had no place to go.

"This has got to stop," I hissed.

"I want to get it on with you. I want to fuck," Colt said in an even voice. He sounded so matter of fact and sensible

423

about it. "And I've seen you. You want it too. I can tell. I can see it in your basket. And you can see I'm interested too." He unzipped himself and fished out a very formidable-looking cock. I shuddered and he saw me shudder.

When I looked away, He had leaned over and placed a hand on my crotch. What he found there confirmed everything he'd said.

"I'm getting off at the Cicero station," he said. "You can follow me off—or not—whatever you want. There's a place there we can fuck." His hand was still on my cock, holding it close through the thin material of my gabardine slacks. And he left it there until we were slowing down in the approach to the Cicero station. And I let him leave it there.

As we were pulling up to the station, which was smack dab in the middle of the smoldering ghetto area, Colt stuffed his dick back into his fly, rezipped, and stood and moved to the door. When it slid open, he glided out. Just before it slid shut, I stumbled to my feet and pushed myself out onto the platform, the door shutting behind me in a curtain-closing little whooshing sound of finality.

We came down off the platform onto a trash-littered street running between a bank of grayish buildings of nondescript function. The building closest to the raised track had its windows boarded up. I walked a good ten paces behind Colt—or, rather, he sauntered and I stumbled along, dragging myself, arguing with myself the whole way.

A block and a half down the street, which was totally deserted, Colt turned right into an alley.

We fucked far back in the alley, in a dim corner behind some big, green trash dumpsters.

He leaned his back against a blackened cinderblock wall, jutted his hips out and widened his stance and pushed me down on my knees between his legs. He unzipped himself and pulled out his long, plump cock and forced my face into it. Just like Jimbo.

When he was feeling hot and serviced enough, he pulled me up to my feet, unbuckled my belt, unzipped me, and pushed my pants down off my hips. I stepped out of my trousers and out of my briefs as well, and then he had me chest and cheek to wall, with my butt and legs jutting out from the wall and his tongue working between my butt cheeks until I was moaning and writhing and begging for him.

I heard him tearing a condom packet and trembled through the moment he took to roll it on and then he stood and nuzzled his young, fat, hard cock up to my now-loosened and moistened crack. I gave a little lurch and groan when he had his cock head inside me. Excited. I was excited. Well past temptation now. No saying no now and walking off, dignity intact. He held there for a few seconds, as he ran his hands up under my shirt and spread his palms over my heaving pecs. Then the long, slow slide into me, as I arched my back and moaned my acceptance. Oh, how I'd missed this. I had no idea how much I had been missing this.

He started to pump me and to pinch and roll my nipples between his thumbs and fingers and to suck on the hollow of my neck. And I was transported into another world. All possession and ecstasy. His heavy breathing was enough to tell me he was lost in the fuck as well. And I started a rhythm with my pelvis and an undulation of my canal walls around his invading dick that had us working as one perfect fucking machine. I turned my head and our lips met and his tongue pushed in. I wrapped a fist around my throbbing cock and started stroking myself off. And I lost all sense of time and place until that series of little jerks, the death of ejaculation. He pulled out of me then, swept the condom off in one swift movement, and creamed the small of my back.

Afterward he told me that this was his weekend El stop. That he lived in one of the downtown hotels and rotated around the restaurants during the week but came back here on the weekends. Then he said he wanted me to come back to his room with him so we could fuck properly.

But I declined. I was feeling guilty now. Temptation had gotten to me, but I couldn't risk falling back like this. This had to end right here. It helped that I was satiated; that I'd gotten my rocks off in the preferred manner for the first time in months.

He didn't try to stop me as I dressed and walked out of the alley on wobbly legs. He didn't come back up on the Cicero station platform while I was waiting for the next train, and he wasn't on the train with me—at least in my car—for the ride back to the Loop.

That night Claudia got the fuck of her life. We probably both thought it was induced by guilty conscience, although she no doubt thought I had guilty feelings over the come-on by Heidi and some sense of reciprocal feeling—after all, Claudia was probably old enough to be Heidi's mother, and Heidi's beauty and allure were still largely natural. But I knew better. I knew that my guilty conscience had the name Colt slapped all over it.

Breakfast at Chicago's Marriott Downtown Hotel was lavish and, for a change, Claudia and I had been able to take it in together. She usually was all powered up and half way through terrorizing her staff at the office before I rolled out of bed. But I had plowed Claudia three times the previous night, in a vain attempt to erase what I was really randy for, and she had called in late (and exhausted) for her morning meetings.

Still, she had eaten her three grains of Rice Crispies and finished two cups of black coffee while I was barely finished grazing the buffet, very much in the need of restoking from even more sex than Claudia was aware of, and had returned to my seat when she pecked me on the cheek, gave me a wondrous smile in which I could see the semen swimming in her eyes, and fluttered out of the room between genuflecting hotel flunkeys.

I had barely dug into a cheese and mushroom omelet when a hotel key was thunked down on top of the neatly folded copy of the *New York Times* at my elbow.

This actually wasn't all that much of a surprise. This happened to me a lot in the dining rooms of New York hotels catering to rich and lonely golf widows. And I'd gotten a whole hell of a lot of experience and variety in playing this game in years past.

But the surprise came when I looked up. Colt was standing at my elbow and staring down at me with laughing—and knowing and possessing—eyes. He was decked out in full waiter gear.

"This is the hotel I stay at during the week," he said. "I'm going off duty. Ten minutes. The room number is on the key."

I took nine of the minutes to wolf down as much of the breakfast as I could. I knew I'd need the fuel. Such a strong web temptation weaves.

The Chance Café

What a neat idea, Ted thought. He'd been down Lexington a couple of times a week all semester from his room to his classes at the university and he hadn't even noticed the Chance Café, down on the lower level under a hippy New Age gear store.

A cyber café, he quickly figured out from a scan of the membership agreement, where you could hook up with other guys in cyberspace in comfort. It was sort of a closed men's club—a dating service, where you checked in at the membership desk—really a private little room—the first time, and someone actually took the measurements himself and filled in the vital information on your club Web site profile and took your picture for posting. Then one could be quite sure who they were talking to and what they looked like and how they measured up. It wasn't subject to personal exaggeration.

It was a closed site only accessible from the other Chance Cafés, wherever they were, and when you wanted to browse the members' pages of those currently on line and chat with them one-on-one, they had cubicles where you could do that—very privately, other than the open door from the corridor. So, if the conversation got hot, you could comfortably get hot too. They had tissue dispensers and everything.

The whole issue of false advertising had been what had turned Ted off about any of these Internet dating services, and he certainly didn't think he had anything to be ashamed of in his own vital statistics, so there was nothing that bothered him about either having a hunky guy gather his statistics—which had led to a proposition that Ted had politely fended off—or having these statistics placed on a profile with his picture—as long as it was a very, very private club and he'd be talking with some guy safely off in Cleveland somewhere.

Ted had fucked with guys before—well, a couple of times. But he'd always found the fantasy of cyber chat and of dirty talk with a guy in cyberspace as so much more arousing than the actual fuck, and a good background for masturbating. Plus, he had this imaginary picture of the guy who would be fucking him—a muscle-bound hunk who would overpower him and sink an extra-long dick in him—and none of Ted's actual coupling partners had lived up to that in any way. He was going to a somewhat geeky school. Very good academically, but most of the men students were the indoor, quiet type who felt well fucked only by a complicated computer program.

But Ted had to laugh at that thought as he stood in the little room off the reception area of the Chance Café and had his dick measured. Here he was not very far from choosing to be fucked by a computer rather than a real man himself.

Ted had been sorely tempted to take the guy checking his stats up on his proposition. He was a nicely bulked-up Scandinavian type with a broad smile and a very nice thick cock of his own, which he had been quite proud to show Ted for comparison purposes while he was measuring and propositioning him.

"I've got my own nice little private cubicle right back here," the attendant had said. "I can hook into a live sex session on my computer, and you can watch it while I bend you over and fuck you deep. How about it?"

Ted had looked at what the guy was packing and was intrigued by the thick gold ball he had pierced to the underside of the cock right under the rim of his bulb. That alone sent little chills up Ted's spine. Nothing like the fucking he'd done in small study apartments with the other computer geeks. He wondered how that gold ball would feel running up and down his inner channel. But Ted was just too shy to more than fantasize about how that might feel.

Alone in the booth and with his still-to-be-completed profile backlit on the screen before him, Ted couldn't get the image of the attendant's gold ball-enhanced cock out of his mind. Why did he shrink from being cocked with something as exotic as that? He knew he wanted more than he'd been getting. That was why he'd checked out this cyber café and continued with the membership procedure after he heard what it was all about. He could find stuff to wank to in the privacy of his own room.

He was here because he wanted to kick it up a level— wanted to masturbate in a more public venue—and to something that stepped it all up a notch—to the fucking words of someone in another Chance Café somewhere, sitting, as he was, in a semiprivate booth in front of a computer with a Web cam. Actually being able to see each other, each other forming the words, as they sat there and masturbated themselves to the fucking words of the other guy in some distant club.

What the hell, Ted, thought, and he threw all caution to the wind. He registered under the name of teddybear4u and tapped in likes and dislikes that described a submissive for muscle hunks. In truth that was his fantasy, so why should he hold back? It was all fantasy anyway. No pretty boys for him. He wanted to see a thug on the screen. And cock? The bigger the better. And, still thinking of that gold bar on the underside of the attendant's cock, he specified that he liked thick cock rings and toys. And forceful. Yes, forceful—don't take no for an answer.

Ted pushed the submit button and laid back in the chair, eyes closed. Waiting to see what, if anything came up in a match. He heard the ding in less than a five-minute wait, but he had no idea what it was.

"Scoot your chair back and take your shirt off."

What? Ted heard the voice, but he had no idea where it was coming from. It seemed to be coming from the computer. He opened his eyes and then he opened them very wide indeed. His profile was no longer what was appearing on the screen.

What he saw was a biker type all leathered out and sitting in a chair away from the video cam wherever he was recording from. It was a cubicle much like the one Ted was in.

That was fast, Ted thought. It was intriguing what the system matched him up with in such a short time. And it was a bit surprising how his profile requests had been interpreted. But from the way his cock was hardening, the match up must have been done well.

Bulky, hard pecs, bulging biceps. Not fat, but a good hard belly that had seen its share of beer. Dark. The overall visage of darkness and danger. Black curly hair, covering pecs and moving down the sternum and belly into a pubic bush from which protruded a thick cock hung down between spread thighs at the front of the desk chair. A thick silver cock ring—just as Ted had ordered. The guy was wearing a black leather hat, a black leather vest that didn't close across his chest, and black shiny boots that reached up almost to his knees. Nothing else, except an insistent, mocking stare.

As Ted watched, the guy leaned forward toward the screen and took his cock in a beefy hand and repeated in a gruff, commanding voice, "Scoot back in the chair and take off your shirt. Now!"

Meekly, a chill of thrill going down his spine, Ted pushed his chair back and lifted his T-shirt over his head.

"Aw, nice little chicken," the computer screen muttered. "Straighten up and lean back in the chair. Now run your hands up your chest. Yes, like that. Finger your nipples. Make them puff out for me. Now!"

Another ding from the computer and it went to split screen. Another hulky hunk. More a bodybuilder this time. Red hair, freckles, lightly tanned hairless flesh where the first guy was dark and hairy. A perfectly sculpted body. Squared-jawed chiseled features on a thick neck. Completely naked and sitting away from the video cam as the first guy was—both guys with computer mouses in their hands on long cords. Heavy-muscled spread thighs, big balls resting on the vinyl of the desk chair seat, stubby little cock in repose, but thick, and crowned with a big gold stud with a ruby-colored gem in the center. This one had already started. He had his hips rolled up and his hand was slowly working a long purple dildo into his hole.

Ted was reacting to the first guy. The second guy just sat there and smiled and worked at himself. Ted was on screens to two other booths somewhere. He was momentarily stunned not only that he had so quickly attracted this attention but that the technology existed to link this way in the first place. This could be a triangulated encounter across the American continent.

"I said Now!" the first voice commanded. Ted started playing with his tits, as commanded. He found it arousing—and more arousing because he was being ordered to do it by a bruising hulk—and not the least so because another guy was watching him do it. Not reality, but close enough to make his cock hard.

"Strip off those pants." The commanding voice again. "Now!"

Ted rushed to comply. It was getting pretty tight in there anyway. He flipped his loafers off with toe on heel and then stood and stripped down his jeans and briefs.

"No, don't sit yet. Turn around."

Ted did so, slowly.

"Now bend down and spread those cheeks."

"What?" Ted asked, shocked at how quickly this was going.

"You heard him. Bend and spread those cheeks." This was the first utterance from the redhead. Higher register voice, but no less commanding, dominating.

Ted turned and bent over and spread his butt cheeks apart.

"Very nice butt and puckered hole," the first guy said. "Been fucked before? Are you a virgin? The hole doesn't looked like it's been used."

"No, not really. Well, not much," Ted answered in a choked voice. "I've done it. But not often, no."

"Nice. It'll be a close fit. Run your finger across the hole," the other guy commanded. "Yes, like that. Nice pucker." Ted could hear heavy breathing. It was coming from that second screen.

"Pretty tight. Ever been doubled?" The first voice chimed in.

"Doubled," Ted asked, confused.

"Two dicks working you at the same time."

"Oh. No." Answered with hesitation.

"Nice. As good as virgin." The second voice commenting.

"OK, turn around and sit down again. Now!" The leather guy commanding. "OK. Here's how this is going to go down. Me and Red here are goin' come in there and give you a fuckin'. Got that?"

A pause and then Ted squeaked out a "Yes." This was so realistic. These guys were going to do him well with just their words. And calling the other guy Red. It was just like they knew each other.

"Yes, what, pretty boy? Yes, sir, don't cha mean?"

"Yes . . . yes, sir," Ted responded in a breathy little voice.

"See this?" the leather guy was saying. He was waving his cock at Ted. It had gotten really big and the cock ring was wobbling back and forth. "You're gonna suck this while Red here is porkin' you and then I'm gonna attach a nice toy to this here ring and give you the thrill of your life. You like toys, don't cha? Your profile says you do."

"Look at Red now, pretty boy. See what he's growin' for you."

Ted's eyes went over to the other side of the screen and got real big. Red's cock was no longer stubby. It had lengthened out alarmingly. And Red had that purple dildo real far up his ass too. Ted couldn't help but gasp with his eyes bugged out. Red looked real pleased with himself.

"Jerk your meat slowly while we talk to you here, boy," the leather man commanded. And Ted took up his cock in his hand and started to pull on it slowly. He was trembling all over. God, this was a great fantasy.

"Red, tell him what you're going to do with that cock."

"Lean over and open the drawer of the desk under the computer," Red commanded. "You should find a couple of nice things there."

Ted did so and found another purple dildo, just like the one Red was using and a bottle of lube and a stack of condom packets. Wow, these clubs are organized, he thought. They are all fully stocked—and the users know that they are.

"Lube up the old purple pleasurer," Red continued. "Do it to your satisfaction. It's going to be in your ass."

Ted covered it real well with the lube.

"Now your hole. And put your legs out wide and role your bum up. I wanna watch this."

Ted did as instructed, and he got a little thrill at the sound of the heavy breathing in stereo from the split computer screen. He was lost in this new experience. It was helping him lose some shyness about opening up. He thought he might get a little more adventuresome in who he responded to on campus now.

"Now put the tip of that purple guy at your entrance and move it around, working it in just enough that your channel gets a taste of it. Lay back and close your eyes. Think of it as my cock. My cock with this here ruby eye in it about to give you a fuck you'll never forget."

Ted widened his stance and propped the heels of his socked feet up on the edge of the computer desk and laid back in the chair, the back of which had give in it, and closed his eyes. He was holding the dildo to his hole and moving it around in a little circular motion, letting it sink in a bit farther with every couple of rotations. He was sighing and moaning now. He'd never done this. He'd have to buy himself one of these. The dildo wasn't all that thick. It felt sort of like Stewart when he was fucking him. Ted knew he could handle this.

"Now, think of me between your legs, right where you are. I've got my cock at your hole just like that. Can you feel the ruby?"

"No." Ted was being truthful. And his voice had a tinge of regret to it; he wanted to feel the ruby.

"Well, you will. Imagine it for now, though. It's slowly working its way in until your muscle grabs it and pulls it in nicely. Happening?"

"Yessss," Ted moaned. His sphincter had caught the bulb of the dildo and drawn it in. He could feel a straight shot

435

up his chute. His walls were actually rippling in anticipation of the journey.

"I'm gonna fuck your mouth while Red's fucking your tail." A gruff, lower-toned voice. The leather guy now. "Keep your hand on the dildo, but put the thumb of your other hand in your mouth and suck it. That's my cock, getting ready for when Red's finished with your hole."

Ted felt his body going into the rhythm of an undulating motion, going with the fuck. He had managed this a couple of times with Stewart. And striving for this feel was the only reason he kept going back to Stewart. And these two were fucking him just as well with only words across cyberspace. He was making slurping sounds with the sucking of the thumb. He'd never sucked a man before. He wondered now what that felt like and decided he'd try it sometime for real.

"Now slowly sink the purple guy all the way in," Red was saying. "That's what I do. I let my partner feel all of me at first. Do it. Now!"

Ted slowly pushed the dildo deep inside him. He was breathing raggedly and shuddering at the exertion. More than once he stopped, and Red commanded him to continue.

When he had bottomed. "All the way out and all the way back in now. Feel me. Open your eyes and see me in the screen."

Ted did so and moaned. Red had lengthened out to at least the size of the dildo, but thicker.

"Now close your eyes and pull it out again—but not all the way. Rest the tip on your prostate. You can find that, can't you? Now slowly rub across it—and think of that ruby eye making love to your spot. Yes. I like the way you move against it. Don't let up. I don't want you to stop until you've creamed yourself."

Ted's other hand had moved to his cock and he was stroking himself.

"Did I tell you you could take that thumb out of your mouth?" The leather guy. Booming voice, cutting across Ted's heightening arousal.

"No, sir," Ted squeaked.

"Three fingers now. Three fingers in your mouth," the leather guy commanded. "Open your eyes and look at me."

When Ted did so, he saw that the leather guy's heavy cock was at full staff now.

"Three fingers aren't enough to be me, but they'll have to do now," the leather guy declared. "No, shut your eyes and don't open them again until you've shot off. I want to hear heavy breathing, moaning, and groaning."

Ted didn't have to be instructed to do this. God what a great masturbation session. This club was great!

Soon, silence reigned with only the sounds of moans and sighs from inside Ted's cubicle backdropped by heavy breathing that sounded so real that it sounded like it was in the room with Ted rather than over the computer. Ted was working the head of the dildo on his prostate and sucking on three fingers and moving his body in the universal rhythm of the full-body fuck.

As Ted ejaculated, though, there suddenly was a flurry of activity in his cubicle. His heels were being swept off the edge of the computer desk, the chair he was sitting in was being leaned back on its back two legs, and his body was being thrown back.

Ted's eyes popped open and he only had time to see a flash of bulging muscle on smooth, freckled skin thrust itself between his legs, when his head was forced back and he had a swarthy-skinned cock with a big silver cock ring being forced between his lips.

Leather guy and Red. Both right here in the room with him; not a cyberspace away in some sister club to the Chance Café.

Red pulled the dildo out of Ted's ass with a slurp and replaced it with his own cock, which started its long journey up Ted's channel. The dildo hadn't been anything like this, really. This was thicker and that ruby eye was gliding along Ted's wall, sending ripples of pleasure all around his pelvis.

But Ted didn't have a great deal of time to think about what Red's sheathed cock was doing to his channel. Ted's mouth was busy trying to take in the leather guy's cock. This was something Ted hadn't done before, and the leather guy wasn't giving him much time or space to figure out what was expected of him.

For the next fifteen minutes, while Ted was tilted back on the desk chair in his cubicle and worked up a second helping

437

of cum, Red's ruby eye was rubbing across his prostrate, demanding more cum, and the leather guy's cock was exploring every inch of Ted's inner cheek walls and upper throat, silver ring occasionally clicking on teeth.

Then, when Ted and Red had come almost simultaneously, Red dove his cock to the bottom again and held, while Ted, in fascination, watched the leather guy roll on a condom with a little special something on the end. It had a clip that latched onto the leather guy's silver cock ring through the head of the condom. And running off this clip were five thin ribbon streamers, about a foot in length and all a different color.

Red picked Ted up from the chair and lapped him in a half-standing, half-crouched position, while the leather guy moved around behind Ted, crouched down, and began working his cock in on top of Red's in Ted's hole. Ted panted and groaned at the stretching of his hole and the feel of two men inside him. This didn't last long—just long enough for Red and the leather guy to show that it could be done.

And then Red had withdrawn from Ted's channel, Ted was lowered back into the chair, the Red came around to hold his shoulders down, while the leather guy replaced him and started fucking Ted deep, swirling those streamers around on his inner channel walls and rubbing that thick cock ring up and down deep inside Ted.

Ted had no trouble coming for a third time.

Later when Ted was alone in his cubicle and contemplating getting up from the floor where he had fallen after being released from his third ejaculation, his mind slipped back into gear and he began to wonder how he had slipped over from self-administered fantasy to full threesome fuck.

The attendant was standing at the door, looking at Ted with some concern.

"What? How? But it was all supposed to be on computer," Ted muttered.

"On the computer only?" The attendant asked. And then he laughed. "You mean you thought . . .? You didn't read all of the provisions in the membership contract, did you? You thought you were just connected to some sort of cyberspace file?

That's not the way this works, fella. When you log on here, you're connected to other guys right here in the club."

Ted looked at him thunderstruck. He'd been had. Or had he? Didn't he really want to go other this threshold. Didn't he really want the reality? And wasn't the reality so much more than the fantasy ever had been? He couldn't backslide now. He needed to forge ahead. He had gotten entirely too much pleasure out of this to backtrack now. And, hadn't the attendant, a luscious Scandinavian hunk with a juicy cock, propositioned him earlier? What would be a better way of forging ahead?

The Scandinavian fucked Ted up against the wall, crouched down, with Ted, belly against the wall, almost sitting on his cock and being thrust up the wall by the strength of the fucking while the Scandinavian reached around and stroked Ted's cock. They finished with Ted bent over the back of the desk chair and the Scandinavian fucking him from behind while they both watched the replay of Ted's session with the leather man and Red as taken shortly before on the Web cam.

And, to be sure, Ted did not tear up his membership card to the Chance Café.

The Commander

"Ahhh, that were very nice," I said with a deep, satisfied sigh, as I spilled my seed down Des's chin. We were in the boathouse on the lower lake, here because Des had wanted me to fuck him. But now we'd have to sit and talk for a bit, listening to the racing shells grind against the dock outside in the bit of a squall that had come up over Sandhurst. It would take me a few to recharge.

"Cig?" I asked, reaching into my pocket and pulling out a pack while he scrubbed at his face with a dirty handkerchief.

"Thanks," he said, reaching out for the fag. He stood and turned, leaning back against the gunwale of the boat I was sitting on. "God, you are built hanging."

"That's what you came for, isn't it?" I asked with a laugh. I was unbuckling his belt with one hand and moving the other down the small of his back and under this waistband, moving into his crack. I'd need time to be in form again, but there was no reason not to prepare him.

"Yes, you are a legend over at New College . . . ugh!" I'd found his hole with my forefinger, and he was rising up on the balls of his feet in surprise. But with a shudder and a little moan, he settled back down on the finger. This is what he'd come here for right after dark. To check out the Sandhurst military academy legend for himself.

"And you're over at Old College?" I asked. He groaned an assent as I pushed the trousers down off his thighs and reached for his dong. Not much more than ordinary, but thickening well. "Valeting for the cadets, are you?"

"Yes . . . oh, shit, oh fuck." I had three fingers in him now. He'd need to be real open for me. "Yes. And you? Over at New College."

"The same."

"Valet for that new cadet, Sandy Coleridge I hear. Father's the big snot for the 6th D.C.O Lancers out in India on the North West Frontier."

"Yes, I do for him."

"And does he enjoy that big cock of yours in him? Particular nice piece of arse that."

"No," I said and then laughed. "I don't do for him that way—would like to, but no. The Lad's stiff as a board proper. Really up tight. A bit of the old man, I hear. A virgin."

Des snorted. "Not a virgin, I hear. I hear he has a regular appointment with his tutor, Percy Hopewell."

"Percy Hopewell?" I asked, incredulous. "Hopewell is almost as stick up the arse as young Coleridge is and puny as a beanpole. And Coleridge is a right tasty piece. I can't see them doing it."

"Well, check it out for yourself. Tuesday afternoons at two, or so I heard. In Coleridge's room. Faithful as clockwork."

"I still don't believe it. But here, you came to get a taste of this," I waved my ready wand at him, and his eyes went wide. "And I don't have all night. So, let's get to it. Here. Hop up on the ledge of the gunwale. Here where it's thickest."

He did as I asked. He was trembling a bit, and he looked scared, his eyes constantly going to my cock, which was hardening up nice, and then looking away. I stripped off his trousers.

"On the small of your back. Yes, like that, roll your arse up to me and hold your thighs out yourself." I let him watch me pull a rubber on, and then I went down on my knees between his legs and lifted his dick out of the way and squeezed it as my tongue went to his buttocks and the crevice between.

He was making little grunting and groaning sounds.

At length, when I thought he was open enough to take me just, I stood, rubbed my cock and his hole with cream, and, taking that big breath that all athletes take before making the big plunge, presented at the rim of his hole.

"Oh god, you're huge," he whined and went rigid as I got the rim of my bulb past his entrance. He had been gasping but now he was still and straining to take me, and his complexion was turning red.

"Here, now," I said. "You've got to breathe. Breathe. Relax. You act like a first-time school girl. You've had it before, haven't you?"

"Yess . . . oh god, oh god . . . but nothing as big as this. Oh fuckkkk."

He'd come for it because it was big; he wanted it. So I gave it all to him in one deep thrust.

"Oh, god! . . . . . Oh GODDDDD!"

* * * *

Turned out Des was right. The next time I was tidying up Sandy Coleridge's room, I flipped open his appointment book and there it was, the notation at two on each Tuesday for "tutorial with Percy."

The next Tuesday at two I made sure I was in the service back hall, with the valet's door into Coleridge's chambers open a crack. I heard voices and soft laughter down the service stairs behind where I was standing, and I went down to find the men in service, Hugh and Cedrick, crouched down on the turn of the stairs. Hugh was giving Cedrick a blow job, and I stood there and watched for a while, pleased by the good, straightforward sex of it. Then I remembered why I was in the back hall and went back to the door into Coleridge's room and pushed the door open to a wide crack.

They were already going at it, if you could call it that. I had to check myself from laughing out loud. They were side by side, close together, in overstuffed chairs, naked. Arms were extended over the chair arms, Percy's hand working slowly on Sandy's cock and Sandy's hand pumping Percy languidly. Percy was reading poetry from a book. Sandy was a real beauty, tanned and hardened from life on the Indian frontier. Handsome as a movie star. Sandy hair—obviously the derivation of the name that had stuck—from head down to the downy tuffs on his sternum leading down his belly and bushing up around a very nice cock. Percy was another matter—an indoor scholar—all angles and height, concave chest, hairy as a dog, dark, and with a poor excuse for a cock. I could hardly see it encased there in Sandy's hand. The only attraction that I could see must have involved seniority—but then, here at Sandhurst, seniority was everything.

Call this fucking? Reading poetry and calmly jacking each other off. Gorsh. I'd say Sandy was still a virgin in any way that mattered. But it wasn't all the fucking they did, and I decided that Sandy, technically couldn't be called a virgin. Percy snapped the poetry book shut and stood up and pulled Sandy up as well. They moved over to the desk in front of the window. Percy gently pushed Sandy's chest down onto the chair that was inserted into the desk hole, and as he did so, Sandy widened his stance. A rolled on rubber and a few minutes of rubbing cream in and Percy was pushing his small cock into Sandy's arsehole. Sandy flinched a bit at the first breaching, but nothing significant or painful looking. Percy bottomed quickly and just held there, moaning softly, his head flung back in what passed for ecstasy for him, while, holding a wash cloth over his tip, Sandy slowly beat his own cock to ejaculation and stared out of the leaded diamond windows of his bay window onto the parade grounds below. Percy was reciting poetry again, and the pace of his voice picked up and he became breathy. There was a slight lurch and a tightening of his thin buttocks, and then the ritual was all over.

It seemed so sad. Sandy looked like he was just marking a "to do" activity off his life's experiences lists. His beautiful body and sensuous lips told me that he wanted so much more out of life.

They dressed in silence, there was one pecking kiss on the lips initiated by Percy, and then they settled down in the upholstered chairs and opened their books for the justifying tutorial session.

That was it? That was all? I thought. There hadn't even been enough for me to take my meat out and beat it. Although I was hard. That was from watching Sandy. As Des said, he really was a nice piece of tail. He deserved better than Percy.

But then I guess that was the way in the British colonial army life. Attend Sandhurst as your father did and his father did, become imbued with the gentleman soldier's training as your father did; become manned by a sensitive but consumptive upperclassman as your father did; find an appropriate bride from a suitable family to marry just before embarking for your colonial posting as your father had; produce sons as your father had—and pick out the best looking of your sepoys and fuck him for your only sense of self and rebellion as your father did.

I turned and crept back to the top of the stairs and did now take my meat out and beat it while watching Hugh splayed out on the stairs on his belly and Cedric crouched over him from behind and fucking him furiously, both of them grunting like pigs. Now that was fucking. A difference between upstairs and downstairs perhaps? I suddenly had a desire to find out.

* * * *

I spent the next night trying to forget Sandy Coleridge— the beauty of his young, supple, yet muscle-hardened tanned body—and not being able to do. I resolved to act and justified it by telling myself Sandy wanted more out of his male-male experience and ultimately would be grateful to me. It was a gamble, and it might lead to me being booted out of a pretty cush Sandhurst job—but it wasn't as if Sandy was repulsed by the idea of being fucked by another man. All of the rationalization came down to the simple fact that I wanted to fuck the cadet from colonial India just to get my cock in him for my own pleasure, however.

So, in the still of the night, I threw some necessities and a couple of toys in a bag, and just in my sleeping briefs, I padded down from my attic room in the New College service area and crept up to the service door into Coleridge's chambers.

All was dark inside, and I could hear him gently snoring. I crept through the door and silently shut it behind me and stood, still, for some minutes until my eyes had fully acclimated to the dark.

Sandy was stretched out on his bed, on his back, his legs tangled up in sheets. He was wearing long sleeping drawers, and nothing else, but his cock was hanging out of the fly and his hand was still on it. The front of his drawers were spotted where he had finished masturbating as he went to sleep. He was as beautiful and sexy in sleep as he was awake—maybe more so, as he looked so vulnerable and peaceful.

I was going to fix that—the peaceful part of that.

The handcuffs made a clicking noise when I took them out of the bag, and I froze, afraid it would wake him. It didn't, though. He just snuffled and turned a bit more on the side away from me and moved his arm over his head. His wrist went between brass railings in the headboard. Perfect. I had that wrist locked in the handcuffs and a good grip on the other wrist before he woke with a start and began the expected confused and indignant objecting to what was happening to him.

I rose off the bed from where I'd gone down on a knee to snap the hand restraints on and turned and clicked on his bedside lamp. I wanted him to see what was going to happen.

"Alec," he muttered in surprise. "What the hell? Release me this instant."

"Sorry, Mr. Coleridge, I've come to give you a proper fucking, sir. It's what you need, sir."

"A proper . . . what is this? Are you joking? I'll have your job for this."

"No I'm not joking. And we'll see about my job. But you can't even say it. Fucking, fucking, fucking. You can't say it, can you?"

"What in the world are you talking . . . no don't do that. Put those back on this instant."

I had been stripping my leggings off, and then I reached over and did the same for him.

"No. Stop that . . . let me go. What is this about?"

"This is about you doing it with a man, sir, but not having any idea what that means, how good it can be for you.

446

I'm going to give you a good idea, and then you can choose whether you want to do it with the likes of Percy Hopewell or with a real man. I think you deserve knowing the difference."

"Percy Hopewell . . . what?"

"I seen you and Percy, sir, and I don't call that fucking."

"Percy and I . . . we . . . we do too do it."

"Do what, sir? You can't say it. Fuck. Say it."

"We do too make love . . . have sex. And that's enough for . . . free me this instant."

I had taken his dick in a fist, and he was writhing around, trying to get away from me. But I could feel him coming to life.

"Bet you can't say this either, sir. Cock. This isn't an 'it.' This is a cock. And this is a cock too, sir," I said, wagging my own proud member at him. "And this cock is going to be in your arsehole. Say the words. Say cock. Say arsehole. Say fuck."

Sandy was still writhing, trying to get out of the restraints and away. I climbed up on him and knelt over his chest, wagging my cock in his face. "Cock. A hard cock. Show me you know what real sex is with a man. Suck it. Suck my cock." I was beating him on the cheeks with my cock, but he was having none of it. His lips and eyelids were shut tight, and he was jerking his head back and forth, still trying to escape my onslaught.

"Aye, well you'll give me suck soon enough—and enjoy it, I'm betting," I said. And then I scurried over him and down behind him and between his legs, swallowed his cock whole, and began pumping my mouth on it. I moved my thumbs to his hole and pushed them in and spread him just a bit. His curses and demands filtered into moans and groans, and his writhings merged into waves of going with the rhythm of the suck as I relentlessly pumped his engorging cock until he ejaculated, which happened quite quickly, this all being a shock to him and him not having been expertly blown before.

Then I rolled his buttocks up and moved my lips and tongue to between his crack, and he was groaning right proper for me, although he occasionally was making an attempt to tell me I had to stop.

He pretty much was under control and his cock had gotten rock-hard solid again when I stopped, slapped him on the butt, and reached down and took a toy out of my bag.

"I bet you don't even feel what that Percy puts in you. I bet my tongue does you better than he does. Can you deny that?"

Apparently he couldn't, because he didn't answer. He peered down to see what I has holding up above his belly, and I felt his whole body shudder. "Wha . . . what is that for?" The shudder told me what he knew what that was for.

"I think you know what this is for," I said. "I call this the Commander—because every moment it's in use you will know the Commander is in control."

"Ahh . . . no . . . you can't," he cried out. And he tightened his thighs together as much as possible and arched his back off the surface of the bed and was rolling back and forth and rattling the handcuffs holding his arms above his head so that they rang hollow, almost musical notes on the brass rails— all of this expense of energy as if that was going to get him out of the predicament.

I held the toy suspended over his belly, and he couldn't take his eyes off it. They were wide with fear. It was twelve inches of cascading rubber nodules, the one at the tip, the first of five, a pointed tear-drop shape about one inch at the upper rim, graduating up in connected tear drops of increasing size so that the fifth, uppermost was a good three inches across at the upper rim. At that point a four-inch rubber lead ended in a strong handle that all four fingers could wrap around for good leverage.

"Tell me. Does this look anything like Percy's cock?" I asked sweetly. "Is he twelve inches and three inches thick at the widest point?"

"Noooo . . ." Sandy moaned, and I didn't know whether he was belittling Percy's dimensions or objecting to the Commander. And it didn't matter.

Sandy groaned and whimpered and begged as I fished cream out of my bag and lavishly greased up the Commander while holding it suspended over his heaving belly.

"Here, I think I'm going to need that pillow," I said, pulling the pillow out from underneath his head and inserting it under the small of his back. "And I think you'll find you've going to want to widen the stance of your thighs just as much as possible."

He, rather, tightened his thighs and rolled his hips back and forth, trying to escape me, as, after I'd greased his hole with some finger work, I placed the tip of the Commander at his rim.

He gasped and cried out and spread his thighs wide, though, as I pressed the tear drop at his hole. The first one was the hardest to get accepted, but, although it was easier with the next two before being quite difficult with the last two, he was as noisy in the invasion of each successive tear drop over the next twenty minutes. As the wide edge of the third tear drop was swallowed by his entrance, he ejaculated again in a great spouting of semen.

"Ah, very good," I said. "And does Master Percy make you come like that? Come. Can you say it? Come. And have you ever come that well for anyone else?"

He didn't answer, but I decided that that was because he was grunting and moaning profusely. No longer objecting. Voicing a little appreciation now for all of my efforts. When I asked him if Percy's cock made him feel this way, he was quick now to acknowledge that Percy couldn't do anything like this.

"No . . . he doesn't." The voice had almost taken on a tone of awe, like he had had no idea how it really could be. That alone told me I was right to do this for him. I did reason that I was doing it for him, although that little voice of truth in the back of my head kept telling me that I was doing it for myself—that I wanted my cock inside this tasty piece.

After the fifth teardrop had disappeared, I moved back up beside him and held him in my arms and looked into his eyes, which were open wider and looking more wild and electric than ever before. He was panting hard and trembling all over, and his expression was flipping through pain and ecstasy and wonder.

"Good for you," I crooned to him. "You've taken it all. You know I'm nearly as long and almost as thick. And I can move it in ways that will send you to new heights of pleasure. What do you think now?"

"Oh, yes, yes," he whimpered. "I want it."

"What do you want?" I asked.

"It. I want it."

"And what's 'it'?" I persisted.

"Your cock."

"My what? I can't hear you."

"Your cock. Your COCK!"

"And where do you want it?"

"Inside me. Oh, please . . . now, oh please."

"Inside what?"

"My arse. My bunghole. I want you to cock me. To come inside me."

"What do you want me to do to you?" I was biting on his nipples and fisting his cock. His back was tense, arched, and his thighs spread wide, the Commander still fully encased in his channel.

"Fuck me. I want you to fuck me!"

I went up on all fours and straddled him in reverse and swallowed his hard cock again. I was pleased to note that his mouth went to my cock, instantaneously, without hesitation this time, and he was sucking me—not expertly, but giving me good suck and extraordinary pleasure nonetheless.

My hand went to the handle of the Commander, and I ever so slowly pulled it out of Sandy's arse. In response he went into a frenzy of passion, sucking hard on my cock and writhing under me. Before the Commander was fully extracted, he had ejaculated again, and I took it at the back of my throat, pleased and awed at the stamina of healthy youth.

I released his hands then and knelt between his legs and gave him a proper, expert, total, working-man's fucking. And he, in turn, gave me the proper lust-released responses for one being well fucked—and now knowing he was well fucked.

* * * *

The next Tuesday afternoon, still employed by Sandhurst, I was standing in the service hall outside Sandy Coleridge's door when I heard the knock on his main entrance. Sandy walked, gingerly, to the door and opened it.

"Oh, Percy, it's you," he said to the one standing at the door, but not given entrance. "You didn't get my message then."

"What message?" Percy said, almost in a huff.

"No session today, I'm afraid," Sandy said. "In fact, we might have to leave off altogether. I haven't been sleeping nights recently, and I feel all fagged out. Sorry. I'll see you at lecture tomorrow."

As he closed the door, I stopped shining Mr. Sandy's boots and gave him a turn of my head and a secret little smile. My chest was puffing up in pride, being as how the dark-hours fuckings he begged me for now were the reason young Mr. Sandy wasn't getting enough sleep at night.

The Thunderstorm

I fully acknowledge my weakness, but I think Janine has a share in the shattering of my vows to her. I'd only had that one fling back in college—with Phil. But Chet and Phil had had an affair after college, and now Chet was living in the next acreage to ours. Obviously Phil and Chet had talked about me, and Chet knew all about me before he moved here, because he had made quite clear to me that he wanted me and knew that I had an addiction to what he could provide. He was one hunk of a man, but I'd left that behind me—had convinced myself it was just youthful experimentation, and short-lived at that—and I was devoting my life to Janine.

I had done everything I could to avoid Chet, who had gotten quite direct in his approach, but it had been Janine herself who set up that fatal day. I had taken off from work to pull a couple of stumps out at the lower end of our yard. Janine was off that week for a visit to her mothers and had pressured me not to work out there alone. I had resisted her suggestions, and, unbeknownst to me, she had asked Chet if he could come down to help me. He obviously was delighted to help.

So there we were, standing next to each other in the driveway in our work clothes, waving gaily to Janine as she drove off, doing all we could to act like there was no nervous tension just under the surface, ready to explode.

I would still see the tail end of her car, and Chet was still waving when he said, in a husky voice, "Let's go into the house."

"God, no, Chet. We've been all over that. I'm going down to work on those stumps. You can go on home. I'll just tell Janine you were a great help."

"That's what I want, Rick. I want to be a great help to you."

"Help? God, Chet, how can you help? I've made a choice, and the only help you could be is just to stay the hell away from me."

"I've seen how you've looked at me," Chet replied. "I know you want it as much as I want you."

"I'm going in the house to get a couple of beers, Chet. It's a real hot day. When I come out, I'd like you to be walking back to your house. I have to get to those stumps."

"It looks like rain. And, you're right; it's hot as hell out here. Not really a day for this; a day to be relaxing in the house."

"Bye, Chet," I said, and I went back into the house and took four beers out of the fridge. Then I thought of the ax and being alone down there with the tree stumps, and I put one back. Chopping wood is no time to have a drunk on. I walked back out of the house, and Chet was gone. What a relief. He was right. No matter what I did to try to stay on the straight and narrow, I ached for him. I tried my best not to admit it, but there it was. I wished that Chet hadn't moved here at all. Everything was going fine until he showed up.

I walked down to the end of the yard, but I could hear the chopping noises before I even got to the garden shed down there. And I knew. Chet hadn't gone home.

He was stripped to the waist, down to his tight, low-slung jeans. He had a bandana covering his head and already was sweating. He was in great shape, bulging muscles of someone used to chopping all of his own wood, going down to a small waist and hips. He was darkly tanned and black hair curled around his forearms and down from his neck and across his chest and trailed down across his navel into his jeans.

He already had chopped one corner out of the biggest stump.

"This isn't really a one-man stump, Rick," he said as he stopped chopping and leaned on the ax handle. "Come on over here and let me show you what a tree stump can be used for. Or an ax handle, for that matter," he said as he winked at me.

"Give it up, Chet," I answered acidly. "I'll just work on this stump over here."

"It's hot as a devil's asshole," Chet said. "At least give me a beer. What, you've only brought three? Let's go up to the house and get some more."

"I don't think so, Chet."

"Well, maybe later."

I turned and started chopping at a smaller stump with my hatchet. Chet was right. This really was heavy work. I heard a roll of thunder from some miles in the distance but couldn't tell if it was just caused by the heat or was warning of a coming thunderstorm.

"Hey, it's too hot for that T-shirt, Buddy. I quickly found it's cooler without."

"I'll manage," I answered.

"Yeah, guess you're right," Chet answered and then chuckled. "I saw you in the gym—you know, before I told you about our mutual friend, Phil. I don't think I could control myself if you took off that T."

"I don't think you're controlling yourself very well now," I muttered under my breath.

"What's that? Couldn't hear you over the thunder."

"Oh, nothing, we'll have to work fast if we're going to beat the rain." But, of course, there was no way beating the rain. It started sprinkling then, but that didn't go long before it came more steadily. We both were immediately soaked to the skin.

"Holy Christ!" Chet yelled, as a lightning bolt hit a tree somewhere close in the forest. "We better get out of here right now; up to the house." And he dropped the ax and headed up the yard.

I just couldn't do it. Instead of following him, I headed for the garden shed, which was the size of a two-car garage, but which was stuffed with all sorts of gardening equipment and supplies. Dark clouds rolled in before I got to the shed, and it was pitch black inside when I got there. I knew we had lanterns around in there somewhere, and I was feeling around for one of them when I heard the shed door open and close, and I could hear Chet's heavy breathing.

"I'm over here, Chet," I said. "Looking for a lantern." I turned, and he was right there in front of me. I felt a hand on my crotch.

"That's me, Chet," I said. "I think the lantern's over there."

"I know that's you," Chet said heavily, and he pushed me up to the wall next to a window. His hand had found my cock through the fabric of my soaked jeans, and I involuntarily responded there, not having a prayer to control my response. "And that's a very nice you," Chet said.

"Chet, no," I said.

A flash of lightning brought light flooding into the shed through the window next to us. Chet was standing very close to me, rainwater flowing down his chest and into his wet jeans. The heaviness of the water in his jeans had pulled the waist down, and if he hadn't had a large, firm butt, they probably would have hit the floor. I could tell my own jeans were having about the same effect from the fast soaking they'd gotten. In that brief flash, I could see the urgency in Chet's eyes. And just before the shed went dark again, Chet leaned in and brought his lips to mine. His were searching, but I resisted him and turned my head.

"No, Chet, I've said no."

He leaned his crotch into mine, and I could feel the rising power of him there. He put his hands against the wall on either side of me, holding me there. I was so weak, however, that I don't think I could have moved if I'd wanted to. Having lost my lips and faced with the side of my head, he buried his face into my neck and kissed and nibbled me there. I moved my hands between us to push him away, but the feel of his chest and nipples sent electricity through me that rivaled the storm expending its fury outside the shed. I couldn't will myself to take my hands away from him.

He was whispering at me. "I've had a hard on for you ever since Phil told me about you. He told me over and over again what a good lay you are. How you took nine thick inches. That you even took it double. What you could do with your sphincter."

"Chet," I moaned. "That's all in the past, and it was just a short fling, an experiment. I'm someone else now."

"Your dick tells me otherwise, Buddy," Chet said and then laughed. "I can feel it grow. It's growing for me. It wants me. It wants me to fuck you."

"No, Chet. No, you're wrong."

Chet's mouth moved down to my T-shirt collar, which he took in his teeth. He brought his hands up to the collar and literally ripped my shirt apart until it was off me. His lips immediately went to my chest and nipples, while his hands roughly undid my belt, unbuttoned my fly in a frenzied motion, pulled the pants and my briefs below my crotch and wrapped themselves around my balls and engorging cock.

"Let me go, Chet," I whined weakly. "I'm not going to do this."

"Strip my jeans off," Chet commanded.

"No, no, Chet. This has already gone too far." So, he released his hands and stripped down himself. His lips came back up to find mine, and I turned away again.

"Touch me," he commanded. "Take my cock." I froze. He took my balls in one of his hands and squeezed. "Touch me, I said!"

I moved both hands down to his crotch and took his cock. He was big and thick—maybe bigger and thicker than Phil. I shuddered, and so did he. This time when he took my lips in his, I didn't turn, but I was as unresponsive as I could be. I felt so weak. I didn't for the life of me want to be doing this. But I couldn't stop doing it. I couldn't help myself. He could feel me relaxing, surrendering.

Once more his lips came down the side of my neck. He took my arms and raised them over my head and told me to leave them there. I did as he asked. He'd brought a bottle of the beer with him, and he popped the top and poured the cold liquid down my chest. His lips did another tour of my pecs and nipples and then up to both of my armpits, licking up the beer. His hands were on my sides and as his lips traveled slowly down my sternum and abs, his hands came down my sides as well. He tongued my navel and then traveled down my belly and into my pubic hair. He wrapped one hand around the base of my cock and cupped my balls with it. The other hand went behind me and caressed my butt cheeks. Then he went down on me, tonguing the helmet first and then the rest of and my cock, swallowing and pumping, nibbling down one side and up another, flicking his tongue around the rim of the helmet and into my piss slit, and then going back to swallowing and pumping.

All the time I was moaning and sighing and admonishing him that this had to stop. I didn't even notice when his hand stopped caressing my butt cheeks and he had started fingering my asshole, but before I knew it, he had a finger past my sphincter and was rubbing my prostate and I jerked and lurched and came in three heavy spasms.

I collapsed against the wall. "That's enough, Chet. That's way more than enough. I've got to go. You've got to leave."

Another flash of lightning revealed the layout and contents of the shed. Chet took me by the hips and pulled me over to the side, where there was a compost drum we had recently bought but not put to use yet.

"On this; down on this with your chest," Chet directed with an urgency.

"Chet, no. Not . . ."

He pushed me down. "Spread those legs." I did as he asked and I felt his lips and teeth on my butt cheeks.

"God, you're beautiful," he said hoarsely. In short order, his lips were on my asshole, followed shortly by his tongue, and he was moistening me up real good.

"Oh, no. Never again," I croaked. But there he was. I could feel the head of his dick at my asshole. He tried pushing it right in, but I wasn't anywhere near ready yet. He took his dick and slapped it against my butt cheeks and inserted first one finger, and then two, and then three and then pushed them apart, opening me up. And then his fingers were replaced by the head of his dick again. I tried to rise up, but he pushed me down with a strong paw on the small of my back. He used his other hand to help gain purchase for his cock, and when he was a good three inches in, he rotated his cock with his hand inside me, opening me more. Another inch and my sphincter took the cock and drew it farther in. As the helmet of his cock dragged across my prostate, I flinched and moaned. He was sighing and moaning as well, clearly enjoying this. He pushed in farther, a good five inches now. He took me by the hips with his hands and rocked me back and forth, more than half in, fucking me in midstream.

"Oh, yes, God that's good. I've anticipated this for weeks. I could come right now." But he obviously decided not to, because he stopped the action and stood very still, holding my hips in place for maybe three or four minutes. And then he just glided right in, all the way, maybe almost eight inches, into me, up to the hilt. I could feel his curly pubic hairs tickling my ass. Memories of Phil flooded back. How could I have denied how this felt?

He pumped me for maybe five minutes, rhythmically, taking long strokes and then short strokes. Then I felt his hand buried in the hair at the back of my head and his other hand just above my belly, and he was pulling me up to a standing position. He just held us there for a few minutes, my back against his heaving hairy chest, as he once again gained control of himself, bringing his breath into a shallower rhythm.

"Not fighting me now, are you?" he muttered. And then when I didn't answer. "You did want it. You can't deny it." I moaned. I couldn't disagree with him. I'd wanted it ever since I tried valiantly to give it up.

He then turned me back to the wall.

"See that pipe up there? Grab for it. With both hands. Hang on." I did as he commanded, and he put his hands below my knees and lifted me off the floor. He was under me now, pumping his dick up my channel from below. This didn't last for long though, broken off by another flash of lightning and another look around the shed. Not far away, burlap bags of grass seed were strung out side by side. Chet turned me again and laid my back on the bags. He stood over me, and only my shoulders were on the bags. My legs were draped up his torso and my ass met his crotch. He held one of my legs against him with one arm and was supporting me by my hip with the other. He had not lost his position inside me, though, and now he pumped down into me for a few minutes. Once again, he had to stop to hold himself in check, and this caused him to cramp up.

He slid me down onto the bags on my back and came down with me, behind me, onto his knees. He took my legs behind the knees and wish-boned them out as far as possible, opening me to the maximum to him. He pumped me deep and he must have grown to almost nine inches, because I felt split in two and did some yelping and moaning and maybe added some sound to the thunder that was still rolling outside. Once again he had to stop to rest and to check himself. He let my legs down, and with one hand he massaged my chest, abs, and belly, and, with the other hand, he slowly pumped my cock back up and caused me to sigh and start writhing under him.

"How's that, Sport? Feel good now? Do you remember how good it feels now?"

I closed my eyes tightly and didn't answer.

"Tell me it feels good. Tell me that you will want me to do this again."

I tried my best to ignore him. He pinched my nipples with one hand and squeezed my cock with the other simultaneously, and I involuntarily sent my hands to both locations. But, when I reached his hands, my body betrayed me, and I left them there, stroking his hands, rather than trying to get them off me.

Chet laughed. "You won't answer, but your body betrays you. I know you've enjoyed this. But I want to hear you admit to it. To tell me we'll do this again."

Silence.

"Okay," he said, taking his hands away from my body. "Here, over on your side." His cock drew out of me completely, and I felt an involuntary stab of regret. I hoped, though, that this hadn't been conveyed to him. We couldn't do this ever again. I couldn't let him through my defenses ever again.

I went over on my side, and he was kneeling there beside me. He tried to kiss me on the lips again, but I turned my head once more. He scooted back to below me, lifted my right leg with his left hand, and glided his cock right back into my ass. He then went back to pumping me slowly but deeply, while his right hand went to my cock and balls. He weighed and cuddled and pulled and rolled my balls until I started moaning again. Then he went back to my cock. He pulled the foreskin back as far as it would go. He pulled his cock out of me briefly and leaned over and kissed my cock head and tongued it until it was moist and I began to grind my hips. His dick entered me again then and went back to a slow, deep pump, while he wrapped his hand around my dick, with his thumb applying pressure to the piss slit and stroked me in rhythm with his own pumping action. I was writhing and grinding myself pretty well and had my torso up so that I could reach his pecs and nipples and shoulders with my wildly wandering hands. I could hear his breathing getting heavier again and I sensed we were both coming to a climax. But once again, he stopped the action and held both of us very still, but only briefly.

He lay down behind me, his cock up me as far as it would go, and brought my right leg down, so that my ass canal closed in tightly around his cock. The muscles in my ass canal were contracting and releasing, caressing his cock. He wrapped his right arm around me with his hand coming back and massaging the nipple on my left breast. His other hand was giving my cock slow, deep strokes. We were both aware that I was about ready to shoot off again. I let my sphincter expand and contract, doing a job on his cock that was giving him a great deal of pleasure. I was remembering how Phil and I had experimented. He had his face in my neck, and he put his tongue in my ear and explored briefly.

Then he said, "Admit it, you have no defenses left. You were wanting me just now just as much as I ever wanted you. Let's have that kiss now."

He raised his head up and I turned and met him this time, opening fully to his lips and tongue, giving as well as I was giving. We were in that position, when I felt his cock jerk inside me and bathe my insides with his cum. Almost simultaneously I ejaculated again myself.

We lay there for a good fifteen minutes, listening to the thunderstorm move off in the distance and to the beating of

461

each other's hearts. He pulled me over him, so that I lay stretched out above him, his cock still up my ass and my cock waving in the air.

"We didn't finish removing the stumps," he said softly, at great length.

A moment of silence.

"No," I then answered meekly.

"We must do that"

"Yes," softly.

"Tomorrow."

"Yes."

"And then I'll fuck you again."

"Yes."

"But first I'd like to show up what can be done with that big stump."

Momentary silence.

"Yes," almost a whisper.

"And maybe the ax handle."

Silence.

"Phil told me about the baseball bat. And I know about the night of the double"

Silence, but I shuddered.

"And maybe the ax handle," Chet repeated.

"Yes," weakly.

"And the day after that."

"Yes," no more than a whisper.

The door of the shed opened and a big, black dude was backlit in the door frame.

"Chet, that you? You told me to come over about now."

"Yep, Ned, it's me . . . and this is the lovely piece of ass I was telling you about."

"No," I moaned, trying to rise up off Chet, but he held me fast, with his arms wrapped around my chest above, with his legs wrapped around mine below, and skewered on his cock, which was on the rise again.

"Yes, I see," Ned said, coming over and looming above us. "Are you sure you were told he can do double?"

"No," I moaned.

"Yes," Chet mimicked my moan.

I lay there, bound and skewered, while big Ned peeled off his T-shirt and his shorts. He stood above us, so that both Chet and I could clearly see him working his tool. He was wiry and lean, but very well cut. But his most prominent feature was his long, thin cock, which sported a large mushroom cap.

Chet grabbed for my wrists and pulled my arms above my head and outward, while Ned pushed our legs apart and crouched there between them.

"Very nice, very nice, indeed," he said and then gave a low whistle. He ran his hands over my thighs and my belly, abs, and chest. He gave me some licking there as well.

"Umm. Budweiser," he murmured.

Despite the predicament, my cock began to harden noticeably. He went down on me then, sucking noisily and twisting and turning my cock, getting it ever stiffer. At length, he crouched over my torso, his legs straddling my sides and slowly sank his ass down on my cock. I lost some of my tension then, thinking that this might not be so bad. I even let him bring his mouth, with his big, thick, sensual lips to my mouth and give me a deep, lingering kiss. His mouth tasted minty, not at all what I expected. While we kissed, he pumped my cock with his ass. I came again rather quickly.

This proved to be a mistake; because it became obvious that now it was big Ned's turn. While still in the kiss, he pulled his ass up off me, took both of my legs in his long slender hands and pushed them up and out. This rolled my ass up and dropped Chet's dick to the lower end of my ass canal. Then, horrors of horrors, I felt Ned's dick head at my asshole, above Chet's cock, He slowly entered me, stifling my screams with his lips and by forcing his tongue down my throat. Chet began to twitch and moan at the sensation of another cock up my ass with his, sliding along on top of his cock. I was panting and writhing, which only helped Ned's tool to move in and up and only excited Chet more. In all the way now, Ned slowly began to pump me, and Chet joined in the rhythm. And I passed out.

When I awoke, I was alone in the garden shed, the door flapping open, and a gentle breeze wafting in and caressing my body . . . and there was a good four inches of ax handle up my ass.

Tit for Tat

There hadn't been much of a firefight at all. The Hondurans hadn't really expected any of our Sandinistan bands to strike across the Rio Coco Segovia, the river marking the Nicaragua-Honduras border, so they hadn't really seriously established a defense of the Gringo mining engineer team at the project in Brus Laguna. The Hondurans apparently hadn't bothered to read our new manifesto for the year about expanding our operations outside of Nicaragua's borders. We really didn't care that much about disrupting the new strip mining operation on the coast of Honduras. But we wanted to make a statement.

We wanted to make the news with the Norte-americanos. We were to capture a few and use them—not kill them—but use them to gain headlines. They hadn't been taking the Sandinistas seriously up North. A point was to be made, and my band was chosen precisely because of the point we could make.

It took a while to settle on the men we wanted. Most of the foreigners working in places we could access in Honduras were Europeans. But we wanted Americanos. And men of prominent, wealthy families.

We found what we wanted at the start-up strip mining project inland from Brus Laguna. Three Americano engineers, one the son of a federal congressman, and lightly guarded.

We had managed the trek across the Rico Coco Segovia from our base in Waspán in near silence and without encountering a single Honduran, civilian or military. The terrain was remote and a true jungle. And we were hardened soldiers now, experienced in the ways of stealth and steal.

At the first sign of an armed attack, the small band of Honduran soldiers guarding the Gringos melted into the jungle. We would rather have taken care of them there and then, though. They retreated in the direction of the army base at Brus Laguna on the coast. This would mean that the trek back to Nicaragua would have to be faster and more stealthy than our march to this point. The escaped soldiers would raise an alarm and the army would soon be on our scent.

We caught the three Gringos trying to hide in one of the mining operation sheds. We'd attacked at night and they were all stripped down to boxers for comfort under the slow-moving paddle fans in their primitive quarters at the height of the Honduran hot season.

The youngest and most fit of the three, a blond Gringo of athletic build and more bravery than the other two, was crouched between the door and his two compatriots when we kicked our way in. He was shielding a middle-aged man who was starting to go to overindulged fat and a younger, dark-haired man of slight height and build. The blond Gringo was holding a knife, at an experienced "kill" angle. He could see that he was not armed to fight with the AK-47s of ten hardened Sandisnitas, but he obviously was willing to try.

I motioned to Hectoro to feint at him from the left, which drew the young Gringo's attention, and then I bore in from the right and caught him in the chin with the butt of my AK-47. He went down with a groan. He wasn't unconscious, but he had dropped the knife.

"David Winston," I barked. "Which one David Winston?" I wanted to know immediately which one was the son of the congressman. He would receive special treatment. And I was the only one in the band conversant in English. This was as planned. I didn't want there to be any chances of the Gringos getting friendly with any of my men. It was impossible to tell, given our specific mission, whether that might become a problem.

The young blond's head lolled up at me. He was groggy from the hit on the chin, but he recognized the name when it was spoken. And he was quick witted. I could see that he understood in an instant that this hadn't been just a random raid.

"What—?"

"No questions," I commanded. "Get up and get those two up too. Where are your boots?"

Winston gestured in the direction of their sleeping hut, just a few steps from the door of the shed, as he whispered to the other two Gringos to stand up, that they were being directed to go back to their hut and dress. But he didn't stop there.

"He asked for David Winston," he was quickly adding. "This can't be an accident. They—"

"No talking," I barked, shoving the butt of the AK-47 into Winston's ribs. "No talking to each other from now on. If you talk we'll gag you. In the wet heat of Honduras, you may not survive that. Think about that. Now over to the hut and put socks and boots on. Now! Move!"

We hustled the three out of the shed and into the hut. Since their guards had escaped, there wasn't much time to get them on the move.

When they got to the hut, the blond started to take khaki trousers and a work shirt off a hook, but I nudged him with the butt of my AK-47 again.

"No, just the boots and the socks," I grunted. "And you won't need this either."

With that, I took the knife we had seized from the Gringo and I ran it under the waistband of his boxer shorts and cut the material to shreds. Winston gasped and tried to cover himself, but I knocked his hands away with my gun butt. He was magnificent. Not only was he built for power in his torso, arms, and legs, but he had the longest, thickest cock I'd seen on a man, and heavy hanging balls.

This mission wasn't going to be hard at all.

I handed the knife over to Hectoro, and he quickly had the other two Gringos naked too. The pudgy middle-aged man was hung nicely too, and the dark younger man had a boyish body that would please a few of my men greatly.

Stripping the prisoners was prudent for more reason than one. It not only served the purpose of our mission, but it also helped make them docile and gave them the proper sense of helplessness. We needed to dominate and control them fully and as fast as possible.

Once they were booted, I made them group together, facing us, with their hands at their sides, and then it was Manuel's turn to ply his craft. Manuel had been the photographer for a newspaper in Managua before joining the Sandinistas.

I had Manuel take several photos of our Gringo prisoners, showing them being held by my men but careful not to show any of the faces of the Sandinistas. He had three cameras; One with good film in it to use later, a video camera, and a Polaroid camera, the latter of which gave us photos to leave for the inevitable Honduran search party to find—once the Honduran cowards had gathered their strength and resolve.

Time was short, though, and I quickly had the band, prodding the prisoners along, their hands tied behind their backs with leather bindings, back into the jungle, for a fast, hard march toward the Rio Coco Segovia River.

We marched the prisoners relentless and mercilessly through the jungle for hours. Twice the pudgy one collapsed and had to be prodded back to his feet. I wanted them to be utterly exhausted before we stopped for the first time. But I especially wanted the blond Gringo, the congressman's son, to be totally exhausted. And he was proving to be strong and up to the task of hiking.

Being naked and trussed, though, finally got to the blond one before any of my life- and battle-hardened Sandinistas had lagged in energy. At the last, as we entered a fern-floored bowl at the base of a rocky hill, the blond collapsed in total exhaustion. The middle-aged Gringo had given out a long time ago. He was being nearly dragged along between two of my men, two who had gravitated to him. I had some idea what they liked, and I was content to let this order be.

The small dark one had also been chosen by natural selection. He was draped over the shoulder of the biggest, tallest of the band, like a sack of rice. The head and arms of the little one were just flopping back and forth between the Sandinista's broad, bulky shoulder blades; he appeared to be nearly unconscious, but I could tell he wasn't completely out, because of the expression on his face. He was in shock and his mouth was open in a look of pain and surprise. This most likely was because both of the big Sandinista's hands were busy. One was squeezing one of the small Gringo's pert butt cheeks, and the thumb of the other hand was buried inside the little one's asshole.

It was obvious that the band was ready to stop here.

I barked an order, and two of the band jumped forward and untied Winston's bounds, turned him over on the moist, fern-cushioned ground, and then retied his wrists over his head and around the trunk of a small tree. Then they both sprang down on either side of the blond Gringo, at his knees, and spread his legs, each taking a well-muscled calf and lifting it up and out, which rolled his firm, rounded glutes up.

Before this, I'd had all of the Sandinistas pull on their black masks, and then I told Manuel to take out the video camera and to get everything from this phase of the mission on tape.

I opened my fly and pulled out my cock. I was proud of my cock, and I stood between the Gringo's spread legs and made sure he got a good view of my cock. I had been mentally preparing for this for many kilometers, when I saw that the blond Gringo was, at last, on the verge of exhaustion. And so my fine cock was standing straight out from my body.

I opened the pack on my back and took out a jar of grease. And then I scooped out a glob and gave it over to one of my men holding the Gringo's legs, and he greased the Gringo's hole while I greased my pole, lovingly stroking myself up and down while standing above the panting Gringo.

The blond Gringo was panting as much now from the realization of what happened next as from his utter exhaustion.

His exhaustion kept him from struggling much, but he whimpered some and bellowed his disapproval much, albeit in very weak, almost-spent tones.

I looked around, hearing other cries and moanings and gruntings and whimperings about me.

The two likeminded band members, we liked to call them the Siamese twins for their special proclivity—the ones who had taken to the pudgy middle-aged one and who had virtually carried him to this spot—were sitting on the ferns not far from me, facing each other close, the thighs of one over the thighs of the other. And with the naked pudgy Gringo sandwiched between them. He was floppy as a rag doll, his head lolling and his eyeballs rolling up in his head. Only his weak cries and whimpers told me he was conscious as, with two pair of hands on his waist and sides, the two Sandinistas were pumping him up and down and their ever-disappearing joined cocks in his single asshole.

The mountain man of a Sandinista band member was walking slowly around the perimeter of the open area, humming and laughing and singing lullabies, obviously pleased with himself. The small, dark Gringo was attached to him at the pelvis, his legs flopping back and forth over the hips of the Sandinista monster man. The Sandinista's big hands were encircling the waist of the small, boyish-figured man, and sliding the small man's ass up and down on his huge tool. The Gringo's body was arched away from that of his ravisher, and his head was lolled back and his arms were flopping down from his shoulders. In spite of his exhaustion, his weak screams were quite energetic and convincing.

I instructed Manuel to make sure he got good coverage of the big man's thick cock appearing and disappearing in the small man's hole.

With a thrill of excitement, I knelt down and placed one hand under the blond Gringo's tailbone and held the base of my cock steady with the other hand. I placed the ruby tip of my cock at Winston's hole, and he whimpered and gave his last argument for being spared, and then I reared my hips back and struck home, strong, fast, and deep.

470

The blond congressman's son cried out and his pelvis lifted up, trying to escape me as I drew back again. But he couldn't evade me. He was fully mine. Exhausted, trussed, dominated, fucked.

"Take that, Norte-americano bastard," I cried out, as I thrust again, and again and again.

The video rolled, as loud cries and bleatings across the clearing turned to whimpers and moans, the heavy grunts to weak groans. The Gringo's ass opened to me. The two Sandinistas at his side worked his greased cock with their free fists, and as they sucked him off, his pelvis started to move with my rhythm. I certainly wouldn't be telling my leader that he seemed to be enjoying his fuck in the end, though.

Both of the other Gringos were unconscious when the video film played out.

The Sandinistas zipped up and took up what were now three burdens, and moved quickly off once more toward Nicaraguan territory.

At the banks of the Patuca River, about half way toward safe territory, we rested for several hours. When we woke, two of the prisoners seemed to be recovering themselves and were whispering stealthy. The pudgy one was still completely docile and doing no more than groaning and moaning, with his eyes tightly shut.

We bustled the prisoners into the three boats, separately, that we had hidden in the rushes upon our trek into Honduras. And when we got to the other side, I let the "twins" double fuck the congressman's son back into submission and I fucked the small one. His ass had tightened up again. I was covering him bent over a mossy boulder on his stomach, and taking him was like fucking a small woman, all gentle curves and slight frame on the outside and all sweet and creamy inside. He even cried softly like a girl as I took him roughly in long, deep strokes, one of my fists between his shoulder blades and the other buried in his hair and arching his head and torso back up toward me.

I had Manuel take still photos of both takings.

The small, dark one soon was completely cowed again and would not, I was sure, be doing any whispering against my command any time soon. I didn't complete my fuck, though, because we heard the sound of chopper blades in the distance, toward Brus Lagunda.

We hurriedly broke off our conditioning and propaganda photo op exercise and gathered up the three nearly comatose prisoners and struggled back into the jungle, running now as hard as we could for the Rio Coco Segovia and the welcoming arms of our well-manned base at Waspán, across the border and in Nicaragua. The return trek was nowhere near as easy as the entry; we were hunted prey now, leaving spoor our trackers could follow—and carrying the dead weights of three fully used Gringos.

They caught up with and cornered us not more than fifty kilometers beyond the Patuca. I sent Manuel and the spent film off on another track toward Waspán. At least the mission we were sent on could be accomplished.

* * * *

I'm not sure what happened to any of the others in my band. I was knocked unconscious early in the hand-to-hand fighting. And I woke up here in a cell—I assume at the army base outside Brus Lagunda. At least I assume I was brought back to where it started. That was two nights before. Since then I've had two, body-crunching sessions with the Honduran soldiers.

I am hunched on a narrow, hard bed against the back wall of the cell. The wall is clammy, rough, badly stacked bricks, but cool against my cut, aching, naked body. They must have tortured me for hours. They beat and whipped and punched every part of my body, careful not to break anything—yet—although I'm not at all sure about two of my ribs. They ache so badly. I am totally exhausted—physically, but not mentally. I am a Sandinista. And I have accomplished my mission—as long as Manuel has made it back. This will be a propaganda statement for the world as has never been made before. The Norte-americanos can be fucked—can be screwed—by the Central Americans. They cannot lift their heads down here in pride ever again now. As long as Manuel and the film made it to safety.

My body aches so badly and I want more than anything else to curl up on the hard wooden bed here and die. But I'm

472

held in this sitting position, my back to the wall, by the shackles at my wrists chained close to the walls and holding my torso up.

I close my eyes, wanting to make it all go away. Listening to every part of my body separately, checking out my wounds, trying to determine whether anything is seriously broken or violated.

But I hear the noise of metal screeching on metal. The door of my cell opening. So, I look up, expecting to see the sneering Honduran captain again.

But there he is. The blond Gringo. The one we'd taken prisoner and fucked for all the world to see. The American congressman's son. He is walking into the cell unsteadily and with a grimace at each step, bowlegged, his ass stretched and worried hard. But he is moving with the resources of determination I had seen from the beginning that he possessed in full measure.

"Winston. David Winston," I croak.

"No, dumbass," he retorts, his voice full of venom and anger. "You stupid insurgents attacked the wrong camp. David Winston's camp is several miles to the east of ours. We are with a Canadian archeological dig."

I want to say something, I'm trying to say something, but he is shouting, "Just shut the fuck up," and then he strikes me hard across the face with an open palm. Nothing compared with what the Honduran captain does.

But then I gasp and watch in horror as he unzips his pants and rolls out that huge, thick cock of his. He is taking a tube of cream from his pants pocket and giving me the most cruel expression. And he is greasing up his monster cock.

My eyes look wildly around the cell, searching for escape, but I know there is none. I hear a noise in the corridor beyond the open door, and I call out for help. But I know there will be no help from that sector.

There, beyond the doorway, crossing the open space, from one side of the yawning opening to the other, being dragged between two burly Honduran soldiers, his feet dragging the ground. Manuel. His head lolling down. Spent. Beaten. His photography certainly unsent.

My legs are being roughly parted and spread and lifted, and my bare butt rolls up and the cuts in my back are opened anew as they scrape along the undressed bricks. And, Yiyiyi! Excruciating pain. The violation of my last protected body part. A telephone pole jamming up into me, running far and deep, swiftly, stretching and splitting soft tissue as it fills me and expands and thrusts deeper. Yiyiyi!

Topsy-Turvy

I'd been working on my Chris Craft on the dock down in the keys for several hours, often looking over to admire the size and lines of a sleek, humongous yacht on the other side of the dock, before I realized that two men were sitting in the covered fantail of that craft and watching me too. I almost regretted that I'd stripped down to the Speedo to do my washdown.

Suddenly embarrassed by their close attention, I went over to the other side of my boat to work. But I took occasional peeks at the other craft, which had the name *Topsy-Turvy* painted on the stern, and couldn't help but notice that both men had binoculars pointed in my direction. From here they looked like Mutt and Jeff. The large guy was a little hard to miss—a bruising muscle-bound hulk in white shorts and a fluorescent-colored Hawaiian sports shirt. The little guy seemed no more than a boy, as spied from down here. He was in gray gym shorts and a T.

The day was hot and I'd been slaving for some time and, having raised my eyes to the boat to see if I was still under surveillance—which I was—I tuned into the fact that I had developed a deep thirst. I came around to the dock side of the boat to fish a beer out of the cooler I had sitting on the dock.

"Care to come aboard for a beer?"

I looked around and up at the main deck of the *Topsy-Turvy*. The big guy was standing at the rail, a beefy hand shading his eyes. He repeated, "I say, you look thirsty; care to come aboard for a beer?"

I was already opening the lid to the cooler, but someone else's beer was always a better idea to me than one I'd bought. "Maybe," I called over to him. "Does the offer come with a tour of the boat? That's some yacht you have there."

"Certainly can, yes," the big guy answered jovially. "We can even take it out for spin, if you like. We were going to cruise for an hour of two this afternoon anyway."

"Sounds good to me," I called back. "Just give me a minute or two to batten down the hatches over here." I'd done all I wanted to do on my Chris Craft that afternoon anyway. And I'd been arguing with myself over whether to take the boat out. It was a gorgeous day, but if I took it out, I'd have all of the scrubbing to do again when I got back to the dock. Now I could have it both ways—a short cruise in a real ship and my own scrubbed down nicely.

A couple of burly crewmen in spiffy whites appeared and started casting off on the *Topsy-Turvy* almost as soon as I got aboard and was moving to the fantail.

"Hello, there," the big guy said as I walked up to him. He was still standing by the rail. The grip of his handshake had power and authority in it. "I'm Tom, and this is Jerry. You tired us out just watching you clean your boat down over there. Come sit and select your poison."

Tom and Jerry. I almost laughed. But then that was better than Mutt and Jeff, I supposed.

I went past Tom as he turned to introduce me to the little guy. The little guy—Jerry—didn't stand up. He looked like he'd fallen down a flight of stairs, rather bruised and battered, and I thought immediately that maybe he couldn't stand. I leaned down, extended my hand, and introduced myself. His hand was trembling and was slightly moist. As I leaned down, I couldn't help but notice red welts on his inner thighs, and I wondered how the hell they'd gotten there. That would be hard to do in a fall down the stairs.

"Hello, Jerry," I said. "I'm Raymond. Call me Ray."

Jerry looked at me wanly. His eyes were glittering and much more expressive than any other part of his face. He responded his pleasure in meeting me in a rather weak voice. His eyes were boring into me, though, and I got the impression that he wanted to convey something to me, almost plead for something. But then Tom spoke again, naming beer brands they had on hand so I could take my pick, And Jerry's gaze snapped away from me and looked beyond me to where Tom was standing. I saw the little guy's eyes blaze up and then dim. Then Jerry looked down in his lap at his hands and said no more for the time we sat in the fantail, Tom and I drank beer and talked about boat maintenance and the Miami Dolphins as the yacht steamed out into the Atlantic.

I had worked hard, and there was a lull in the conversation, and both the sun I'd already taken and the beer I was drinking too much of got to me. My head went back into the cushions as the yacht steamed along and I dozed off.

My dreams were disturbed. I heard noises, disturbing noises, groans and moanings and sharp little cries. I jerked awake at the sound of a louder, muffled scream, my mouth sour from the beer, my head throbbing a bit from having had too much sun while scrubbing down the Chris Craft, and the sensation of not knowing whether the cry had been in my dream or was part of my sudden wakefulness.

Tom and Jerry were gone, but one of the white-clad crew members was standing at the door into whatever lay inside the ship's main cabin beyond the fantail porch. He was looking at me, and when I was fully awake, he pushed the door into the salon open with a hand and pronounced in a low, gravelly voice, "They are in here."

I stood and walked over and through the door and then stood there, immobilized for the moment in shock. Then I turned, wanting to get out of there—and off the ship, not giving a thought to the fact that we were a good two miles off the strand of Florida keys now.

But the crewman, who was nearly as big as Tom, was blocking the door and staring at me in a way that I knew would not permit exit.

Tom turned around and gruffly told me to take a seat and watch. I collapsed into a tub chair near the door.

Then Tom turned back and flicked Jerry's naked buttocks with a leather whip, raising a little cry tapering off into a gurgled whimper. He then thrust his engorged cock inside Jerry's ass and began pumping hard in long strokes.

It was a regular S&M movie set. Jerry was naked and bent over a padded, brown-leather-covered gym pommel horse type apparatus that was closer to the ground than usual and didn't have the handles of a regular gymnastic pommel horse. He was barely in contact with the floor on his stretched toes. His wrists were cuffed to the legs of the horse on either side and his legs, straining back from the apparatus as he reached for the floor, were separated by a steel extender rod cuffed to his legs underneath the knees. This was holding his thighs wide in involuntary spread. His cries were muffled, because his head was covered by a leather harnessing that held a plug in his mouth. His buttocks and back and the backs of his thighs were red with welting from where Tom was whipping him.

I sat there aghast, unable to take my eyes away from the tableau. Tom, decked out in only black leather pants missing a crotch and black storm trooper boots, was fucking Jerry hard while flicking his legs and torso with the whip. With each upper thrust of his cock, Tom was lifting Jerry's scrabbling toes off the floor. The action stopped long enough for Tom to pull his cock out and strap a ribbed silicon extender over his already-huge member that increased its width and length appreciably, and then he reared his hips back and slammed the pole into the channel of the much smaller man. Jerry writhed under the augmented attention and turned his head back and looked at me—his eyes full of his pain and pleading.

I started to rise, to try to go to his aid, but the crewman at the door leaned over and pushed me back into the chair with a meaty fist to my sternum. The look in his eyes told me I'd better not move again.

As the fucking continued, Jerry began to writhe under the attention and to moan ever louder. I was embarrassed, but I had to admit to myself that something was stirring inside me—that I found this arousing. I turned and looked at the crewman at the door, and that didn't help a bit. He had his cock out and was beating it. My hand went involuntarily to my own cock, which was hard and throbbing inside the restricting pouch of my Speedo.

Jerry was moving his hips in a frenzy now, and he arched his back and bellowed under his mouth restraint as he jetted out cream under the powerful, relentless thrusts and whipping of Tom. I didn't know how the little guy managed it. He looked far too fragile and vulnerable against the brutish hulk of his oppressor.

After Jerry had come, Tom pulled out of him and just let the small guy collapse against the apparatus in muffled moans.

Tom turned to me and said, "You now. You fuck him now."

"Me?" I croaked in shock.

"Yes, you."

"I . . . I can't do that," I managed to blurt out. Possibly the severe tenting of the crotch of my Speedo and the spot of precum there somewhat belied that statement, however.

"We're not going back to land until you do," Tom declared ominously with glowering eyes. "Stavos," he bellowed, and the crewman at the door, who was busy stuffing himself back through his fly, came to attention. "Supplies for our guest."

I looked around as the guy at the door dug in his pocket. He came up with two condom packets and flipped them over to me. I let them fall at my feet and looked down dumbly at where they lay. A big hand—Tom's—reached down and picked them up and tucked them under the rim of my Speedo and then he stormed out of the door. The crewman shut the door behind Tom and then turned again, crossed his arms, and resumed his guard stance inside the door.

Jerry was whimpering and moaning. I rose and went over, and, as gently as I could, freed him from the collection of restraints, and half dragged, half carried him over to a bed at the side of the room.

"Thank you," he whispered. I turned to leave, but he clutched at me. "Please don't leave. Hold me. Please."

I sat down on the edge of the bed, and he curled up to me in a fetal position and wrapped his arms around him. I

479

encircled him with my arms. I don't know who started it, but we began to rock back and forth, and he had a hand down the front of my Speedo and was squeezing my cock. The sensations of arousal and lust welled up inside me.

"I must go," I murmured, trying to pull away from him. But he held me fast, suddenly quite strong.

"No. You have to take me. You heard him. You won't get back to land . . ."

"Hush," I said, putting a finger over his bruised lips. "Don't try to talk. I . . . can't . . . I . . ."

He was pulling my face down to his with the back of his hand, the other one still encasing me cock. "Fuck me," he whimpered. "You must fuck me. It's the only way." And then he had his lips to mine and his mouth was opening to me, and we went into a passionate kiss.

I adjusted our bodies, coming up more on the bed, moving his buttocks to presentation position for my cock. When in a natural position for fucking, I opened a condom packet and, with a sigh of resignation edged with a chill of thrill, I crowned my cock.

"No . . . no . . . Bind me," Jerry whispered when I had the bulb of my cock at his rim. "Both wrists to both ankles."

"What?" I said, loud enough for the man at the door to take notice. "I can't . . . I couldn't . . ."

"He's watching; he'll know if you don't." Jerry was whimpering, pleading with me, reaching for the leather thongs on the bed coverlet.

So, I bound him, ankle to wrist on each side and rolled him onto his back, trussed like a sheep for shearing. And I put the palms of my hands under his buttocks and presented the bulb of my cock to his Tom-stretched anal entrance. And I fucked him. And he moaned and told me how filling and manly I was and how much he loved my cock churning inside him— loud enough for the monitoring crewman to catch it all. And, sad to say, I enjoyed it immensely.

When I was lost to any qualms about what I was doing and was fucking him vigorously in long penetrating strokes, he cried out, "Slap me. Punish me, Daddy. Slap me." He had to say it a couple of times before I complied, but when I did slap him on the buttocks and on his nipples a couple of times, he became frenzied in the fuck and his cock hardened. And he ejaculated up his belly.

Ashamed at having enjoyed myself, but unable to deny that this had been one of the hottest fucks of my life, I untied him and we went back into a rocking embrace.

"The punisher," I heard him mutter after several minutes, while our breathing was returning to normal.

"What?" I responded, in shock. I'd heard him perfectly, but I didn't quite believe what I was hearing.

"The punisher, Daddy, I want you to do me on the punisher. The apparatus. Put me on the apparatus again," he was pleading. "I want you to fuck me again on the apparatus. Please, Daddy, please." Jerry was licking his lips and giving me an intense, dreamy look full of lust and determination.

I sat up and away from him, staring down at him. Seeing him for the first time since I had boarded this boat.

"Tom," I said, accusingly.

"Tom works for me," Jerry said. "This is my boat. I told him to get you aboard." His face was set in a determined, suddenly strong expression. His voice now was equally hard. "Fuck me on the apparatus. We're not going back to land until you fuck me on the punisher."

I required Salvos's help in hooking Jerry up to the apparatus correctly, during which time Jerry became increasingly docile and started to tremble in anticipation, his cock hardening as we finished. After I had fucked Jerry on the apparatus, just as Tom had, but without the whip and the mouth restraint, substituting hand slaps in response to Jerry's angry declarations that he couldn't come if I didn't punish him, and I had unhooked him from all of the restraints, Tom reentered the room. He was still in those black leather, crotchless pants, big, thick cock at full staff and flicking his whip. And he had a mean expression on his face.

"Salvos," he bellowed. "Help our guest get hooked up to the punisher."

"Nooooo," I cried out. But Salvos already had me in his grip.

Wrong Choice

It was the wrong choice of swimwear, and I was headed back to the guest room to rectify that, when the cause of it all stopped me in the hallway. The new owner of our company had invited me to his country place for a weekend to discuss some details of a project we were working on, and it turned out there was a pool party included. But, not knowing that, I hadn't brought my suit. I had assumed this would be all business. So there I was, having to pick out a loaner suit from Thad, my boss, and I'd picked the wrong one. The choice really was between a pretty skimpy Speedo and something that looked like boxer silks. I'd rejected the boxers because they didn't come with a supporter, and I was afraid that all I'd have to do was go into the pool and I'd come out showing everyone everything. I didn't think this was the right impression to be making on the new owner of my company. Turns out that wouldn't have been a real problem, because Thad had only invited men to this party—and certain kinds of men at that—but, then, I didn't know that when I put the suit on.

Thad, counter to everyone else, had come to the party decked out in a gladiator costume. His great pecs were crossed and highlighted with leather straps, the waistband of a short pleated skirt thing dipped well below his navel in front, and there were leather wrist shields and sandals with leather straps winding up his calves. Thad was a heavily muscled hunk and I'd about spill my seed in meetings with him for the three weeks he'd been on board, but this Roman costume, which showed off curly chest hair I'd never seen before to match the curly dark hair on his head and the curls showing above the waistband of his skirt really was too much. My interest was just too obvious when all I had on was that Speedo. So, I was heading back down the hall to put those boxers on over the Speedo when I nearly ran into Thad himself heading up the hall.

As I was about to pass him in the corridor with no more than a smile, he put one arm against the wall in front of me, and the other hand came out to stop me. Unfortunately, it came out at a pretty low level, and there I was, trying to take care of the start of a hard on for my boss, with my boss standing close to me with the palm of his hand spread out on my lower belly.

"Here you are, Tim," he said in a casual voice. "I saw you outside, but then you were gone, and I wanted to talk to you about an idea I had on the Robinson project."

I tried to remain nonplussed and to at least appear more attentive to what he was saying than to the growing tenting out between my legs of the Speedo, but I wasn't doing a very good job of it. I could feel my engorging cock, which really was too big for a Speedo in the first place, pulling the hem of the suit down beyond my pubic hair line. It must have been my imagination, but I got the sensation that Thad's hand had moved down farther as well.

"But you're not completely with me here, are you, Tim?" Thad was saying as I snapped back into the conversation.

"Well, no, Mr. Stevenson, not actually. There was something I needed to do back in my room, and I'm afraid I was focused on that."

"It's Thad to you, Tim . . . and that something you needed to do wouldn't have to do with this very interesting hard on you've got, would it?" That was another thrilling thing we'd all learned about Thad at work. He was very direct.

I mumbled something that even I didn't understand.

"Because if it's got to do with this hard on, I think I could help you with that. I'd really like to do that. Would you like me to do that, Tim?"

I mumbled in confusion and consternation some more. He had turned my back into the wall with that tantalizing hand on my belly and still had the other arm against the wall to prevent me bolting in the direction in which I had been going.

"I'll tell you what, Tim. I'll do a little fast inventory, and any time I'm doing something you don't want, just let me know and we'll go on about our business as if this never happened. If I like the goods and you're interested, we can just slip into my bedroom right here for a few moments of mutual entertainment. Is that okay with you, Tim? I think you'll find it very career enhancing."

My mouth felt like it was full of cotton, and my cock was rising at the very thought of this totally unexpected turn of events. I mumbled something incomprehensible again. But he had me at "career enhancing."

"I'll take that as a yes, shall I?" Thad said, and he moved his hand until it loosely covered my tented package. My knees wanted to give, but I braced them by moving my pelvis forward, which Thad took as an affirmative sign.

"Ah, is that your 'yes,' Tim?"

"Yes, I guess so," I managed to whisper.

He moved his hand back up on my lower belly but only so that he could then work his fingers under the waistband of my Speedo. He moved straight down to my balls and weighed them in his hand and then came back up to my cock and measured the length of that. I heard the intake of his breath.

"My God, you're a stud, Tim. Just as I'd hoped. Is this your full hard?"

"No, I don't think so," I replied in a low voice. That disconcerting direct approach again.

"Any objection to going behind this door here for a short while?"

"No . . . No . . . But won't your guests . . .?"

"Fuck my guests, Tim. My guests know how to amuse themselves in my absence for short—or long—periods. My pool guy might come looking for me, but that wouldn't be a problem either. So, here we go then. I'd much rather that we were fucking."

I moaned about having it out in the open—where this was going. And so baldly stated. No subtlety. I wouldn't be able to expect any in what he did with me. It would be whatever he wanted to do.

He removed his right hand from my crotch and opened the door that was beside us and ushered me through with his other arm. He didn't let me actually move any distance into the room, though. As we went through the door, he closed it firmly behind us and just turned my back to the wall beside the door.

"You don't have any trouble with fast reloading at your age, do you?"

What a strange question, but I didn't, so I simply answered. "No, no problems. Rather quick, actually."

"I thought so. You obviously keep in great shape. I only ask because I've ached for you from the first day, and I need to start with a quickie unless that would spoil the fun for what I have planned later."

"Ached for me?" I asked weakly. If only he knew how close I was to being able to say the same thing about him.

"Yes, ached for you. Ached for you to have a good package, and you're triple A there. And, if so, ached to have you in me—in my mouth and up my ass. Am I being direct enough with you? Am I clearing up any confusion you might have about the latitude you have with the boss?"

"Yes . . . Thad," I said weakly. But it was a relief. I'd be fucking him; not he me. I'd go either way to enhance my career, but . . .

"The only thing is that the first time, I am completely in charge. Understand? If there's a next time, we can share the direction more. Understand?"

"Yes, Thad."

"Can I kiss you now?"

"Yes, Thad." Upon which, he took both of my arms by the wrist and raised them over my head and leaned in and gave me a lip lock that very clearly supported his claim to have ached for me. Holding my wrists in place with his left hand, he then lowered his right hand and quickly and very expertly examined my arms and my torso and traveled down to my lower belly and around to my firm, round butt cheeks, pushing the Speedo down below my buttocks. He briefly had his finger on my asshole, measuring the pucker there, and then, with his hand under the rim of the Speedo, he moved around to my crotch, and my dong popped out of the suit. He wrapped his hand around my cock and started to gently stroke and pump it. I cooperated by groaning for him appropriately. His left hand started traveling down my arm, and I lowered my arms, thinking I'd do some exploring on him, but he quickly pushed my arms back up, so I kept them over my head. This stretched my torso out nicely for his exploration. He pulled away from the kiss and my mouth and continued his kissing down the side of my neck, around to under my chin, and then to my pecs and nipples. He fairly quickly descended to my sternum and abs, dwelling for a bit in kissing the cleft of my belly, tonguing my navel, and letting his left hand play some follow-up on my nipples and armpits.

This seemed to be a man on a short-deadline mission, though. He didn't spend long anywhere, but his visit would be fondly remembered everywhere he'd been. He quickly exchanged his hand wrap around my cock with his mouth. He did some quick preliminary work there, seeing how hard he could make me and being pleased with the results. He had pulled my Speedo down and off my legs and had cupped one hand on a butt cheek and had that other hand in that tantalizing place across my belly. Some quick work on my shaft and then he came up for air.

"Very nice. Very nice, indeed. You were right. You weren't nearly as hard as you could get yet. Now turn and take that stance they talk about in cop shows."

I turned around, facing the wall, arms above my head and splayed out, steadying me, and my legs spread apart. He almost brutally forced my butt cheeks apart with his hands and buried his face in my butt crack. He was tonguing and kissing my ass, rimming me and pushing in with his tongue and generally slobbering and making me all wet and slippery. I began to pant and moan and writhing a bit in my stance, which only excited him and increased the pleasure of the motion for both of us.

"Now, turn again. Quickly, turn now." When I turned, I saw that he had pulled his own dong out of the thong he was wearing under that skirt and had been pumping himself as he tongued me. I started to say I wanted to help him with that, but Thad obviously had an agenda and a close deadline. He positioned himself on his knees in front of my right leg and a little off angle from me, but very close into me.

"Your right leg. Over my left shoulder." I did as he directed, and he snaked his left arm up behind my waist and held my hip to him. During the rest of the operation, my own hands moved around along the wall and to his head and back in an effort to maintain my balance in the face of increasingly rubbery legs. He took my dick back into his mouth and he started pumping, first with short strokes going half way down the shaft and then with deeper throating. Off and on his tongue did a job on my glans and piss slit. I moaned in appreciation and did some minor gyrating with my pelvis. Very quickly his right hand went between my legs, and, with the heel of his hand behind my balls, his middle finger moved to and into my asshole.

"Uh, Thad, I don't know if . . ." But he ignored me, and the finger went in smoothly enough because of the water work he'd done on it earlier, which both caused it to loosen and lubricated it enough for me to accommodate his finger without much pain. His finger slid right in up the sphincter muscle, which accepted it, sucked it in, and helped the pad of the finger land squarely on my prostate gland. I gave a little lurch and yelp. Thad's only response was to plop my dick out of his mouth and my balls into his mouth. He was gently rubbing and applying pressure to the prostate and sucking and extending my balls and thus was working on the root of my semen production plant from both outside and inside. I moaned and twisted and thumped my shoulders against the wall, and panted and begged for relief, but he held me firmly in place at the hip.

Very shortly, waves of pleasure, something that went beyond the normal jacking off and lasting longer, started to flash through my pelvis. I felt like I had to piss, but then that changed to the sensation of precum oozing out of my cock. Thad took that as a signal, and, without giving my prostate relief, he swallowed my cock to the root again and began brutally and furiously sucking me off.

I hadn't utterly failed to defend against this full-scale attack very long before I huskily warned him, "Oh, God, Thad, I think I'm about to blow. You'd better pull off now."

I knew he heard me, but he wasn't having any of that and in short order, I came, sending the semen he had helped produce down his throat. He pulled out then, gave a little cough and, releasing my right leg from his shoulder and allowing me to take my full weight on the ground, quickly kissed his way back up to my mouth. His finger came out of my asshole with a squishy little pop when he could no longer hold it there on his kissing and tonguing journey up my body.

After a deep kiss, he said, "That was great. Now we can take it more slowly. The urgency of the wait is gone now. You are one sweet stud. I knew I was right about you." He took me by the hand and led me over to a gigantic bed and told me to lie on my belly on the middle of it.

"I figure about a fifteen-minute timeout should do it," he said, and then he scurried around above and beside me on his knees in the bed and began massaging my aching muscles, from my heels and my tense calf and thigh muscles to my back and shoulders and biceps and arms. This alone probably took the fifteen minutes.

"Turn over," he said. "Ah. Beginning to come back to life already, I see."

My half hard on was flopping around on my belly. Before he had finished massaging my feet, toes, belly, abs, pecs, neck muscles and temples, though, my flag was back at full staff. As he had leaned over me, I had played with his pecs and abs through the tantalizing straps across his torso and had gone under the skirt and ripped his thong away by snapping the strings on either side. He had given me a big smile and a longing look with his eyes when I had done that and had sighed and moaned when I latched onto a pretty big—and quite hard—penis. While he was fussing around with the rest of my frontal massage, I did what I could to keep hold of his rod. He crawled over to a nightstand and came back with some lubricant and a condom.

489

He rolled the condom onto my tool, took a big gob of the lubricant in his hand, handed the tube to me, and knelt above me, his butt facing me and his knees close in on my sides. "Here, lather me up, while I take care of this monster cock," he said. So, while he rubbed the lubricant up and down my sheathed pole, I spread his butt cheeks and lubricated his hole, around the rim and in a good bit, leaving a good-sized gob to be pushed farther into the hole by, I strongly suspected, me. I also took hold of that skirt on either side of his waist and just ripped it down and off him. When that was done, he moved his butt down, positioned his asshole right above my shaft and started working on descending on me. I was squirming.

"Hold still," he said. "Hands above head and legs spread." I did as he directed, and he continued to work his butt down into the hollow of my belly. When he had accomplished this, he did a little pumping, but not for long. He then did something that astonished me. He laid back on me full length, his arms extended on top of mine, his hands holding my wrists in place, and his legs stretched out on top of mine. He moved his butt up off my pelvis and a little way farther up my belly and then whispered. "Fuck me. Pump me." I found that, with a little effort from my butt muscles, I could do that and that the new sensation was quite pleasurable. He was tighter inside now than he had been when he impaled himself. I would have reached around him and stroked his cock for him, but he had me in a wrist hold above my head again.

That's when and where the pool guy found us. I was later to learn that the pool guy was also the driver guy and the gardener guy and that much of the driving he did was into Thad's ass and that one of the gardens he was assigned to plow was Thad—regularly. His was a light-skinned black guy with handsome Jamaican features. Lean, but well muscled in the pecs, washboard abs, and bulbous butt. Ropy arteries stood out on his pecs and arms. He was wearing a wild-colored cousin to those boxer silks I should have worn, and I saw that they would not have solved my problem, because as soon as the pool guy came upon Thad and me on Thad's bed, his trunks began to tent out awesomely at the crotch and the waistband in front was pulled down to where I could see a very formidable cock.

"Ah, Clem," Thad announced calmly. "Perhaps you could join us. My dick seems to be in the need of attention."

Without need for a written invitation, Clem grinned and dropped his trou. I thought I might faint. His cock must have been a good ten inches engorged, and, although not thin, its length kept it from appearing to be too fat. It rose up in a little curve near the business end. He wasn't circumcised and he hadn't filled out yet enough for his helmet to burst forth, but I could see evidence of a pinkish mushroom cap. The contrast in color between the cap and the cock brought your attention right directly to the business end of the pool boy.

Clem quickly joined us in bed. He straddled Thad in a 69 position and started working on face fucking his cock. Thad did the same for Clem, but I was also available at that angle and must admit that Thad shared Clem with me. No way I was going to swallow that whole, though, I thought. I can't even imagine burying it in my ass. All this time I was fucking Thad for a while and then resting for a while.

"Ah, I see what you doin', Mon," Clem spoke, and I felt fingers going to my ass. "And I see a tube of sex goo right here, very near," he went on to say. I felt the coldness of the lubricant as Clem lathered up my hole.

"No, please," I said weakly. Clem's only answer was to stand up on the bed, his feet close in at Thad's and my sides, roll a condom on his rod with great difficulty, and hover there over us, a big grin on his face and his dong looking like a rigid telephone pole. He started lathering up his rod, and I lost all interest in fucking Thad.

"Well, now, I haven't given you a big island welcome to our house yet, Mon. I'll take care of that right now." He back-peddled down to beyond Thad's and my midsections. I felt my butt cheeks rise as he slid his knees below us, my cheeks resting on his well-muscled thighs. He fingered my ass for a bit with long, thin, sensuous fingers, while I moaned and quietly begged him not to carry through with this. I struggled to bring my arms down, but Thad held me in a strong grip. He also had gotten his ankles wrapped around mine, so that I couldn't move them any distance. Then I felt the head of Clem's dick at my hole and he

491

pushed in a good two inches. I moaned and twitched my dick around in Thad's ass, which made him moan as well.

And then I felt both my legs and Thad's being lifted and wish-boned out and then Clem started the long slide into me. I felt this descent had gone on for several minutes and that he must be nearing my stomach. He did a little languid pumping there, and the sensation of his uncut foreskin through the ultrathin and stretched sheath against my ass channel walls was quite new and pleasant. Even if he hadn't declared himself, I might have called this fucking style the "Jamaican Welcome." He slowly pulled his rod out with a sucking sensation and then came back in just to where he could feel my prostate with his bulbous now-extended mushroom cap.

He rubbed that with his dick head until I came inside Thad in the peaceful release of flowing semen into the expanded bulb of the condom, after which Clem slowly went deep again and fucked me slowly and deeply with that loose-skin feel for several minutes before giving a series of little lurches that told me that the Jamaican Welcome had been achieved, upon which, with a grunt and a sigh and Clem had collapsed on top of Thad and me.

When we had caught our breaths, Thad bounded up off the bed, headed for the door, and told Clem and me to meet him at the shallow end of the pool. With a sigh, I struggled off the bed and hobbled toward the door in a rather bowlegged gait, with the aid of Clem's spread hands on my butt cheeks. I was beginning to realize that my new boss was going to be a real taskmaster.

~

About the Author

Habu is one of the pen names of a former supersonic spy jet pilot, intelligence agent, male model, movie actor, and diplomat. A wild youth in South East Asia was spent enjoying whatever sexual opportunities came his way, and much of his gay male writing is about recalling incidents from those days and inventing ones he'd perhaps have liked to experience. He now leads a very quiet and ordinary happily married family life.

An American, he is a published mainstream novelist and short story writer under another name and in another dimension of his life. He has written or cowritten (with Sabb) over 500 published short stories and nearly 100 published erotica e-books, primarily of gay fiction but also memoir, straight fiction and ménage fiction. His hand and creative writing can be seen in stories and books by habu, sr71plt, Dirk Hessian, Shabbu, and Stephen Kessel—among unrevealed others that might surprise readers. The fictionalized GM memoir *Flying High, Diving Deep* is loosely based on his life experiences. He can be found at the adults only gay male site www.BarbarianSpy.com, which he shares with Sabb and Dirk Hessian.

Our authors always like to receive feedback, and appreciate it when readers post reviews at Goodreads, and other sites

BarbarianSpy

FOR LITERARY HEAT

Not all books listed below may currently be on release.

BOOKS BY DIRK HESSIAN

Xtreme Erotica

The King's Men
Shores of Tripoli
Prophecy of Noto
Pretender's Fate

General Erotica/Romance

Constantinople
The Beautiful Way
Blue and Gray
Colonel's Treasure
Beginning of Time
Labyrinth

BOOKS BY HABU

Gay Erotica

Memoir Faction

Flying High, Diving Deep*

Xtreme Erotica

Second Coming
Vortex: Sacrificed by Curiosity*
Dark Angel Sounding *(included in Sounding:Ultimate Control)**
Sounding: Ultimate Control (Print Only)*
Sounding Five (E-book only)

General Erotica

Romance

Lower Than the Heart
Brambleton
Gotta Keep Trying
Finding Amnad
Platres Conclave

Other

Anything for Ambition
Rough Riders

Dance of the Ravishers
Beyond the Beaded Curtain*
Hard Knocks U*
Habu's Christmas Balls
My Neighbor's Spa
Man's Man*
Trip Money
Clint Folsom Mysteries Compendium Volume 1*
Death to Blonds - Stolen Judgment (Clint Folsom Mystery)
Clint Folsom Mysteries Compendium Volume 2*
Grab Bag 1*
Grab Bag 2*
Grab Bag 3*
The Indian Doctor
Sailorboy
Home to Fire Island
The Sporting Life*
Fetish Galore!*
Choke Hold
Literary Gay Erotica
Cairo Surrender*
The Handyman*
Homeward Bound
Journey to Mirage*
Menage Erotica
13 Ways for Halloween
Luther*
The Indian Prince
BOOKS BY SHABBU
Finding Jason
Dirty Pool
Operation Black Jade
Cigars!*
Angel in the Barn
Gayly Complicated
Despoiling David
The Tree of Idleness
I Met a Man
The Interview

Rough Road to Happiness
BOOKS BY SABB
Hiring in Hollywood
The Legend of Holleystone Grange
Surprise Encounters
She is He
Wrong Man
Loyal to his King
Barbarian Tales - Book One - Traveler's Tales*
Barbarian Tales - Book Two - Journeys Begin*
Barbarian Tales - Book Three - The Inheritance*
Barbarian Tales - Book Four - Road to Persepolis*

~

* indicates the book is available in paperback and e-book.

www.ingramcontent.com/pod-product-compliance
Lightning Source LLC
Chambersburg PA
CBHW020824030726
47496CB00001B/78